Blood

Blood

Patricia Traxler

St. Martin's Minotaur ▄▄ New York

www.minotaurbooks.com

Excerpt from "Night" from *The Blue Estuaries* by Louise Bogan. Copyright © 1968 by Louise Bogan. Copyright renewed 1996 by Ruth Limmer. Reprinted by permission of Farrar, Straus and Giroux, LLC.

Library of Congress Cataloging-in-Publication Data

Traxler, Patricia.
    Blood : A Novel / Patricia Traxler.
        p. cm.
    ISBN 0-312-27484-X
    1. Women painters—Fiction. 2. Female friendship—Fiction. 3. Radcliffe College—Fiction. 4. Cambridge (Mass.)—Fiction. 5. Adultery—Fiction. I. Title.
PS3570.R354 B58 2001
813'.54—dc21

                                                                              2001031942

First Edition: September 2001

10 9 8 7 6 5 4 3 2 1

To my husband, Patrick

Author's Note

Although this novel makes passing reference to various public figures from the worlds of literature and the arts, all of *Blood*'s characters are entirely fictional, as are the events portrayed here. And though the Larkin Institute of this story bears many superficial resemblances to Radcliffe's former Bunting Institute, it will be obvious to anyone who was at the Bunting during the period when I was there that none of *Blood*'s characters is modeled on, or even resembles, anyone from that time and place. Similarly, the murder depicted in *Blood* is in no way based on the still-unsolved killing of a Bunting colleague during my first year there, although that event did provide the seed of an idea for this story. Indeed, the only aspects of the tragedy that make their way into this narrative are the shared grief, loss, and fear that followed in its wake.

Acknowledgments

I'm grateful to many people for their support and advice as I worked on *Blood*—among them, Angela Johnson, Susan Traxler Pompo, and Eileen Traxler for reading early drafts and making helpful comments. I'm grateful to Martha Rhea, the Salina Arts and Humanities Commission, and Horizons Fifty for technical support and project grants, and for a long and sustaining association. I'm indebted to Robert Pinsky for his wisdom, his generosity, and his indispensable eye. I thank Polly Rosenwaike, formerly of Brandt & Hochman, for finding this manuscript in the pile and passing it along. To my agent, Gail Hochman, my real and lasting gratitude for her energy, perspicacity, tenacity, and winning results. To my editors, Melissa Jacobs and Kelley Ragland, enormous thanks for insightful readings and superb ideas, and for their faith in this book. My enduring gratitude to Margot Livesey for her splendid observations and advice, and her very generous support. To Kim Cooper, who read the entire manuscript four times in various drafts—my eternal thanks for her friendship and inspiration, her keen editorial eye, and her stubborn faith, which helped me to keep my own alive. And finally, to my husband, Patrick, too many thanks to enumerate—just thank you, thank you, endlessly.

— O Remember
In your narrowing dark hours
That more things move
Than blood in the heart.
      — Louise Bogan, "Night"

Blood

Prologue

Though it's true there's a killing in my story, its principal violence is, I think I'd have to say, the violence of love. And even after all that's happened, I don't begin to know what love is—only what it does. When I have it in my life, I live with it gratefully but warily, the way I live with electricity or wind. That is, I can't comprehend electricity, but I know it has the power to kill, or to light a room; I don't understand the origins of wind, but I've seen how it can ravage the landscape, and have also felt the voluptuous relief of it on hot August days.

I was a late arrival to love—maybe because painting filled my imagination and used me up, and I wasn't particularly aware of any void in my life. For a long time I saw sex mostly as fleeting pleasure. After a decade of empty dalliances in my twenties, a couple years of celibacy, and two brief live-in relationships that expected too much, I fell in love for the first time when I was thirty-four, really in love—with a married man. It was only then that love presented itself in all its unruly splendor.

Once love happens, sex feels like a sacrament—even when it could be called adulterous by the Church. Or your mother.

My mother was a strict Irish Catholic, an old-fashioned woman who quit teaching when she married, to become what people used to call a "homemaker." My late father was her polar opposite—Jewish intellectual, a psychiatrist who agreed with Freud that religion is "an illusion." I can't imagine what brought the two of them together. I pray it wasn't sex—I've got enough of my mother in me that I really don't like to think of anyone's mother having sex. Mother provided my sex education in one anecdote: She told me she'd made my father kneel down beside the bed and pray with her on their wedding night before she would "consummate the marriage." Daddy was an athiest, but apparently he knew where his bread was buttered because nine months later I was born.

Obviously, sex is a mysterious force. Until Michael, I don't think I had a clue about the real power of erotic desire. With him I learned that you can disappear there, can lose yourself in the wilderness of mutual skin, and before you know it, your world has lost its shape and its boundaries. All that matters is the next touch.

I often had to wait for that, though, because now I was what people like to call the "other woman," a term that makes clear that no matter how real the love, you're a spare—like a summer house in the Hamptons or the shoes he saves for formal occasions; something he doesn't actually live with, but which he keeps just outside his field of vision, his real life, in case he should need it.

In that state two perfectly nice people can turn a world inside out and scarcely notice. At some point they may look around the ruined landscape and find they can't quite orient themselves to what they've made. The married party has another life and goes back to it after each assignation; the unmarried one becomes more and more solitary, spends too many free hours waiting for the married lover to appear. People speak of adultery as a double life, and I found it did add up to two lives: Michael had a life and a half to deal with; I had half a life. Even with the demands and pleasures of work, it began to seem as if the meaning of my existence could be summed up in one question: When will I see you again? It's not encouraging to realize your life's meaning has been reduced to the title of a bad song from your early dating years.

I'd show up at art openings and social functions alone, and when friends tried to fix me up with available men (often, oddly, with the words, "He's a big teddy bear," or, "He's a bear of a man," as if I were looking for someone to hibernate with), I'd turn them down with vague explanations. I couldn't tell them the truth: I'd promised Michael I would talk to no one about us until he'd found a way to tell his wife he wanted to leave the marriage.

It didn't take long for me to see how, caught outside the flow of ordinary life, a person can end up inhabiting a false universe. In time, as I became increasingly distant from my friends, that universe began to seem real, and it was hard to remember that I was only a viewer of

Michael's world, not a participant in it. I knew every drama in the lives of his two kids, Finnian and Bridget—their problems and triumphs at school, their growing pains, every detail of the Thanksgiving when eleven-year-old Bridget unexpectedly got her first period at the dinner table and thought she was bleeding to death, and later that same evening when sixteen-year-old Finn showed up with a pierced tongue and announced over pumpkin pie that he was "primarily hetero" but considering his "sexual options." I fretted with Michael when Bridget refused to leave the house till the bleeding stopped five days later; I gloried in Finn's first poetry publication in a campus literary journal; I knew their lives as intimately as if they were my family, yet they didn't know I existed.

I remember sitting alone in the living room of my Cambridge apartment high above Brattle Street one night that fall thinking *Winter's coming,* and I didn't mean only the weather. The moon was big. I heard my own whisper leaping out into the room, *I want to go home,* as if the words had formed independent of me, frost on a windowpane, a chill. *I want to go home.*

All my life I've heard those words in my head, and I know I'll hear them till I die, no matter where I am. I've no idea where home *is.* But the words are always in my mind, except when I paint—they're what sends me to the canvas in the first place because they fuel that need, the hunger that ultimately feeds me, makes me know I'm alive. Alive and impermanent—the awareness of finitude is important there—it gives desire the edge of necessity.

I want to go home. The words sang in my blood, pumped through it each time I fucked Michael, *I want to go home,* and I climbed him like a ladder, fervid, hungry to reach the top, to know everything, every cell of him, to have it, have it, *I want to go home,* and the explosion then, that strange ecstatic apogée of having, the settling of the pulse into the air of the moment, that brief harmony of need and knowing, a perfect clarity, home.

Then the calm rolls in like fog, and nothing in the room, in your life, has edges. You think right then you might want it to last forever.

Lucky it doesn't. If that calm were a lasting state, no one would paint or write, design a skyscraper, or build a bridge. Erotic torpor. It's a killer. Sometimes when I was with Michael the words would go away for days at a time. Without them, I didn't paint, didn't need to.

3

And then he'd leave me to go back to his real life, and I would lock myself away with the words and the paint, and desire would reconstitute itself. Everything began to be red in those days, blood reds shading into odd reds I'd never seen. I think infinite shades of red must exist that I've still not seen. For a long time I tried to locate more and more of them in my palette. I filled canvas after canvas with unnamed reds, the reds of my longing and anger, of need and grief and jealousy. But the hardest reds to look at were the clear, sudden reds of knowing.

When I was a kid in Catholic school, we were told that in taking the sacrament of Holy Eucharist, we were eating and drinking the body and blood of Christ. I was so young when I learned about it—six years old—that it never seemed extraordinary to me, the idea that Jesus would want us to take him into our own skins that way, corporeally whole and entire, in order that he could take up residence, as the nuns told us, "in our hearts."

"That's how great is His love for us," Sister Mary Agnes would say.

Sometimes I wonder if I've taken my idea of romantic love from that early catechism lesson. Probably because I'm a painter, I tend to cast abstractions into visual images—it's how I understand them best. And the way I imagine it, desire rides on the blood, follows it through our veins and arteries to the heart, and when it finds its way at last into that soft chamber, it takes up residence there. Sometimes it can't get out again.

I'd like to understand such longing better. I've come closer to comprehending it in my painting than in my life, but for the most part it's remained a mystery to me. Still, I feel I can't give up till I've found my way to some kind of clear and solid truth about the desire love fuels, that longing beyond mere arousal and more than just *of the flesh*.

If I could do that, sometimes I think it's possible I'd learn to trust it again.

Then I think of the events on Brattle Street and remember it was disappointed desire, distorted desire, that turned all the world the color of blood, and I have to wonder if anyone could ever be safe in such a wilderness.

Is it strange then for me to say that even considering its capacity for damage, I believe love should never be regretted? I do believe that. Regret is unbecoming. It's a way of not taking responsibility for what you've done.

Long ago I read about how Edith Piaf, "the Little Sparrow" of Paris, climbed to the top of the Eiffel Tower late one night and sang out over the streets of the city, in her unforgettable voice, the song, "Non, Je Ne Regrette Rien."

I'd like to be that way, regretting nothing. I'm aiming for that.

A late night motor trip in early childhood—my mother asleep in the front passenger seat, and I, probably four years old, in the backseat awakening to the bluish lights of a nighttime freeway in Northern California, the passing flash and roar of each oncoming car, the sight of my father's hands on the steering wheel, the springy black hairs on his lean wrists, the tensile strength in his fingers as he steers, moving us through the night toward our destination.

Looking back, I believe this was a foreshadowing of adult female longing, a kind of desire, though even now I can't say for what exactly since I knew nothing yet about the things men and women do together. I only know I couldn't take my eyes off my father's hands. My mother was asleep, which meant that I was alone with him in the tiny, rolling universe of our family car, alone with him in the grown-up world for the first time. I didn't need to speak, and I didn't. It didn't matter that he was unaware of my wakeful presence there in the seat behind him. All that mattered in that moment was that my father was carrying us skillfully through the darkened world to wherever it was we were going, and that I was seeing his hands and wrists, really seeing them for the first time and they were beautiful to me, they were telling me something about what a man is and something about me—and I was caught there speechless, in love, my eyes wide open in the dark.

1

I'd spent most of the week packing my worldly belongings for the move to Brattle Street, and by Friday night I was nearly finished. I found it unsettling, how easy it was to sort my life into boxes I arranged in rows on the floor. I hadn't moved in a while—several years, in fact—and I'd forgotten how this felt.

As with every life decision I made, I was tormenting myself in its aftermath, plagued by what my pal Liz liked to call "buyer's remorse." (She used the term for everything but real estate, which thus far had played no meaningful part in her life or mine—in particular, it was how she described her own feelings in the wake of any new romantic commitment she ever made.) Actually, I'd been happier with this Watertown house than with any place I'd rented before, so it was easy to feel remorse.

Increasingly in the last few days, I'd found myself wandering through the familiar rooms at odd hours to appreciate the wonderful light in every room and contemplate the beauty and integrity of the architecture. I was just renting half of the house, and I shared that half with a housemate, Jill; but the rooms were huge, and with two stories we each had loads of room to ourselves. The best thing about the house, for me, was the sunny studio I'd set up on the second floor. For years before moving here I'd dreamed of having a home studio. And now I was giving it up.

Of course, I had to remind myself that the advantage of a home studio was severely mitigated by a housemate like Jill, who tended to walk right in on me without knocking while I was in the throes of painting and practically levitating, most recently to share with me a *Newsweek* story on

"Breast Cancer Among Childless Women." ("Childish women *deserve* it," I'd responded, deliberately misreading the *Newsweek* headline she'd thrust into my field of vision.) Jill was the creative equivalent of a cold shower.

It would be good for me to get into my own apartment, even if moving to Brattle Street did mean giving up the studio, for it would provide me with the solitude that would allow me to paint undisturbed during my Larkin Fellowship year at Radcliffe. This was the chance I'd never had before to be a full-time artist, and I was eager to discover what it was like to live alone and be truly immersed in painting. I wanted to test myself, to see how far I could go in my art with nothing to impede me.

My desire for privacy was compounded, of course, by Michael's presence in my life. We'd been involved for over a year now, and it was never easy finding a way to be alone together. Jill worked the same hours I did and went out infrequently beyond that. Clearly I needed to live alone for the sake of both love and work, and the low rents Harvard Housing offered its students and fellows would enable me to rent without a roommate. I simply couldn't afford to live by myself anywhere else in or around Cambridge on the modest stipend the Larkin offered.

"Well, great!" Liz had said when I told her what Radcliffe was giving me to live on for the year, "So, what *car* are you planning to live in?!"

And she was right—it wasn't much money, not enough to live on in any deep comfort. But I'd taken a year's leave of absence from my graphic design job at Aperçu Archive and was determined to make it on my Larkin check so that all my work time could be given to painting.

As I got the last of my books into a box and taped it shut, I saw it was nearly seven o'clock and realized I was hungry. I'd forgotten all about making some arrangement for dinner, and it occurred to me for about the millionth time how nice it would be to have a normal boyfriend I could go out to dinner with on Friday nights. But there was no point in feeling sorry for myself in this relationship; I wasn't a kidnap victim.

Sometimes I couldn't quite believe I'd put myself in this situation. I could clearly remember having my first inkling that I'd fallen in love with Michael before it had ever occurred to me that the two of us might be heading toward more than friendship. Even then, I didn't give him any indication of how I felt. Although I believed in lots of things other people might not, I didn't believe in affairs with married men.

At the beginning, I couldn't imagine that my feelings for Michael might be reciprocated anyway—he was an increasingly successful fiction writer and I was just the woman who had designed the cover for his book of short stories and was working on a cover for his upcoming autobiographical novel, *This Cold Heaven*, which was a lyrical, rowdy, and poignant account of growing up Irish in South Boston's projects. Everyone at Aperçu knew this would be Michael's last book with a boondocks house like us; it was inevitable he'd go on to bigger things.

Everything changed between us one Monday evening when he was leaving our office after a long meeting with his editor. He saw me walking to the bus stop in a pouring rain and offered to drop me off on his way home. I knew he had no idea I lived way too far to "drop off."

"I live in Watertown," I told him.

"What? I can't hear you."

"I LIVE IN WATERTOWN," I yelled, leaning from the curb toward the open window of his car, rain flooding my mouth as I spoke.

"SO WHAT'S YOUR POINT?" he yelled back, grinning. "HOP IN!"

I did, and by the time we pulled up in front of my house on James Street, the rain was beating down on the car like a million tap-dancers, and he suggested I wait until it slowed a bit.

We sat outside in his car laughing and talking far beyond the rain, far beyond good sense—long enough for me to know he felt the way I did. At some point, the inevitable moment of silence occurred, during which he looked at me so intensely and ardently I had to avert my gaze.

"I think this may be dangerous," he said after a moment, his fingers tapping the steering wheel nervously. "I think we'd better try to control our imaginations, Honora."

"What," I said lamely, falling shy suddenly.

"We both know what. I think I love you or something. I have to try not to."

It was six more months of torment before we gave in to our feelings, and both of us knew two things immediately after our first tryst: We were made for each other, and we felt guilty as hell. I'd never allowed myself even to consider being involved with a married man—cheap, needy women did that, women who didn't care about other women. Women named Honora definitely did not do that. (All my life, I'd carried my first name the way an ant carries a large bread crumb, made humble by its heft.)

Michael had never "stepped out" on Brenda before, he told me, and he'd always supposed he never would. In addition to his disquiet in the role of adulterer, he was finding our eleven-year age difference a continuing source of angst: "It's such a cliché of midlife crisis," he moaned, "the seedy, long-in-the-tooth, very married writer falling for a young, beautiful woman just as he's achieved some middling relief from insolvency and obscurity." I told him that the only compelling evidence I saw of a midlife crisis was his view of himself as "seedy" and "long-in-the-tooth" at forty-six and of me as "young" when I was thirty-five and likely heading for a bout of midlife distress myself. Charitably, I let the "beautiful" slide.

We decided over and over again not to see each other anymore, not even to talk on the phone. Each time we came to that point, I knew I couldn't be the one to break that resolution no matter how I missed him. He was the married one, and I wasn't going to argue him away from his marriage—that would be wrong. Of course, it was true I'd been committing vigorous and enthusiastic adultery with him every chance I got, and most people would call that wrong, too. The thing about adultery is, it's full of moral rationalizations and ethical contradictions, and if you're going to be in it, you have to choose your wrongs. Prioritize your rights. Looked at objectively, it's not pretty. In any case, it's a stomachache.

So we would resolve to stop, and we'd mean it. We would live through three days, five days—one time even eight days—of torture, and then he would call me, and we'd fly into each other's arms again.

Somehow, after more than a year of it, we'd gotten to this place.

Now, just as I bent over the last packing crate with a marking pen and scrawled BOOKS, I heard the screen door open and close behind me. I straightened and spun around to find Michael standing in the doorway across the room, grinning his lopsided grin.

"What are *you* doing here?" I asked, shoving a strand of hair behind my ear. Why did I never remember to lock the front door? At least that would have given me a moment to collect myself. Michael's auburn hair was tousled as if he'd run all the way to Watertown from Brookline.

"Can I take that to mean you're glad to see me?" His eyes strayed to my shorts. "Wow," he added and then shook his head. "I can't believe I said 'wow.' I hate that word. But you look great."

Goddamn shorts, I thought. I had an ass like two prize watermelons, and I didn't like imagining the eyeful he must have had while I was bent over the book box with a marking pen.

"Don't even start with the Irish flattery," I told him. "I look like hell tonight."

"If that's hell, I'm feeling better about the afterlife all the time," he said. "You look adorable, you idiot. I've never seen you in shorts."

"My point exactly."

"What's the big deal?" He laughed. "I've seen you stark raving naked after all."

"You could have called, you know. Don't you children of Irish immigrants ever phone before visiting? Or knock before entering?"

"Nope," he said cheerfully. "We've had no proper upbringing. Most of our formative years were spent cleaning chimneys for those Protestant bastards in the Back Bay." He paused, turned serious. "You know, I could see you in here from way out on the sidewalk. Don't you put down the shades at night, Norrie?"

"Not always," I admitted, surreptitiously tugging down the legs of my shorts in back.

"But anyone at all out there could see you larking around in here, you know."

"I wasn't actually quite so much larking as *packing.*" I said. "I'm sure no one was out there watching, Michael." As always, I was both warmed by, and resistant to, his protectiveness of me.

"Sometimes I worry about you, that's all."

"We have my mother to do that," I said. "And she puts lots of time into it, so she's even better at it than you are. You could say she has a vocational calling."

"Well, I'm suddenly thinking the woman may have a point with her cautionary phone calls." He brushed a lock of hair out of my eyes; his voice softened. "I was hungry to see you."

"I thought you were going to write tonight," I said into his mouth as I kissed him.

He pulled me close, letting his palms rest on my offending rear. "Yeah, I kept trying, but I couldn't quite get you out of my mind no matter how I tried. So I threw aside my darkly brilliant manuscript and gave in to the siren song."

"It must've been some other siren. I was definitely not singing you to me tonight. I've got to move out of here tomorrow." I glanced at the stairway, then said in a lower voice, "Jill's home tonight, you know."

"Yeah, well, I figured as much," he said in a kind of cheerful resignation. But he let go of me and stepped back a bit. "I just wanted to see your face." He brushed my upper arm with the backs of his fingers, and then he looked over at the rows of boxes on the floor.

"So you're moving tomorrow? I thought that was next weekend."

"Well, it was. But they're letting tenants move into the vacant apartments early if we want, to avoid congestion next weekend when everyone in the world will be descending on Brattle with moving trucks."

"Surely you're not going to try doing all this yourself?"

"I'm fine," I said. "I've got a truck coming first thing in the morning for all the furniture and boxes. I'll move the stuff from the studio myself over the next few days. I don't trust them with that. Jill says I can use her car."

"Jesus, Norrie—there's a lot of stuff up there—easels and lamps and dozens of paintings, just for starters. I'll come and help you with that. Otherwise you're going to have to make about a hundred trips over to Cambridge and back in the car."

"That's sweet of you, Michael, but I can manage it. I really can."

"Tell me, is there anything you can't manage alone, Honora? Ever?"

"What do you mean?" I asked. Actually, I knew what he meant, but I didn't know how to talk to him about it. I was leery of becoming dependent on him. When you allow yourself to depend too much on a man and then he goes away, you're left sprawling and helpless, as if your skeleton had been removed. I could still remember watching our neighbor, Mrs. Mumford, teach my mother how to use a checkbook after Daddy died. Mother wasn't stupid—it was just the way she'd been raised, to let a man take care of her. Night after night I'd wake to find her hugging my doorway in the dark, wraithlike in her long flannel gown, telling me she'd "heard a noise." She had no idea how to live without Daddy, and she lost years and years adjusting to life after he was gone.

I think it was only after I won a four-year scholarship to the Rhode Island School of Design and moved away from her—three thousand miles away—that she learned to be alone and to enjoy it. I'd taken a lesson from all that and made a point of being self-sufficient from the get-go.

"You never let anyone help you," Michael was saying. "And, hey—you know I won't try to run the show. I promise to take orders as docilely as a tiny lamb, while at the same time employing my considerable brawn for the heavy lifting, okay? I can rent a U-Haul trailer, and we'll get everything over to Cambridge in one trip tomorrow afternoon, singing camp songs all the way."

Except for the camp songs, it did seem like a good idea. I wouldn't have slept easily on Brattle Street tomorrow night, knowing that all my paintings had been left behind. I looked up at him and grinned. "You're not going to give up on this, are you?"

"No, ma'am, the Irish never give up. Does the potato famine ring a bell? So, okay, I'll arrange a U-Haul for tomorrow afternoon?"

"That'll be swell. Thanks." We grinned at each other. He knew he'd won this round.

Just then Jill came down the stairs, her car keys in one hand and a large, hardbound book in the other. She must have her book discussion group tonight.

She stopped when she saw us and said, "Oh," with no particular inflection.

Awkwardly I introduced her to Michael, wondering what she might've overheard, and midway through the introductions I recalled that I'd introduced them the last time she'd come upon us together in the living room.

She acknowledged him and then smiled nervously, looking down as she left the house.

"I thought that went well," Michael said, raising one brow.

"Right. You know, I think she recognized you."

"Well that wouldn't take a brain surgeon. After all, you *introduced* us—twice."

"No, I mean, *you the author*—I think she heard your name just now and in that second she recognized you from your jacket photo." Michael really laughed at this.

"You think everyone's read my book. Several people haven't, you know. You're just letting your paranoia blossom again, darling."

"Oh, Jesus, didn't I tell you? Maybe I didn't—I found Jill reading *This*

Cold Heaven a few weeks ago for her Episcopal women's book discussion group."

"How depressing," he said, "I'd hoped for more of a Hell's Angels kind of constituency."

"Whatever," I said. "I'll just be glad to get my own place so I don't have to think about what a roommate has or hasn't noticed. The new place is really private."

The six-story, Harvard Housing building I was moving into was right on the edge of Harvard Square. It offered one-, two-, and three-bedroom floor plans, as well as two studio apartments per floor. I'd taken one of the few still vacant one-bedroom units. I loved the fact that there were only three apartments in my little cul de sac off the middle of the fourth-floor hallway, and my apartment was the one deepest inside—spanning the foot of that short hall—which made it all the more secluded. Better yet, although I knew it wouldn't last, the other two apartments—both studios—were empty right now. I'd been told that the tenant in the one on the right side had a Fulbright or something and would be away a lot all year, and the apartment directly across from that had not yet been rented.

"Speaking of privacy," Michael said softly, "am I hallucinating again, or do we have this house all to ourselves?"

In minutes we were upstairs in my bed, one of the few times we'd had a chance for unhurried privacy there. For once, I didn't bother to entertain nervous thoughts of Jill's unexpected return. All that mattered was the long-legged, ardent man who was putting himself inside me before I'd quite managed to get my shorts off—an unusual approach for Michael, who usually tended to browse awhile. As much as I liked his leisurely and inventive lovemaking, it thrilled me when occasionally in the flush of lust he just pushed himself inside me this way, urgent and hard, and brought us both home without art or deliberation. I'd felt myself go wet from the moment I led him up the stairs to my bedroom, and now in the rhythm of his thrust I was quickly at the cusp of orgasm and then awash in it with a gasp. Immediately, as if he'd only held back by force of will, Michael called *Oh* and let himself go, too, and in that moment as we tumbled mindlessly together toward the edge, the leap, and the blind, spinning fall, I would not, could not, have stopped if the house were on fire or an intruder had held a gun to my temple.

"When you come," he said afterward, nuzzling my ear, "that's the sexiest part of it all for me, even more than my own coming—selfish beast that I am notwithstanding." His fingers ranged over my hipbone, my belly, reading my body like Braille. "I've never seen a woman come the way you do, with such abandon. It gets me."

"It's just with you," I said, a little embarrassed. "It was never this way before." That was the simple truth, and it wasn't as much his considerable skill or his beautiful body or his words in my ear as the fact that it was him inside me, him.

He held me for a long time then, and neither of us felt a need to talk.

"How d'you suppose this happened?" he asked after a while, stroking my shoulder with two startlingly long fingers. "How did you become my one?"

Just as I turned my face to his, I saw his eyes flicker toward the clock. He couldn't help it, I knew—he had to keep track of the time. But still, it reminded me that when he untangled his limbs from mine, he would be going home to her, as always.

At the door he held my face in both of his hands and kissed it all over very softly.

"It's just getting across the river that's hard," he told me, "once I've got to the other side, we'll be together all the rest of our lives."

After I'd shut the door behind him, I listened to the clatter of his old VW starting and then accelerating as he pulled away. Such a bucket of bolts. It seemed ages before the sound of it died away in the night.

The time you made every letter of the alphabet for me with your naked body and I watched from across the room, caught mute by that sublime contortion of male limbs and torso, quick and limber, A to Z, your body breathtaking from any direction. I could never have been beautiful in every pose the way you were, stooping, bending your limbs at awkward angles, lying on your back and putting your feet in the air as you did on the W. Your M was amazing, your O was sublime. Your S made me weep. You were so innocently, stupidly happy as you went through the alphabet, so pleased with your clever mime's ballet that you were oblivious to your own startling beauty. And I was grinning as I watched, grinning like an idiot and breathless with love.

2

By the end of my first week on Brattle Street I was settling happily into the solitude and sunlight of my small, fourth-floor apartment, but whenever I went out into the hall or down to the lobby I felt conspicuous, in the way an outsider is conspicuous. Everyone in the building seemed to be younger than I was, for one thing—most were in their early twenties while I was thirty-six. And although it may have just been in my mind, it seemed to me they all knew one another already; I don't know how many times I found myself going up or down in the elevator with people who seemed to be well acquainted with everyone getting on at each floor. Also, it appeared that most of the other tenants were sharing apartments—so I was always alone, while they moved about the place in chatty couples and threesomes. Not that I wished for a roommate, but I did feel rather solitary in their midst.

I told myself I'd better just get used to it, since solitude was the whole point of this move. Anyway, I was seeing Michael more now. He'd been dropping by to see me nearly every day since I'd moved, even when he only had a few minutes. We'd spent a couple of long, idyllic afternoons together here, and he was coming over tomorrow at noon to prepare his legendary linguini with clam sauce for the two of us. We also had plans to go to the Museum of Fine Arts next Tuesday morning and then come back to my bed. We were discovering that privacy can be voluptuous, to say the least; but even more precious than the sexual freedom was the normalcy it afforded us, the unhurried conversations spoken in normal tones, the meals cooked and eaten together, the sense of the ordinary— that was the best part. We could be together now without it being a special occasion. Brattle Street was the first place Michael and I had had to ourselves without the worry of a roommate coming home unexpectedly, since I'd never slept with him in his house—their house . . . I wouldn't have even if he'd asked me to, which he hadn't.

Their house, that phrase was painful to say or think. It brought to mind the fact that I was in love with another woman's husband.

How can I explain why—or how—it didn't feel like that? Once Michael and I were in love, we were each other's. Love seems to confer a sense of belonging on two people (some would say "ownership" but I prefer "belonging"), and it's hard to think beyond that "we" the two of you have become—impossible to understand from the depths of that attachment that the other half of your "we" is simultaneously one half of another entirely separate "we." Even saying it now, all this time later, it stings—more than stings. But once you're in it you only know you're in it, and you tend to close other people out of that little universe you've created together.

I'd told no one about Michael, not even Liz, my closest friend. God knows I could not have told my worrywart mother who called every day from Santa Monica to reassure herself that no one was at that moment trying to break in and kill me. (Liz often said that my mother should simply call each day and ask, "Are you dead yet?") I was quite sure that if Mother knew about Michael she would say I was headed for hell; she'd been considering that a distinct possibility for years anyway, since the first time I lived with a man without, as she put it, "benefit of wedlock." And simply the fact that I'd never married made my life unnatural to her.

"Your father," she'd said more than once, "would roll over in his grave if he saw how his only child is living her life!" This image, the grave rolling, was in direct conflict with the facts as I knew them. First of all, my father was in an urn on the top shelf of my mother's bedroom closet and had been since I was twelve years old, so he was not likely to roll. Second, Daddy died atop a woman named Betty Arnold at a Holiday Inn in the throes of something in no way akin to moralistic piety or guilt, as far as I can figure.

Mother still, to this day, didn't realize I'd known before she did about Betty, who was the appointments secretary in Daddy's psychiatric office. But even though I was only a kid at the time, I'd found out about the girlfriend weeks before the final tryst when I overheard Daddy talking to her on the phone about getting away with her some weekend soon, and about the things he would like to do to her "right now," if only he could. I'd sat there trembling on the extension phone—which I'd picked up to try a radio station's "Guess This Song Played Backward" contest (it was, I'm embarrassed to say, the Ricky Nelson tune "Travelin' Man")—and I was so afraid he would hear me hanging up and thus realize I'd overheard them that I sat paralyzed and mute, the receiver in my lap, until they finished talking—audibly, even from my lap—twenty minutes later. I learned more about sexual variety from that one conversation than I ever learned in any other way until quite some time after I lost my virginity at nineteen.

Everyone had known about Betty, it later turned out; everyone but Mother. I felt guilty for not having told her what I knew, but I'd been so terrified by what I'd heard my father saying and by what the woman had said to him. It had been so graphic, so lewd—so absolutely new and unthinkable—that I couldn't have brought myself to repeat it to anyone. That had been the first real secret of my life, a very painful and isolating one to carry around.

And now here I was, carrying a similarly isolating secret around and *simultaneously* inhabiting the despicable Betty's role with another woman's husband. I couldn't think about it like that or my head would explode. Or my heart. Or my soul.

Sometimes I found myself obsessing on minor issues as a way of avoiding such daunting or confounding aspects of my life. This may have been why the whole subject of my Larkin studio had become so disproportionately upsetting to me. By the time I moved to Brattle, it was all I could think about. It really had begun to feel like a threat to my *privacy*. That word again.

The previous spring, when I'd received the telephone call announcing that I'd been accepted as a Larkin fellow, I was told straightaway that I'd be given a studio on the grounds of the institute in one of five renovated Victorian houses that had been moved to the parklike Cambridge location a few blocks outside Harvard Square, where they were set around a picturesque green. For years I'd passed Radcliffe's Larkin Institute and longed to be one of the women who were invited there to devote themselves to their life's work for a year. Yet now, on reflection,

I had doubts about working communally, and I told Jane Coleman, the Larkin's director, that I didn't think I'd be needing a studio since ordinarily I painted at home. Jane had laughed genially and insisted I at least give community life a try.

"One of the reasons the Larkin is such a rich experience for everyone," Jane said, "is the sort of cross-pollination that occurs when people of different disciplines work side by side. All the Larkies say it's wonderfully enriching. I think you'll find that to be true, too, once you've acclimated." At any one time there were as many as forty-five women at the Larkin Institute from all over the world, women who had distinguished themselves in a variety of fields—medicine, law, science, history, literature, music, government, and art. That year there were to be forty-three Larkin Fellows, all working in offices or studios in those houses surrounding the green. It was an idyllic setting and it would be an honor to be there; but somehow I couldn't make anyone understand that the circumstances under which I'd made the art that supposedly justified my presence at the Larkin were circumstances of extreme solitude. That was how I worked.

The Larkin year had begun that week with a three-day orientation and a dinner, and after socializing with the other fellows ("sister fellows," they were called around the institute), I found it even more awkward to resist the idea of working there. I hated the idea of seeming an ungrateful or grudging member of the community. But for me the gift of my fellowship was not so much *community* as *money,* the money they were paying me to paint for a year. It was simple: Money bought me time. I'd never had that before—the luxury of time away from a wage-earning job.

Though I'd earned my MFA at Brown after finishing RISD and could easily have landed a decent university job, I had been put off teaching altogether after a series of teaching assistantships in college made clear to me that teaching drew from the same pool of creative energy art relied on.

Over the years I'd worked dozens of tedious, low-paying jobs to support my work as a painter, and in fact, until I'd landed the job doing art and graphics at Aperçu Archive five years earlier, not one of my jobs had made the slightest use of my artistic talent or even had anything to do with art. I'd once worked as a secretary to three morticians in South Boston! And wherever I'd lived, I always had to have a roommate to share expenses with me. I was never able to just be alone, and I'd always felt that I would work more and better if I could be. Now here I was in my own apartment on Brattle Street, being paid by Harvard University each month just to do my art.

I'd promised Jane Coleman I would try using my assigned Larkin studio for painting and had meant it when I said it. To convince myself of my good faith, I'd even taken a small box of art supplies, two canvases, and my second-best easel over to the studio, which turned out to be a charming attic space in the yellow Victorian at the center of the circle of old houses, light streaming in on three sides. But I didn't see how I was going to work out the logistics. The Larkin Institute was an eight-block walk from my apartment, and I nearly always paint at night, often until two or three in the morning. I didn't have a car, and even as cocky as everyone thought I was, I wasn't sure I'd feel safe straggling home on foot from a studio at all hours.

Several of the staff had assured us during orientation that first week that Cambridge was safer than most places, as long as a woman was careful. There hadn't been a murder there in eighteen years, they said, though of course there were rapes ("a normal number of rapes," said the Harvard policeman who'd been brought in to speak at our orientation session). Women should be street smart, we were told, walk in well-lighted areas, stay in groups or twos at night whenever possible, carry a body alarm, and so on.

Well, you could say that was true pretty much anywhere these days.

But beyond the issues of personal safety, I just wasn't comfortable with the idea of painting at the Larkin—day *or* night. I couldn't stand being in the middle of a painting and having someone interrupt my concentration. I imagined my fellow "Larkies" wandering in and out of one another's offices and studios every minute of the day, though I knew that was probably a silly thought—these women were as serious about their work as I was about mine. Still, when people are working all around you, interruption is always a possibility, and that can be as hard on concentration as an actual interruption would be. I thought of all the times Jill had interrupted me when I was painting, and how hard it had often been to regain my focus afterward.

When I'd called Liz a few days earlier to give her my new phone number, she'd expressed surprise that I had taken a one-bedroom place instead of a studio, considering how tightly budgeted I was going to be all year. I told her that I needed a room at home to paint in without fear of guests seeing my work.

"You know how it is," I said. "I'm sure you can't write just anywhere."

"Honey," she laughed, "I wrote a chapter of my first novel on the back of a Harley-Davidson during rush hour in Rome." That was Liz—unflappable. I'd really missed her easy-going presence since she'd left to take a two-year residency at San Francisco State. "I bet you'll love having a studio to go to," she said.

"It's just I've never painted away from wherever I've lived," I said. "I'm used to working at home—always in my bedroom, in fact, until Watertown."

"Sure you're used to it," she laughed, "because you've always been too poor to rent a studio like other painters do. Now Radcliffe wants to *give* you one for a year, and you don't want it?"

"I'm afraid I'll feel the psychic weight of Radcliffe's expectation if it just sits there all year and I'm not working in it."

"Oh, please," Liz snorted. "You *have* to take it. I mean, it's *free,* for God's sake, and it's *yours.* And you may find you actually like working in a studio a couple of times a week for a change—it might keep your creative spirit fresh."

"But, Liz, how could I leave a painting half-finished at the Larkin and come back to my apartment to sleep? All night I'd be thinking about the work I'd left there, thinking about a shape or an angle or a shade, and I couldn't just leap out of bed and go to work while a fresh idea was still alive and kicking."

"Actually, I can understand that," Liz admitted, "wanting access to your work at night. I mean, I always try to keep my current manuscript next to the bed at night, just in case. I can remember sometimes when I've wakened in the night with an idea and failed to jot it down out of laziness, you know, and fallen back to sleep so sure I'd remember it. But then in the morning I'd find I'd completely lost it. All that's left then," she said, "is the *sense* of the idea, like that little trail of white exhaust in the sky after an airplane has moved out of sight."

"See—you do understand. So I'm not just being willful or eccentric."

"Yeah, I understand. But sure, you *are* willful and eccentric. That's what I love about you—your passionate heart."

That's what Michael would say. I started to tell her and stopped myself just in time, my lips making a sound like *thfff*. It was awful keeping such a big thing from my best friend.

At that moment, in an absolute non sequitur that made me think she'd read my mind, Liz addressed the issue. "You haven't mentioned a man in a long time," she said, "and whenever I ask how your love life is, you just say, 'Nothing to write home about.' "

"Really?" I answered edgily, "I say that?" *Nothing to write home about.* A classic Catholic girl's evasion of the truth. I could imagine myself saying it while thinking, It's not a *lie,* really, since I *couldn't possibly* write home to Mother about an adulterous love affair.

"Well, so what's the deal?" Liz pursued. "Are you seeing anyone?"

This was the first time she'd come right out and put it in a way that could only be answered yes or no. It was an awful moment. Liz and I had been each other's sounding board and support system since grad school at Brown—it was she who'd convinced me that her native Boston was the place for me to settle after graduation—and though I knew she'd never been involved with a married man, I also knew I could trust that she would try to understand the situation and not judge me. It would have been a comfort to confide in her.

From Michael's point of view, though, Liz was one of the worst people I could tell because the two of them were acquainted. Liz had even published her first novel with Aperçu right around the time they had brought out Michael's short story collection.

"I know she's your closest friend," he'd told me, "but if you could please just hold off for now until I've found a way to talk to Brenda." He was right when he said Cambridge was a village; everyone there seemed to be a writer, and every writer knew—or knew about—every other. "If you see some guy walking down Mass Ave with a bad look on his face," locals liked to say, "you can be sure it's because his book isn't being reviewed." The Boston-Cambridge literary scene was overpopulated with gossips, and slander was a kind of parlor game. "People dish for sport around here," Michael said, "and I don't want Brenda to find out that way."

Liz could be trusted not to repeat a confidence, I'd pointed out, but Michael had argued that simply telling Liz would be wrong in itself. "She's acquainted with Brenda," he said, "and it's just unfair to let anyone in our circle know about this before Brenda does." I doubted that Brenda and Liz had ever spoken two words to each other, but I could see Michael's point and I'd promised not to talk to Liz about us.

The phone was sweaty beneath my hand now as Liz waited for my answer, and after the approximate length of time it takes for one lifetime to unreel before your eyes, I spoke. "Not really. No one in particular." I heard my lie straggle out in an unintentionally wispy voice. It was the first time I'd lied to Liz in all the years I'd known her.

After we hung up I would think it through all over again. Couldn't I have just said yes, I was seeing someone? But then she'd have asked *who*. And when I said I couldn't tell her who, she'd have guessed instantly that he was married. Considering the predictable rhythms of my life, which moved back and forth routinely between Aperçu and the room I painted in, she'd know it was likely someone I'd met at work. It would be a baby step from there to Michael. To tell Liz anything at all would be to tell her everything.

But it had been one thing to keep my relationship from Liz; now I'd lied to her outright and I feared that would inevitably, irretrievably, and by infinitesimal degrees corrode our friendship. After we hung up, I sat in the chair beside the phone for a long time, trying to figure out what was happening to my life—no, what *I* was *doing* to my life—in the name of love.

My life and my work: The more mute I was forced to be around friends, the more stalled I was beginning to feel as an artist. I'd been painting less in recent months. I hadn't painted for two weeks before the move to Brattle, nor had I painted since—a total of three weeks.

Sure, I'd been packing and preparing to move, but that kind of thing had never stopped me before—*nothing* had, really. Painting was a daily thing for me—or nightly—even when I worked a full-time job.

I'd already received my first monthly stipend check, which was paid through Harvard University's Payroll Department, and I was worried sick at the thought that they could end up paying me for a year while all that time I was not painting. Would I actually waste the creative opportunity of my lifetime and maybe have no new work to show at my colloquium exhibit before the assembled Larkin fellows?

There was a lot to think of right now.

Of course, I had no idea how much darker and more difficult life on

Brattle Street would become before long. I didn't know then that I'd come to yearn for those early days in my sun-filled apartment, for the hopeful quality of its light, the freshness and possibility of each day there, for the relative simplicity of a time when whether or not to paint in a studio provided free of cost by Radcliffe seemed a problem worth chewing over for half an hour on the phone with Liz. Most of all, I would long for the days when I wasn't afraid all the time, for the time when I'd felt safe.

That afternoon, a Saturday, I was making my way to the elevator with a basket of dirty clothes and towels I needed to wash in the basement laundry facility. When the elevator door opened, a small yellow-and-orange sofa appeared to walk out of the elevator on end, nearly knocking me down. I gave an involuntary yelp as I jumped out of the way, and then I heard a voice exclaim, "Oh, I am sorry!" Even in those few words I could hear a Spanish accent. The walking sofa wobbled to a standstill before me, and a round female face peered around it in alarm.

"Oh," I said stupidly, "I didn't see anyone there." And I set my laundry basket down.

"Hello," a young woman said as she stepped around the bulky piece of furniture that still stood on its end. She was sturdy looking and garbed simply in green slacks and a plain white shirt with the sleeves rolled up. Her shortish, wispy black hair was pulled back in an elastic at her neck, where it stood straight out behind her head like a toddler's ponytail. This woman certainly didn't look frail, but I couldn't imagine how she was strong enough to carry a couch around by herself. Or even a love seat, I thought, appraising its size downward.

"Can I help you with that?" I offered. "It must be awfully heavy."

She laughed, and it was nearly a giggle—an incongruously girlish sound coming from such a solid, unadorned woman. "Oh no," she said, "it is not heavy at all . . . try it and see." With that, she lifted the sofa and then set it back on end beside us. I hesitated and she urged, "Really— try it."

My customary social awkwardness made me obey her, and when I tried to lift the sofa I discovered that it weighed very little indeed and was just essentially three blocks of foam rubber covered with a '70s flower-power-patterned upholstery—a downright ugly fabric, now that I was really looking.

"It opens," she was explaining, "to make a *bed!*" She said it in a kind of wonderment, as if she'd just discovered fire or ice. I couldn't help grinning along with her. Then she nodded toward the little cul de sac just across from the elevator, the recessed area where my apartment was. "My new place has no bedroom, so I had to find something I could sleep on at night and seat visitors on in the daytime. This was quite cheap, and I could carry it back here by myself!" She was clearly so delighted by the unattractive couch that her broad, plain face had become appealing, almost pretty. I couldn't help feeling a kind of admiration for her spunk. But another thought was edging out whatever else I felt: So this was to be my new next-door neighbor. I suppose I'd always known the apartment next to me would rent eventually, but all the same I felt my guard going up even as I smiled and said, "Welcome to the building. I'm Honora Blume—Norrie."

She was fishing for her keys but looked up, a little startled. "Honora?"

"Norrie," I said again. "My friends call me Norrie." I always felt embarrassed by the ponderous sound of my given name, but usually people were able to get past it without looking so uneasy. "Awfully heavy name to carry around—Honora. Kind of brings a burden of expectation with it!"

"Oh no, not at all. I just . . . have not heard this name before. Thank you for welcoming me! I'm Clara Brava."

"I guess I live next door to you," I added.

"Oh, but that's wonderful! I am so glad!" When she smiled I saw that one of her upper front teeth was edged with gold. "When I'm all settled," she said, "you should come over for a glass of wine or a cup of coffee." Her smile was sweetly persistent, and I was caught in my usual existential ambivalence at that moment; on the one hand, I was leery of any next-door neighbor's potential intrusion into my life when I wanted to devote my time here to painting, yet I was also oddly warmed and heartened by the idea of having a neighbor—a woman who appeared to be in her thirties, as I was—someone I could say hello to in the hall or maybe invite out to a movie. It made me suddenly not the outsider I'd felt myself to be for the last week or so.

"Of course, at this precise moment," Clara was saying, "I *have* no wine—*or* coffee!" Her smile became a grin, "*Or* cups. *Or* glasses!" She laughed and her front tooth glinted in the hall light. I knew I should invite her over to my place for coffee, or even for dinner, since I was all settled in and she wasn't, but somehow I just could not.

"Let me lend you a few things," I finally said. I could hear the compensatory, falsely hearty tone in my own voice. "I have a few dishes and glasses and other things I could spare." I didn't, but if it got me off the hook, it'd be more than worth it to run over to the Coop and buy some new ones after I'd lent her mine!

"Thank you so much," she said, "but just now I purchased some kitchen things at the Crate and Barrel store. They are holding them until I come back to pick them up." She looked at the hideous love seat and said, "This was all I could bring back with me at one time."

"You got that at Crate and Barrel?" I asked, trying not to sound incredulous; they usually had more minimal, attractive things.

"Yes!" she said. "On *sale!*" No doubt. I looked at the love-seat-bed again, and imagined Clara lugging it back alone, peering around it as she went. Crate and Barrel was just a block and a half up Brattle Street, but even so I was a little amazed that she'd schlepped such a big item back to the apartment by herself, including up in the elevator. There was no doubt that Clara was a person of determination. Again, I found myself admiring her spirit.

"Do you need some help carrying the rest of your purchases back here?" I heard myself asking her.

"Thank you so much," she said again, but this time she stopped there. My heart sank as I realized she was accepting my offer. As she unlocked the door to her apartment, I noticed it had a peephole. I needed to ask Harvard Housing to put one in my door. Clara tipped the love seat onto the hall floor into its upright position and began pushing it inside, over the bare and rather worn oak floor. All the floors in our building seemed to need refinishing. "Come in, please!" She smiled back over her shoulder. "I only want to get this into its place, and then I'll be ready to go back for my other things." She eyed my laundry basket. "Maybe you were busy," she said.

"Oh, I can do laundry anytime," I told her, and picked up the basket. "Let me return this to my place, and I'll meet you here in five minutes."

Back inside my apartment I saw that the phone machine in the bedroom was blinking. I wondered if it was Michael but felt I couldn't take the time to find out or Clara might come over to fetch me. I was strangely reluctant to have her in my place so soon—after the previous two years with Jill, I was jealous of my newfound privacy. I hurried back next door. Maybe I would invite her to eat dinner with me in the square. Perhaps at Casablanca, where they had great crabcakes.

She was adjusting her love seat below the window when I got back; a small boom box and a stack of CDs sat on the floor beside it. I noticed a Paul Klée print taped to a side wall in the nearly vacant room. Coincidentally, it was the same Klée print I'd bought at the Coop for my bedroom. I liked it for its mischief, its bold color, its nerve. Clara saw me looking at it.

"My only amenity, thus far," she laughed. "I liked the spirit of it—so free and maybe even fearless." Not a bad description of Klée, I thought.

"I have the same poster in my apartment," I told her, "for the same sort of reason."

"Oh yes? From the Harvard Coop?" She pronounced it "co-op," though Harvard people pronounced it "coop," as in "chicken coop."

"Yep, from the Coop," I smiled.

"Oh . . . *Coop* . . . I'm still learning the, the, how do you say it . . . strings?"

"Ropes?"

"Yes, ropes." She looked around her one rather shabby little room, her plain face animated by real pleasure. I liked her very much in that moment. "It's very nice, no? Is yours like this?"

"Well, no, it's a little larger," I began hesitantly. I was always uncomfortable having more than someone else. "I took a one-bedroom because I need a work space to use when I'm not at my studio." If I should ever actually *be* at my studio, I thought.

"Studio?"

"Yeah, I'm a painter." Her face took on an odd aspect I couldn't quite define, as if something had surprised or unnerved her. Or maybe I was reading into things again, as Liz always said I did.

"A painter, how wonderful," Clara said, but her voice had suddenly hardened, gone cold, belying her words. "I have never known a painter before. And you even have a studio—you must be very successful." In the wash of her sudden coolness, I found myself making excuses, though I had no idea why I should.

"Well, actually it's just a studio I've been given for the year by the Larkin. I don't even know if I'll end up using it, to be honest."

"The Larkin?" An edge of vitality came back into her voice.

"Institute. I'm a Larkin fellow."

"But what a coincidence this is. I, too, am a Larkin fellow." She was warm again now, enthusiastic. What a strange creature she is, I thought.

"Really? But I don't recall seeing you at orientation last week."

"No, I am arriving late. Perhaps you can show me around the institute tomorrow."

"I'd be glad to if I were going to be there tomorrow, but the thing is, I have to be somewhere else—" I was meeting Michael for lunch. "And actually, Clara, I don't . . . I just really don't go over there very often."

"You don't?" Clara looked shocked, maybe even a bit scandalized. "But there are so many brilliant women there from all over the world. This experience will only be given to us once! Surely you might change your thinking about this."

"Well, I'll definitely be going to most of the weekly colloquium presentations on Wednesday afternoons, but other than that and the odd special occasion, I doubt it. I plan to use this year for painting. I've waited years for the opportunity to take time off work to paint."

"You are so lucky to have that talent," Clara said, as if she saw that it was best to shift the focus of our conversation. "Everything for me depends on words. I think it would be a relief to rely on visual images sometimes instead. It must be wonderful to express oneself without language." Before I could think of an answer, she said, "I guess we should go now before the shop is closing." I knew my attitude about the Larkin had disappointed her.

As she walked to the elevator beside me, I saw that Clara was much shorter than I, and built very compactly; she was even rather muscular. Beside her I felt long and stringy.

"Where are you from?" she asked me as we crossed Brattle. The street performers were already out around Harvard Square, and near the door of Crate and Barrel I could see a three-piece combo playing what sounded like some kind of Latin music, maybe Peruvian.

29

"California, originally," I said, as we pushed the glass doors open and walked into the wonderful world of housewares, "but I've lived here for years."

"In our building?"

"Oh no. I moved to Brattle Street about a week ago. I meant in the *area*. I was sharing a house in Watertown before I came here."

"And you will go back there when you've finished at Harvard?" Clara asked. "Back to the Water City house?"

"Watertown," I said a bit abruptly. How could I answer that question honestly? I hoped to be living with Michael by the time my Larkin year was through. He and I had discussed the fact that I would have to move again when this academic year ended, and he'd resolved to make a clean break by then so that we could begin our new life together. "Well, I don't know where I'll be living after my Larkin year, actually," I finally said. It struck me then that Clara had asked a lot about me and I hadn't reciprocated. My social skills were a little rusty these days, and in general I seemed to have a low threshold of people. "What sort of project has brought you to the Larkin?" I asked, hoping my tardiness hadn't been as obvious to Clara as it was to me.

"I'm a journalist," she told me, as we wandered past shelves of kitchen things. "I'm working on a book about the advent of feminism in Chile."

"That sounds interesting. What inspired you to write it?" I was more comfortable with inspiration than with theory, and anyway, feminism wasn't exactly a new idea to me.

I was startled when Clara stopped dead in her tracks to answer me. Her voice became solemn and deliberate. I remember we were standing by a sign that said MIRAGE VASE, and beneath the sign were a dozen or so handblown glass vases with cobalt shapes floating up the sides.

"My father was a wonderful poet," she said, "and he would have been happy to do only that. But he had inherited a newspaper that belonged to his father before him, and a sense of family duty made him take up the reins after Grandpapa died. When my father's conscience gave him no choice but to speak out against Pinochet's regime in his editorials, he was killed, brutally assassinated, and his newspaper offices were burned. I was just a child at the time. My mother did not know how to live in the world without him. Her parents took us in and we had all we needed materially, but it was too late for my mother. She didn't like the world anymore—she was afraid of everything. I think I grew toward feminism as a result of seeing how helpless she was then."

I was struck by how much it sounded like my own mother after my father died, but though I'd been privately critical about those years of Mother's inability to cope, something kept me silent now. I found I felt defensive of my mother, inexplicably wary of mentioning her. I fell mute.

Clara, too, was quiet for a moment, and then she went on. "I didn't want to be like that, not ever. My mother died in her late-forties, just three years after my grandparents were killed in an automobile accident outside Santiago. I was twenty-five and I knew I would have to live the rest of my life with the knowledge that my mother *wanted* to leave this world, even though her daughter—her *only* child—was still alive."

"She took her own life?"

"Not directly. She simply died inside first, and then allowed ill health to consume her. It was a way out, that's all it was." Clara's face had taken on a bitter look that once again transformed her plain features, this time rather unpleasantly. She certainly had a mobile face, I thought. She would be a challenge to paint.

"What did she die of?" I asked, feeling increasingly uncomfortable.

"The doctors said cancer, the coroner's report said cancer, but I knew it was the desire for death, a failure of spirit." There were tears standing in her eyes, but her face was hard as stone. "She was weak!" Clara fairly spat out the words, and then she paused and drew a deep breath before going on. "My mother was everything to me. I had no one else in the world. I can never forgive her for leaving me."

I didn't know how to respond. I felt sorry that Clara had lost both of her parents so young, but sorrier in a way for her dead mother—to be judged so harshly and absolutely by her surviving daughter after what must have been a painful and possibly protracted death from cancer.

At that moment a saleswoman came over and asked if she could help us, and all at once I was struck by how bizarre it was to have had this conversation in the middle of a Crate and Barrel. Odder still that Clara had emptied such a potent, long-harbored bitterness into a moment of budding acquaintance. I heard her now explaining to the saleswoman about the things being held for her there; her voice was perfectly normal again. Just for a second, in a sort of idle non sequitur of the mind, I wondered what the unequivocal Clara would say about my relationship with a married man.

31

I looked around the store, stifled a sigh. Then my eyes settled on a red glass pitcher on a shelf by the front window, the sort of fat-bellied, forward-leaning pitcher you might see in a Dutch still life. I'd never before seen one like it made of glass—only of clay or ceramic pottery. It was a deep and gleaming clear red glass through which the last rays of daylight refracted. I forgot Clara for the moment and walked over to the display; it was, apparently the only red pitcher left, though there were several in celadon, which I also love. But the red was spectacular—a rich, deep red that was, I'd say, the color of blood, if blood could be spun into glass and filled with light.

This might spur me to paint. I picked the pitcher up without even checking the price and carried it back to the counter, where Clara was standing and watching me, an odd, quizzical expression on her face.

"Look!" I said, "isn't it great? I've never seen a pitcher of this style made out of glass!"

"Very nice," she said, but I heard the restraint in her voice. Just then the saleswoman and a male stock clerk brought out Clara's paid-for purchases.

"I'd like to buy this," I said, and when the woman took it from my hands to ring it up, I experienced a sort of absurd separation anxiety. I wanted it back. I never wanted to let go of it. Even when I saw the price—enough to buy my groceries for several days—I didn't care. I watched the woman wrap the pitcher in layers of tissue and then put it into a white paper bag with the store logo in black on both sides. I took it from her hands carefully and with pleasure. Maybe I would paint again soon. Maybe tonight.

"*Expensive,*" Clara said in a light, rather amused tone I found annoying, "especially for something not essential. Well, I have heard you Americans are profligate!" I felt a flash of anger.

"I'm a painter," I said hotly and maybe a little haughtily. "What may not be essential for you might be an absolute necessity for me."

"Oh," she said, "Oh no, I hope I haven't offended you, Honora . . . Norrie. I'm sometimes so stupid in the things I say. Forgive me." She looked so worried and contrite that I softened.

"No, really, forget it. You may be right about us profligate Americans, but honestly I think this wonderful red pitcher will make its way into a painting I'm working on."

In my mind.

Will soon be working on in my mind.

It amazed me what a fraud I felt, calling myself an artist when I hadn't painted in weeks.

Clara and I examined her four huge bags of assorted utensils, cutlery, pots and pans, dishes, glasses, some small stacking units, and bedding. All essentials, I noted, and from among Crate and Barrel's plainer, more modestly priced items. But if she was so frugal, she could have bought most of this in the basement of the Coop for less, I thought. It would have been less stylish, but cheaper. I contemplated saying so and then was ashamed of the petty impulse.

I took two sacks and Clara took two. Carefully I put my wrapped and packaged pitcher into the bedding bag I was holding; it would be easier to carry that way.

It was getting dark as we walked back out onto the street, and the Latin combo had shifted from their up-tempo sound to a slow song I found rather spooky and mournful. Clara and I both fell quiet, and the music seemed a lugubrious sound track written to accompany us on our trek home. The bags were so big they interfered with the movement of our legs as we walked. I was tall enough that at least mine didn't drag on the ground, but Clara had to constantly heft hers upward to keep them from hitting the sidewalk. Suddenly I was glad I'd helped her. It would've taken her two trips to bring all this stuff back by herself. At the same time all I wanted was to get away from her, and I couldn't quite have said why.

"I would love to visit with you again sometime soon," she finally said as we walked through the courtyard at the front of our building. A young, athletic-looking couple were just coming out and laughing heartily about something; his arm was slung carelessly around her shoulders, and she leaned into him as she laughed. "You are *so bad*," she said in a flirtatious tone. I wanted to be one of them; at the moment it didn't particularly matter which one. "You are so *easy* to talk to," Clara was saying. "We have only just met today, and I can't believe how much I have told you already."

Neither could I. And I couldn't imagine reciprocating.

Wordless, I just smiled and nodded and put my outside key into the front door of the building to let us into the lobby. We crossed to the elevator, the Crate and Barrel bags bumping our legs as we went.

"Would you like to come in for a while?" she asked as we got off the elevator on the fourth floor. She had to be wondering why I wasn't extending that very invitation to her since I was already settled into my place.

"No thanks," I said. "I have plans for tonight."

I did have plans—to be alone and try to paint. I could have kicked myself for not simply telling her that. I resolved to get over such senseless reticence. My art wasn't some flimsy social excuse; it was my *work*.

"Oh, too bad," Clara said. "Maybe after you get back tonight you would like to come in for a cup of tea? I have a few tea bags on hand—and now I even have cups!" Right then I could easily have corrected her misimpression that I was going out for the evening, but I was in a posture of retreat, and that was all I cared about at the moment.

"No, it just wouldn't work tonight. But maybe another time." I supposed it was quite possible that my resistance to Clara said more about me than about her.

"Good, yes," she said. "I would love that."

We said good-bye and then as I stood at my apartment door, key in hand, I heard Clara calling my name again and I turned around.

"I just wanted to say that I'm very glad you live here," she said. "I feel we will be the best of friends."

"Thanks, Clara." I smiled to ameliorate the noncommittal sound of my words, but I could not make myself respond in kind. Clara returned my smile and then dragged the Crate and Barrel bags into her apartment. Immediately I felt bad that I hadn't been able to agree with her that we might end up the best of friends. Maybe we would, but for now I was in a wait-and-see mode.

Inside my apartment I noticed that another lavender memo from the management had been slipped under the door and lay at my feet—the Harvard Housing people seemed to find anything an occasion for a memo—on Monday it had been something about water pressure at peak hours of usage and on Wednesday it had been about visitors leaving bikes in the lobby. I folded the memo, pushed it into my pocket without reading it, and went to the answering machine.

The message was from Michael, who was going to a wedding this evening with Brenda.

"I'll be thinking about you tonight," he said into the air of my bedroom. "Oh well, big news, I think about you every minute anyway."

Along the opposite wall stood my easel with a blank canvas on it. All my life I'd loved the feeling of opportunity a fresh canvas offers, but my mood had soured and I suddenly doubted I would paint tonight. It wouldn't be fair to blame it on Clara—the longer I went without painting, the more the idea of it felt like a failed obligation. I wasn't used to that. I'd never had a real creative block in my life. Tonight an empty canvas didn't look like opportunity to me; I hated the sight of it. I threw my red silk kimono over it so that I wouldn't wake up in the night and see its stark whiteness lurking.

I guess it was the kimono's color that made me think of it then: the red glass pitcher. I couldn't believe I'd left it in the bag with Clara's bedding. So badly had I wanted to get away from her in the hallway that I'd forgotten all about my wonderful red pitcher. Now I stood just inside my front door, hesitating. What should I do? I wouldn't go over and get it now, I decided, because I couldn't bear to start up a fresh conversation with her.

But what if she should come to my door with it? No, that wouldn't happen. She thought I was going out for the evening. Then I had an uneasy thought: In order to depart or arrive at my apartment you had to pass Clara's door. She might notice when I didn't leave all evening after telling her I had plans. And, of course, no visitors would be coming to knock on my door either. Would she realize I was alone in my apartment, that I'd more or less lied to her—or anyway, intentionally misled her? I forced the thought out of my mind; I didn't need to start imagining Clara's eyes on me.

If she came to my door tonight with the red pitcher, I'd just not answer her knock. I'd reached my maximum daily requirement of Clara. I could go over and get the pitcher tomorrow.

I eyed the kimono spread over the canvas like a lover. It made an interesting image.

In the bedroom I changed into a nightgown. I could feel my mood spiraling downward and was determined not to give in to it.

It was when I was putting my jeans over the back of a chair that I noticed the lavender memo protruding from the pocket. It was a warning to tenants that there had been several burglaries in our building recently. They advised keeping your door locked whether you were home or away and asked that tenants not prop open the front door of the building as some had done recently when having parties. "The door to the lobby should remain closed and locked at all times, and visitors should use the intercom to gain entrance to the building. By doing otherwise, you are putting your neighbors at risk of material loss or bodily harm." Great, one more thing to feel wary about.

In the kitchen I emptied a take-out carton of leftover corn chowder into a pan. I would watch television in my bedroom while I ate, just to help me relax, and I'd keep the sound low enough that if Clara came to the door she wouldn't hear it and realize I was home.

Before I ate, I played Michael's message once more, and then I erased it. Life felt both empty and crowded.

The TV was on, but I couldn't have said what was playing. After a bit I switched it off and walked to my easel, where I pulled the red kimono off the blank canvas and draped it over a chair. At the very least I should face up to my failure. I sat on the side of the bed and sipped my soup, watched the canvas the way a person might watch a movie, waiting for something to speak.

From the first time we brought our two bodies together, I knew I wanted to have you in every possible way. Sometimes it felt like greed: The more I had of you, the more I hungered for you. Never was that feeling more acute than the first time we went away together on a weekend trip to San Francisco. I guess because we'd never before gone out into the world together, far away from familiarity and expectation and into a place where neither of us had any significant history, it cut us loose, intensified our erotic fusion.

We were staying in Liz's third-floor apartment on Chenery Street while she was away in London. It was late spring, and the wind blew in through an open kitchen window and drifted across our bodies in the darkened living room where we lay together on the opened-out sleeper couch. All Liz's living room windows were bare of curtains or shades—that's so Liz—and I remember there was a sort of lavender light at the edges of the darkness that caught your long limbs beautifully, and when you shifted once on your back to stretch I was beset with desire, I wanted to have you in a new way, wanted what I'd not done with anyone before, hadn't been inclined to try. I didn't know what it would be like, or if it would hurt, and I was even a little afraid. But it was you there, splendid in the hungry light, and I wanted you, wanted it, wanted every kind of knowing between us. I'll never forget how, when I asked, you said "yes" just as I said "ass," so that the two words fell into the air with absolute synchronicity in one sibilant sigh.

I didn't want to tell you I was scared a little, scared it would hurt, because I didn't want to ruin it. I waited on hands and knees as you came up behind me on the opened-out sofa mattress and then I leaned forward to rest my arms on the back of the sofa. I felt you hard against me and when you pushed tentatively, gingerly, I felt my body opening and you asked if you were hurting me, I said no, yes, no, do it, I want it, and then you came fully into me opening me and it hurt a little but I wanted it and when I felt you push in all the way O the shock of it shock of knowledge, of you deep, deep inside me where no one had been before, and I heard your voice behind me. It's like honey, you said, and I felt it too, wanted you there, felt you move gently very gently inside me at first, then more insistently, and finally thrusting thrusting until suddenly I began to come, without warning I began to come though I hadn't thought I could come that way but I did, I came hard, hard, and then you came, too, exploding deep inside me, and I knew right then that I would do anything with you, knew that I wanted all the knowledge desire invites.

3

I woke on Sunday after a night of fitful sleep just as morning began seeping through the muslin curtains on my east window. Still tired and way too unmotivated to get up, I closed my eyes again and tried to replay the dream I seemed to have wakened in the middle of but could only reconstruct it elliptically: In the dream I was in a hospital bed and could not move my arms. Then suddenly my father was standing in the middle of the room and holding out a smooth, clear, dark red stone about the size of a robin's egg on the palm of his open hand, which was extended toward me. I could see he wanted to give me the stone—and something told me that having it was crucial to my recovery from whatever ailed me—but I couldn't move my arms to reach for it nor could my hands have grasped it if I had, and I was too weak to get out of bed and walk to it. Daddy didn't seem able or willing to speak or to move closer and place the stone beside me on the bed. Throughout nearly all of this seemingly endless dream, I did nothing but strain to reach the stone again and again. Even after my father had given up on me and disappeared from the dream, I continued trying to reach the stone, which hovered in the air where his hand had been; but my limbs were useless and without sensation. The lovely red stone, clear as glass, remained in the path of my vision but impossible to reach.

What a dream, I thought—like a bad Bergman film! Did this painter's block have to plague me even while I was asleep? Beneath the sheets I stretched my body like a martyr on a rack. Then the thought of the red glass stone reminded me of the red glass pitcher, and I realized the image had probably come out of my distraction about the pitcher before I went to bed last night. I would have to retrieve it from Clara this morning. Somehow I felt as if it held the promise of artistic inspiration, that maybe my fixation on it was some sort of evidence to myself that I was still an artist. Odd, and maybe pathetic, how one can imbue an inert object with such power when self-confidence is flagging.

I thought then of the lost green glass ring of my childhood. Mother and Daddy and I had been at a church bazaar at Our Lady of Saints one spring evening when I was five, and I'd won the ring at a "Go Fishing" booth. It seemed a wondrous object to me with its large, emerald-cut stone, like something a fairy-tale queen might wear on her index finger. I'd put it away for safekeeping in the small, brown paper bag full of loot I'd amassed at the festival that night. Then somehow I became separated from my parents and began wandering around the school grounds to find them, treasure bag in hand. I remember my interminable search around the schoolyard that night, past other children whose parents were beside them.

As I wandered I began to cry, and I remember little from that point until the moment when I spotted my mother and father walking quickly around the booths, their faces caught in expressions of panic as they looked for me. I ran to them—I remember trying to make my legs go faster and faster—and I'll never forget the joy I felt when Daddy swept me into his arms and Mama hugged me as he held me. It was only when we got back home that I realized I must have dropped my brown paper bag somewhere on the school grounds during my search.

All I thought of for days after that was the lost ring. I wanted it vehemently, hungrily; I felt a loss I hadn't known before in my young life. I chafed and was baffled by the idea that something of mine could somehow be irretrievably gone. For years to come the green glass ring would return to my thoughts at odd moments, always with a fresh stab of grief, and when Daddy died during my seventh-grade year I began thinking of the ring again for the first time in years as if somehow the loss of it were tied to his death. Of course, now it seems to me that it was natural to have thought of the ring after his death, for it represented the first deeply felt loss of my childhood, and when Daddy died, that earlier loss returned with the kind of force and power his death had now brought to the sensation of grief. And thinking of the ring helped me in an odd way to deal with recurrent thoughts of him. For a time I think I actually imagined that if I could only find the green glass ring, my father might come back somehow. Even in my adult years I'd occasionally had the sensation that to find the ring again would set everything right in my life.

I looked at the clock now. It would seem intrusive to knock on Clara's door before ten on a Sunday morning. I showered and dressed and waited for it to be ten, idly musing on the two treasured glass objects, pitcher and ring, and thought how odd that both had slipped from my possession while in bags that had been meant to safeguard them.

It was getting close to ten when the phone rang. When I picked up, I heard Michael—unusual for him to call me on a weekend morning. "Last night I dreamed you were on a beach fucking someone else," he said without a prefatory hello.

"Hmmm, I don't believe I was. Let me think." I paused. "Who is this again?"

"Have a heart," he said. "Listen, I can't really talk right now, but I just wanted to say it made me crazy. I woke up ready to find the asshole, whoever he was, and beat him senseless."

"Whoa, big fella. I think you're confusing yourself with Schwarzenegger. You're the evolved, nonviolent type, remember—the man of letters?" I'd always loathed the idea that some women like their men to fight over them, and I wasn't about to encourage this alpha-male behavior by revealing how it was exciting me. I was a little unnerved to see how acute was my response.

"Oh, I had my days as a kid in Southie," he said. "I thumped a few heads. We all did—you had to, to survive in the projects. Anyway, as for being or not being a 'violent type,' I don't think it's as simple as that. I mean, I think anyone might be capable of violence if what he desires most in the world is taken away. But my point is, I honestly can't recall ever feeling like this before. I can't stand to think of you with someone else. I seem to covet you in the extreme."

"At Catholic school they taught us that 'to covet' meant to greatly desire something that belonged to another," I told him, "and *I* belong to no one else. So if one of us covets the other, wouldn't that have to be *me* coveting *you?*"

Just then, as if to illustrate my words, Brenda called out to him from another room.

"Yeah, be right there," he shouted, and then to me, "I have to go."

"I rest my case."

"No matter what you think about all of this," he said, with uncustomary fierceness, "I belong to *you*." He hung up. I knew that in a sitcom the audience would be laughing at us. That's the problem with growing up in Los Angeles—you often tend to see yourself through cameras.

Again I thought of Brenda's voice calling through the house to Michael with all the quotidian humdrum expectation one has a right to in marriage, and I felt a keen, fresh unease at the idea that I desired a man who was someone else's. In the true liturgical meaning of the word, I *coveted* Michael, for he was her husband. Covetousness was one of the Seven Deadly Sins the nuns had taught us about at Our Lady during my childhood: pride, covetousness, envy, lust, gluttony, anger, and sloth.

Sometimes when I was a kid it had seemed to me as if any honest emotion at all must be a sin, and I'd wondered why God had given us these feelings if they were wrong and could land us in Hell. Was He tricking us? I wondered. Why would He want to do that? Most of the Seven Deadly Sins had to do with desire of some kind: lust, gluttony, envy, covetousness—even pride and sloth. Hell, even anger if you thought it through. At one time or another I was feeling any or all of those emotions in connection with Michael. I wondered if early religious teachings could ever be purged from the mind, and if they could, why had I never managed to liberate myself from my Catholic upbringing?

It was ten, so I took leave of my spiritual crisis and went to Clara's to get my red glass pitcher. There was no answer when I rapped on her door. I couldn't believe she'd left, possibly for the day, without first trying to return my package. There could be no doubt she'd have discovered it last night in the Crate and Barrel bag where I'd left it, since my bag was in the bag that had held her bedding. I returned to my apartment feeling frustrated and a little annoyed. I had plans for later in the day and wanted to get the pitcher back before I left.

At eleven I returned to her door with the idea of inviting her for lunch if she answered. Ransom, I thought as I knocked. Still no answer. I made another fruitless try at noon and left frustrated by the thought that I wasn't going to be able to check back again until very late in the day because I had to leave for Brookline soon. I imagined my red pitcher on the floor of Clara's living room, catching and holding rays of midday light.

I was going to see Ida Czernak, mother of Henry Czernak, a man who'd lived with me in the Watertown house several years ago, just after I'd moved there. I always visited Ida on Sundays if I could, and had called the Brookline Manor Nursing Home to let the staff know I was coming today so they could get her ready. Ida still had a fair amount of female vanity at eighty-four and hated for me to come unannounced and catch her not looking her best. Ida's son, Henry, a fine arts professor at Tufts, had broken up with me after I told him I wasn't inclined to get married and have children—possibly ever. ("I want to find someone more life-affirming," he'd said the night he ended our two-year relationship; that comment had stung me far more than did the breakup itself.) Henry had been killed in an auto accident on an icy Vermont road just six months later as he drove to see a woman he'd begun dating, apparently someone more life-affirming than I—though a lot of good that quality did him, as it turns out.

During the two years Henry and I were together, I'd gone with him regularly to visit Ida in her cluttered Brookline apartment on Sundays and had become quite fond of her. After Henry and I broke up, I'd continued to see his mother, but on Saturdays to avoid running into him. When Henry died, Ida had no one left. She'd been a widow for many years, and Henry was an only child. Now that I'd become the old woman's only visitor, it seemed important not to let her down.

Ida was diabetic and had chronic kidney trouble; last year after a fall had broken her left hip, she had given up her apartment and moved to the nursing home. She'd deteriorated noticeably since giving up her in-dependence; and though she still had good days and bad days, lately there seemed to be more bad than good. Last time I'd gone to see her—two weeks ago now because of the move—it had been a bad day for Ida. Throughout our visit she'd been very confused about everything, had even believed that Henry was still alive and I was married to him.

"Why am I being held prisoner here?" she'd asked me as I stood to leave that day, her fingers working frantically, pleating and unpleating the skirt of her navy blue crepe dress. "I've done nothing wrong. You must tell Henry to talk with a lawyer about this and get me out of here, posthaste!" I'd blinked away tears all the way back to the T stop.

I knocked on Clara's door one last time as I left to catch the T to Brookline, and when there was still no answer, I set off to visit Ida. Today was a clear, warm day and the streets of Cambridge were bustling in that indolent Sunday Cantabrigian way. Here and there musicians and evangelists performed without benefit of an audience, except for the occasional small knots of quiet Asian tourists with cameras. I passed panhandlers at the doorway of nearly every storefront, and in front of the Coop a skinny, male tightrope walker sang "God Bless America" as he swanned across the wire he'd set up in a portable frame along the outer edge of the sidewalk.

At Nini's Corner I bought *People, Star,* and *Royalty Monthly* for Ida (she loved gossip and was fond of the British Royals). Then I picked up some sugarfree raisin scones at Warburton's Bakery just down the block. All the way to Brookline on the T, I kept my eyes closed, imitating sleep, as a way of avoiding conversation with an array of seatmates.

When I arrived at the nursing home, I found Ida blessedly clearheaded and very glad to see me, but I was distressed to see that she was quite weak and seemed to have lost weight. In fact, she looked jaundiced and rather skeletal against the pillows of the recliner chair someone had transferred her to in anticipation of my visit. She was wearing the magenta velveteen robe I'd given her for her last birthday. Usually she insisted the nurses put her into a proper Sunday dress for my visits, and I knew she must be in more pain than usual or they would have. Her white hair had been nicely brushed and arranged, as always, and she was wearing her customary lipstick. But it was clear to me that a nurse had applied the lipstick this time because it followed the natural line of Ida's lips, rather than curving above her top lip, 1950s' style, which was how Ida liked to do it.

I explained to her, in case she'd forgotten, that I'd missed my visit last weekend because of the move, and I explained again about my Larkin Fellowship (also in case she'd forgotten, which she apparently had).

"My, such an honor for a young artist!" she exclaimed. "I'm very proud of you." I grinned; I supposed thirty-six was young to Ida. Then she looked into my face with a kind of curiosity. "Are you getting to be famous?"

"Not a chance," I laughed. "But I guess you could say my work is getting some notice. *ArtAmerica* recently listed me in their rundown of twenty-five up-and-coming American painters."

"My word," Ida said, and then her face took on a musing expression and she fell silent. I took that moment to excuse myself on the pretext of using the restroom. I wanted to talk to the duty nurse and see why Ida looked so frail. Marge Flannery, my favorite of the Manor's nursing staff, was on duty today, and I knew that if I asked her for information about Ida's condition, she would give me no trouble about my not being a blood relation. Marge had worked at the manor for as long as Ida had been there, and she knew quite well that the old woman had no visitors but me.

I found her at the nursing station, talking on the phone. She motioned for me to come around and sit down with her behind the counter till she was through. "That's right," I heard her saying as she tapped a chair beside her and mouthed *Hello*. "He is doing fine today, Mrs. O'Malley. I know he would just *love* a visit whenever you can manage it. Oh yes, I can imagine how busy you must be right now. But one of these days you may wish you'd made the time." She looked at me and rolled her eyes. "Yes, I'm sure you will. Yes, I'm sure you do. Good-bye." Marge didn't have much patience with those errant sons and daughters who rarely visited their parents at the Manor.

After our routine greetings, I asked what was wrong with Ida today. I was stunned when Marge informed me that Ida was going to have to begin dialysis treatments because her kidneys were failing. "We're lucky there's a wonderful center just a block away," she said cheerfully, "and they'll come and get her in their ambulance three times a week and bring her back." I was about to ask why no one had called me, then reminded myself that since I wasn't a relative, they had no duty to notify me. Also, it struck me that no one there knew my last name anyway, though by now many of them called me by my first name. So when Ida died, there'd be no one to call and inform except the coroner. How sad. How unacceptable.

"Look, Marge, I know Ida isn't my own flesh and blood, but she's got no one else in the world now. Couldn't you list me as the one to call if she takes a turn for the worse?"

"Of course I can." She immediately went for Ida's records, asking over her shoulder for my name and phone number, then noting the information in several places.

"And if she needs or wants anything that's not billable to Medicare, would you call me, Marge? Maybe I can help." I knew Ida couldn't have a lot of financial security; she'd sold the Brookline apartment to pay for a place in the Manor.

Marge assured me that she would have someone call me if Ida needed anything. "But those weekly visits are what she needs most, and you're already doing that." I felt a stab of guilt for not coming last weekend. I could have made the effort, I knew. I'd just let fatigue get the better of me after getting everything moved into the apartment on Saturday and then staying up all night unpacking. But that wasn't the whole story. I was pretty much all moved in by Sunday midday when Michael had called, and I'd succumbed to the chance to see him alone in my new apartment for the first time instead of making the trek to Brookline for Ida. It had been the only Sunday visit I'd missed in nearly a year, so it hadn't seemed like the end of the world. But as it turned out, the end of the world for Ida might not be too far away.

Over tea brought in by a nurse's aide—instructed, no doubt, by Marge—Ida and I chatted while we nibbled the raisin scones. I was relieved that today she remembered her son was long dead. In fact she seemed only to want to talk about Henry suddenly—what a talented painter he'd been and what a shame he'd never had time to pursue his art seriously, what with his teaching responsibilities and everything.

"He'd have been famous by now," Ida told me, "if only his life hadn't been snuffed out before he had a chance." I didn't tell her that Henry had never painted a thing after he'd gotten out of grad school, and that although he was a terrific art teacher, he was really quite a mediocre painter. Even Henry had not considered himself to be an artist. But all I said was yes, I guessed it was a shame he couldn't have had more time to pursue a career as an artist. In all, it seemed a pleasant-enough conversation. Then Ida asked me why Henry and I had never married—a question which, oddly, she'd never asked me before, and I'd always just assumed Henry had told her.

"I thought the two of you were so appropriate for one another," she said, "both being artists."

Henry had wanted to get married and have children, I explained to her, and at the time I wasn't sure I wanted that.

45

She allowed that I'd had a right to my own feelings about marriage and children, whatever those feelings might be, but said she couldn't help thinking that if I'd married Henry he would be alive today instead of "dead on a road in Vermont." Ida said this matter-of-factly rather than in any obvious anger, but I was stung, even as I imagined Henry the way she described him, still dead on a road in Vermont after all these years.

When I reminded Ida that Henry was the one who had left the relationship, she said, "Well, you didn't give the poor fellow much choice, did you?" And before I could come up with an answer, she added, "Maybe you didn't like the competition of another artist in your life. But how sad for Henry that he should have to suffer and die for that."

Just then the nurse came in with Ida's meds and it seemed a good time for me to go. I kissed Ida's forehead and she said, "Come back soon—I get lonely for you." She seemed innocent of the effect her comments had had on me. I was hurt, and no matter how I tried to tell myself that Ida was old and confused, it seemed to me that even in words that sprang from dementia there had to be the seed of some real conviction, didn't there? Was it possible Ida would die believing I'd somehow shortened her son's natural life out of selfishness or professional jealousy?

Altogether it was not a happy visit, and I was gloomy as I headed back up Brookline Avenue to the T station. More than likely, though, the next time I came to visit Ida she wouldn't remember having said those things to me. But I kept wondering, did she have such a low opinion of me or was today just some sort of synaptic fuse blowing?

I got off the Redline into Harvard Square in no mood to fix myself dinner, so I stopped at a little café on Mass Ave and ordered a spinach omelet and some cottage fries—a comfort meal—and then headed home.

By the time I got back to the apartment building, it was nearly seven P.M., and I went straight to Clara's apartment and knocked. She came to the door right away.

"Norrie, how nice to see you!" Her collar-length hair was down today, and it slimmed her face, made her look more feminine. "Come in," she invited, smiling broadly. I'd been prepared to be irritable, but I found it hard to resist her friendly grin. I even decided to wait a couple of minutes before mentioning the red pitcher which, I noticed as I scanned the room, was not out in plain sight anywhere.

"I've just bought some wonderful Chilean merlot," Clara said, "down at Sage's Market. I was surprised to see what a fine selection they have in their wine cellar."

"Yes," I agreed, "they do have a good selection. But I don't think I've tried any of the Chilean wines—I wouldn't know which were the good ones." I followed Clara into her small kitchen, still looking around for my red glass pitcher. A small, white plastic shelf unit she'd bought yesterday had been assembled and placed against a wall of the kitchen near the tiny gas stove. On it stood a cutlery-filled knife block and a small, lucite wine rack that held several bottles of wine. On the second shelf stood a group of storage jars she'd purchased at Crate and Barrel, filled now with coffee beans, pinto beans, rice, tea bags, and pasta. There were a few dirty dishes in the sink, which was filled with soapy water. Apparently she'd eaten already, too.

The red pitcher was nowhere to be seen.

"I always tell people they should just look for the labels that have 'Saint' before the name, like Santa Rita and Santa Carolina," Clara advised as she took a bottle of wine from the rack and expertly removed the cork, "or try Casillero del Diablo—it's a real bargain." She filled two stemmed glasses and handed me one.

We settled on the love seat I'd seen her carrying the day before. I looked around the room. The boom box and CDs were now against the side wall below the Klée print and had been neatly arranged on another white plastic shelf unit she must have assembled last night. The whole room was amazingly tidy, and the Crate and Barrel bags were nowhere to be seen. Clara noticed me looking around.

"How does it look?" she asked with a hopeful expression on her face.

"Wonderful," I told her honestly. "So orderly!"

"Oh yes," she laughed, "I have been told that I'm orderly to a fault. But when you live in small apartments, you must keep things in order or you might go crazy, I think."

"Absolutely . . ." I hesitated, then made the plunge. "Clara, I wonder where my red glass pitcher is?"

"What?" she looked startled. "What do you mean?" My heart sank at her words. That had been the last one of the red pitchers in the store; I might never be able to find another like it. Had she taken it to punish me for my American profligacy? My native paranoia had boiled to the surface, and I could hear its effect in the slightly elevated tone of my voice as I replied.

"Surely you came across it when you took your bedding out of the Crate and Barrel bag last night." I heard myself say this in a way that reminded me of Perry Mason's court scenes. Would my red glass pitcher end up just another goddamn lifetime icon of careless loss, like the green glass ring?

"Oh! You put your pitcher into my bedding bag?" She walked quickly to a door next to the Klée print and the new CD stand. When she opened it, I could see what was a fairly generous storage closet, and in the middle of it, two large Crate and Barrel bags sat, apparently still unopened since yesterday when we'd brought them back here. She bent to check one of the bags and retrieved the small sack inside it that held my precious pitcher. "I am *so* sorry," she said. "I had no idea you had put your bag into my bag, and I was so tired last night when I finished putting my shelves together that I just fell asleep on the sofa without even opening it out into a bed or getting out my new bedding."

It couldn't have been very comfortable sleeping on this love seat that way, I thought. She must have been exhausted. I was regretting my paranoia as she handed me the bag.

I immediately opened it to look at my red glass pitcher, whole and unharmed in the thick tissue the Crate and Barrel clerk had wrapped around it before she'd slipped it into the bag. "Thank God!" I blurted, then amended in a more casual tone, "I really would like to paint it."

"It's very beautiful," Clara said. I resolved at that moment to make up to her for my suspicious thoughts.

The two of us drank the remarkably good merlot and listened to one of Clara's CDs of Aldo Ciccolini playing the piano music of Erik Satie. I couldn't believe Clara loved Satie, too. I didn't think I'd ever met anyone else who felt about his music the way I did. And about Ciccolini's intuitive interpretation of those eccentric compositions. "Le Piège de Méduse" was playing—it was one of my favorites. I loved Satie because he was a rebel, and also I felt empathy with him for being such a recluse. When he died in his tiny lodging in a Paris suburb, thirty-two identical black suits with white shirts were found in his closet—his daily apparel. He knew what he liked, apparently.

As Clara and I drank, we talked about the Larkin Institute, our hopes for the year, and about our shared feeling of diffidence in the illustrious company there. One of the fellows this year was a former governor of Vermont, and another was an ambassador to the United Nations. Clara mentioned that there was also a poet from India named Devi Bhujander who had been nominated for a Nobel Prize for her powerful poetry about the women's struggle in India.

"She lives in this building," Clara said, "but I haven't met her yet. Have you?"

"No, I haven't, but I did see her at orientation last week. She's very beautiful."

"Oh?" Clara's expression changed just slightly, although I couldn't interpret the change. "I must meet her. Her poetry means the world to me."

"You said before that your father was a poet. I guess you inherited his interest in poetry."

"Oh yes, to love it is my legacy. In fact, my father chose to name me after two poets. Clara is for Claribel Alegria, and my middle name is Gabriela, after Gabriela Mistral, the first Latin American ever to win the Nobel Prize for Literature. Poetry is revered in my part of the world. We consider poetry an important tool of resistance, and it has been quite a powerful influence for change in Chile, where Neruda is a national hero. But tell me, do you know Devi Bhujander's poetry?"

"Actually no, not well. Do you?"

"Oh yes, very well. It's brilliant. Quite stirring. She is one of the youngest poets ever to have been nominated for a Nobel Prize, and many believe she will win it one day, though of course she's much too young to get the award now." Clara leaned toward me just slightly then and said, "I've only seen the same small photo on all of her book jackets. What is she like?"

"She's very petite and kind of fragile looking," I told her. "I'd say she's no more than five feet tall and she couldn't weigh even a hundred pounds." Clara waited as I paused to summon other details from my memory of the Larkin's three-day orientation period. "She has long black hair past her waist, and she keeps it in a braid. She mostly wears traditional Indian garb, but I saw her from a distance one day last week in a calf-length skirt with a loose tunic top over it."

Clara was fixed on me as I talked; and when I paused again, she said, "Yes, go on . . ."

"Well, I'd say she has a strong face for such a delicate woman, a straight nose . . . and the thing I most clearly recall, besides her lovely hair, is the beauty of her eyes. They're, well, *dramatic*. I actually thought she might be the most beautiful woman I'd ever seen."

Clara expelled an audible breath. "I can't wait to meet her. One of the things I've most anticipated about my Larkin year has been meeting Devi Bhujander."

"So you knew she'd be here at the Larkin this year?"

"Oh, yes. As a journalist, I've followed her career closely."

"But what good luck that she's here the same year you are."

"Luck. I don't believe in luck," Clara said matter-of-factly as she poured us each a second glass of wine. "I believe in fate."

I could feel the effect of the first glass of wine already, so I forced myself to slow down and sip the second. I was finding it surprisingly pleasant to be here talking with a new friend and listening to music I loved. Conversation was easier between us tonight than it had been yesterday. I should try harder not to make premature judgments about people.

At some point in the conversation Clara asked me if I was "seeing anyone." I debated whether I should say yes and then decided I couldn't because she was likely to see Michael visiting at some point, and she mustn't know he was my lover. His face was recognized more and more by people who followed the literary scene. I decided to find a way of answering without lying. "I was engaged," I said, "but my fiancé died in an auto accident." That wasn't a lie. Except for the part about being engaged. Which was, on reflection, nearly all of it. Lucky lying wasn't one of the Seven Deadly Sins.

"Oh, I'm sorry, Norrie. Actually, I, too, was engaged once, but he was not prepared for such a commitment and it ended rather abruptly."

"It's painful when love comes to nothing," I said.

"Yes. You and I have much in common," Clara answered, and I heard myself agreeing immediately and enthusiastically, my rusty social skills lubricated by wine. I realized my second glassful was gone. So much for sipping.

"I'm glad to have you for a neighbor," I said, remembering how restrained my response had been yesterday when she'd said the same thing to me. "It'll be nice to have someone to share the Larkin experience with."

"Do you enjoy going to films?"

"I adore it. Some people have told me I'm addicted to the movies!" My mother.

"Have you heard about the Harvard Film Archive?" Clara asked. "They have an excellent series on Wednesday nights. This month they're showing Ingmar Bergman films."

"Really! I've often wondered how I would feel about Bergman now. I don't think I've seen one of his films since college." Unless you counted the dream I had last night, I thought. "Which one are they showing this week?"

"*Wild Strawberries,* I think. Would you like to go with me Wednesday evening?"

"I'd love it," I said. "Maybe we can go out for dinner before the movie."

"That would be splendid." Clara poured the last of the wine into our glasses, taking care to divide it equally. "I'm feeling very happy right now," she announced suddenly.

"You know," I answered, "I am, too." Then I glanced at my watch and saw that it was nearly 10:00 P.M. Time had melted away.

Soon after that I excused myself to return to my apartment with the red pitcher. Clara gave me a little hug at the door and I had no trouble returning the embrace, even with the pitcher firmly in my grip. After all my dread of being too friendly with anyone who lived next door, I thought, wasn't it ironic that the time I'd spent with Clara tonight was the only part of the entire day that hadn't been frustrating and unsatisfying. It occurred to me that, between my work and my secret life with Michael, I might have become too isolated, even for a person who valued privacy as highly as I did.

When I got into my apartment I walked around searching out the perfect spot for the red glass pitcher and finally decided to put it on the bookcase below my bedroom's south window, where it could catch the changing light each day. This room was where I'd be painting, and also I loved the idea of looking at it from my bed when I opened my eyes each morning. I tried turning out the light and then looked at the pitcher where it sat before the night window. In the dark it only showed red around the upper edges where it caught a faint beam of light from a sliver of moon.

On my machine there was a message Michael had left earlier in the day to say that he and Brenda were going to visit her sister on Martha's Vineyard for her birthday and would be back late tomorrow.

It bothered me that he was taking a trip with her, that he would be sharing a new bed with her—there was something sexy about a strange bed, I always thought. The idea of their everyday marriage bed was bothersome enough.

I erased the message and got ready for bed. I was tired of myself, of my jealousy and sourness, my creative paralysis, my apparent collusion with whatever was stalling creativity in me. I remembered something I'd once heard Michael say about how after years of procrastination and feeling "stuck," he'd finally reached a point where he *had* to write his novel—that or not be a writer. He said, "It suddenly hit me that maybe inspiration comes *during* work, rather than *before* it. And so I just sat down and wrote the damned thing." He'd written the first draft of *This Cold Heaven* in four weeks and then had spent the next ten months going back over it, "sanding it," as he liked to say, "until I found the grain."

With sudden, half-formed resolve, I took off my nightgown and put on my old painting clothes. Maybe I wouldn't paint anything worth showing, but at least I would be working again. Process, not product, that would be the point for now. I got out my paints, most of which were still in the closet in the boxes I'd used for moving them, though I'd taken a few things over to my Larkin studio. I cleared off the table beside the west bedroom window and covered it with the paint-stained dropcloth I hadn't had occasion to see for weeks. Relief spread through me at the familiar sight of it. Once my supplies were set up, I would leave them out all year, whether I had good results tonight or not. I would leave them there with the expectation of using them every day. Even if I ended up using the Larkin studio sometimes, I still needed to be fully set up for work here where I lived.

I went into the living room and got the Chet Baker CD Michael had bought me for my birthday and brought it into the bedroom, where I put it in the little boom box beside the bed. The room filled up with Chet's sweet and moody sounds. I, too, felt sweet and moody!

When I moved my gooseneck lamp so that it shone down into the red glass pitcher, the light filled it like water.

Though I'd told Clara I wanted to paint the pitcher, I didn't necessarily. It had just felt too hard to explain that really, most of all, I wanted to look at it; that looking was, to a painter, legitimate work.

And that was what I did now. I studied the red glass pitcher for a long time, and while Chet was singing "My Funny Valentine," I began mixing colors. The aromas of paint and linseed oil brought a flood of nostalgia for my old self, the self who painted no matter what else was happening in her life. I thought of Michael in bed with Brenda on Martha's Vineyard tonight; I thought of our lovemaking, of what I wanted, what I hungered for, what I coveted.

I found myself mixing reds, shades of red for which I had no name, and then applying them to the canvas, timidly at first like some tyro; it had been too long. The oils went on thick and voluptuous and with the depth of tone that was the reason I'd never bothered with acrylics. I began to apply the paint in a rush then, a push, changing in the midst of it from my large ermine brush to a palette knife so I could get gobs, globs of those reds onto the canvas and move them around, shape them, rough them up, smooth them. Somewhere in there the phone rang, and I couldn't leave what I was doing to answer it though I knew it must be Michael and I wasn't trying to punish him or fuck with him now, wasn't trying to do anything to him, wasn't even particularly relieved that he'd somehow found the privacy to call me from the Vineyard; I was just painting like a fool an angel a criminal, manipulating all the reds and then mixing more of them but this time with black, I was mixing a lot of black into them, *noir*, like old blood. I kept painting though I knew what I saw on the canvas wasn't my best work, wasn't even very good, but I kept going, kept going all night, and if it was lousy this time I didn't care, it didn't matter, this was what I wanted, what I needed to do, and I had to have it, I was greedy for it the way I was greedy for Michael's body, but I did not have to covet this, for it was already mine, it was mine.

It's possible it all began in childhood with the mystery of the Church and the hold it had on me then: Good Friday, the Stations of the Cross, the ritual clouds of incense, Dies Irae, Sanctifying Grace, chaste nuns discussing the Passion of Our Lord in schoolrooms. The hold it still has on me, despite everything: fear, devotion, a caged passion, a longing to be raised above the earth. Baptism, "the indelible mark" the nuns said it leaves on you, like a tattoo, it always seemed to me as a kid, a tattoo on my heart. And then the longings of my body began and with them an adolescent's question: Why is the death of Jesus referred to as His Passion?

I decided that the day you begin to understand the nearness of passion to death is the day your longing-to-be-raised is the very power that raises you. The Church holds that one cannot freely give in to passions of the body and still have purity of soul. Passion makes you outlaw, excludes you from the world of Sanctifying Grace. But the body is incapable of lying to us, even when we're able to lie to ourselves, and ultimately it may seem that there is no true choice except the one your body makes.

Then the same fear and longing that once bound you to the Church commit you to erotic desire. You live for the moments when pleasure seems eternal. Afterward you feel afraid, guilty, certain your immortal soul is damned. All night you compose mental letters to God and other strangers, explaining everything. Then you stop praying—afraid no one will listen, afraid someone will hear.

And finally one night you pray anyway because it seems that after all these years you have to, and while you pray, your lover's scent drifts up beneath your nightgown, rising between your breasts. You breathe it in like incense, breathe it in and pray at one and the same time and somehow your shame is gone. You realize that all human passion, whether of body or mind or soul, is simply the longing to be raised above the earth.

After that you can pray again, but you keep your longings out of churches, keep them in the open where they can rise. But always, no matter how far you think you've moved from the rituals and teachings of your childhood, no matter how far you've tried to stray from God's House, your heart beats the pattern of the indelible mark, the tattoo that rests on it like a scar, warning you each time you rise above the earth just how far you may have fallen—and still you rise, you rise, you rise.

4

It was Friday night. I was pacing the long narrow hallway of my apartment, counting places where the wood was broken or chipped. Every once in a while I wished I had not declined Clara's invitation to go out and eat with her and some friends who were visiting from Santiago, a married couple who had worked with her at the newspaper. It had been sweet of her to ask me, but I just didn't feel up to meeting new people tonight and also I knew that the three of them would've had to speak English all evening on my account. My awareness of that would have left me feeling like odd man out the whole time. After an incident that had happened with Michael earlier in the week, I didn't think I could stand feeling that way.

So I paced, feeling regretful of all the times I'd been privately judgmental of women friends who fell for unavailable men and then whined about how their lives were going to hell. It had been so easy to tell myself that these friends were self-destructive, spineless, antifeminist, looking for trouble. How many times had I advised women I knew to "just leave" the men for whom they were putting their lives into suspended animation? How often had I repeated the single women's adage: If he hasn't left his wife by the end of the first year, he never will?

Now I saw how hard it must've been for these friends to try to explain to me the hold their lovers had on them. And it wasn't some kind of abusive hold, though I think I often saw it that way. It was something perhaps even more tenacious—the grip of *desire fulfilled*. Erotic fulfillment was, I was learning, so much more than just sexual. It implied union, complete trust, unboundaried intimacy, imagination's flight, a safe harbor from the world, absolute acceptance. In this surrender to sexual longing there was a kind of relief that accompanied the release, something that came unknotted inside you. It was just unfortunate when those feelings were inspired by the love of a married man.

I paced. Each time I reached the north end of the hall, I had the choice of settling into the living room or, at the south end, of going into my bedroom and giving myself over to the fiery reds of a canvas I'd begun the night before, but at the moment I didn't feel up to confronting its anger and hunger and longing. Finally I settled on the living room sofa with a book of Devi Bhujander's poems (now I could see why Clara had called them stirring; they were passionate, lyrical, deeply engaged with social concerns).

In a while, though, I would have to face my own work. Things had become more complicated with Michael this week, more fraught, and that had put me in a mood that made the work itself feel loaded, dangerous. But wasn't I the one who liked to say that art should be dangerous? That may have been me.

Earlier I'd gone on a walk, browsed a couple of bookstores in the square, picked up the Bhujander book. The stores themselves hadn't been the point, though, the point was the walk—the idea of falling into step with the Friday evening crowds along Mass Ave. I guess I'd thought it would help me to feel less solitary, but it had had the opposite effect, which only made me gloomier. Everyone was walking in twos or threes, except for the jugglers and the street musicians and the misfits.

I walked past the Brattle Theatre four times, each time wishing I had the heart to get in line for the Preston Sturges festival, but—and this was truly silly since Michael lived in Brookline—I kept imagining he might be in there with Brenda. They rarely went to the movies together, but I had become paranoid. And with good reason, I felt.

The previous Tuesday night I'd unexpectedly ended up at an event where Michael was in attendance with his wife. I'd gone over to Aperçu that afternoon to discuss some last-minute design details about Mark Gold's book with my boss, Ed Hershorn, and Ed had reminded me that Mark was reading at MIT that evening and suggested I go, since he couldn't make it himself. "Just to show house support," he'd said. Mark was going to be an important poet, and Hershorn was pleased to have signed him for this second book.

Sometimes I thought Ed was testing me during this year's leave just to see if I was still a loyal part of the Aperçu team, and it rankled a bit. After all, I'd worked several eighty-hour weeks to wrap up all urgent design work before going on leave and had continued checking in with Ed every couple of weeks. Still, I had nothing going on that evening, and I said I'd fill in for him, wording it just that way to remind Ed it was a favor, not something he had a right to expect of me right now. I decided to go directly from Aperçu to MIT, and it never occurred to me I'd see Michael—much less Michael and Brenda—there.

I can't remember a single thing the poet read; all I remember is the shock of seeing Michael there as part of a couple when I'd never before seen him with any woman but me. They were four rows ahead of me, and all during the reading I couldn't take my eyes off their backs. I was watching for clues in the tilt of their heads, waiting to see if their shoulders touched. I've never felt so alone. I didn't go to the reception afterward, though I'd promised Hershorn I would. I couldn't bear to be in a room with them and didn't see how I could behave normally.

The only thing I knew right then was that I didn't ever again want to be part of any group that included the two of them looking for all the world like a practicing couple, their friends swarming around them. To see other people regarding them as a pair, that was more painful than seeing them that way myself, I think, because it was a confirmation of Michael's other life, many would say his *real* life. That put me on the outside of his world, erased me from it, when for over a year it had felt as if I were residing at the heart of it.

Earlier that day we'd been together. First we made love in my bed while rain beat down on the windowpanes and the street below. Then we went to see the Impressionists at the MFA, and after that we wandered around the Back Bay, choosing windows. It was a game we played, imagining which windows would be *our* windows if we lived together, describing each of our rooms in detail. It began to drizzle again and we ducked into a bakery, got blintzes and coffee.

"I admire your fingers," he said; "anyone would know you're an artist." And he closed his own fingers around mine, laughing at his "humongous, insensitive mitts." I loved his hands. They looked like the hands of a laborer, not the little pinkies you might imagine on a writer or a scholar, effete and straying frequently to the brow, the upper lip. They always put me in mind of the jobs he'd taken during his teen years in the South Boston projects, working as a grave digger, a hard hat, and a night-shift janitor.

When we got back to my apartment, we made love again, long and slow and sweet in the cool, gray afternoon, the sounds of traffic on Brattle Street an accompaniment to the traffic of our hands and limbs, the rush of our twin breaths, the feel of his urgent cock filling me then, pushing in to where pleasure is nearly pain, and finally the explosion, the sudden release I felt all along the length of my body, in my brain, in my bones and veins, no boundaries, no borders right then between the two of us. Afterward we stayed in each other's arms for a long time, and neither of us spoke a word or needed to. It seemed to me right then some kind of idyllic state, the most completely merged the two of us had ever been, nothing outside of us intruding or threatening to intrude. He never once looked at the clock. Finally, he said, "You know, for a long time I've known I didn't want to live without you. I suddenly realize I *can't* live without you, and it scares the hell out of me."

And then four hours later I saw him become part of a *them,* greeting acquaintances who shared some history I was no part of.

It was an unseasonably cold night for September, and he was wearing a big dopey blue-and-black alpaca cardigan. She was blond and thin and pretty, though she had what seemed to be a permanently unpleasant expression that detracted from her beauty, made her seem aloof and brittle. She, too, had on a large, bulky alpaca sweater, a blue-and-white pullover in much the same pattern as Michael's. I couldn't believe it— the two of them in nearly matching imported sweaters: the intellectual equivalent of his and hers bowling shirts. They looked like a couple of schnooks.

As they were standing to leave, Michael turned and saw me, and our eyes locked. I felt the swell of our gaze holding us in some horrible paralysis that felt like epiphany. Even from several rows away, I could see him wince. I felt my reduced standing right then, my solitary humiliation.

* * *

And so tonight I passed by the Brattle Theatre without stopping, even though I knew there was no way they'd be in there. I just kept walking, hunched into myself like an outlaw or a spy.

As I passed Radcliffe Yard, a doper on a bench said, "Aaaay, looking good!" Before common sense took over, I felt a rush of gratitude to him for inviting me back into the human race, and without thinking I said, "Thank you." I can't believe I thanked this guy for hitting on me.

"Wanna share a joint? he asked me then, apparently encouraged by my appreciation, and I actually answered, "No thanks, I'm engaged."

No thanks, I'm engaged? My God, what *was* that? *I'd be happy to do drugs with a total stranger except I happen to be engaged?* I hurried back to my apartment, knowing I wasn't fit to be out in the world right then.

When I got back inside, I resolved not to give in to despair, reminding myself that, all in all, it hadn't been a bad week.

For one thing, I'd gone over to the Larkin with Clara on Wednesday afternoon for the weekly colloquium. The presentation was by a science fellow from Vancouver, Mary Wilkins, and I didn't understand a lot of it, but to hear her speaking so passionately about the stages of micro-structure evolution in chemical vapor–deposited diamond was oddly compelling at first. After a while I began to glaze over.

Clara, beside me, sort of gasped when Devi Bhujander walked in and seated herself alone on the other side of the aisle, one row up. "It's her, isn't it?" Clara had whispered, and I'd nodded. Clearly my neighbor was starstruck, I thought, and as I looked over at Devi I could see why she might evoke that sort of response. She sat in an almost rigidly upright posture, small hands folded on the lap of a plum-colored satin sari edged in gold, her thick and shining black braid falling past her waist and bound with an elastic from which tiny saffron beads sparkled when she moved. There was a look of deep concentration on Devi's face, in profile, as if she were aware of no one in the room but the speaker, and she seemed genuinely caught up in the presentation. At this moment Mary Wilkins was saying that the morphologies and sizes of the diamond particles and the substrate topography had been examined as "a function of deposition time." I looked at Devi; her face was alight with interest. I was bored out of my skull and perfectly willing to concede that this disparity of response was quite likely indicative of Devi's superior intellect.

Just then, as if reading my thoughts, Clara leaned over and whispered,

"She is brilliant." I knew even before I saw Clara's eyes on Devi that she was not talking about our brilliant speaker.

There was a question-and-answer period after the presentation, and when Devi slipped out before it ended, Clara was visibly disappointed. I knew she was desperate to meet the poet from Delhi, and I felt amused at such fan club behavior. There was a sort of appealing naïveté about Clara; clearly she was the type who, when she liked or admired you, became devoted. I was a little ashamed now at how negatively I'd reacted to her the day we met. Now it seemed we were actually becoming friends, and I thought I might learn to like her very much.

Following the colloquium we went to dinner and then to see Bergman's "Wild Strawberries," and afterward we found a tiny underground Spanish café where we drank coffee and talked about the movie and about what Clara called Bergman's "eroticism of death." I didn't see it quite that way, and we had a friendly verbal bout. We decided we would go out on Wednesday evenings after the colloquia whenever our work schedules permitted.

It had been a nice evening, but I didn't feel entirely at ease with Clara yet. I think it was mostly because over dinner she seemed to ask a lot of questions about what I was doing, where I'd been, where I would be going, when we could get together again. I had to allow that this all might just be a function of my own current social reserve and privacy mania.

In several ways it had turned out to be quite a good thing I'd gone over to the Larkin with Clara. I'd found it much easier to relax this time because I wasn't alone, and I saw that I could take real pleasure in feeling part of that community. An odd thing: I was scanning the notices and announcements on the bulletin board in the Administration Building and discovered that someone had clipped and pinned up the *ArtAmerica* article, "Twenty-Five Up-and-Coming American Artists," and circled my name (we were listed in alphabetical order, so I was near the beginning) and had also circled the accompanying color photograph of my oil painting, "Time Reduced." It made me happy, reassured me, to find that someone at the Larkin who hardly knew me (and really, almost no one there knew me beyond "Fine, and you?") would go to the trouble of sharing my little triumph with the rest of the Larkin community.

Another positive turn of events that came out of this visit to the Larkin was that before the colloquium I went up to my studio alone while Clara was setting up her own office in another building, and I found that it actually felt good to be standing in that sun-filled attic space. Maybe, I thought, looking at the easel I'd set up a while back, *maybe* I'd be able to paint there sometimes during the day. I would do my primary work at home, but it could be interesting to see what might develop in this different space, with its wonderful daytime light. I unpacked the box of art supplies I'd brought over with the easel and spread them out on the work table the Larkin had provided.

Which leads to the main development of the week: I'd been painting at home every night—my creative dry spell was ending! I couldn't say I'd done anything worth keeping yet. Mainly I was experimenting with reds, mixing a lot of them, and using those reds on canvas in different ways. And though at first I'd just globbed them on with a palette knife to see how they looked and what I could make of them, now it felt as if I might actually be getting somewhere.

On Thursday night I'd begun a figurative work, which I thought might just end up a keeper. It was a nude (a self-portrait, though I wasn't going to title it as such), very slightly stylized, just a bit elongated, and all on a field of red—the blanket, the walls, the curtains, all in varying shades of red, ranging from pale melon red to a dark red I named *blood*. Even the night sky out the window, which from a distance appeared to be black, was actually one of the blackened reds I'd mixed. The figure was in normal flesh tones and the hair was auburn, like mine, the eyes hazel. The range of reds on red did something to the air of the room in the picture—made it seem about to explode around the figure of the woman, though there was the sense that the air was simply taking on the heat and longing of the woman herself. She was recumbent, and there was an expression on her face that I'd seen on my own when I'd glimpsed it unexpectedly on Tuesday in the window glass of the T train underground. It was a hungry look I found unsettling—even unattractive—but also, once I'd begun painting, had found it necessary to record.

In the painting, just behind the figure, is the easel with my red silk kimono clinging to the canvas in the way I'd observed it a few days earlier—like a lover. In the picture the red of the kimono is nearly the same hue as the red of the blanket the woman is reclining on, but the satin sheen of the kimono and the embroidered dragon on the back make the kimono distinct from the velvety blanket, while at the same time a part of the voluptuous swarm of red around and beneath the woman's body as if she's caught in it, awash in it, and together the elements become a picture of desire, of a kind of dangerous hunger—covetousness.

Once as I stood back to absorb the painting, I thought that maybe the reason that kind of desire was designated a Deadly Sin was because it takes over like kudzu, immobilizes your body and soul, closing out all but the moment of wanting and the object of desire.

Mother called while I was painting, to ask why I hadn't been home when she'd phoned earlier, and I realized I'd forgotten to return her call when I got back from the square. She asked where I'd been, and when I told her I'd just gone for a stroll around Harvard Square, she began telling me of all the murders that had happened recently in Los Angeles when women had been foolish enough to venture out alone at night.

"You're taking your life in your hands," she said ominously, "a beautiful young woman like you out there alone, larking about on dark city streets at night." It amused me to hear my mother say "larking"—one of Michael's favorite verbs. I blew a strand of hair from my face, my free hand covered with red paint.

"That's just where I like to keep my life, Mother," I told her cheerfully, "in my hands."

"I can never make you listen," she said. "You've been this way since you were small. You're not careful. You just take everything for granted, as if you were Hercules."

It was a struggle not to laugh out loud right then at that image of me. "I'm very careful, Mother," I said. "And you'll be pleased to hear that I'm growing more paranoid all the time."

I didn't mention that I'd locked myself out of the apartment this evening and had had to call Harvard Housing's emergency number when I got back from the square. They'd beeped the super, a genial Irish guy in his sixties, and it had only been a couple of minutes before he came up and let me in with his master key. Turned out he'd still been in the basement putzing around—marvelous luck for me—I didn't remember ever before having a super who would be caught anywhere near the premises after five on a Friday. I could imagine what my mother would have said at the thought that someone—*a man!*—had a master key that would open my apartment door. Mother doesn't understand apartment living, having lived in the same two-bedroom Santa Monica house since she married my father when she was twenty.

Michael called very late, and we were a little quiet and awkward at first, as if regarding each other in a new and larger context that disoriented us momentarily, jarred us from the intimacy we'd taken for granted in our small, private world. Now other presences had intruded on that world—not just theoretical presences suddenly, but incarnate ones—a wife, their friends—a whole community that considered them a pair while I lurked alone behind them—and why shouldn't they? I asked myself. He was married. What did I expect? As it turned out, Michael hadn't gone to the reception either, thinking I would be there. Clearly neither of us could bear to witness the two worlds colliding again. It was as if we'd been living on some moon somewhere for fifteen months and suddenly had to readjust to the atmospheric changes of earth.

On my way back from the bookstore earlier, as I'd walked up Church Street in the crisp night air, I'd heard the violin strains of "Stardust" moving through the dark from somewhere. Then I saw the skinny street musician, a sweet-faced young black man standing alone on the sidewalk with some kind of electric violin. His music was beautiful and painful to hear. I could hardly stand it, couldn't bear the vulnerability I felt as it washed over me, sending a frisson of loneliness over my shoulders and down my back. The long, shuddering notes were piercing as I walked past him in the dark and dropped a five-dollar bill into his money basket, my eyes glued to the sidewalk. It seemed, in that moment, as if my loneliness and foolish longing must be visible to him, to everyone I passed. I couldn't wait to get back into the apartment where I had only my own eyes to meet. That was hard enough lately.

Awake all night thinking. Are you taking me to hell with your body? Are you? If there is no afterlife, no heaven or hell, then is hell the loss of honor? Am I losing my honor by loving a man who has promised himself to another woman, a man who has to lie in order to see me?

I read once that sin is whatever obscures the soul. That makes sense to me. Is allowing myself to love you obscuring my soul? If it is, then why am I so awake when I'm with you?

Is loving you a sin only if I sleep with you? Or is it a sin just to love you?

Maybe there is no such thing as sin.

But supposing there is an afterlife, a system of eternal rewards and punishments. Am I going to hell then? Are you?

How can I fear sin, even theoretically, when sometimes I'm not sure I believe in any definitive or specific deity? Would I fear sin if I hadn't been raised to fear it? Nearly everyone who believes in a God believes adultery is a sin. But what about intention? How much does that factor in? If I don't believe it's a sin to make love with you, is it still a sin?

The nuns said that if we thought it was a mortal sin to throw a pebble into a pond and we did it anyway, then we had in fact committed a mortal sin even though the act in itself was not inherently sinful. All the light would go from our souls then, they told us, just as if we'd committed one of the most serious sins, like murder or adultery; and then if, say, we were hit by a bread truck or a bus on the way to school and died in that state, we would burn in hell with all the hardened felons of the world from all the years of humanity's stay on the earth. Forever.

Shouldn't it also work in the reverse then? So that If I don't believe a designated sin is actually a sin, then it's not?

Maybe. But that's if there's a God. If there is no God, then I have to depend on myself for mercy and understanding. It might be dicier that way.

I torture myself all night like this until without warning and still awake I dream the arc of your arm coming round me, your long body enfolding mine, the voice of God unintelligible then and my own self-doubt and judgment in abeyance as the cells of my body take on the imprint and heat of your cells and I fall toward sleep at last as if I were only me again loving you and not a sinner at all.

But not quite. Because halfway there it occurs to me to wonder if anything can be true and right when it takes two people to make it so.

The long hours alone in the dark, when the soul talks too much——I think anyone would prefer noisy neighbors, barking dogs, midnight freight trains passing the bedroom window a foot away. Anything at all would be better than this.

5

For over a week I'd been painting pretty feverishly. It was going so well now that I was loath to chance jinxing it by stopping; I even regretted sleep. I'd nearly finished the painting of the woman in the red bedroom and realized it would be the first in a series of figurative works I would set in red rooms. When I wasn't working on that first painting, I was making notes for the others to come. Liz agreed that I shouldn't break my pace when I was kicking ass this way.

"The French say that if you leave art for one day, it leaves you for three," she informed me.

"I love the way you attribute a single quote to an entire nation, as if 'the French' all go around saying it every day."

"They have to have something to do when they're not eating," she said.

Three thousand miles apart, we were both getting ready for our evening's work, she on her new novel and I on the painting, and this prefatory telephone conversation was our twisted way of saying, "Go out there and win one for the Gipper!"

"I don't see how you can paint at night the way you do," she commented. "Normal painters don't paint at night, do they?" Then she snorted, "Normal painters? What am I saying? Talk about an oxymoron."

She was right that it was a little unusual to paint almost solely at night. I only knew a couple of others who were nocturnal painters like me. After all, light was supremely important to us. We'd kill for a space with good light to work in. Originally, I'd gotten into the routine of painting at night because I'd always had a day job; ultimately I'd come to prefer it. Though I usually mixed and tested my colors in the afternoon when light was true, I always found myself doing my best and most dangerous work at night.

I said this to Liz now, adding, "Art needs to be dangerous—not just pleasing to the eye."

"Oh sure," she said, "I firmly believe art should make everyone uncomfortable."

" 'The ugly may be beautiful, the pretty never,' that's how André Gide said it. He may have been an asshole, but he was right about that. By the way, you'll notice that I narrow the sources of my aphorisms to one person, rather than crediting them to an entire nation."

"Still, he's French," she pointed out. Whatever.

Nights were hard now, even though I was working so well—or maybe because I was working so well. Art was opening me up, as it always did, making me feel things more acutely, and lately while I was working after midnight, I found myself troubled by images of Michael in bed with Brenda and by the occasional out-of-nowhere conviction that they were at that moment having sex. I tried to push those thoughts out of my mind and just paint, but the more I painted, the more that image plagued me. I knew I was running out of patience. Michael needed to do something decisive soon, or I'd have to tell him it was over. Bad enough our affair had deformed my social life and made me lie to my best friend; now it was threatening to interfere with my work.

After so many nights of picturing him asleep beside Brenda while I was waiting for our life to begin, it wasn't so difficult to imagine telling Michael I was through. What was hard was thinking of the days and nights afterward. I couldn't visualize my world without him in it, couldn't imagine my body bereft of his. Still, I felt myself moving inexorably toward telling him.

It seemed fate, then, that just at the beginning of this work cycle he'd come over unexpectedly one morning when I was in no mood for love. I'd been up all night with bad thoughts, as well as in the throes of the most god-awful period—heavy cramps, free-floating pervasive horniness, and torrents of blood, my stomach puffed up like a blowfish and my back aching like hell. I'd just stepped out of the shower when he rang; I hadn't even had a chance to dry off. Grumpily I buzzed him up, threw on an old terry-cloth bathrobe, and went to the door, not caring at all that my hair was a bird's nest and my face was bare of makeup. Maybe

I was trying to scare him away so that I wouldn't have to be the one to end it.

"Look at you." He grinned when I opened the door, and before I knew what hit me I felt my damp, untidy person encircled in a pair of big man-arms. Immediately my pathetic, no-pride body responded, but I wasn't letting on. Why should I give him that satisfaction when I'd been alone and awake with *no* satisfaction all night while he snoozed in the marital bed with Brenda?

"Let me see you," he said, trying to tip my chin up so he could examine my naked face. I resisted. I was not in the mood for a Julia Roberts moment; there was no way I was going to go all dewy eyed today.

"You can come in, but keep your eyes averted if you have a shred of decency."

"I haven't," he said, holding me at arm's length now to get a better look. "You look about twelve years old."

"Is that supposed to be a compliment?" I asked, leading him to the living room rather than to the room I ordinarily led him to. Why was it that men always thought you looked younger without makeup? And who was it, again, that we were wearing the stuff for? Obviously not them.

"Sit," I said, pointing to the couch. "I'll make you some coffee." Today might just be the day when I'd tell him I couldn't wait around anymore. As I turned to go, he took my wrist and pulled me onto the couch beside him, folding me in his arms again and kissing me very slowly indeed. Michael was the best kisser I'd ever known, and I'd always loved the way he started softly, holding back, his mouth opening gradually against mine, like a secret. So many men led with their tongues, as if that were a mark of virility. They didn't understand what Michael knew—that even with kissing, getting there is half the fun. Despite myself, I began to return his kiss. *Fine,* I thought, *I'll fuck you, but I'm not going to be friendly.*

"Forget the coffee," he murmured, "I'd like more of this, please." I let him lay me back on the sofa. He spread the top of my robe open, licking my nipples erect and then sucking them in turn, causing acute answering frissons of pleasure in my groin, which suddenly put me in mind of the fact that I hadn't yet inserted a tampon. I could feel the blood warm between my thighs.

"Bloody hell," I said. *No way I was doing this.*

"What?" He was still north of trouble, in the demilitarized zone.

"You don't want to know." I tried to get up, but he kept his face in my bosom and gently held my shoulders down with his hands.

"Arrmmum," was all he said.

"That's easy for you to say, I'm bleeding all over myself."

"Oh God," he said, "I want to see you, Honora." Before I could answer, he undid the sash of my robe and opened it wide, running his tongue slowly down my ribs and abdomen and then lower, moving between my labia, wet with blood. No man had ever put his mouth on me during my period, much less in the midst of my heaviest flow, and I desperately wanted him to stop and not stop! He pushed his mouth against me, urgent and eager, opening me more and more, his tongue surging into where my own blood filled me, and I couldn't stop myself from moving with him, moving against his lips and tongue, couldn't stop myself, I came quickly, intensely, and he kept his tongue stirring inside me as again and again I felt my own blood-wet reverberations against his mouth.

He tore his shirt and jeans off then, his shorts, and I saw my blood on his face, I'd have been mortified if I'd had time to think about it but I wanted him and he was fervid, pushing into me, driving us hard while I bled into my robe and the sofa beneath us till he came convulsively with a shout that reverberated through my body.

How could I live without him? And how could I afford a new couch? Answers: (1) I didn't know because I couldn't imagine it; and (2) I absolutely could not. Try slipcovers.

A couple of nights later I'd decided to let the first painting sit for a while so I could gain objectivity about it, and I started working on what I was hoping would be the second painting of the series. I was at the point with this new painting where mild interest has just given way to focus and intensity when Clara knocked at my door. I knew it was her because no one else would have been able to get to my door without first buzz-ing me from downstairs—and really, no one else would have been coming to see me at that hour anyway. Up to my elbows in paint, a CD of Maria Callas arias playing full blast, I was completely involved in what I was doing, involved in the way I pray to be involved when I begin painting each night. I couldn't leave it to answer the door or I knew I'd lose that focus—and very likely the entire night's work. So I didn't answer the door.

She just kept knocking. I couldn't believe it. She wouldn't stop knocking—just stood out there in the hall rapping away with her knuckles, as if one more knock might bring me to the door.

Within a couple of minutes I felt I couldn't take it, but still I didn't go to the door. I could feel my resentment surging. Obviously, Clara could hear the music playing and knew I was in there. So what, I thought—it should be clear that if I wasn't answering the door, I must be working or just needing privacy. Couldn't Clara understand that? Apparently not. It was amazing she hadn't yet come to call when I was in bed with Michael, nor had she seen him arriving or departing—at least I was pretty sure of that. As she knocked insistently now, I began wondering how I would handle that situation when it inevitably arrived.

After a long time—and I mean maybe six or seven solid minutes of knocking—she went back to her apartment, and as I let out my breath I realized I'd been standing tensed and hardly breathing, paintbrush in hand. I turned back to the canvas and after a few minutes of gawking at it I realized I couldn't regather the intense involvement I'd had before she knocked. I found myself staring, just staring at the canvas.

Then the phone rang. I let the machine take it, as I always did while working, and Clara's voice filled the room.

"Norrie," she was saying, "are you okay? I heard your music but you didn't come to the door. You must pick up so that I know you are okay." *Must.* I picked up, just to put a stop to her dogged pursuit.

"Yes?" I heard the impatience in my voice and realized I hadn't even said hello. I didn't care.

"Are you all right?" she asked again.

"Sure I'm all right," I said. "I'm just trying to work."

"Oh," she said. "Well, I'm wondering, can you take a break?"

"Actually, no. I can't. I'm in the middle of my night's work, and if I stop I may never get back to where I was." It was already too late to "get back to where I was," but I wasn't going to encourage future interruptions of this sort by being available whenever it occurred to her to knock.

"I wish you had simply opened the door and told me that," she said. "I just wanted company tonight."

70

"But, Clara, I'm working. I can't just open the door and then go back to what I'm doing. It doesn't work that way when you're painting. This is the middle of my workday, nighttime or not."

"Well, people take little breaks from their workdays," she persisted.

"I don't know what 'people' do, Clara." I felt weary all of a sudden. "You can't always just take arbitrary breaks when you're trying to make art."

"Oh, *art.*" I heard the edge in her voice. There was a silence on the phone line between us until she spoke again. "Well, *I'm* writing a *book,* but if you needed me I would be there, no matter how deeply involved I was at the time. I'm your *friend,* Norrie, and I will be there for you anytime you need me."

"But I would never call you away from your work, Clara," I said firmly, "never. I wouldn't think of it."

"I am telling you that you *can,*" she insisted, and the silence I couldn't fill with a reciprocal declaration was excruciating. I knew I'd made a mistake in allowing things to get to this point with us. I decided in that moment that I couldn't go on with our standing date for Wednesday evening dinner and a movie, though I'd enjoyed it; the routine had only given rise to expectation. I would tell her I had to work next Wednesday night, but that I would still accompany her to the afternoon colloquium at Radcliffe. I didn't want to cut her out of my life, only to temper things a bit.

The following Friday afternoon when I was out in the square I noticed a playbill in the window of the American Repertory Theatre. *The Homecoming* was playing, and I'd always loved Pinter. Going to a play seemed a perfect diversion for me right now—and it might even feed what I was doing with my art, especially that particular play with its characters' battle for sexual dominance, which I thought might add an interesting wrinkle to my interpretation of erotic desire.

On impulse I stopped in to see if the box office was open, found that it was, and bought a single ticket for that night's performance. I'd never before attended a play alone, and it had occurred to me that I could invite Clara to go with me, but I was on guard now and had decided that the best thing I could do was have activities separate from her just so she knew we didn't do *everything* together.

It seemed a little gloomy that evening, the idea of dressing to go to the play by myself; I wished Michael were going with me, but of course we couldn't go out together in public—or anyway, not for such a "date-like" event. An occasional lunch out or a daytime trip to an art museum could be explained away, but not this. Besides, he and Brenda were going to a dinner party tonight at the Cambridge home of economist John Kenneth Galbraith and his wife—"Ken" and "Kitty" had been friends of Brenda's family for years and years.

I walked up Brattle to the ART wondering if anyone else would be alone there on a Friday evening, but once I got inside the auditorium and found my seat, I realized it wasn't so bad being alone there, really. Other ticket holders drifted in, couple by couple, with a trio of women at the end of my row (which was, I realized, why there was such a prime seat still available in the center of the fourth row), and soon I was just a member of the audience.

It was a terrific production, and I had a fine time. I felt proud of myself for going to the theater alone. On the way out I grabbed a flyer about an upcoming Karen Finley performance. I'd just go to that, too. I was sure Karen would be painting her naked self with chocolate, as usual, or shoving a yam up her ass—a more recent performance piece. Imagine, I thought, an artist who never seemed to be blocked—except, from time to time, by a yam. And she got applause for that.

I walked slowly up Brattle to my apartment building, enjoying the late night breeze, which smelled faintly of the Atlantic. All the stores were closed and the street entertainers had left for the night. Just a few people strolled here and there, some walking dogs. On his customary bench just outside Radcliffe Yard, smoking a reefer as usual, sat the cheerfully in-dolent ragbag of a man who had lately been introducing himself to passing females as "Mutton."

"Hey, honey, wanna suck on this joint?" he asked, holding his hand-rolled number out to me in the light of the streetlamp. I shook my head and kept walking.

"Well then, wanna suck on *this* joint?" I heard him say as I passed him. I didn't turn around to see what he meant, didn't have to. I shuddered. His laugh seemed to splash against the stones of Brattle Street as I hurried my steps toward home.

When I got inside my apartment the phone was ringing, and I saw that my answering machine already had three messages on it. I hurried to pick up the phone.

"Hello?" I said a little breathlessly.

"Oh, I was worried about you," Michael said. "Were you out when I called before?" He seemed increasingly worried lately that I might get tired of my lonely weekends and find someone else. He was right to sense my discontent, and this time I let him suffer a little when I answered.

"I went to a play," I said, not offering more detail than that. Let him think I'd had a date.

"A play? Really!" His voice was slightly elevated to affect enthusiasm, but it only sounded anxious. When I didn't answer immediately, he said, "Huh. No kidding, you went to a play."

"Yeah," I finally said, *The Homecoming*, at the ART."

"With your friend Clara?" he asked, his voice clearly showing strain.

"No," I said, then stopped, reluctant to give him the relief he was asking for. Let him see how jealousy felt. Let him see how it felt to be on the outside of your lover's life.

There was a momentary silence on the line, and then, just as I started to say, "I went by myself," he said something that sounded like, "Fine. Would hate to pry into your private life."

Then the two of us said, "What?" at the same time and both fell silent again.

"You go first," he said at last, in a voice that sounded tired and uncertain now, not young. I felt ashamed of my high school tactics.

"I went by myself," I told him. "I took myself to the theater, and . . . and it was very nice, actually. I had a good time." I felt strangely proud saying it and figured he'd be relieved and happy that I hadn't been on a date. He sounded distressed instead.

"Oh, Norrie," he said tenderly, "Oh, baby, I feel like such a shit, leaving you alone all the time like this."

It's funny how little pleasure or satisfaction there is in making someone you love feel bad. Still, my endurance was wearing thin these days, and I was afraid I'd probably do it again if I had the chance. Jealousy seemed to fuel all sorts of bad behavior.

* * *

73

Quite early the next morning I went down to the basement to do my laundry, hoping to find an empty machine. People in the building tended to leave their things in the washers and dryers forever, and as the day wore on it would become harder and harder to find an unused machine, especially on Saturdays. When I got into the laundry room with my basket of towels, I saw a woman in a chenille robe standing at a washer with her back to me. I knew instantly it was the Indian poet, Devi Bhujander— I recognized the braid that fell to her waist—but was also a little disconcerted to catch the glamorous Devi in such downhome apparel. She'd seemed so reserved at the Larkin that immediately I was tense, not sure what I should say to her—if anything. But then she turned around and saw me and smiled a lovely, open smile.

"Oh, hello! You're the artist." I was surprised she knew who I was. "Honora, isn't it?"

"Yes, but my friends call me Norrie. And you're the poet. I've been reading *Of Earth and Sky,* and I think it's wonderful."

"Oh, thank you," she said. "I'd love to see what you're working on these days. I saw a book with your cover on it a few months ago and saved it just for the cover art. I thought it was marvelous." I was surprised—it always seemed to me that people took cover art for granted. I was dying to know which book it was, so I asked her.

"It's a book called *The Night Room,* a collection of poetry by Marie Sarvosa. It had the most wonderful cover I've seen in a long time—very erotic, too—and when I checked the credits I saw that you'd done the artwork."

At her praise, I felt myself flushing with pleasure. I'd spent many hours working on that cover—a watercolor on rice paper, blurry and impressionistic in style, in tones of rust, peach, teal, ivory, maize, violet, and dark gray. In it a barely discernable couple stood by a night window, both of them nude and twined together, he behind her, and the picture was just abstracted enough not to be pornographic. You really had to look at it to know that it was erotic.

"Since then I've kept your name in mind," Devi was saying. "I thought how wonderful it would be to have you do the cover art for one of my books sometime." *I tought how vonderful it vould be* . . . She had an elegant Anglicized Indian accent—probably educated in London, I thought.

74

"I'm glad to finally meet you," I began, preparing to explain that I'd been working at home rather than at the Larkin.

"Oh, it's my fault we haven't met sooner," she said ruefully, "I've been to my office at the Larkin so little so far. I'm hoping that will change soon."

"I was going to say it's *my* fault we haven't met—I've only been there for the Wednesday colloquium presentations. Jane Coleman told me last week she'd never seen such a bunch of isolationists as this year's Larkin class."

We began talking about the solitude we needed in order to do our art, and Devi said she had an October publisher's deadline and was finding it easier and more fruitful to write at home; she said she was feeling a little guilty that she hadn't been around the institute more.

"I just can't work well with other people around," she said. "I don't know why that is."

"That's exactly how it is for me," I laughed, thinking of the studio I'd gone into just twice.

Devi told me then that she was uncomfortable with the attention she'd received in the last year, because she hated the feeling "of being watched." I noticed that she was too modest to mention the reasons for that attention—the Nobel nomination and Britain's Standish Award, which she'd won for the book I was currently reading.

As I began putting my towels into an empty machine, Devi asked if I would like to come and have dinner with her the next evening.

"I love to cook," she said, "and maybe you like Indian food?" I adored it, and told her so. "It's agreed, then." She smiled. "We'll eat together at my place tomorrow night. Seven o'clock?"

"Yes, that's perfect," I said, and just then a man I recognized as the super came walking into the laundry area. When he saw Devi, he beamed at her.

"Well, well! Hello there," he nearly shouted, his Irish brogue quite apparent. "I've got something for you," he told her. She smiled in the way a queen might smile at a favored servant.

"Oh, Joe," she said with obvious pleasure, "my toaster is repaired?"

"You bet," he said. "If I'd known you were down here I'da brought it with me. But I'll take it up to your apartment later."

"Oh, that's splendid, Joe," she said, "and then maybe you could look at my hair dryer? It just doesn't work properly anymore."

"Sure," he said, "I'll look at it for you, but I don't know much about hair dryers."

"Ah well, maybe you can just try, and see how it goes," she encouraged him, seemingly unfazed by the fact that superintendents aren't expected to repair things not attached to the building. And Joe didn't seem to remember that either, so smitten was he with the lovely Devi. I hid my amusement, though it really wasn't necessary since Joe wasn't looking at me; he only had eyes for Devi. I supposed everyone was in love with her.

The next night she received me in a long violet cotton dress, feet bare and hair hanging thick and loose down her back, several inches past her waist. On each wrist she wore ten or twelve fine silver bangles; I could hear the soft jingle of them each time she moved her arms. Devi was feminine in a way Western women weren't, I thought, suddenly aware of my own Levis and long-sleeved thermal top. I'd been painting since returning home from a visit with Ida this afternoon to make up in advance for any work time I might lose by going to Devi's tonight. I'd run from my easel to her apartment, only stopping to brush my teeth and change from a stained chambray painting shirt into this clean white top.

"Would you mind taking off your shoes before we go to the living room?" Devi asked me. "You can put them there." She gestured to a spot on the hall floor where several pairs of her own shoes stood in an orderly row. Obediently I took off my clogs, setting them at the end of her row of footwear and wishing I'd worn socks. As we walked barefoot down her hall toward the living room, I noticed that Devi's toes were small and evenly tapered in length, the nails unsullied by polish. My second toe is longer than my big toe. The puce nail polish on my left big toe was chipped. I tried not to look down. The apartment was filled with the most exotic and delicious aromas. I felt a sharp hunger pang and realized I'd forgotten to eat lunch again, between the trip to Brookline and my painting.

Brookline had taken a lot out of me, I realized suddenly. Ida had been weaker today and quite gloomy. She hated dialysis.

"Why am I still alive?" she'd asked me. "I never had any desire to live this long." The lipstick a nurse had applied was garish red against the sallow skin of her face, which had sunken in around the bones of her skull. She had tears in her eyes as she said, "I never wanted this." It was so unlike my sharp-tongued, buoyant friend to talk that way that I hardly knew how to answer her, and what could I say?

Finally, clumsily, "I'm sorry it's so hard, Ida, I truly am."

"It's not the *hard* that bothers me," she said, "it's the *nothing*. The nothing doesn't justify the hard."

Shifting my eyes upward now as Devi and I entered her living room, I was jolted by the force of color—there was red everywhere: crimson silk scarves over the two lamps; several burgundy votive candles on the mantlepiece, all lit; a variegated red hooked rug in the center of the room; and large, scarlet cushions on the floor. Red-and-purple-striped Indian gauze curtains were pulled back at the sides of each window, and the sofa was covered with some sort of exotic carmine woven throw, gold-embroidered at the borders. There were even pots of red-leaf coleus on the windowsills and the floor beneath the windows. The effect, once I'd adjusted to it, was elegant, warm, and welcoming. It was also a little disconcerting, considering the work I was so deeply involved in right now—the colors could have been my own.

Devi had the same one-bedroom apartment I had, and it was in the recess of the hall on the third floor, which meant she was directly below me. Her apartment was identical to mine in layout, but somehow it felt rather regal by comparison. Even her floors were freshly sanded and finished. There was a low fire in the fireplace, though I'd been told we weren't supposed to use our fireplaces until after they'd been inspected and repaired, which didn't seem to be on the management's agenda anytime in this century. There was sitar music playing quietly on a little stereo in the corner.

"It's beautiful," I said. "And your floors, Devi! They're gorgeous. Mine look like someone had a tractor pull on them." I wondered fleetingly if Devi'd ever heard of tractor pulls.

"Well, I told the managers," she said conspiratorially (*Vell, I dold the managers,* it sounded like), "that I *must* have better floors because I'm always barefoot here and could get splinters in the soles of my feet. It's

77

a cultural issue, I told them, going barefoot indoors, and in respect of that, the floors would have to be sanded and refinished."

"And they did it?"

"Yes," Devi said, "of course."

She took her place on the sofa with easy grace and gestured for me to sit beside her. I felt awkward, unkempt, and suddenly inarticulate.

"You're quite straight," Devi said cheerfully.

"What?" Was she referring to my sexuality? My comportment? What?

"Your posture," she said, "is very straight. I've noticed it several times when I've seen you at a distance around the Larkin. You carry yourself like a dancer." Before I could embarrass myself with some sort of awkward response, she asked, "Would you like some tea?"

There was already tea steeping in a small teapot on the table, alongside two cups, mismatched. One was chipped. Then I noticed that beneath the elegant red throw, Devi's sofa was threadbare and upholstered in an ugly mustard tweed—probably purchased at a yard sale in the neighborhood. The curtains were made out of the bright, cheap Indian bedspreads available all over Cambridge. I realized with admiration how magically she had transformed this mundane place with her exotic sense of beauty, using inexpensive objects and a few things she must have brought with her from Delhi. We sipped our tea and swapped details of our lives and work.

At dinner Devi ate with her fingers in the traditional Indian style. I was relieved to see she'd provided me with a fork. There was yogurt in little bowls as dressing, and five or six dishes of succulently seasoned food, including the best *dhal* I'd ever had. There was no meat—Devi explained that she was a strict vegetarian—but I rarely eat meat anyway and didn't miss it. We both forgot to talk for a while, so comfortably engrossed were we in the meal.

As we finished dinner, I told her that I thought I might have begun the painting series that would make up my Larkin project. I still felt somewhat tentative about claiming that what I was doing was *definitely* my Larkin project. All that really mattered, I kept reminding myself, was that I was painting—*process, not product.* It was lucky I felt that way, since the second oil I'd begun had come to nothing after the night of Clara's persistent interruption. Still, I thought I probably had the first painting close to done, and I knew it was good.

"When is your colloquium presentation?" she asked me.

"I requested May," I said. "I think it occurred to me that I would rather fall on my face at the end of my Larkin year than at the beginning."

"Oh, surely you don't believe you will disappoint them," she said.

"Force of habit, I guess, arising from my native diffidence. When they let us choose the date of our colloquium I just went for the latest date possible."

"Actually, my own colloquium is sometime in May, too. You know, I would love to see some of your new work if you'd feel comfortable showing me," Devi said.

"Would you like to come upstairs and see it now?" I asked her. My answer was so automatic that I seemed to hear it at the same time I said it. I realized I wanted very much for Devi to see the new painting, and to see it through her eyes might help me to evaluate it and move on to the others. I was pleased when she took me up on the invitation.

"Your apartment is directly above mine," she exclaimed when we got to my door. "What a coincidence."

I felt nervous that Clara might hear us there and come out, for I knew that would force me to include her in the invitation to look at my painting, and I just wouldn't be comfortable yet having her see it. I hurriedly unlocked the door and let us in.

When Devi saw the woman in the red room, she was quiet for a long time. I began to be uncomfortable but managed to stay silent, giving her a chance to take it in.

Finally, she turned around to face me, her eyes alive with feeling.

"Oh, Norrie," was all she said at first. I looked at her, not at all sure what she was thinking and afraid she might not care for it. Then she faced the painting again and went on. "It's amazing work, really powerful. The way you've used color to create light and heat. And so much desire in the face—it almost hurts to look at it." She turned to me. "It's brilliant work."

I let my breath out in relief.

"It's you," she said then—didn't ask—as she gestured toward the woman in the painting. "She's you."

I nodded, a little embarrassed.

"What happened?" she asked quietly, her eyes again on the figure of the woman. "What made you feel this way? Surely only love could have done this."

"I don't know," I said. "I mean, well, I can't really talk about it, Devi. I wish I could."

"Of course," she said. "I understand."

And I knew that she did. But suddenly, overwhelmingly, I needed to stop hiding. I'd needed to tell someone for ages. But I couldn't betray my promise to Michael. I decided I could tell Devi about us without giving any identifying details about Michael.

"I love a man who's married," I finally said, feeling both fear and relief in the words themselves and in the act of revealing such a long-held secret. "We want to make a life together. But I've lived in secrecy for over a year and it's difficult. Getting more difficult lately."

"Yes," she said, "I know how hard it is to contain such a powerful enormity as love in such a small room as the human heart. You need to sing, but you're forced to whisper."

"If even that," I agreed. "Often I've felt mute, absolutely mute."

"This isn't good for you as a woman," she said, "but clearly the blossom that's been pinched back in your life has bloomed in your art." No one but Devi, I thought, could carry off such lyrical language without looking silly. Her voice became a little shy. "I fell in love with a man in London— I've never loved anyone this way—but it's not possible for us to have a life together. That may be why I understand the need and hunger in your painting, the raw desire." I tried not to show how startled I was to hear Devi speaking of "raw desire." Why should I find it surprising that the lovely, iconic Devi might be as much a sexual creature as I was? Yet I did find it so.

"He was married?" I asked.

"No, no, he wasn't married. But he wasn't an Indian. I could never marry a non-Indian. My family would never accept it. And since my arrival here in the U.S., I can see that all the more clearly and have made the decision not to see him anymore, no matter how painful it is for both of us." She trained her eyes on the floor. "I miss him every day. It's very difficult to love without hope of a future." Perhaps, I thought, this relationship was more purely romantic than lustful.

"Are you still in contact with him?" I asked.

"Oh yes, we write and sometimes we phone. But I've made clear to him that it isn't possible to go on with it in any meaningful way. Family is everything to me, and no matter how much I love him, I couldn't hurt my parents and disrespect our family traditions and our bloodline for the sake of my own desire."

"You have such self-discipline. It makes me ashamed of how I've given in to desire."

"No, no, you mustn't think more of me than I deserve, Norrie. To be completely honest, I must say also that I only had the strength to end the relationship after I'd arrived here in the United States and was far away from him. I'd been tormented for a long time by what I was doing and how it would affect my family, but as long as Paul was near me, I found my will unequal to the dictates of my conscience."

"Even so, Devi, I don't think I could have done it." We both fell quiet for a moment.

"I'm working on a poem about desire," she said, finally. "I'd love to show it to you soon. Do you know about the concept of chakra?"

"Well, I've heard of chakra. Isn't that what the Third Eye is?"

"Yes, exactly! That is one chakra of seven in the human energy system—root, sacral, solar plexus, heart, throat, crown, and Third Eye. My poem is about the sacral or Swadhisthan chakra, which is the center of creativity and of sexual energy for women—two forces that have merged so powerfully here in your art. So you will instinctively understand my poem, I think. It's not quite ready yet, but I'll be grateful to have someone I can trust look at it." She embraced me quickly, then let go.

As we were saying good-bye at my door, Clara came out of the elevator with a basket of laundry, and when she entered our cul de sac off the main hall she stopped abruptly, looking stunned at the sight of Devi in my doorway. She was mute, clearly at a loss. I felt a surge of sympathy for her and quickly introduced the two of them, telling Devi how highly Clara had spoken of her poetry. Clara relaxed a little at that and smiled; but then she made an unfortunate miscalculation, and it seemed to me that anyone else might have known that it was the wrong approach to take with the reclusive Indian poet.

"You are my hero," Clara said. "I am your biggest fan. I have been looking for you for ten years. I can't believe I am meeting you now, right in front of my own apartment. This is the greatest honor of my life." Any one of those statements would have been more than enough, I thought, cringing a little. Poor Clara didn't know when to stop.

Devi looked uncomfortable but was gracious. She put out her hand to Clara, and Clara took it—and kissed it. I couldn't believe my eyes. Quickly masking a startled look, Devi smiled and said, "I must go now. I'm very pleased to have met you, Clara."

"Would you like to come in for a glass of wine?" my neighbor persisted. She looked at me then and added, "Both of you, of course."

In perfect synchronicity Devi and I answered, "I can't," and then Devi added, "I must get back home to work tonight." I was relieved someone else was saying those words to Clara, who looked first at Devi and then at me, uncertainty gripping her broad countenance. She seemed a lonely figure to me in that moment, slouched in her baggy sweats, the laundry basket at her feet. She's one of those people who never seem to fit in, I thought, maybe because they want to so terribly much.

And she wasn't giving up. "Perhaps you would like to go to dinner and a film with Norrie and me on Wednesday night?" That was when I realized I still hadn't told Clara I wasn't going to be keeping our regular Wednesday night date anymore.

Hurriedly I said, "I won't be able to make it this Wednesday night, Clara. Actually, I don't think I'll be able to go out much in the evenings at all anymore—I'm getting pretty immersed in my painting, and night is when I work."

Clara looked hurt, then bitter. "Oh, your *painting*." Our eyes held for just a moment. Then she turned to Devi, but Devi had anticipated her next question and said, "I work at night, too, Clara. I rarely do anything after five." I could see from Devi's expression then that she and I were simultaneously thinking of the fact that it was now 10:30 at night and the two of us were obviously ending an evening together.

"Tonight was quite a departure for me," Devi said kindly to Clara. "I've known Norrie's work for some time and wanted to talk with her about doing a book cover for me." That seemed to first appease and then disturb Clara. I thought she was probably feeling a twinge of jealousy that Devi knew of my work.

"I hope you'll be going to the Larkin with me on Wednesday afternoon," I told Clara. "I'm still planning on it, if you are." Her face eased a bit, and she turned to Devi.

"Would you like to walk over to the Larkin with us on Wednesday?"

"Sure," Devi said, "that would be lovely."

When Devi left, I went back inside my apartment quickly, hoping to avoid questions from Clara about how I'd happened to spend an evening with her favorite poet. I felt sorry for her and wondered if she had the slightest idea how off-putting her behavior was—how self-defeating.

I'd just begun sketching out another figurative scene when the phone rang. I knew it was probably Clara, and after what had happened tonight, I knew I had to speak to her.

Our hellos were strained. Then the questions started.

"I was wondering how this happened," she said. Instantly I felt fresh resentment.

"What do you mean, Clara." I left the question mark off to show my impatience.

"I mean, very simply, you didn't know Devi Bhujander and now you are her friend."

"Yes," I said slowly, "I guess that's right."

"That seems rather odd, doesn't it? How did you get to know her so well?"

"I wouldn't say I know her so *well*, Clara. I met her by chance down in the laundry room yesterday, and we struck up a conversation."

"Oh yes, I'm sure the two of you have much in common," Clara said, "being *artists*." There was a flat tone to her voice on the last word. What was this thing about artists? I knew we were, as a group, pretty insufferable, but Clara's manner put me off.

"I guess we do," I said, deliberately offhanded. Then I begged off the phone to do my work. "I'll see you on Wednesday afternoon," I said, forcing cheer.

"Yes," she said quietly, "I suppose you will."

When you came to see me in the middle of the night last night without warning, I was taken completely by surprise. You'd gotten up out of bed at 1:00 A.M., you said, and had driven straight over to see me because you felt you had to. You didn't say what you told your wife when you left, and I couldn't bear to ask. Maybe she was asleep or out of town.

The buzzer rang just as I'd just stopped working for the night—I was done much earlier than usual because I'd finished my painting of the woman in the red room. There hadn't been much left to do, as it turned out—mostly just a few things I'd noticed when Devi was looking at it. I knew for certain it was done now and was feeling that initial elation along with the usual inchoate panic and regret that come when an engrossing piece of work is completed. When I heard your voice over the intercom I thought something awful must have happened—you'd never come over at this hour before.

I answered the door in my paint-covered clothes. You scooped me up in your arms and when you kissed me I forgot everything else. I hadn't seen you in several days and I was hungry for you—had been hungry for you the last few hours as I put the finishing touches to the painting. All of the nights I'd been painting the woman in the red room, I'd felt my hunger going into her, and tonight when I looked at her face in the finished piece, I'd seen the cumulative effect of those nights. I'd seen, as if for the first time, what Devi had seen in it and it frightened me, that much hunger, that much want. I felt all of that surge through me again as you kissed me, and I couldn't believe that just a kiss could hold such trans-formative erotic power. Suddenly I was pure muscle, my entire body was one muscle of wanting and I took you to my bed, pulled your clothes off, and then took my own clothes off while you watched me, and then I fucked you. That was how it was—I fucked you sitting astride you on the bed, equestrienne style, no foreplay and no tenderness. We both came so hard it rattled the lamp beside the bed. You'd never seen me this way, you said later. I'll tell you now if you still don't know it—you have no idea of the power of my stored desire. You have no idea.

Afterward at some point you became aware of the painting. It was the first time I'd left it facing into the room that way when you were here and she seemed to be looking at us, to have watched our lovemaking. You looked at her for a long time, as Devi had, but when you turned around and faced me again, your face was quiet and your eyes looked too bright.

God, you said. My God, Honora, it's hard to look at it.

You don't like it.

Like it? It's amazing, it moves me—it has power. But I don't like what I see in your face there. It scares me to think I've done that to you.

Michael, it's a painting.

It's life, and you know it. I'm ruining your life.

After you left I stood before the painting for a long time, looking at it with your eyes, and I saw what you'd seen.

I hated the woman then, because I knew she was making you think of going away from me.

Then of course I remembered she was me.

6

The night I went to see Karen Finley's performance at American Repertory, the house went wild when she did her yam schtick. Why couldn't I be more like her, I wondered? Why was everything in my life so fraught, when she was getting the glory with some chocolate and a tuber? I hadn't been able to work at all since the night Michael had seen the first painting and found my ruination in it, at his hands—and other body parts.

And it wasn't just my work; everything was stalled since that night. Michael and I had reached a kind of impasse, and it wasn't like I hadn't seen it coming. More than ever, he was plagued by guilt and indecision, vacillating between distancing himself from me and returning in passionate reconciliation.

For my part I continued to torment myself with images of his marital intimacies. The idea that I was sharing his sex, even marginally, with another woman tormented me. In dreams sometimes I would see their— what could I call it? Not *fucking* . . . and I refused to call it *lovemaking*— but I could see them in that act as if with a close-up lens: her belly, and below it her pubic hair, his penis entering her there. It was awful, clinical and awful. I always woke from such dreams with the certainty they'd had sex that night. I actually began to believe that I knew when they were having sex.

Despite the fact that our sex had intensified beyond imagining, or maybe because it had, we were both more and more painfully mindful of the fact that Michael was living a double life. I, for one, felt need of a clarifying discussion—what Michael would call one of my "seminars"—

and the sooner the better, which was how the moment arrived, or how I chose it.

It was a Thursday night and Michael had stopped by on his way home from a class he was teaching at Harvard Extension. We were sitting in my living room on the newly slipcovered couch (I'd bought it in a dark reddish brown color), and I had an old Van Morrison tape playing, "Inarticulate Speech of the Heart," as if it might offer him some warning of what I was about to say. We'd barely seated ourselves on the couch before I spoke.

"Do you still have sex with her?" It may have sounded like a non sequitur, coming as it did on the heels of "How are you?" but I knew Michael knew it wasn't. I waited for his answer with my stomach clenched.

He looked startled, then embarrassed. Now my heart clenched.

"Rarely," he said uncomfortably, "very rarely. And it's not, well, the sex is not the way it is with *us*. More routine, I guess you'd say."

"How can you do that when you're sleeping with me?" I demanded. Though I'd been with my share of men, I'd never slept with two at one time in my life; it was something that had always seemed sloppy to me, sloppy personal ethics. To be fair to Michael, though, *I'd* been single when we fell in love; I was not prepared to swear to what I'd have done—or not done—if I had been married as he was. Still, I said it again, "How can you do that."

"I . . . oh, God," he said, looking rueful. "Look, nothing excuses it, but it doesn't . . . it doesn't happen much. Hardly ever, in fact. But when she makes an overture I just, I guess I know that if I say no to her about that, it means the marriage is over, and I don't seem to be able yet to tell her that—or to tell it to my kids, frankly."

"Well, I can't stand to think about it. It disgusts me that you would go from one of us to the other."

"First of all, it's never been like that, and I'm sure you know that, Norrie. Please don't make it sound any worse than it already is." He looked miserable. "Past that, I don't know what to say. I'm not going to try to defend what's indefensible. You know I love you. And I truly want to be with you—*only* you—but so far . . . so far I'm finding it very fucking hard to tell Brenda it's over after she's spent most of her life with me, and had two kids with me." His speech became more intense, even as his voice went quiet. "But even more than that, I'm afraid of alienating our kids, unsettling their lives. Finn may be at NYU now, but he still thinks of our house as his home base, and I *want* him to. He's only seventeen, and skipping his sophomore year of high school has forced him out of the nest awfully young. As for Bird, she's just—she's so wired, such an emotional type, such a *kid,* really, for being nearly thirteen! She probably comes to me fifty times each evening with questions or 'unbelievable' news . . . she calls everything 'unbelievable' these days . . ."

He trailed off, blew out a puff of air. "And I'm also afraid of what our friends and relatives are going to think of me if I leave my family. You know, I was the only kid I knew in the projects whose dad hadn't taken a hike. The only men in any of those households, besides the occasional grandfather or disabled elder brother or uncle, were boyfriends, and they never lasted long. Somehow through all the troubles we had in our house, all the struggles, my dad managed to stay with us when everyone else's old man had deserted them." I started to protest, to point out that Michael wouldn't be deserting his kids by making a life with me; but even though I believed in the truth of that, saying it would have felt too much like a sales pitch.

"I'm afraid of the pain, Norrie." His voice was quiet. "I'm afraid of the pain."

Though I'd believed him when he said he wanted to be with me, what I could hear clearest in his voice was the enormity of his fear, the stubbornness of his desire to protect his kids, to keep his family together. How could I blame him for that? And I was well aware how much he didn't want to become the bad guy to everyone they knew. How had either of us ever thought we could make it, that we could have had a future together? I didn't see how I hadn't seen this all along.

Suddenly I felt anger at Michael. If this was how he felt about it, what had he been doing with me in the first place? The tape stopped playing and the silence grew. I had to face the fact that all I could control was me.

"Look, I understand your desire to protect your home and family, Michael—anyone would understand that. But meanwhile I have no life, and even what little I have of you I seem to be sharing with Brenda. I can't do it anymore. I don't quite believe I'm actually saying this, though God knows I've thought the words often enough. I just really think we need to stop."

My words hung there like a banner.

Michael looked stunned, looked down, then back into my face. Our gazes met and merged, seemed to swell the air between us.

After a moment he nodded, one quick nod of resignation. "How can I argue with you when I don't blame you for how you feel?"

I didn't speak. Maybe I wished he was fighting this edict of mine instead of understanding it. After what seemed a long time, he added, "Yeah, all the deception, all the doubleness—it's been wearing us down, killing our souls, I know."

Sin is whatever obscures the soul.

I didn't have to answer. Anyway, I was afraid to speak.

We sat silent together in my living room for a long time, the moon out the window laying a sulpherous light on the edges of our bodies, limbs, and faces, and in our silence I could hear the traffic reasserting itself four stories down on Brattle Street. Somewhere a car alarm.

Finally, Michael asked, "So what now, Norrie? What do we do now? Do we just stop making love—or do we stop talking altogether?" Before I could answer, he hurried on. "No, forget it. I can't go that far. I can't stop knowing you."

He turned to me on the couch and was about to embrace me; then he dropped his arms, shrugged, blew out a defeated breath. "Obviously, *touching* isn't going to make things any easier if we're just, just going to be friends now," he said ruefully and maybe a little bitterly.

I wanted his arms around me, wanted it so much I felt an ache in my chest when he pulled away. But I couldn't ask him to hold me; I was no good at asking. Whenever I felt I was losing someone, my modus operandi was just to let them go.

Could we be friends? I wondered. I didn't have the heart to voice the question.

It was late October, and Michael was about to leave on a book tour of England and Ireland for his British publisher. When he left my apartment that Saturday evening it was with the understanding that though we would no longer be together in the physical sense, we would try to preserve our friendship in some form. He was departing from Logan early the next day and wouldn't be back for two weeks; when we met again, whenever that might be, it would not be as lovers. As we said good-bye at my apartment door, we held each other for a long time. I'm not sure how that happened, but I think it was me—I think I just sort of poured myself into his arms and we clung to each other there in the doorway like Hansel and Gretel lost in the woods.

After he left I stood completely still for a while just inside the door I'd closed against the view of his retreating figure. I wasn't thinking or crying or waiting for him to come running back; I was just standing. After a while I went into the bedroom, put on my painting clothes, and got out a fresh canvas. I knew my work was all I had to count on. I began mixing oils, feeling in a hurry, wiping tears. Again my palette would be a series of reds, but not the reds of the first painting. I added bold yellow to the mix now, with just the slightest touch of gray to temper it, so that the red took on a flamelike quality—not orange, more the shade of red you see in a house fire. From that I reduced the red gradually, taking it to apricot and then to a clear, pink-tinged yellow. After that I lightly sketched on the canvas a rough outline of the scene I was imagining. I'd thought of setting this painting in a kitchen or living room, but once again the woman was in a bedroom, and I saw that I may as well just set all of them there.

The nude figure would be viewed from the rear this time, and again it was just slightly elongated. In the woman's posture was a hint of sadness or fatigue. She was standing at the window looking out with the drapes framing her, their red startling beside the pallor of her flesh. On the floor was the blanket, a harsher red this time. She was holding the kimono in her left hand, and it hung in shining folds along her thigh, the sash dragging on the floor near her feet.

I began to apply the paint I'd mixed. The light in the woman's bedroom was intense in the way artificial light can be, and almost painfully bright—an assault on her skin, which had taken on a chilled quality, for which I mixed just a touch of robin's egg blue into the palest flesh tones, and a deeper blue into the shadowy grays that filled the hollows of her body. Out her window the moon was a red so pale—no, not pale, but so *thin*—that it was nearly not-red, and yet it was radiant in the night sky.

In this room I wanted to achieve a quality of light that was not inert

90

on the canvas but was active, a light that would seem oppositional to the woman's physical presence, her flesh, as you viewed the picture whole and entire, watching how she stood, chilled and blue-tinged, too naked in the raw, hot brightness of the room. Even the moon would seem hard and unrelenting in its brilliance.

At 4:00 A.M. I stopped painting, then turned my phone ringer off, and slept till Sunday noon. It took me a while to wake up enough to think of checking my phone machine, and when I did I found three messages from Michael, trying to tell me good-bye before he left for London. As I listened to his three attempts to reach me, I felt a bloat of grief; playing them a second time it hit me fully that he was no longer mine, and I slid into a kind of quiet gloom that may have been just as much my simultaneous realization that he never had been.

I ate breakfast at one, then dressed and left for Brookline to see Ida. All the way there on the T, I tried not to think of Michael but felt my mind returning to the sorrow again and again, the way a tongue goes repeatedly to a chancre in the lining of the mouth. How had I managed to work so well last night? It was as if, in the wake of an unthinkable event, I ran for refuge in my painting as the only place where I felt safe from the ruined landscape of our love. What a laugh, to think of art as a safe harbor! Art, which was so full of risk, the unknown, and uncertain results. But I did feel safe there, maybe *because* of those risks, mysteries, and uncertainties. They engrossed me, challenged me, and I knew I was up to those challenges, whereas I had no such confidence exploring love's terrain.

Ida seemed physically weakened today, but mentally she was quite alert. Once again she was in the robe I'd bought her, but today she wore no lipstick. It was the first time I'd ever seen Ida's lips bare of makeup; they looked thinner than I'd realized, and today they were the same color as her skin, which was tinged with gray. Marge wasn't there when I checked the desk; I decided I would call during the week for an update.

Today Ida talked about the old days, the Depression era, how people had to "make do" then and "didn't expect to have so much as young people expect now," and how children had made their own toys and games. "Everything wasn't electronic then," she said, with a kind of cheerful scorn or pity for the youth of today. "You had to have an *imagination* in those days."

91

When I hugged her as I left, her body felt light and hollow as if made of the finest, thinnest sort of papier-mâché. It made me sad to leave; now each time I told Ida good-bye, I found myself wondering if she'd be alive for our next Sunday visit.

At home I got straight into my painting clothes and ate a quick peanut butter sandwich. Clara had gone away for the weekend to some journalism conference in Chicago, and I felt relieved that I wouldn't have to worry about her knocking on my door at inopportune moments. As always, I was feeling ambivalent, conflicted, about my neighbor. I felt sorry for her; I really did. I'd seen her alone in the square twice recently, seeming more to wander than to walk, holding her books against her chest like a schoolgirl, lank hair flapping in the breeze. Both times I'd turned toward a shopwindow to avoid her.

I got right to work on the woman in the window, which was how I'd begun to think of the figure in the new painting. When I found my thoughts drifting to Michael across the Atlantic in London, no longer my lover though still my love, I squeezed those thoughts out of my head and added a touch of yellow ochre to two of the reds, which gave them more of the weight the mood required. The figure of the woman made me sad as I shaded in her limbs, her shoulders and torso, the split of her ass. She was full of loss and she was me. Fine, I thought, so shut up and paint.

All night I painted, not stopping till full daylight was pouring through my bedroom window. I saw that it was ten o'clock and realized I'd painted for sixteen hours straight, only leaving the canvas twice, to pee. When I finished I was parched with thirst, and as I walked to the kitchen to get a glass of water I felt light-headed, unsteady on my feet. I stripped off my paint clothes and fell into bed soon after that without even washing my face, brushing my teeth, or putting on a nightgown. It occurred to me then that I should turn off the ringer on my phone, and I managed to lean across and complete that one Herculean task just before I dozed off.

It was two in the afternoon when I woke, and my answering machine was blinking like mad beside the bed. I turned over and went back to sleep until four.

When I finally got up I felt woozy, wobbly on my feet. I knew I might've pushed it too hard last night, but when I looked at the painting—nearly finished, which was remarkable considering my normal snail's pace—I knew it had been worth it. I began to feel excited about this series. I decided I would call it *Hunger*.

There were two messages from Clara, who'd arrived back late last night (the first message "just to talk" and the second, in which she said, "I really need to talk to you"); one from Devi (to say she had found some information on the function of Agnya, or the Third Eye, which was going into a poem about time and memory, and then she would be ready to show it to me); and two from my mother (the first one saying to call her, and the second one asking why I hadn't yet called her).

I phoned my mother and told her about my nearly all-weekend painting marathon; she was pleased if I was pleased, she assured me, "But you know what you're going to do to your body if you keep this up—not to mention your mind."

Then I called Devi and got her machine; I told her I couldn't wait to see the poem.

I was relieved when I got no answer at Clara's, and I made a split-second decision based on my need to finish this painting uninterrupted. I spoke into her phone machine in the rapid-fire style I can't seem to avoid when I'm making excuses. I welcomed her back and told her that I hoped she'd had a good trip; then I said I wouldn't be able to talk to her for the next couple of days because I'd be painting furiously, but that I'd see her for our regular Wednesday afternoon trip to the Larkin. I added that I'd be interested then to hear how her conference had gone. At the thought that I was free of Clara for another couple of days, a kind of relief filled me that seemed a bit out of proportion to the situation.

But, I thought, look how much I'd accomplished in one weekend of solitude—this second painting was nearly done. In the space of two days I'd worked on it for twenty-five solid hours, the same number of hours I might ordinarily be able to give to a work in progress over a period of ten days when I was working my job at Aperçu. If I could only keep up this pace for the rest of my Larkin year, it could change my life as an artist.

That evening I decided to go out for a walk before I settled in to work, figuring it's never good to stay at it for too many days straight without diversion; you can get stale and you'll bring that to the painting. I decided I would spend a couple of hours in the square—have dinner somewhere and then maybe browse a couple of bookstores, stopping to hear street musicians along the way. As I left my apartment I walked quietly past Clara's door, hoping I could avoid an encounter with her. I was tired from the last two nights and sad about Michael; I just wanted to be alone tonight.

Actually, I realized as I was going down in the elevator, I just wasn't feeling all that great, period. When I hit the sidewalk just outside the building, I actually felt weak. Was I getting too old to work so obsessively now? I was only thirty-six, for God's sake. Or was this something other than fatigue? As I walked, it became clear to me that it was indeed something else. I, who almost never got sick, was sick. And with every step I took, I felt sicker. My head was beginning to ache, even my skin ached, and I felt hot and cold at once. I'd gone less than a block when I gave up and turned back toward the apartment building, hoping I hadn't caught the awful preseason flu that was making the rounds of Harvard and Radcliffe. My walk had lasted all of two minutes. Unsteadily I took a shortcut through the alley and went into the building via the rear entrance to save strength.

By the time I got back up to the fourth floor, my head was pounding and filled with pressure. In my apartment I made a beeline for the bathroom, where I got out my thermometer and some flu medicine Michael had brought me as a joke a few months ago when I'd told him, "I'm not sure if this is love or the flu"—inadvertently useful, as it was turning out. When I took the thermometer out of my mouth, it showed a temperature of 103.1. I couldn't believe it—I never got fevers. The last time my temperature had gone over 100 had been in college.

I'd only been back inside the apartment for a couple of minutes when I heard it, and if I hadn't been walking through the hall from the bathroom to my bedroom I mightn't have heard it at all; someone was quietly trying my doorknob. Was it just my imagination, my foggy head? Then I heard the sound of metal sliding into the lock and my heart began to pound. Whoever this was thought I was out! I stomped loudly across the wood floor toward the door and yelled, "WHO IS IT!" The tool or key was pulled quickly from the lock, followed by the thump of running feet out in the hall. It sounded like one set of feet, I thought. Why the hell wasn't there a peephole in my door like there was in Clara's? I would ask Harvard Housing to put one in on Monday.

But right now I was calling the police. Should I call the Harvard police? No, I decided, I wanted to talk to *real* police. I dialed 911 and got the Cambridge Police Department. By the time they arrived, I was shaking all over with fever and the realization that if I hadn't heard the sound of the key (and it amazed me that I had, really) I would have encountered a burglar face-to-face and there was no telling what might have happened to me. The officers—a middle-aged black man named Greene and a youngish, overmuscled red-haired guy named Porter—took my report (Greene listening carefully and Porter printing laboriously his distilled version of what I was saying). When I'd finished telling my tale, I realized I was sweating profusely and feeling faint.

"Are you okay?" Greene asked me.

I told him I thought I was coming down with the flu. Inexplicably, Porter chuckled, which riled me—what the hell was so amusing about the flu? Greene moved away from me just a bit on hearing I was sick and said he hoped I didn't have the bug that was making its way around Cambridge and Boston right now. "That is one damn doozy," he said, shaking his head and also chuckling. Somehow it didn't bother me so much when Greene chuckled, since he'd bothered to ask if I was okay in the first place. I gave Porter a snotty look.

The two men then prepared to depart, offering me differing professional opinions as to what had actually happened. Porter said he thought some other tenant "probably just got off the elevator on the wrong floor and thought they were opening their own front door." He clapped his hands once—loudly—as he practically shouted, "Happens all the time!" I flinched. Jeez, this guy aimed to be bigger than life, and I just didn't have the constitution to take too much of that right now.

"If it was something as innocent as that, why would they have had to *run away?*" I challenged the Schwarzenegger clone.

"Oh, that was just embarrassment," he said, standing with his Popeye arms akimbo, hands on his waist and his big legs apart. My whole body was sweating and every inch of my skin ached. If this guy did one more annoying thing, I was going to find a big rock and kill him.

Greene posed a scenario more in keeping with what I'd decided: "I think whoever's been burgling these apartments all year without getting caught is maybe watching you tenants to see when you go out—or maybe having somebody else watch and then call him." It was interesting how in any postulated crime theory of this sort, the theoretical perp was always a *him*. I liked to believe that we women could be just as felonious as any man.

"You'd left a few minutes before this happened," Greene mused, "about ten minutes *tops*—right?" I nodded and he scatched his chin and looked at my ceiling, thinking. I didn't realize people actually did that outside of cartoons. My temples and neck were pulsing. "So," he said, "that makes me think the MO for this series is one guy watches the place and calls another guy to come and do the actual dirty work—that would account for the time lapse between your leaving and the perp arriving at your door." He said it was a common modus operandi in this type of crime. "Could be another tenant, or maybe a janitor, a super—whatever. And I'd say when you came back through the rear entrance you threw them off—they thought you'd be coming in the way you went out." That made sense to me. I'd be keeping my eyes open going in and out of the building from now on.

As I let Greene and Porter out, I suddenly felt alone and fearful, and very, very goddamn sick. I double-locked my door and pushed a chair from the kitchen up against it. That took all my remaining strength. I fell onto the bed without eating any dinner and was asleep until the phone woke me at 1:00 A.M.

It was Michael. It had taken me so much effort just to lift the receiver that I found I could hardly speak. My whole head was pounding; my throat was burning and seemed to be closing up.

"God, I hate this," he said without any prefatory niceties. "I can't not be with you, Norrie. Ever since I flew out of Logan I've been thinking about you—you're the one I want to come home to. I can't stand having the fucking Atlantic goddamn ocean between us." I made a sound that came out kind of barklike, and he asked, "Are you okay?"

When I tried to speak I found I had nearly no voice. "Not really," I finally croaked and with the effort began to cough. That was interesting—I didn't know I had a cough. Shit. I wasn't just sick, I was *fucking* sick.

"I'm sick," I said weakly when I'd stopped coughing, but by then Michael was drowning me out with, "Norrie? Norrie? What's wrong?" so all my effort was for naught.

My sigh made me cough again. It was all so difficult. I imagined tapping Morse code into the phone with my index finger, it would be easier than talking. But I didn't know Morse code. Michael was still calling my name, and I was pretty sure I hadn't answered him yet. I inhaled deeply, summoning all of my vocal power. My chest and neck hurt as I pulled in my breath sharply.

"SICK. HAD A BURGLAR," I barked.

"A burglar? My God, Norrie, were you hurt?"

"Nope," I mumbled and then began to rest my eyes. I woke with a start when the phone dropped onto my lap. When I got it back to my ear, Michael was there, yelling my name.

"What?" I inquired.

"My God, so you're sick as well?"

Sick as well. That was kind of funny. If I had an actual voice I'd be telling him how funny that was; instead I managed to hiss Yes. Somehow, across the entire Atlantic Ocean, he heard me.

"D'you think you've got that goddamn flu that's going around Cambridge?" he asked me.

"Yep," I sort of belched.

"You sound like shit," he said. "I just can't leave you alone! Before I can get to a phone you've got burglars breaking in and microbes invading your sweet body. Are you taking that flu medicine I got you as a joke?"

"Muh."

"That's good. Now who broke into your apartment?"

"Tried," I managed to say. Of course, with a voice I'd have said, "How the hell should I know who it was?"

"Must be part of that series in your building," he concluded brilliantly. "Shit, now I'm going to be worried about you every fucking minute till I get back." I very kindly refrained from pointing out the fact that I wouldn't be any safer *after* he got back since he lived somewhere else entirely, with the little woman. Maybe that occurred to him, too, because right then he sighed. Amazing how the sounds of hisses and sighs could carry thousands of miles. "I can't concentrate on anything I'm doing over here," he lamented. "I don't even want to be here."

"Sorry," I said. Somehow we said good-bye and I walked to the bathroom, holding the hall walls all the way and then landing hard on the toilet seat, whereupon I discovered I had diarrhea. Great. I wished the fucker *would* break in and kill me, whoever he was. I limped back to bed with a bottle of Evian, turned off the phone ringer, and fell back to sleep.

I dozed on and off all night, and at 6:00 A.M. I woke with a feeling like being hit in the head with a hammer. When I managed to sit up in bed and open my eyes, I knew my fever was back with a vengeance because I kept seeing raccoons hovering in the darkened air of my room, just sort of floating above the bed. I remember yelling at them once, and who could blame me for that? I tried to get a drink of Evian from the bottle on the bed stand and spilled at least half of it on my paint-covered chambray shirt. My paint shirt. I wondered when I'd put that on. No idea. It was soaked and sticking to me; I seemed to be nude underneath it, but then people are always nude under their clothes, I reasoned, so why think about it? I was shivering and sweating and shaking and then I fell asleep again, every inch of me aching, including my head. As I drifted in and out of sleep, I hated pretty much everybody and everything, especially the raccoons.

On Tuesday morning, night, or noon I woke in my Evian-soaked sheets and wet chambray shirt, shaking like hell. Fuck, I was fucking dying. I looked around for my thermometer but couldn't find it anywhere. Maybe that was just as well. I wasn't in the mood for bad news.

I saw the phone machine blink blink blinking, goddamn phone machine. I straggled out of bed and shed the wet shirt, put on some ancient gray sweats, the pants of which had long-since shrunk to calf-length. I was still shivering so I pulled on my red kimono over the sweats and I walked to the bathroom with great effort, drinking half of a fresh, tall bottle of Evian as I sat there on the can. Thank God the diarrhea was gone.

The first message on my phone machine was from Michael, who must've called back almost immediately after we hung up last night, just after I'd turned off the phone. He'd forgotten to give me a contact number, he said, so that he could be reached if I "should need" him, and then he solemnly recited a long overseas number—and repeated it. I began to giggle hysterically; even as sick as I was, it seemed to me 911 might be a better bet.

Liz had called: "Nothing important." Fine, then I wasn't calling her back.

Another call was from Clara (naturally she wasn't honoring my two-day Leave Me the Hell Alone request). She wanted to know if I thought she should invite Devi to go with us to the Larkin again tomorrow. "I didn't think she was very relaxed the last few times," she said on the tape. *No shit,* I thought. With Clara fawning over her the whole time, relaxation had probably been a challenge. It occurred to me I was going to have to call Clara to let her know I was too sick to go to the colloquium tomorrow. Hell. Bloody fucking hell. I didn't want to call Clara.

She answered right away and when I explained about my flu, she said, "You sound terrible! Have you had anything to eat?" I realized I hadn't eaten in a couple of days, and with that realization came the further realization that I was hungry. After being sick for two days, I'd become so accustomed to discomfort that I hadn't sorted out the hunger pangs from everything else.

"Actually, no," I croaked weakly, knowing what would come of that revelation. But I was so tired and hungry that even Clara coming to my apartment with covered dishes was better than feeling like this.

"I will be over in five minutes," she said. "I have some soup left over from my dinner."

"What? What time is it?" I asked, disoriented.

"It is six o'clock in the evening," she said. "Norrie, you are *really* sick."

When she arrived I led her to the living room because I didn't feel up to her seeing my two paintings yet; I'd closed the bedroom door just to be sure she would not. She was carrying a tray with a bowl of soup on it and some toast on a paper napkin beside it. There was a tall glass of milk, too. I was so glad to see food that I began eating the beef vegetable soup without second thoughts of my semivegetarianism. It was hot and tasty, and as it entered my empty stomach I began to feel almost human. She'd set two shortbread cookies on the tray near the milk. I wasn't a big milk drinker, either, but milk and cookies after the soup sounded comforting.

I looked up at Clara as I wolfed down the food and was caught by the look of affectionate concern on her broad face. What a shit I am, I thought. Oh God, what a shit.

"Clara," I said, full of contrition for all my past, present, and no doubt future negative thoughts, "you're an angel."

"I don't think so," she said, smiling gratefully. "Oh—and you know, I called Devi Bhujander to invite her to walk to the colloquium with me tomorrow, and when I mentioned that you weren't going, she said she didn't think she would be attending this one." The implication was clear from the rueful expression on Clara's face; she was sure Devi didn't want to go if I weren't going. I wondered if indeed Devi *was* avoiding Clara the way I had been until five minutes ago.

"Maybe she has writing to do," I tried to reassure her. "I know she's been working hard on a new poem and was just at the point of making a breakthrough a couple of days ago—something about the Third Eye." I'd hoped to soothe Clara's bruised ego by convincing her it wasn't personal, but she didn't look reassured by my words; in fact, I saw a shadow cross her face as she absorbed them, and I realized she was thinking about the fact that I was on personal enough terms with her idol to know something like that. I tried to imagine her thoughts: *I knew and loved her work before you did; she is my hero, and you have appropriated her.*

"I don't think she likes me," Clara said. When I started to answer, she hurried on. "It doesn't really matter so much. I would rather spend time with you anyway."

"Clara," I said sincerely, "you're a very good person, and Devi is, too. I think she's just pretty reclusive."

"Yes, I know she is," Clara said, a little bitterly now, "But she likes *you*—she wants to spend time with *you*."

"Oh, I don't know how much she likes me *personally*," I said, "I've only seen her alone on a couple of occasions since I met her, and we talked about work almost the whole time." Suddenly I thought how much this sounded like what one might tell a boyfriend after being seen out to lunch with another man. Here I was again, explaining myself to Clara. I looked down at the half-empty soup bowl and felt a combination of guilt and wariness. I looked up at Clara then and saw her expression—there was a kind of anger in it that seemed to be mixed with ardor. Maybe she was in love with Devi, or thought she was.

"I will go and let you finish your meal in peace," she said, and I heard a note of self-deprecation or self-pity, maybe both.

"You don't have to go, Clara," I said feebly.

"Yes, I must, I have work to do. I *am* working on a book, you know."

"Of course," I said. "I hope your work goes well tonight."

After Clara left I got up and locked the door behind her, then carried the tray to my bedroom and finished the soup, the toast, the milk and cookies, feeling guilty the entire time though not certain why.

I went to bed, turned off the phone, and fell asleep quickly; I didn't wake until Wednesday morning when Clara knocked on my door loudly with a breakfast tray in hand. I dragged myself to the door, taking stock as I went: My head and throat and skin no longer hurt, but I had a cough deep in my chest and I felt as if every muscle in my body had been removed by scientists while I slept.

The breakfast sausage and eggs smelled so ungodly good to me that I hovered around the tray in Clara's hands like a big, overeager mutt. I even craved the sausage, which I'd long made it a rule to avoid. It seemed possible I was guilty of at least three of the Seven Deadly Sins just in the brief moment before Clara handed me the tray.

"Oh my God," I said as I took it in my hands, "How can I ever thank you!" It was not intended as an earnest query, only a rhetorical convention used in the expression of gratitude. But Clara treated it like a question.

"You can be my dearest friend," she said quietly. "Nothing more."

And there was something so heavy, so intense and final in her tone that I felt as if I'd sold my soul for a breakfast.

How could I have heard the phone? I had the ringer turned off and was fast asleep, and then the next thing I knew I was awake in bed holding the receiver to my ear and your voice was pouring into me like nectar. And sick as I was, all of a sudden I was hot. So hot. Your voice was the touch, and I felt my body opening, I was drenched with desire.

In the morning I didn't remember anything you'd said, only the sound of your voice and the hypnotic rhythms of your words pouring into me in the dark, and I wouldn't have believed it had really happened but for the fact that my body felt sated and I was aware of that slightly swollen morning-after-orgasm effect. When we talked the next night I was too embarrassed to mention it, I thought maybe it had been a dream. After all, how could I have known to pick up the phone when it had no way to ring? Then after we'd talked awhile, you said, That was amazing when I woke you last night—it was morning here and I really didn't mean for it to turn into that, but when you said it I had to do it, I wanted it too.

When I said it? When I said it. Yes, I remember now the sound of my own voice: Fuck me, please fuck me I need you I have to have you. Fuck me.

7

When Michael got back from England, everything changed; that is, everything changed back. He said he'd realized while he was so far away from
home that the woman he wanted to come back to was me; the life he
wanted to live was with me. We would be a couple again after he talked
to Brenda. Then we would begin planning a life together that included
his kids. We would start looking for a place to live, with a spare bedroom
where Bridget could sleep whenever she was with us; we'd get a sleeper
sofa for Finn's less frequent visits home from NYU.

He mused aloud again and again about what he thought he should tell
Brenda and not tell her. He didn't want to start our future together
under the weight of her bitterness and anger, but he didn't want to lie
either. I tried to listen to him without making suggestions, which was
never easy for me in any situation, but I knew that this was one conversation I had to stay out of. He decided to do it gradually: First, he
would tell Brenda his feelings had changed. He would begin sleeping in
his study. If the marriage could end gradually, he hoped they might avoid
the violent tearing that occurred when such decisions were made and
acted on overnight.

Rather than sell the Brookline house, he decided, he was going to give
his interest in it to Brenda so the kids wouldn't lose the familiar home
base. He'd also give her half of the advance on his next novel, as soon
as he got it. She actually made more money than he'd ever made, but
under the circumstances he knew he owed her.

"I made a promise to her long ago," he told me, "and now I'm about to break it. I want her to be okay, and I need her to know I feel that way. I need the kids to know that, too."

For so long I'd been waiting for Michael to take decisive action; for over a year that had been the dreamed-of resolution, the golden ring. I was confused now by my feelings when he left my apartment resolved to talk to Brenda as soon as he got home; now was the time, he told me somberly, while Bridget was away for the night at a slumber party. After he left, I found myself too shaky to paint; I paced instead. A marriage was about to end; a family was about to have its expectations and its continuity broken. I had a wild impulse to phone him and tell him not to do it. Just forget it, I could tell him. *Don't do it!* I stood by the phone, reaching for the receiver once, and then putting it back in its cradle without dialing.

I paced my hall back and forth until a realization settled in me and stilled: the realization that it would be false to call him and say such a thing, because I knew he would still go forward with his decision, only then he'd be all alone in it. I would have effectively abjured myself from the proceedings, and that would be a denial of my complicity, my own responsibility in the matter.

For hours I walked back and forth through my apartment, too nervous to light anywhere, trying to think everything through again and again.

Brenda was not some sort of monster, I knew that. It would have been easier to bear the thought of what was happening tonight if she had been because then there might have been an edge of righteous pleasure in thinking she was getting her due. But the truth was, she was a perfectly good person—a devoted if somewhat rigid mother, a successful invest-ment banker, and, in all likelihood, a faithful wife. A former Back Bay debutante, she was a bit of a social butterfly who tended to become petulant when they didn't go out often enough to suit her, and as she'd become more and more successful, she'd had an ever-growing number of old-money friends and business associates with whom to exchange invitations to dinner parties, in addition to the elegant evenings her par-ents hosted. Michael found it a torment to sit through dinner with most of the people Brenda knew (although he happened to be quite fond of the Galbraiths). He said he'd often wondered what his parents would have made of the sight of him there in such elevated company.

When they'd married in their twenties, Michael had just landed his first job teaching comp at Tufts, and Brenda was following in her father's footsteps by getting her degree in finance at Harvard. Later, after winning some important awards for his short stories, Michael began teaching fiction writing at Emerson; around the same time, Brenda was hired at Shearson Lehman, a respected Boston firm. Finnian came along when they were both nearly thirty; Bridget five years later. Michael and Brenda had probably seemed a fairly ordinary urban couple in those days.

As Michael became increasingly immersed in his writing, Brenda grew more successful in the world of finance; inevitably she became the better wage earner of the two. This disparity in their income had long bothered her, Michael said, but a worse problem for him was the sense that she considered his professional position to be not in keeping with her own. For years his literary life had been what Michael called "the Great Unspoken," but now, since his novel had begun selling quite briskly and was getting raves from all the right reviewers, Brenda had been bringing up the subject of his work frequently in dinner-table conversations with her friends and colleagues. In my hearing Michael had rarely sounded embittered about anything—it wasn't really his nature to be sour—but when he talked about this, I'd heard the acid tone in his voice and, beneath that, the hurt.

I could only imagine how Brenda would see Michael's announcement tonight: Now that he was finding success as a writer and attaining a stature more compatible with her professional standing, he was leaving her. How could she not find this a cruel irony? Maybe the discordance between their two worlds hadn't been as apparent to her as it was to him. Why should it have been when they lived mostly in her social world? But Michael hated that world, had long found it unbearable. ("I hate the bloody Dow," he always said.)

It was four hours later when Michael finally called me from a downstairs phone at their Brookline house, and I was a wreck by then but managed to put on a calm front. He sounded worn down, and I could only imagine the scene he'd been through.

For a long time after hello he said pretty much nothing. We just listened to the other's breaths and the empty telephone air. It was some kind of comfort simply to be there within reach of each other.

Finally he said, "It was awful. She completely lost it. She threw a cookbook at me, just like in Dagwood and Blondie. *Let's Cook Italian.* Then she pummelled me and started to cry. She's in bed now." He paused, blew out a puff of air. "I feel like a criminal."

"God, Michael. Oh, God."

"It was awful," he said again.

"You told her you're leaving?"

"No, I just told her I thought we should try an at-home separation until I figured out what to do. I told her that I care about her, but that I'm not in love with her. I'm sure every asshole in the fucking world who leaves his wife says that. And I announced I was going to start sleeping in my study. It's all such a fucking goddam late-twentieth-century cliché."

"Then don't do it, Michael. Don't do it if you feel that way." Now it seemed my duty to say it, but it was hard to know what was right. If anything was, at this point.

"Norrie—you know I don't feel that way myself—I'm just saying that's how it's going to look to everyone who knows me. Especially when . . . oh, I don't know."

"When what?" I asked, alarmed. I knew this had something to do with me. "When what?"

He didn't answer. Unless a sigh is an answer. I guess it is.

"When they see you with me?" I asked.

"Something like that, I guess."

"Why? I'm not a floozy—I'm a perfectly nice person."

"You're the most wonderful person I've ever known. I actually *mean* that, you know. You are. But you're only thirty-six years old, Norrie. It's all such a fucking cliché of midlife crisis."

"Because you're forty-seven, you mean?"

"Yeah, but more because *Brenda* is forty-seven. And let's face it, you look even younger than you are."

"I do?" That was news to me.

"You're such a sweet-faced, natural type—you could easily be a college coed." He had such a quaint way of expressing himself some-times. A college coed—what a goon. My heart melted. "I guess it's an image thing," he said, "an ego thing. I like being admired and thought of as a great guy. I'm not really wild about being seen as Humbert Humbert."

"Jesus, Michael, I'm not goddamn Lolita. I could be Lolita's mother! If this were the Appalachians, I could be Lolita's *grandmother.*"

He laughed, sort of. "Oh, I know," he said wearily. "Look, I'm frazzled. I'm sure I'll see this in a more hopeful light tomorrow. The main thing I called to tell you is that I love you very much. I love you so much that I'm still sane, even now after all of this. Barely."

"'*Still* sane' implies a preexisting condition," I reminded him. "I'm not sure you're eligible to claim that."

"What would I do without you?" he said, and actually kind of chuckled.

I sighed. "Not this, I guess."

For the next two days Brenda didn't get out of bed, and Michael got very scared. He brought her warm milk and rubbed her shoulders but didn't back down on any major point. He still meant everything he'd said the other night, he told her contritely but unwaveringly. Bridget was allowed to stay on at her friend's house for another night because Mom was "sick."

On the third day Brenda got up and went to her office. She called Michael from there at noon and told him she hated him. That night she tried to sleep with him.

By the sixth day they were coexisting in their Brookline house, keeping up appearances around Bridget, and had even gone out to lunch together twice "to ease the tension," Michael said.

"What am I going to tell the kids?" Brenda asked him over salmon bisque on Thursday.

"It's not the time to tell them anything at this point," he said he'd told her. "Let's just worry about us right now—we'll figure out the rest of it later."

The *us* hurt when he repeated the conversation to me; there was a take-for-granted intimacy in it, an implied history. Of *course* there was. Still, something in me flinched when he said it.

* * *

Things started to normalize after that—whatever normal was. Michael even became cheerful and began talking about where we might live when all of this was over, how many rooms we'd need in the new place: plenty of room for Bridget and Finn's visits, and a room for me to paint in— a room with a door that closed. There would be adjustments for all of us in this situation, and Michael and I had to be sure, as the adults (and the instigators of the change), that we'd prepared a setting that would help everyone to be as comfortable as possible. We weren't going to have a lot of money, he reminded me; neither of us cared about that, which was lucky.

We looked at apartments and duplexes for sale in Somerville and Watertown, just to see what was out there. Each time we walked through a place we could imagine living in together, it smoothed and unknotted me, calmed the nervous hesitation I always tended to feel about letting go and trusting love. Michael was visibly cheered to see a concrete future embodied in the rooms we walked through arm in arm behind a real estate agent.

Our spirits lifted by the day, and he came over more often—mostly, as it happened, during the hours when Clara was away. She'd been au-diting classes at Harvard (a free privilege of Larkin fellows) and was not at home now on most weekdays. I actually began to stop worrying about running into her.

Then one afternoon as Michael and I left the building, we encountered Clara walking into the lobby. Nervously, I introduced the two of them. Clara showed no sign of recognizing Michael's name, which relieved me. I told her the truth, or part of it: Michael was one of Aperçu's authors, and I'd worked on his book cover and design. She only looked at Michael when I was talking to her; oddly, when he spoke to her, to say he was happy to meet her, she looked into my face as if to ascertain the truth of his words. I turned as we exited the courtyard at the front of the building and found her still standing on the steps watching us. I waved, to cover the awkwardness. She nodded and went inside.

"Odd duck," Michael said when we got halfway down the block. I didn't reply.

* * *

It was a week later that Michael and I went dancing at a club in Allston, a mostly black club with some kick-ass, live rock- and jazz-flavored blues and a nice big dance floor. We wanted to be careful; there was no point in making public appearances together anyplace where we could be seen by people he and Brenda knew. This was safe, he said, since none of their friends went dancing, and he didn't know anyone in Allston. I'd found out about the club from Liz last year when she was dating a gorgeous black saxophonist who played there. Liz has always had the most beautiful boyfriends—and nary a one of them married.

I was really excited about this occasion, which felt like a first date, and I spent a couple of hours getting ready for it. I even bought a black silk, wraparound skirt and a stretchy, black silk-and-lycra ribbed T-shirt with three-quarter sleeves. And the major thing I did in preparation for our date was, well, to depilate my nether regions. I'd never done this before, for anyone, but it seemed like a nice surprise to give Michael. I wasn't going to say a word about it—he could just find out through his own initiative.

After my bath, I rubbed lotion all over my body and walked around naked for about twenty minutes so it would soak in before I got dressed. Then I pulled the black top over my head and smoothed it down over my torso—it was a real body hugger—and put on the black silk wrap skirt, which was longish and bias cut, clingy in just the right way—not to mention the fact that walking or dancing would reveal a nice flash of leg. I put on some black sandals because no other shoes looked right with these clothes. And that was it. I have not mentioned the underwear I put on because I did not put on any underwear. Michael was to have a double surprise tonight—no underwear beneath my silk clothes and, well, the smooth-as-silk pussy.

The club was dark and kind of smoky, and though I didn't like breathing smoke, tonight I just didn't care. We took a little table along the wall and ordered drinks, which we barely sipped because we seemed to be out on the floor dancing to nearly every song, fast and slow and in between. In-between tempos were actually very sexy to dance to. In fact it was after one of those that we got into a little bit of trouble, Michael was a great dancer, and we moved very well together—the problem was, if it was a problem, we seemed to get hotter and hotter as we danced, especially to the numbers that called for a bit of slowed-down body contact *and* a certain amount of movement. The in-betweens, as I said.

It was after "Sunshine Superman" that we returned to our table and Michael pulled me onto his lap. I felt his erection through the back of my thin silk skirt. I remember the band was playing a sexy version of "Round Midnight" with a vocalist who sounded so much like Bobby McFerrin I couldn't believe it. Michael slid his hand over my upper leg and, finding the split in the skirt, moved his hand up my bare thigh beneath the skirt, and then up to where it became quite clear that I was wearing no underwear and had no pubic hair.

"Oh, God," he breathed, "I don't believe you." His fingers stroked my smooth exterior and then interior lips, and he whispered, "You're so wet!" Yes, indeed I was. He pulled his hand away then, and I wondered if something was wrong. He was shifting around on the chair, and then I realized he was unzipping his jeans. I had to assume, then, that he was fully exposed behind me—I was very glad the club was so dark. I felt the slick material of my skirt being pulled up beneath me—because it was a wrap skirt, nothing was revealed in front—and the next thing I knew Michael was inside me. Inside me. It was the first time he'd ever been inside me without a condom, which was in itself exciting. And then he stayed perfectly still like that, deep inside me but not moving—that restraint was one of the things I'd always found sexiest about Michael. I tried to keep still, too, though I knew I had less self-control than Michael did and it was an enormous effort for me. I hovered on the edge of orgasm as we sat like that through "Angel Eyes," and by the time they got to "Body and Soul," the feeling of him inside me, bare and tumescent, was too much to bear.

On "How High the Moon" even Michael could take it no longer, and he began to move inside me. I was so hot and so wet, he was so hard and so hot—the denouement was inevitable.

"OH!" he gasped and then came and came and came inside me. I happened to be coming at the same moment, so his OH went for both of us. Even after we'd come, he stayed inside me and I squeezed him with my superior vaginal muscles in time with the music, until the next thing we knew he was hard again and within a few minutes coming again. That went on for two hours, and later he would tell me that he'd never known he could come four times in a row. It had never happened in his life, he said. That was later in the car, parked by the Charles River, when we were embarking on number five.

When he left that night and I was getting ready for bed, I realized I'd never had so much cum inside me in my life. I was about to get into the bathtub and then I changed my mind. I wanted to feel it between my legs as I fell asleep, wanted to breathe in the scent of it all night long.

We seem to be going further and further sexually, doing things neither of us has done before with anyone. I wonder why. Is it that we sense freedom ahead after hiding for so long, and we're drunk on the idea of it?

Or is this newly intensified lust fed by the awareness that we are finally only each other's and not sharing ourselves physically with anyone else? Does that somehow confer on us a kind of privilege, a sense that there are, as the fighters say, no holds barred? That if we belong to each other, then we are each other's to do with as we wish? Maybe. And just thinking about it that way excites me.

Am I saying, then, that monogamy is sexy? It may be so. That's an idea for the books. But apparently for us, anyway, that old truism about the lure of the forbidden doesn't obtain. Our sex is no longer "the forbidden," and it's more urgent, wilder, than ever before.

When you left tonight I wondered for a moment if we should be more careful with our sexual experimentation, our exploration of each other's bodies—not only careful in the obvious ways, but careful about understanding, protecting, and observing some mutual sense of limitation.

And then I thought, Why should I pretend regret or an inclination to moderation? I know that if you were here now, neither of us would hesitate to do anything the other wanted. Anything.

It seems I think about you all the time now, every minute of the day and night, no matter how I'm occupied or where I am, I feel you inside me.

And that almost-constant state of arousal has made its way into my painting. How could it be otherwise? I want to show her to you, the woman in the red room, I want you to see her in this new painting so that you'll understand how my desire for you feels to me. I want you to feel it too, as if we were one skin.

She's on her back on one side of a dishevelled red blanket, the skin of her face and body awash in the glow of lamplight, flushed, blooming. Her eyes are closed, as if she's in some state of thrall, her lips slightly open and her long legs parted just enough to suggest recent sexual activity, her knees bent slightly. Her clothes lie in a heap on the floor nearby.

The red silk kimono is thrown over the back of a chair, and the black satin sash is missing from it. If you look carefully you can see the sash just beneath the woman's neck. Her arms are opened out on the floor as if to fly, as if she might have recently experienced the headiest sort of thrill and now cannot bear to return to conventional pleasures.

I mixed some vivid reds for this scene, rich and radiant reds for the drapes, the blanket, the kimono, and the moon, which is not a full moon tonight but just a slice of moon, so hard-edged, such a thin, sharp slice that it looks like a scythe blade, a dangerous weapon that could slice that warmed and satisfied flesh. This is the only element in the picture that seems ominous, as if it might be a warning about the dangers of the flesh, the danger of letting desire take you too far. And yet the color, the lambent red of that slice of moon, says, Don't stop don't ever stop.

And I know I can't. I don't want to, of course, but that's not the point. I mean I can't. I can't. I can't stop and I won't.

8

As fall wore on I saw Devi more often, and we found a close friendship developing—not yet as intimate as my friendship with Liz, but Devi and I were close in the same sort of way that Liz and I were—a comfortable, sisterly kind of familiarity.

I'd told Liz about Devi and was dying for the two of them to meet. Liz told me she knew Devi's poetry well and admired it a lot ("Once again you've demonstrated excellent literary taste in friends," she'd said). A week or so later I was thrilled when Devi mentioned that she'd read quite a lot of Liz's fiction in recent years and always found it "spell-binding."

The three of us made a plan to meet for dinner when Liz came to Boston on her book tour sometime after the first of the year. The tour dates weren't even set yet, and we were already planning where we'd eat.

I tried not to talk to Clara about my friendship with Devi because Clara was so jealous and insecure. To complicate matters, Devi continued to be unresponsive to Clara's overtures, which made for a certain level of tension when the three of us happened to be together at the Larkin colloquium presentations each Wednesday. Indeed, what may have put Devi off might have been the fact that there were so very many overtures from Clara and that they were so self-consciously courtly. Devi had never spoken ill of Clara to me, but I sensed her coolness—and so did Clara.

Finally one evening I decided to broach the subject to Devi. I was eating dinner at her place again; she loved to cook and I loved to eat, so the arrangement had been working out rather well. I came right out and asked if she disliked Clara. Devi answered straightforwardly.

"Of course not," she said, "but she treats me like a celebrity rather than a person, and it makes me uncomfortable. She's the epitome of everything I don't enjoy about the literary attention I've received lately. I don't like to feel pursued."

"I understand. I just think maybe she'd calm down a little if you gave her a chance."

"Norrie, I don't tell you how to live your life or who you ought to spend time with—or not spend time with. Those judgments are highly personal for each of us, don't you think?" Devi's voice was gentle but also firm. I felt like a klutz.

"Yeah . . . of course, you're right. And anyway, I avoid Clara myself—every chance I get. To tell the truth, I think that what I said to you was just my own guilt talking."

"To tell a truth in turn," Devi said, "I can hardly bear to be around her lately. Last week at the Larkin she came up to me just after the colloquium and told me she'd been dreaming about me and felt as if we might have been close to each other in an earlier life."

"God."

"Yes, it was rather upsetting to me. She watches me all the time with those hungry eyes. I've seen her looking at you in exactly the same way."

"What?"

"Yes, I mean it, Norrie. She was staring at you when the fellows went to dinner afterward. You were talking in a lively sort of way to Serena Holwerda, and the two of you were laughing. I happened to turn toward Jane Coleman and saw Clara next to her. Her eyes were on you and her face was rapt, but also I would say tortured. It was a look I found very unsettling."

I felt a little unsettled myself, just hearing the description of Clara's eyes on me. "Are you saying she has romantic feelings toward us?"

"Oh, who knows? It matters very little to me what the source of this behavior is. I can't take the time to fret about it."

"Well, Clara has had a hard life. It might explain some of this."

"Oh?"

"Yeah, she lost her parents very young—both of them. Her father was a prominent newspaper editor in Santiago who was murdered for his political outspokenness. Her mother died of cancer ten years later, and Clara was quite traumatized by that. She's all alone in the world."

"How sad. It's really too bad. But, Norrie, we've all suffered in one way or another in our lives. That doesn't give us the right to possess and control others." She paused. "Think about this, Norrie," she said. "You and I have become, I would say, very good friends. Yes?"

"Absolutely."

"And your friend Liz was very happy at the thought of meeting me, wasn't she?"

"Yeah, sure. She knows I like you and find you good company."

"Exactly. And I'm excited about meeting Liz for the same reasons. If she means so much to you, I feel she'll be someone worth knowing. But Clara is not that kind of friend, Norrie. Surely you see that. She looks at us with suspicion when she sees us talking, and she even looks angry sometimes. That's not friendship. That's possession. I will not be possessed."

"Maybe she feels left out," I said, but I knew I'd lost the enthusiasm to defend Clara.

"Her behavior causes that," Devi answered, casting an eye at my plate.

I looked at it and saw that I'd eaten almost nothing. I seemed not to be as hungry as usual.

"You're not eating, Norrie. Isn't the food good tonight?" Devi asked, concern on her face.

"It's wonderful, as always," I assured her, "but I don't know, I just . . . maybe it's all this talk about Clara. I feel kind of upset to my stomach, and it's hard to have an appetite."

Devi looked at me for a long time then, as if she wanted to speak but was afraid to.

"What?" I asked. "Don't do that. What?"

"Nothing," she answered hesitantly. "Nothing, really . . . I just keep looking at you, and to my eyes you seem different. Also, you haven't been acting as peppy as usual, and now I see your appetite is down. I've noticed this difference in you for at least a week now. I've even wondered if you might be . . ."

She didn't have to finish her sentence; I knew what she was thinking and simultaneously I knew it was true. I was pregnant. My mind instantly retrieved the image of Michael inside me in the dark jazz club four weeks ago—inside me without a condom. Mentally I counted weeks. My period had been due last week. I'd not felt great for a couple of weeks now that I thought about it. I looked at Devi and couldn't speak at first. She and I had not spoken of my relationship with Michael since the night I'd told her about it without identifying him.

"Jesus, Devi," I finally said, "what are you? A gynecologist? Some kind of holistic oracle? While you're at it, do I have any teeth that need filling?"

"Oh, Norrie . . . I'm sorry if I'm being intrusive," she said. "But you don't seem yourself. When I know someone pretty well, I can often detect early signs of pregnancy. I've known all four times my sister Rina has been expecting, even before she knew it herself." She blushed. "My God, listen to me. It sounds like I'm bragging! Oh, Norrie, are you all right?"

I breathed deeply and took inventory. "Nope," I decided. "I'm not all right. Jesus, you'd think I was some idiot high school kid. How could I have let this happen?"

"It takes two," Devi reminded me, just as Liz would have. If she'd known. But Liz didn't even know I was seeing anyone.

That was something I could worry about another time. I had other things to think of. If I was pregnant, I couldn't imagine what Michael would say—couldn't imagine.

As if his life weren't complicated enough right now.

And he'd been handling things so well lately; he'd even begun making some decisive steps toward our future. He'd found a house for sale in Watertown— half a large house, rather like the one I'd rented with Jill— and had called me eagerly the previous day to ask me to go and look at it with him. We'd met with the realtor in the afternoon, and she had taken us through the place room by room. Though it wasn't so distinguished a house as my former rental, it had charm, lots of sunny rooms, and a generous terrace just off the upstairs master bedroom.

Michael and I had stood close together by the French doors that led to the terrace, imagining our life together in that house. He'd put his arm around me as we stood there and pulled me against him. Michael had a way of making me feel safe, and it embarrassed me to admit to myself how much I liked that protective aspect—it was something I'd avoided all my life.

We left with the asking price written on the woman's business card. The owners didn't want to close till after the first of the year, and Michael felt that militated in our favor because he wanted to wait until after the Thanksgiving and Christmas holidays to make the final break with Brenda. "A lot of buyers wouldn't want to wait that long," he pointed out. He would check with a bank about a mortgage and make an offer as soon as he had the necessary preapproval. "So many people fall into depression during the holidays," he added, when we got out to his car, "and Brenda's fragile already. I don't want a meltdown going on at our house when Finn gets here for the holidays." He sighed, pulled me to him. "Anyway, my Irish mother always said bad news should wait till after Christmas."

I had an Irish mother, too, I thought of pointing out, and she enjoyed passing along bad news anytime of the year.

Ever since we'd come back from looking at the house yesterday, I'd been riding high. Now I was nervous again. Back home from Devi's, I stared at myself in the bathroom mirror. I had no idea what sort of change she had seen in my appearance tonight. To me I looked the same as always. But it was true I'd been a little listless, and my appetite, generally like a stevedore's, was now more like that of a supermodel. My breasts had been a little sore, too, now that I thought of it. Also, yesterday morning I'd thrown up some eggs I'd scrambled. I'd figured the eggs might be stale and had thrown out the rest of the box.

I wanted to call Michael now, this minute, but I always had to wait for him to call me, to be sure Brenda wasn't within earshot. I prowled my bedroom, slowing each time I got near the phone and staring at it, jumpy and anxious.

Once one thing got under my skin, I tended to worry everything else to death. Now I began thinking how things hadn't changed in any noticeable way at their house since the night of their blowup—what Brenda had taken to calling "The Saturday Night Massacre." (That's one thing I may have neglected to mention about Michael's wife—she had a sharp wit and could be quite funny sometimes.)

Michael was still sleeping in his study, but that study was right off their bedroom—it had been a sitting room originally—and the two of them shared one bathroom. I could imagine Michael standing in front of the basin in his boxers with a toothbrush in his mouth, while she sat on the toilet nearby and peed.

That gave me another uneasy thought: Hadn't I been peeing more than usual?

I stewed. Paced. Waited for Michael to call. Put on my painting clothes. Didn't paint. Tried to figure out what I would tell him. I could always wait until I'd been to the doctor to say anything about this—or at least I could wait till I'd taken a pregnancy test. But Michael and I weren't like that with each other, and I wasn't used to keeping things from him. That was too *I Love Lucy* for me. No, I would have to tell him I thought I might be pregnant.

At midnight my phone rang and I picked it up on the first ring. I would tell him slowly, so as not to shock him.

"Hello," I said in my calmest voice.

"Tell me, dear," he crooned in his hokey Elvis imitation, "are you lonesome toniiiight?"

"Not so much lonesome as pregnant," I said. That was about as long as I could wait.

"Jesus," he said, shedding his Elvis persona. "Really?"

"I don't know."

"Norrie, talk to me."

"I think I may be pregnant. Tonight Devi asked me if I was, and she always knows when everyone is pregnant before *they* know."

"Well, I'm sure Devi is a wonderful person, but that's not exactly a scientific diagnosis."

"Okay, but my period's late, I'm sleepy all the time, my breasts hurt, I'm peeing pretty often, and I threw up my breakfast yesterday."

"That's more the sort of evidence I was looking for," he said, and blew out his breath in that way he does when he's in a bind. "So how far along do you think you'd be?"

"Oh—I was just now figuring—I guess it'd be four weeks, or maybe five."

"Really? I thought women just somehow always knew immediately when they were pregnant," he said, the implication being (in my prickly state of mind): *Brenda* did. That really made me mad. It felt as if he were saying that I was falling down on the job of being a woman, was not as in touch with my body as good old Brenda, the Renaissance Woman.

"I've never had a baby, Michael." I made my voice flat.

"Right," he said, "I didn't mean—"

"I'm a spinster, okay? And an only child! I never even saw my mother pregnant. Or a sister, since I don't have one."

"Sure, Norrie, calm down. Let's get you to the doctor. Then we'll figure out what to do."

I felt reassured by the *we,* but not by the rest of the sentence. I wondered what he meant by "what to do." I'd always believed in choice (despite my mother's militant pro-life stance: "Only witches in a coven believe in abortion," she always said), but I was healthy and this pregnancy had been conceived in love. How could I justify abortion under these circumstances? Suddenly I was afraid Michael was going to suggest it. Wouldn't I almost have to do it if he insisted since he had a say in this, too? But then again, if he did insist, I wouldn't want to be with him anymore anyway. That would be it for me. Would I raise the baby alone then?

As soon as we hung up, I burst into tears. Then as I blubbered into the sleeve of my painting shirt, which I had obviously put on for nothing, I remembered that crying is also a sign of pregnancy. I wondered if paranoia was?

The phone rang again.

"Hello," I wept.

"Oh, Jesus," he said. "That's what I was wondering. If you were crying."

"So that pretty much clinches it?" I sobbed.

"I'm afraid it does, darling. Irrefutable proof." His voice became serious. "You know, Norrie, I just called to say . . . to point out that we do love each other, after all."

"No shit, Sherlock." I blew my nose hard.

"I mean, scary as it may seem to both of us at the moment, what can be so bad about this turn of events, other than the timing? If we're having a baby, well then——" he did that air puff thing again. "——we're having a baby. Let's get you to a doctor and then we'll sit down calmly and figure out the rest of our lives." His voice was both tender and kind of nervous.

"Okay," I said. Thank God. I shouldn't have doubted Michael.

"So, really, you have to try to calm down."

"Okay," I said again. Clearly I'd switched from crying to obedience. And wasn't obedience also a sign of pregnancy?

"Do you need me to come over for a few minutes and hold you?" he asked. "Let me do that—let me come over and fold you up like a little seed." I couldn't believe he would offer to leave the house after midnight in light of the current situation with Brenda—that would be a sure sign to her that there was someone else in his life.

"I guess not," I said, "but thanks for the offer. We've got enough to worry about already. You'd better stay home."

"Are you going to be all right?"

"Sure," I said. "I might even paint." But even as I said it, I realized I wouldn't. I was hammered, emotionally and physically flattened.

"Paint?" Michael said, "Now? Don't you think you ought to get some sleep? Anyway, you're going to have to talk to the doctor about the wisdom of inhaling paint fumes."

I started laughing. I don't know why. I laughed all the way to the bathroom, where I threw up again. But that didn't necessarily mean anything.

Maybe it was that image of yours about folding me up like a seed that did it. I only know that when I went to bed last night and closed my eyes, I kept seeing it——too small to call fetus or embryo——more a tiny seed inside my womb, preparing to germinate. It made me think of the mustard seed bracelet Daddy gave Mother when they were first dating. She saved it and has always kept it in the jewelry box on her dresser, though she never wears it. When I was small I used to sneak into her room to look at the little yellow seed floating pure and solitary in that crystal orb, and as I gazed into the glass it seemed like a whole infinitesimal universe in there. Now it seems I have a seed-baby floating in the universe of my uterus. Poor little bastard.

I'm feeling so tender of it——of him or her. Himher. It . . . I'll call it it, because right now I see it as a seed. A dinky kernal of life floating in the womb that has so recently been at the receiving end of raucous and unremitting sex. I shudder to think what your penis must have felt like to that little seed——a battering ram, I guess. I feel guilty when I think of it, but of course we couldn't have known.

For hours last night I lay in bed awake with my eyes closed, knowing it's in there all alone without a clue. Will I be a good mother? Yes. I will because I will love this little creature that you and I made together in a smoky blues club on a night when I wore no underwear and had shaved my pubes slick as a baby's. Thank God it was too busy being formed to stop and observe the goings-on. Still, I feel a little embarrassed at the thought.

Creation: The word has such a dignified ring. Leave it to humans to turn a sacred moment bawdy.

But it was an ecstatic occasion. What better way to welcome new life?

9

At week's end the realtor called Michael to let him know that another couple had bought the house we wanted—for cash. Michael had been waiting to see what CitiCorp would say about a loan. So that was that. We both felt very let down about it, and I thought of suggesting we go out looking again; but then it seemed there was enough to think of right now, for both of us.

I had an appointment to see my gynecologist the following Tuesday, and until then I couldn't concentrate on my work. It was awful waiting, but I wanted to see my regular gyno, Dr. Margaret Vesta, and she was away on a skiing trip. I hadn't painted since that night at Devi's. I couldn't seem to gather the creative energy. At the moment, all my energy was going into tormenting myself, which takes a lot out of a person.

It seemed I was pregnant; every day I became more certain of it. I vacillated between tenderness for the seed-baby growing inside me and terror that it was there. What in the world would I do with a baby? Sometimes it seemed already to be a cherished part of my life; at other moments, however briefly, I wanted it out of me, wanted it gone.

While I was waiting to see Dr. Vesta, I decided to try a home pregnancy test. I ended up buying three of them at once on my trip to CVS, figuring I'd go with the best two of three.

All three turned blue.

Something happened to me when I got those three positives—I went quiet inside, stone quiet, and knew I wouldn't want to announce the results to Michael, tentative as they were. He and Brenda had been having marathon arguments that went on into the morning hours all week, and he was a wreck. How many times and ways did I have to tell him I was pregnant, anyway?

If he didn't have enough to worry about, now his book, so wildly loved by critics and readers alike, had become the object of vitriol for some South Boston residents who, after reading a long excerpt of *This Cold Heaven* in the *Globe*, took umbrage at Michael's gritty depiction of life in the projects. No one was disputing his account of things in Southie, but his descriptions were seen as disloyalty or, as one woman put it, "taking leave of your own blood."

One sixty-seven-year-old man wrote to the *Globe* that he considered Michael Sullivan "an infidel." A woman who called herself "just an old Irish rip who thinks loyalty needn't be out of style," wrote: "Shame on you, Michael Sullivan, for you have shamed us all, even your own dead mother and father, by making us sound crude and rough and promiscuous. Wasn't it enough that you made it out of Southie? You should face the truth that once you crossed over the Broadway Bridge, you became an outsider. You needn't have come back to humiliate those who once were your very family, the ones that gave you your start."

To make things worse, Aiden O'Connell, an irascible, reactionary radio host who had an afternoon call-in show, had jumped on the bandwagon, encouraging residents of Southie to phone in their condemnation of "this money-grubbing opportunist," and the word had spread so well through the Lower End that people who seemed not even to have read the book were weighing in on the matter.

Michael was shocked and hurt—and angry, for he felt the charges were unjust.

Sure, he told me, he'd written of his childhood and teen years in South Boston with an "unblinking" eye, but not without respect and compassion for family and neighbors. And sure, there was more than passing mention of the poverty and violence in Old Colony and other heavily Irish projects in Southie, and he'd written of the promiscuity and alcohol that relieved boredom and discontent for some, as well as the drugs that organized crime had brought into the neighborhood. (On this subject, Michael had made special mention in the book of the man behind that drug trade for many years, Whitey Bulger, who went from Southie's resident hero to notorious traitor when it was discovered that he'd been an FBI informant all along.)

Michael included in the book certain events that occurred after he left Southie to go to Columbia University on scholarship, incidents such as the 1974 busing riots, because he felt that the roots of these things could be found in the conditions he'd lived with as a child growing up among the misunderstood working-class Irish of the Lower End, those who had been branded "lazy," "ignorant," and, worst of all, "racist."

It had always seemed to me that Michael felt he had a very personal debt to pay in writing the book. His fourteen-year-old brother Kevin, had been fatally knifed one Saturday night when he'd wandered too far outside the Old Colony projects, and Michael still felt guilty that he'd been away at college then and not around to look after his little brother. Now he was especially stung by the woman who accused him of "taking leave of his own blood."

"I thought," he told me, "that in many ways *Heaven* was a tribute to the spirit of the people who live in the place where I grew up. I was just trying to do it honestly—trying to avoid 'thinking with the blood,' as Kipling called it. It'd just have been a fucking sentimental gloss if I'd done that." He was more upset than I'd ever seen him, and I knew it wasn't just his injured pride but also that he felt so terribly misunderstood.

He obsessed on this situation, talking about it all the time, until at my urging one afternoon he phoned Aiden O'Connell's show. I left him on the bedroom phone and waited in the living room so that I could hear his words as they came out over the air in the context of other people's comments. O'Connell, clearly excited that the author himself had tuned in, put Michael on right away. "Well, so this is himself," O'Connell said with dripping sarcasm, "the very man who's been writing about you people."

"First of all, this is a novel—not a memoir," Michael said. "But I have tried honestly to keep my depictions of Southie accurate, and I can only write from my own experiences there. From what I remember, from what I know firsthand or saw happen to members of my family."

I could hear the strains of Southie in his speech, as always when he was upset or impassioned.

"It was a world closed off from the larger world," he said. "There *were* no 'haves' in the projects at all, only 'have-nots,' and every waking minute we knew we had enemies out there who didn't understand us, who would stab us in the back if they got a chance. We stayed close to home as much as we could so that we could stay alive. There was a class war going on in Southie, and my little brother, Kevvie, was killed in it. My cousins Tommy and Liam, too. My sister and my aunt both committed suicide, and I consider them to be casualties of that same war. Everyone I knew lost at least one loved one to street warfare or drugs or alcohol. I have as much right to talk about Southie as anybody else does.

"I wrote this book for Kevvie and Tommy and Liam," he told the listening audience. "I wrote it for my sister, Maureen, who took an overdose when she couldn't stand her life anymore, and for Aunt Molly, who hanged herself ten months after her two sons—her only kids—were murdered, and most of all I wrote it for my mother and father, who worked so hard through years and years of grief and deprivation and then died too young, just from exhaustion and despair.

"You know, I haven't tried to hurt anyone. I've just tried to tell the world how it was for me and my family and how it may still be for some of you who live in Southie. I got tired of hearing the Irish of South Boston condemned. A woman who wrote to the *Globe* about *This Cold Heaven* criticized me for what she called 'taking leave of my own blood.' I just want to say that I couldn't do that if I wanted to—and I've never for a minute wanted to."

After Michael rang off, O'Connell's callers moved to the subject of Whitey Bulger, and I told Michael I thought that was a sign he'd made his point well. He didn't answer.

A few days later I pointed out to him that the angry letters to the *Globe* had tapered off. "There's only been one this entire week," I said. But even one Southie resident's resentment was hurtful to him, and often in his quieter moments I could see that in his face.

One day at lunch he mentioned that Ed Hershorn had called him, full of glee about the brouhaha. "It's great for the book," he'd told Michael. "You should be glad people are talking about it!" Then, Michael said, Ed had gone on about how Philip Roth had endured a similar attack when a number of Jewish people had written letters to the *Times* accusing him of representing Jews negatively in his stories. "He wrote a great essay in rebuttal," Ed had pointed out.

"Of course I know the essay Roth wrote about that," Michael told me, "and it's a great riposte. But somehow that doesn't make it any easier to hear the things people are saying about my book."

"People," I said. "Michael, hardly anyone has had anything but praise for *This Cold Heaven!* It's just a small, small group of people who are put out by the book."

"Yeah, Norrie," he said, "but they're *my* people." I couldn't think of anything to say. This wasn't vanity or pride; it was hurt.

Of one thing I was certain, there was no good reason to add to his worries without a doctor's confirmation that I was pregnant.

Though I didn't intend to, I began to imagine the life growing inside me. *If you're a girl, embryo dear,* I whispered one night as I fell asleep, *don't ever fall in love with a married man, even a kind and beautiful Irishman with a touch that turns you to putty.*

And one morning when I was walking back from Sage's Market I stopped on the curb at the red traffic light. *Wait,* my mind said when the light turned green, *here, take my hand, watch for right turns. Be careful crossing, look both ways.*

This bonding with the seed was obviously nature's design, but knowing that didn't make the feeling easier for me to handle—if anything, it made it much worse. I stayed home from the Wednesday colloquium at the Larkin, pleading work. *Your mother's a coward. Don't be like me.*

I was a walking aphorism, my head abuzz with advice for the fetus: *Today is the first day of the rest of your life. It's always darkest before the dawn. Oh, what a tangled web we weave, when first we practice to deceive. A stitch in time saves nine.*

When Liz phoned on Thursday I didn't pick up and didn't return her call—how could I? How could I talk to her when I was probably pregnant now, and she still didn't even know there was a man in my life!

I wasn't returning Clara's and Devi's calls either. Devi took the hint, but Clara kept phoning and leaving whiny messages. I almost began to enjoy the feeling of not responding to her; it felt like retribution for all her torture. If there was anyone I couldn't bear to talk to this week, it was my noodgy neighbor.

Whenever my mother called, of course, I had no choice but to answer. If I had let her calls go for too long without responding, she would have called out the militia—and I know that sounds like a joke, but actually I'm not kidding. One time when I dropped out of sight for a week in

Montana after meeting a lovely cowboy type at an art festival, Mother actually got the Missoula police searching for me. Somehow they found me at the cowboy's house in flagrante delicto. To this day I had no idea how they'd tracked me down. Ever since that incident, I'd picked up the phone whenever my mother called.

It wasn't really so hard talking to Mother in this situation as to Liz anyway because I'd *always* lied to Mother, for her good almost as much as my own. *You won't need to be like that with me, you can tell me everything. But I won't pry.*

All week I was nauseated; I had what could be called morning-noon-and-night sickness. Then, if that wasn't enough, on Friday night I began having cramps. I started to wonder if I was just going to be sick the whole nine months. My Larkin project couldn't possibly get finished— and be good—if I were sick all the time; I don't paint well when my body is screaming for attention. Which meant that even if I didn't end up sick the whole time, even a healthy pregnancy would break my concentration as an artist. If I had any sense I supposed I *would* get an abortion. But I couldn't do that. Couldn't. I seemed to have feelings for the seed.

I went to bed tired and crampy that night, privately pissed at Michael for being at a dinner party with Brenda—not one of those parties with Brenda's dull finance friends, oh no, this was a party where Martin Amis would be one of the guests, a small, hip dinner party given by Tom Beshears, a British novelist-in-residence at Emerson. Michael had struck up a real friendship with Tom and liked him a great deal; he'd told me several times that he wished Tom could meet me because he knew we would hit it off.

Even beyond my petty jealousy I felt that his taking Brenda was a bad idea, though I didn't feel like telling him so: Why should Brenda become acquainted with Michael's new friends at this point? She and Michael were separated! Soon enough I'd be accompanying him, and everyone who saw him with Brenda now was just one more friend with whom I'd be forced into the awkward role of *successor*. Come to think of it, maybe this part was petty jealousy, too. I couldn't sort it all out anymore.

Although I said nothing, I guess Michael could tell I wasn't thrilled to hear that the two of them were going to Tom's party. Over lunch at Balducci's, he told me it seemed to him a good idea to take Brenda because they'd been fighting all week, and he thought she might mellow a bit if they did something social together. Brenda loved parties. (Odd, I thought, since she didn't seem to love people.) I picked up my wine glass, set it down without taking a sip—oops, not good for the seed. *I didn't have any, don't worry.*

"I'd just really like Brenda to see that we needn't be enemies," he was saying. "If she sees that we can still be friendly with one another, can even have fun together, maybe she'll stop the nightly reign of terror. Poor Bird keeps asking us what's wrong. I'd like things to settle down a bit before Finn comes home for Thanksgiving." He regarded me over the rim of his wine glass. "I'm sorry if it upsets you, Norrie. I just think I have to do it for the sake of the family."

"What. I didn't say anything."

"I know your face."

"Maybe I think this merlot is insipid."

"Come on, Norrie, I know you."

"I'm not going to nag you about this, Michael—we've got a whole lifetime ahead of us for that." I took a faux sip of the merlot, smacked my lips audibly, and winked at him. I had my pride. *Always keep your dignity, embryo dear, and never put yourself in a situation that's going to make you feel small.*

Just before 3:00 A.M. I woke in terrible pain, immediately aware that my thighs were wet and sticky. I sat up and felt the sheet wet beneath me, too. There was the smell of blood in the air. I threw back the blankets and got up out of bed, immediately doubling over in pain. In the bathroom I sat on the toilet and watched between my thighs as blood drizzled out of me and occasionally blood clots plopped into the toilet water. My lower back was killing me, and the abdominal cramps were ten times worse than any menstrual cramps I'd ever had.

I stood up from the toilet and immediately blood ran down my legs and onto the tile floor. How was I going to stanch this flow? My mind felt foggy and it was hard to think: I had only tampons on hand, which I knew would not do. I grabbed a hand towel from the rod, rolled it up, and stuffed it between my legs, walked knock-kneed to the bedroom, and turned on the overhead light. In my bureau I found a stretched-out pair of bikini underpants that might accommodate the bulging towel and hold it in place. I pulled them on then and turned around and waddled toward the phone; that was when I saw my bed in full light—the whole center of the sheet was soaked with blood. It looked like the scene of a murder. At the sight of it my head cleared and focused for the first time. The seed.

Are you gone? Have I lost you? Have I lost you?

I didn't know who to call. It was after 3:00 A.M. and I couldn't call Michael—at least I knew that much. As a Larkin fellow, I had low-cost Harvard Health Insurance, and a trip to their emergency facility at Holyoke Center would get me the best medical care in the world for about five dollars. I had a little sticker on my phone with the number of the Pink & Black cab service. I rang them quickly and told the dispatcher I needed to be taken from Eighty-two Brattle to the emergency room at Holyoke, and I asked them to hurry. The dispatcher said they had a cab available right now, so I told him I'd wait outside on the sidewalk. I pulled on my shrunken sweatpants, tugging them up over my towel-enlarged lower body. Holyoke was probably a five-minute cab ride from the apartment, tops.

All the way down in the elevator I kept one hand on the rail to steady myself, feeling dizzy and weak. There was an absence in my body. I knew it was gone; I could feel it.

Out on the sidewalk I found the air surprisingly cold, and the wind came in the sharp kind of gusts that just bypass your skin and go straight for the bones. I'd forgotten to put on a coat, and now if I went back upstairs I might miss the cab. I stood near the sidewalk just inside the archway of our front courtyard, shivering as I watched down Brattle Street for the lights of a cab. I waited. No cab came. No cab came.

Then I saw a man approaching on foot. I thought it odd to see anyone walking down the sidewalk alone at three in the morning, but then I was never outside at this hour—maybe people strolled these sidewalks all night. As the man passed where I stood and saw me in the archway, he slowed and spoke to me. He had a voice that came from deep inside his throat, as if he were speaking into a can.

"How much?" he asked, as if I were a prostitute. I immediately turned and ran clumsily back inside the building, pushing the front door closed and automatically locked behind me. I trembled as I rode back up to the fourth floor in the elevator. There was something about that man, something low and sinister. What was he doing out at this hour? Maybe he was a burglar. Maybe he was *our* burglar. When I got back into the apartment, I called Pink & Black cabs to tell the dispatcher the taxi had never arrived. I could feel the flow of blood into the towel increasing as a result of my attempt at running.

The dispatcher checked for me and then said, "Where were you, lady? Cab went to Holyoke to getcha and you weren't there."

"No," I said, "because THAT'S where the CAB was supposed to TAKE me! I told you I needed to GO to Holyoke from Eighty-two Brattle." I was shaking with panic-induced anger. Later—much later—Liz would ask me why I didn't just call 911, and I would honestly tell her I never thought of it. I guess the trauma affected my thinking somewhat, but really, even now I don't think people call 911 for a miscarriage, do they? That service has always seemed to me more appropriate to a house fire, a heart attack, or a choking infant.

"Well," the dispatcher was saying, "that cab now has another fare."

"But this is an emergency," I said, "and I *told* you that when I called the first time."

"Look, lady, this is business. You weren't there. He got a call and took another fare. I'll see what I can do. Will you be waiting out front?"

"Yeah, sure." With a blood-soaked towel in my underpants, you criminally stupid weasel.

"Now look, I'll try to get someone over there for you. But you're gonna hafta be where he can see you."

I went back down in the elevator then, and once again I waited in the archway near the sidewalk. What if the creep came back? I thought. If he did, I answered myself, I would deck him. Finally a hot pink and black checkered cab pulled up and I got in. Once in, it took about two seconds for me to figure out that the driver spoke no English at all. I mean nothing beyond *Hello* and *Where you go?* He had a West African accent, I thought. A couple of blocks away from Brattle I noticed that he was driving in the wrong direction, away from Holyoke.

"Hey," I called, "this is the wrong way."

He turned and looked at me and then just kept going; he didn't understand a word I was saying.

"NO," I told him, "Holyoke Emergency Room." He turned toward me again and I gestured in the other direction. "That way," I said. Immediately he turned sharply onto a one-way street—in the wrong direction.

"ONE WAY," I told him. He didn't seem to hear me. I tried again and after I'd made two or three fruitless attempts, the matter was addressed when he saw the headlights of two cars coming toward us and hooked a radical U in the middle of the block, nearly hitting both of the oncoming cars as he turned in front of them. Throughout these near-catastrophes he said nothing and showed no emotion that I could discern from the backseat.

"Holyoke Center!" I said, "Please. It's an EMERGENCY." Just then I felt an enormous blood clot passing, accompanied by cramps so powerful they made me swoon. "Please," I almost wept, and then I just couldn't talk for a while. If I'd had any doubt, I had none now. I'd lost the seed.

For the next ten minutes this man drove all over Cambridge except anywhere near Holyoke, while I sat in the backseat, mute and hunched in pain.

Finally I saw that we were on a street I recognized as a couple of blocks from Holyoke Center, and I realized I would be better off getting out here than hoping this driver might still find the way.

"Out—Please—Let me OUT!" I said. "I'll walk." He kept driving and took a turn in the wrong direction, away from Holyoke again. I got a twenty out of my purse and banged on the plastic partition between us, then waved the money at him through the opening.

"HERE," I said, "OUT, I want out!" He reached up, took my money, and came to a stop right in the middle of the street. He sat there then, waiting for me to get out. I couldn't believe it. I opened the door and stepped out unsteadily onto the street. Before I'd even gotten my balance, the cabbie drove off with a little squeal of his tires, apparently not yet having learned the words for *Sorry I took your money for nothing and am leaving you alone and bleeding in the middle of a street at 3:45 A.M., but I am a world-class asshole.*

It was pitch dark out except for streetlights, and I saw people here and there in the doorways of storefronts, nearly all of them men and most of them drinking from bottles in paper bags. I was in so much pain that I didn't bother to be afraid one of them might mug me; actually, I don't think most of them even looked at me as I stood there in the middle of the empty street.

I staggered to the curb and began making my way up the sidewalk. A man in a doorway I passed asked me for money, and that was when it hit me: The cabbie hadn't given me change for my twenty, though the cab ride from Brattle to Holyoke should have been three or four dollars at most.

"Sorry," I told him, "I don't have any money on me."

Another man in the same doorway said, "Fuckin' bitch." That did it.

"You got THAT right!" I roared, and he shut right up. I could see that my upset was turning to anger, and I would dare anyone to mess with me. I think these guys—and everyone else along the street—sensed that I was trouble because after that not one person said a thing to me as I lurched up the sidewalk with a bloody towel bulging at the front and the back of my shrunken-to-the-calf sweatpants. Frankenstein. That was the image. So what. I wasn't going to the prom.

Holyoke was probably three or four blocks from here. I could make it. I was okay, I thought, though more and more bent into the pain as I walked. And, God, it was cold. Where was Michael when I needed him? What would he think if he saw me now? And what about the seed? It was gone, of course.

I began to cry then. I had no idea I was going to do that, but suddenly I was in a quiet but messy crying jag. At one point I fantasized finding a doorway of my own and just sitting down in it. That would be the beginning of my life on the street. Maybe the people out here were more loyal and trustworthy than the fuckers in my world, who were too busy rubbing shoulders with Martin Amis to help out in time of miscarriage.

Finally I arrived at Holyoke and walked like a crab into the emergency room, doubled up and weeping, shaking all over. The nurse at the desk looked up when I walked in, and before she could say anything I blurted, "Help me—I'm bleeding." I saw her eyes giving me the onceover to see where the blood was, so I pointed to my crotch and said, "Please— hurry!" I wasn't going to mess with filling out forms right now.

She took me into a cubicle with a curtain around it and told me to take off my clothes.

"I can't," I said, "I'm bleeding too much; it'll get all over everything." She told me to lie down on the examination table and a doctor would be right in. She called for the doctor from a red phone on the wall, and then she didn't stay around to chat. No one wants to chat with a bleeder.

In no time I was up on a table, bare and bloody from the waist down, and being examined by an Indian ER doctor named Souza, who, after questioning me about dates and recent symptoms (I mentioned the three blue pregnancy test results), informed me that I'd "had an abortion."

"What?" I said. "I did *not!*"

"A spontaneous abortion," he said, "what you may call a miscarriage. I'll give you an injection for pain and to calm you a bit." I was comforted by the fact that his accent sounded like Devi's, and I decided not to give him shit about the "to calm you" remark. He said *bain* for *pain*. Bane or pain—either word seemed appropriate to the occasion.

They let me stay on a bed in the emergency room until the bleeding seemed to have abated a couple of hours later. The injection had made the cramps somewhat milder, but my back still hurt. When I was ready to go home at about 6:00 A.M., Dr. Souza gave me a pain prescription and suggested I take iron for a couple of weeks to make up for blood loss.

"Not enough loss to require a transfusion, I'd say," he told me, "but enough to make iron a good idea." Whatever. He should see my bedsheet. But since I consider anyone else's blood inside my body an invasion of privacy anyway, I wasn't going to argue. "And no sex for at least two weeks," he said to me in a way that sounded scolding. I looked down, embarrassed, and nodded like an errant teen.

On my way out, the nurse gave me a sample pack of superabsorbant pads. "You'll probably need these, hon," she said, and patted my arm, at which kindness I burst into a flood of tears and walked rapidly away. I found a pay phone in the reception area and called Michael. This time I didn't care if it was a good time to call him or not.

When he answered, he sounded as if he'd been asleep. The minute he heard my voice, he said, "Norrie! What's wrong?"

I began to sob again. "It's gone," I said.

"What? Norrie, where are you? Are you okay?"

"No," I said, "I'm not." I told him I was at Holyoke emergency room. "Come and get me." I was not asking; I'm sure he heard that in my voice.

He was there in about ten minutes, which is how long it takes from Brookline if you drive like a bat out of hell. When I saw him coming into the emergency area in his old leather jacket and jeans, so long and lean, his hair still tousled from sleep, my heart contracted with love. All I could say when he came over to me was, "It's gone." He kept his arm tightly around me all the way to the car and helped me into it like an invalid. I felt moved by his solicitousness and put my head against his shoulder in the car.

We drove a couple of blocks without talking. There wasn't much traffic this early, and the air was still misty, just short of being foggy. Michael stopped the car at Mount Auburn Cemetery, where we'd often gone on happier occasions to watch the birds and be alone together in the outdoors. This time it seemed macabre. I didn't want to be in a cemetery, but there we were.

"It's gone," I said, looking straight ahead through the windshield, not at him. "I lost it."

We both cried then. We held each other and wept as we sat in the car watching the mist burn off in the dim, early morning sun, over tombstones and urns and a million birds hopping around in wet grass. For about a minute of the crying I bawled like a baby, right out into the air. I hadn't done that since I actually *was* a baby. Michael just cried in that silent, damp-faced way that men manage to do in times of tragedy, and I felt a surge of pity and tenderness for him. I would not want to be a man.

When we got back to my apartment, he came up with me but remained standing.

"There's no way I can stay," he said apologetically. "I'm really sorry, Norrie, but it's going to be hard to explain to Brenda and Bridget where I went this early in the morning. If I get back fairly soon, maybe they'll still be asleep since it's Saturday."

I was too tired to ask him why it really mattered at this point what anyone thought; it seemed a little late for that somehow. After all that had happened, being together in this seemed to be more to the point.

"Please don't go," was all I said.

"Maybe I can stay another few minutes," he replied, which was just a nice way of saying no. "And I'll come back this afternoon with your prescription and anything else you might need. Why don't you give me a list in fact?" I looked at him in what I imagine was some kind of disbelief. A list?

"I can't give you a list right now," I said, "because I can't think."

"Of course," he said, "I'll just use my imagination."

"Honestly, Michael, I have plenty here. I guess all I really need is sleep."

"If you change your mind, let me know," he said.

I didn't quite feel up to reminding Michael that I couldn't really let him know anything since I wasn't supposed to call him on the weekend when Brenda was home.

"It's time for me to talk to Liz," was what I said to him instead. "I have to."

"What?" He looked confused, and I'll give him that it must have seemed a non sequitur. But to me it was very much in keeping with everything else at hand.

"I have to talk to Liz," I repeated, looking down at the worn place on the knee of my shrunken, blood-smudged sweats. I needed to say this and I didn't want to look at him for fear I might back down. "She's my oldest friend," I added, "and I need to talk to her. Our friendship is very strained right now. I never seem to call her back anymore, and that's because of us— you and me. I've been avoiding her because I can't stand holding out on her this way. It's like every word I say to her is a lie." I hated lying, though I'd done more than my share. I didn't want to lie anymore. I made myself look him squarely in the face to be sure he knew how serious I was. "I have to tell her about us. That's all there is to it. It's my life, too, you know. Every-thing can't be in the service of your life and in total disregard of mine." That was the most I'd said in hours. Maybe years.

He was silent for a minute. Probably a whole minute. He expelled his familiar puff of air and slid his fingers through his hair.

I was just getting my hackles up, when he spoke. "No, no—of course I know you have a right to talk to your friend." He hesitated. "I . . . I'm sure she'll be discreet. I know we can trust Liz." He turned to me then and pulled me to him. He said into my hair, "I'm so sorry, sweetheart. I'm sorry I've made your life such a mess."

"It's not your fault," I said. "Someday maybe we'll speak of this as that fire we went through to get to where we are."

"I hope so," he said sort of glumly. Then he stood up.

"You could sound more hopeful and positive," I said then.

"I feel like an utter asshole and a miserable failure," he said. "Look what I've done to you, look what I've done to Brenda. How heedless

I've been about my kids through all of this. I feel like I'm the fucking Black Plague."

And then he left, first kissing my cheek at the door. I walked to the living room window and watched his car pulling away.

"Don't you dare," I whispered to him through the glass. "Just don't you dare."

I go to bed on the couch in broad daylight and lie there under about a million blankets, curled into a fetal pose, frissons of grief skittering over all my surfaces. O God—I've lost you, and I feel it was a failure of my heart, of my strength and goodness. If I hadn't had those occasional thoughts fearing you and regretting you there inside me, you might have stayed put in me. I know you would have grown into a wonderful child. But you never put down roots in my body to hold you there, to keep you from washing away. I can't help thinking that may have been because I wasn't equal to the situation and you knew it. Forgive me, seed, little one, please forgive me.

10

My mattress was soaked in blood and I couldn't lie on it after Michael left, couldn't bear even to look at it, so after I'd showered and put on clean underpants and a pad, I rolled up in all of my blankets on the living room couch and slept away the entire day wrapped like a burrito.

When I woke near midnight and went to the bathroom, I found I was still bleeding but remembered that Souza had said I should expect that.

After drinking a glass of milk in the kitchen, I went back to the couch, the sounds of Saturday night traffic lulling me like music, my own pulse in the pillow providing the backbeat.

I was almost back to sleep when I heard something else.

Something awful.

It was the sound of my own breathing, of myself inhaling and exhaling.

How disgusting and pathetic it was. What a helpless creature it made me seem. How easy it would be to die.

I listened to it coldly, in the way a species not dependent on oxygen might observe it—with alienation, repugnance, pity. Just as modern-day moviegoers have looked on the slimy, oozing spawn of the creature in *Alien* with disgust, I saw myself as some revolting biological mass feeding greedily and indiscriminately on the air.

After what seemed a long time, I began to slip in and out of sleep uneasily, now and then distracted by the sense that there was something I ought to be doing. When I woke on Sunday morning I still felt that way, but I couldn't think what it might be.

As I became more fully awake, I found that I had some appetite, and also that I was desperately thirsty, probably from the loss of blood. I drank a tall bottle of water and fixed myself a bowl of oatmeal, the instant kind. At all times I made an effort not to think about the seed. Periodically I became acutely aware of my breathing again—in . . . out . . . in . . . out . . . that silly, striving labor—as if it were something I was merely trying out with an eye toward finding a less primitive method of staying alive.

I showered again. Though I'd showered twice before going to sleep, I couldn't seem to get the smell of blood off me. Afterward I found myself shivering and realized I had no choice but to enter my bedroom in search of something warm to wear. I think even in my sleep I'd dreaded going back in there, ever.

Bedroom, dreadroom, I found the huge bloodstain on my mattress had dried to a dark brownish-red. Of course everyone knows blood does that, everyone knows that blood doesn't stay bright red, but the sight of it now—darkened beyond puce and in places nearly black—entered my skin as both shock and information simultaneously, and though it was horrifying to look at, I found myself studying the variations of color for a moment in the late morning light, examining the permutations of blood.

And then, freshly shaken by the loss it signified, I found an old double-size beach towel to put over the stain, the thinned and faded terry cloth imprinted with the legend SANTA MONICA PIER above a lone surfer shooting the curl.

With great deliberateness, I spread my red blanket on the bedroom floor and settled myself in front of the TV, my back against the side of the bed. At first I channel surfed, and then I settled in and watched the Sunday morning evangelists, one after another, as many as I could find. One of them had thin, red, head-hugging hair and the knot of his tie was pulled loose as if he'd yanked at it during some prior ecstatic experience that now qualified him to speak to the masses. It pissed me off to hear him preaching about love while at the same time asking for money, but then he read a quote from the Bible—Corinthians—that was so beautiful I forgot all about him as I replayed the passage over and over in my head: *Love bears all things, believes all things, hopes all things, endures all things.*

I'm not saying I exactly believed the words might apply to my life in any transformative way, but I did take hope from them. Although things had fallen into darkness and I was filled with doubt, I supposed it was still possible that everything would work out with Michael and me. It was still possible we would get married and make another seedling that would grow into a fine child, though we would never forget this one, our first. Those Corinthians were in the right line of work, that was for sure.

It was thinking about a lost child-to-be that made me try to imagine the pain of losing a child who'd been alive in the world with you for years—a child with a name, a familiar voice, a certain way of moving his limbs. And that made me think of Ida, how sad she still was over the loss of her Henry, insufficient as I'd found him in several ways. And then, Goddammit, I realized it was Sunday and I'd forgotten all about her. I knew I was in no shape to go to Brookline.

I called Brookline Manor to see if Ida was strong enough to talk on the phone without too much strain. Luckily it was Marge today, and she said she would go into Ida's room and make it easy for her to talk.

"If she's weak, I can just hold the phone up to her and she can talk lying down," she said. "I know she's going to want to talk to you . . . So what's up? Got that flu that's going around?"

"Something like that," I mumbled, wondering how I would ever keep my vow to lie no more. It was proving to be a tricky promise to hold to during any human interaction at all, however mundane.

Ida answered the phone in a small, hoarse voice that sounded surprisingly timid. Of course she hadn't talked to anyone on the phone in a while—I usually didn't call, and who else was there to phone her? When I told her it was Norrie, it seemed to take her a minute to place me. After a long pause, she spoke. "Oh," she said, "you're the one who wanted to marry my son."

I hesitated. "Yeah, well, Henry was quite a guy." That wasn't actually a lie, since it meant nothing, really. Sort of like the ever-useful, "Oh my, now that *is* a baby!"

"Oh yes," she said, "he took after his father, Henry Senior, who was called Harry. My Harry was quite a guy, too."

"How are you feeling, Ida?"

"Well, you know, a person is not *supposed* to feel good at my age, and I feel terrible. So I guess I'm doing a good job of being old." That sounded more like my Ida.

I promised her I'd try to visit during the week, as soon as I felt better.

"What's wrong with you, Honey?" she asked, sounding even more herself. "Are you sick?"

"I've been having a . . . kind of a . . . a little female trouble." At least that wasn't a lie.

"Oh my," she said, "aren't you a little young for that sort of thing?"

"Well, not really," I answered, unsure what to say.

"This may have been why Henry had to break it off," she said. "It's possible he felt you were too old for him. Men are like that, you know."

That Ida, she was okay.

After Ida I decided to phone everyone I owed a call, saving Liz for last because that would take a while. First I called Devi, and when she answered the phone I was so happy to hear her voice that I broke into a grin and it felt strange, as if I hadn't used these particular muscles in a while.

"Norrie!" she exclaimed, "I thought you were mad at me."

"What?"

"When you didn't return my calls, I thought I'd made you angry by speaking out of turn that night you were here," she said, sounding contrite. "I wouldn't blame you."

"Devi," I said, "if you hadn't spoken up, I might have been even worse off last night than I was—because I wouldn't have realized what was happening to me."

"What happened to you last night?"

"I had, I had a miscarriage. A very bloody one. I had to go to the emergency room."

"Why didn't you call me, Norrie? I can't believe you didn't call me!"

"I didn't think of it, honestly. And since you don't drive, all I'd have done was wake you up for nothing—this was three in the morning. I called a cab."

"But I could have gone along with you in the cab and given moral support, you know. Oh, Norrie, you are hopeless. There's something unhealthy about such a degree of pride or isolation! You won't even ask a friend for help when you're bleeding to death!"

"I wasn't bleeding to death," I said. *It just looked like it.* There was truth in what she was saying about me. I'd have to think about that— later. "I'm okay now."

"All right then, Norrie, I want to see you," Devi said, "so I can determine that for myself."

"Well, I'm not really feeling chipper enough to go down to your place—and if you come up here, Clara's going to see you and then the next thing I know she'll be in here, too, and I don't think I could handle that right now."

"Clara's at the Larkin today. I know that because they're having a Women's Culture Festival and she asked me to walk over with her, but I declined. I explained to her that I was using today for my writing. The festival lasts until eight o'clock tonight."

Women's Culture Festival. I loved the Larkin and felt very grateful to it, but that was the kind of thing I was finding, well, *self-conscious* about it. Everything was about women. If a woman had written it or painted it or thought it, it had to be good. Considering that there was the threat of a Harvard-Radcliffe merger in the offing, with the Larkin possibly to become coed—or defunct—as a result, I'd have thought they would be trying a little harder to open themselves up to a two-gender world.

"That must be why she was trying to reach me," I said. "She left *four* messages on Friday, and I got so frustrated listening to them one after another that I made up my mind not to call her back for a day or two. Why isn't one message enough? I hate that." Then I realized Devi's point was that with Clara at the Larkin, she could visit me unnoticed. "Come up and have a pot of tea with me," I invited. "Immediately!"

And she did, carrying an assortment of small glass refrigerator dishes filled with her wonderful cooking.

"I made all of this just yesterday," she said. "I think you might find yourself getting a little hungry by tonight." At the thought of Devi's cooking, I found it likely that I would indeed be hungry by tonight.

Looking back on our visit, it seems as if I started talking the second we sat down, just began burping out my recent personal history, and Devi listened, simply listened, there beside me on the couch. I didn't even remember to get us that pot of tea. I just babbled. What a friend. She let me talk and talk; she wanted to hear. I told her about the miscarriage and my experience out in Cambridge in the middle of the night. I told her about my feeling for the minuscule life that had been growing inside me. As I was telling her that part, I found tears leaking into my eyes and I looked down so she wouldn't see. When I felt ready to look at her again, I saw that she had tears in her eyes, too.

"I'm not surprised to hear that part," she said. "It's very like you to feel that way, I think." She took my hand, and I felt her hand, small and cool against mine. "I'm sure you'll be sad for a while, Norrie. But please don't be a hermit. I want you to call me whenever you need to talk about it—or even if you just want some company, with no talking."

When Devi left a couple of hours later, I thought how admirable of her it had been that she had never once asked me about the man who was my partner in the pregnancy. Without my saying a word, she knew that I didn't want to talk about that right now.

It was only about 2:00 P.M., so I had time to do the rest of my phoning. I called Clara and left a message telling her I was sorry to have been so out of reach in the last week. I told her I would be busy painting this week (I fervently hoped that was true) but would love to have a good long chat with her as soon as she had the time. I resolved that when Clara called me back, I would take the time to do just that.

I rang my mother back then, and she told me that brown recluse spiders had made their way from the eastern seaboard and the Midwest all the way to California. "I can't believe it," she said. "It's never going to be safe to clean out a closet again." Then she added, "They're also called violin spiders, you know." My mother felt you were safer if you knew all of a spider's aliases. Just for a moment, in what I took to be a kind of emotional dementia, I felt an intense yearning to tell her every-thing, to say, *Mama, help, I'm sad, scared, there was life in me and I lost it.* I even fleetingly considered the possibility that she might commiserate with me because the fetus was three-quarters Irish. *Your grandseed, grand-fetus. It's gone.*

Quickly I rang off, afraid I might begin hemorrhaging details into the phone. Clearly I wasn't to be trusted just now.

I went into the bathroom and shut the door, sat on the closed lid of the toilet for a while, stayed there till I heard the phone ringing.

The machine came on, and I heard Michael saying, "Your phone was busy for hours."

"I've been catching up," I said, picking up.

"You've talked to Liz then?"

"Not yet." I didn't feel like discussing that with him. Just didn't. "What are you doing today?" I asked, as a subject changer. The minute the words fled my mouth, I regretted them. I knew that any information Michael could offer on this subject would only make me unhappy in one way or another. It was the weekend, after all.

He said that he and Brenda had gone out to get groceries for Thanksgiving. Yep, that made me unhappy all right. Thanksgiving. It was this Thursday. I had no idea where I'd be on Thanksgiving. Pushing aside the image of Michael's domestic feast, I told myself that maybe I could go and see Ida, bring her some turkey. But where would I get it? Maybe I could find some kind of Thanksgiving take-out somewhere. I would check around on Monday to see what might be available.

"Norrie?" Michael said. I realized I'd been spacing out for a time.

"I'm kind of tired," I said. "Let's try to talk later." I was feeling distant from Michael, and I wasn't sure if it was some kind of subconscious resentment or if I was just being cranky because I didn't feel well. I only knew I felt a stone in my heart.

After Michael I called Liz, my fingers trembling as I punched in the familiar number. Her machine came on and I spoke into it because I knew that Liz never answered the phone without screening her callers.

"Pick up," I said, "it's me." She picked up the phone immediately.

"Where the hell have you been?" she asked.

"Hiding out."

"From what?"

"The world," I said. "But now I need to have a long talk with you. If you don't have time right now, then figure out when you can make time."

Her voice changed from light to serious. "What's wrong?"

"Do you have the time?"

"Goddamn it, if I didn't have the time, I wouldn't have asked what's wrong."

"Okay. I've been lying to you for nearly two years."

"What?"

"By omission."

"What kind of Catholic bullshit is this?"

I just ignored that and rolled right on through. "I've been having an affair," I said.

"Big whoo," she laughed.

"He's married."

"Oh. Well, that's not good. Somehow I wouldn't have pictured you doing that." That would be, I knew, the extent of Liz's reproof.

"Yeah, well," I said, "neither would I."

"Well, but why didn't you tell me? Have I ever given you the impression I was a saint?"

"You know him," I said flatly, and took a deep breath. "He asked me not to tell you because you know him."

She was silent for a minute, and I knew she was doing the mental list-scanning I'd always figured she'd do once she had the slightest idea what was going on. I wondered how long this would take. I was prepared to sit in silence for the duration.

"Michael Sullivan," she said, about ninety seconds later. "Goddamn, it *is,* isn't it. It's goddamn Michael Sullivan!" I just decided to sustain my half of the silence and let her have her say. "Well, I can't blame you a hundred percent," she finally said. "because he's one beautiful man. I was even tempted once myself."

"What? You and Michael?" My heart stopped.

"Not exactly," she laughed, "more me and my imagination. He's very sexy, very smart, and . . . well, a damn nice man. Except for that last part, he'd be just my type." We both laughed. Liz had a history of falling for brilliant, sexy men who weren't all that nice to her.

"Yeah, he's quite a guy." I remembered I'd said the same thing about Henry earlier on the phone to Ida. But now I found it actually meant something when I said it about Michael. So had it been a lie before? Honesty was hard.

"He's married to a brittle blond financier, as far as I remember," Liz was saying. "I met her a couple of times. Does that woman ever smile?"

"Investment banker," I said. "And apparently she does smile, but only if you've earned it."

"I'm not that wealthy," Liz said.

"They're separated now." I didn't feel comfortable dishing on Brenda, though I appreciated very much Liz's willingness to do it for me.

"Really? I guess I always thought Michael was the married-for-life type. To be honest, I'd never have thought he'd be unfaithful."

"Well, he never has been—before. He's serious about this. We've even been looking at houses to buy. And he stopped sleeping with her—

he stays in his study at night now. He's told her he feels he'll have to change his life."

"Boy, things must be fun at their house right now."

"Oh God, it's marathon fighting every night." I instantly felt guilty for telling Liz this. It was one thing to tell her my part of the story, another to tell her Michael's business. "I love him," I said. "I've never in my life loved a man this way. I'd marry him tomorrow and have his babies."

"Get out," Liz said. "Who *is* this? What number were you calling?"

"Shut up," I said. "That isn't all."

"Good God, what else?"

"I got pregnant a few weeks ago. Had a bloody miscarriage last night. Had to go to the hospital in the middle of the night."

"Oh, Norrie," she said. "Oh, God, that's rough. You okay?"

"Yeah, I guess."

"Well then . . . I don't know . . . don't you think maybe it was for the best right now?"

"No. I—I have to say, I wanted it."

"Jesus." She was quiet for a minute and then said, "Well then, I'm sorry it ended up like this, honey. I really am. Are you sure you're okay?"

"I'm having cramps and some bleeding. But it's under control. I missed you."

"You mean when you weren't answering my calls?"

"Yeah, sorry about that. I just couldn't stand lying to you anymore. I'm never going to lie again."

"You sure about that?"

"Well, except to my mother."

"Oh, well, that doesn't count."

"No, that's what I thought."

She sighed. "Well, hell, since you're on this honesty kick and seem to be observing that Jesuitical concept, *sins of omission,* I guess I want to tell *you* something."

"What?"

"Well, not *want* to tell you, really, more like *feel I should* tell you."

"You're gay."

"Don't get your hopes up, Gorgeous," Liz said. "Just that I was in love with a married man once, too. Do you remember the poet Richard Lash?"

"The one you taught with at BU? He moved to Washington state, right?"

"Yeah."

"Did you sleep with him?"

"No, but not for want of trying. Somehow he just managed to resist my wiles. We kissed once at an MLA shindig. Well, actually, we made out. That was after he'd moved to Washington, and we hadn't seen each other for I guess six or eight months. Then after that for quite a few months we . . . we talked on the phone a lot."

"Phone sex?"

"Not for *him,* I don't think." We both laughed. "Like I said, he managed somehow to resist my wiles."

"That's hard to imagine—any man resisting your wiles."

"Isn't it? But it's true. God, I was in love with him. And I knew he felt something, too."

"Thanks for telling me. I don't feel quite so Scarlet Letter."

"Yeah, well, it didn't seem fair not to say something, in this mea culpa atmosphere."

We got onto our work then, and Liz told me about her novel-in-progress. She was hoping to have it to her editor by the end of the year. I told her about the series of oils I'd been working on, and that I'd been unable to paint since I realized I was pregnant. I described the three I'd finished.

"I can't wait to see them. What are you calling the series?"

"Hunger," I said.

"I don't have to ask where that comes from."

Michael called again in the early evening, after I'd finished Devi's food and was belatedly nodding off over my Sunday morning *Globe.* On a full stomach, I seemed inclined to be a little more friendly toward him than earlier. Or maybe I'd been softened by the fact that he was ordering me a new mattress, which would be delivered on Monday or Tuesday. But after we'd talked awhile I felt myself slipping back into a looking-for-trouble mood. I asked him if he was relieved.

"Relieved? About what?" he began, and then his mind clicked on what

I meant. He sounded honestly stunned. "Norrie. *God.* How can you say that?"

"I'm not *saying*—I'm asking."

"No!" he said in a wounded voice. *"Jesus,* Honora."

"Sorry. I just had to know."

"To tell you the truth," he said, "it's more the opposite. I've been feeling kind of a letdown. I guess I have to say I'm disappointed."

It warmed me to hear that. "Really? I can't believe it."

"Of course. You know, it's hard to find the strength to change my life—there's going to be so much pain, and I can see it takes enormous fortitude. But I know that once I just *do* it, I'll be with you the rest of my life." He hesitated, then said, "I keep thinking that if you were still pregnant I'd have *had* to do something."

Maybe he didn't realize how that would sound to me. I couldn't speak.

"Norrie? Are you there?"

"What are you saying?" I finally asked him. "That a baby would be a good excuse to change your life, but that our relationship by itself isn't reason enough?"

"No," he said, "Norrie—"

"What you're saying is that you were yearning for a deus ex machina, right? I thought you literary types considered it a cop-out to rely on those. That's it, isn't it? You were hoping for something larger than yourself that would just *force* things to the conclusion you've been wishing for but haven't had the strength to accomplish." I should have said *huevos* instead of *strength*, I thought. I was getting kind of worked up; I could see that.

Michael sighed. "Well, something like that, I guess," he said in a surprisingly reasonable tone, as if he didn't think it should offend me. "Jesus, Norrie, you've never been married, never had kids. You don't know how hard it is to dismantle an entire life."

"There's truth in what you say," I admitted. I knew he was right on that count.

"But I didn't mean to insult the baby or you." The baby. No one had put it quite that way before. *The baby.*

"I dreamed of him, the . . . the baby, Friday night," I said. It was funny how dreams did that sometimes—reconstituted themselves suddenly and without warning in your waking hours though you hadn't once recalled them before. "It was, you know, before I . . . woke up bleeding." In my heart I was still back at the place where I'd said *the baby*.

"Really?" Michael said, surprised. "I had a dream like that, too, only mine was last night. So . . . you saw the baby as a boy?"

"I know he was a boy. I could see him clearly in my dream." *him. you.*

"Isn't that magical thinking?" he asked.

"No, it's Irish thinking."

"Can't argue with that," he said.

"Do you want to hear what he looked like in my dream?"

"No," he said, "I don't think I could handle that right now."

It was an hour or so later, around 8:30, that the phone rang again. I knew it would be Clara, and I was dutifully prepared for a good long catch-up chat. But Clara was crying—she sounded almost hysterical.

"I have been robbed!" she cried. "My computer is gone! With my book on it! It's gone!"

"Oh no! From your office at the Larkin?"

"No," she wept, "I brought it back here so that I could work at home the way you and Devi do." She sounded angry now, as if this fact made Devi and me at least partly to blame for the theft. "If I had left it in my office at the Larkin, I would still have it."

"Oh God, Clara, I can't believe it. When did this happen?"

"I don't know. Today sometime. I have been at the Larkin since this morning. When I came home, I found my door unlocked and my computer gone. And my CD player. Everything I had is gone."

"Hold on, I'm coming right over," I said. We hung up and I washed my face and put on a big sweater to hide my swollen abdomen. I didn't know why a miscarriage should make me swell up—I had no prior experience with maternity matters—but it had, and I found I couldn't zip up my jeans all the way.

I found Clara sitting on her flower-power love seat, weeping. She looked up when I came in.

"This is the only thing they didn't take," she said, gesturing at the love seat. Not surprising, I thought, with a sudden burst of tenderness for Clara. I sat beside her, put an arm around her. She was trembling. I asked if she'd called the police yet. She had, she said, and they'd already come to take the report.

"They told me they came to your apartment a few weeks ago," she said. "They told me you also had a burglar. Why didn't you tell me?"

"I thought I had," I said. I really did. But then I had been avoiding Clara so much.

"What will I do?" she cried, and then began sobbing again. Jesus, I thought, these guys were at work right outside my door, maybe while I was asleep—which was a lot of the morning, now that I thought of it. And it could've been this afternoon, too—maybe while Devi was over. We were talking and I had music playing. I guess we wouldn't have heard anything. Or later, while I was on the phone. I looked around the little studio apartment and saw that the shelf unit Clara had put together now stood bereft of the CD player, and in the kitchen the wine bottles were missing from the rack. More was missing I thought, but I couldn't place just what—the whole apartment looked pretty empty.

"My microwave oven is gone, too," she said as she saw me taking inventory. "And my coffeemaker. But the worst thing of all is my computer. My entire book was on it—all the work I have done. My life here is ruined. I may as well go back to Chile, because I can never replace everything I have lost."

"Clara—hadn't you printed off hard copy?"

"For some of it, yes. But there was much I hadn't been able to print yet because I have no printer. For that I was taking a floppy disk over to the Larkin library every Monday and using one of their printers. I have been writing all week, every evening, and I have no paper copies of any of that. It was three new chapters. Gone now. I can never get them back." I patted Clara's shoulder as she sobbed.

"There's got to be a way to help you," I promised. "Don't worry, Clara. We'll find some way to fix this."

"You're wonderful to say that, Norrie, but that would take money. Neither of us has any."

We were musing about the break-in and the fact that with so many students moving into and out of the building all the time it was easy for thieves not to be noticed.

"It seems like every weekend there's a moving truck here," I said. Just then someone knocked on Clara's door.

"Oh, maybe that's Devi," Clara said, and her face brightened. Knowing what I knew of Devi's feelings about Clara, that didn't seem likely, but when I got up to answer the door, there, sure enough, was Devi. She looked worried.

"What happened?" she asked. "I was out at the grocery and then when I returned I found a message from Clara—she was crying—she said it was an emergency." I motioned her in, thinking how clever that even in her misery Clara had already thought of using this misfortune to play on Devi's sympathies. I immediately killed the observation, which seemed petty.

Clara and I filled Devi in on what items had been taken, and Devi's beautiful face took on alternating expressions of anger and compassion as she listened. When Clara spoke about her lost chapters, she began to cry again and Devi's eyes filled with tears, as they had a few hours ago for me. When Clara got to the part about how she might as well return home to Santiago because her life here was over, Devi cut in abruptly.

"NO!" she said, "No. You must not give up, Clara. I'll help you. Obviously I can't do anything to retrieve your lost chapters, but I have some money and I'll lend you whatever it takes to replace the stolen items. This is a setback, but you can recover."

Clara's eyes widened. She looked awestruck. "But—I don't know when I would ever be able to repay you," she said. "It could take a long time."

"I don't care," Devi said. "Money is *for* things like this. Nothing else is as important right now." She smiled at Clara. "I want you to take the money. I don't care if it takes you thirty years to pay me back."

Clara hurled herself into Devi's arms then, and I felt caught between amusement at the sight of it and sympathy for Devi, who tended to use physical affection sparingly. I saw her face pressed to one side below Clara's shoulder, looking helpless and slightly caught.

Eventually Devi found a gentle way to extract herself from Clara's fervid embrace, saying she had to go back to her apartment to put away her groceries.

"But when you've figured out what it will cost," she said, smiling again, "you will tell me, and I'll immediately write you a check. And we won't talk about it after that. Not ever."

I knew that this last admonition was as much for her own sake as for

Clara's. I was certain that the idea of Clara's undying gratitude had put the fear of God into Devi.

And although I was relieved that Clara had a way out of her troubles now, I couldn't help wondering if Devi might yet regret her generous impulse. I'd already learned that a kindness to Clara could only lead to impossible expectations. And I'd never extended a kindness of such enormity as this to her. I could only imagine what was in store for Devi over the coming months. One thing I knew—it would be difficult for her to extricate herself from Clara's embrace.

The wind howled all night last night, and each time I woke I thought it was me. I'd put a clean sheet on the bed, but I couldn't forget that beneath it was the blood that had dried to a dark brownish red in the shape of some horrible blossom. No matter how I tried, I couldn't cleanse my mind of the stain and what it meant—the vestiges of something alive now irretrievably lost.

All night I drifted in and out of sleep that felt like a darkened landscape, risky terrain. I woke once when the phone rang and I heard your voice over the wire, tender in my ear: I love you, you whispered, I do believe we can make it.

Both love and anger stirred in me as I felt my flesh, my entire body, pulled toward your voice, your words. Tell me—how did you earn such power over me?

I looked at the clock and saw that it was 3:00 A.M.—the exact hour when I heard a stranger on the street asking me, How much?

Save me, I thought, but didn't say out loud into the phone. save me.

Who was I addressing in my mind—was it you? God? the seed?

I keep picturing it afloat in eternity like an image from 2001: A Space Odyssey. I have no real reference point for infinity.

Save me, I said in my mind.

It's possible I was talking to myself.

11

As winter neared and the world turned colder, I remained distracted by an awareness of the absence in my body—I could feel it every day, not there, the baby we'd begun. *Him.* I tried to paint, but desultorily, and as the absence overtook me I found there was nothing there in me to bring to a canvas. I was a husk, dry and empty, and though I had moments of wishing I was working, most of the time I didn't truly care. I went to the Larkin on Wednesdays for the colloquia with Clara and Devi, absorbing the ideas and passions of women whose worlds were shaped by law, science, literature, or medicine, and their worlds provided respite from my own. I let their words soak into my parched brain.

Sometimes now I also attended the Larkin brown-bag lunches on Thursdays, and though I didn't get too close to anyone, though I joked a lot and avoided the subject of my own work, I was finding covert comfort in the presence of the other women. Sometimes I wished I could open up and let myself know them better, but to do that I'd have had to let them know me, and always I felt conscious of an essential part of myself I had to hold back.

Michael was tender and attentive when he was around, but he couldn't be with me as much now as before—his world had begun to change dramatically. In November his novel crept onto the bestseller lists of both the *Boston Globe* and the *New York Times,* and he was getting calls to do interviews and book signings all over the place. A friend of his at Columbia University who knew someone on the Pulitzer Prize board told him in confidence that his book was definitely in the running for the award—against all odds for a first novel from a midsize literary press outside New York, even a novel with A-list rave reviews like *This Cold Heaven.*

I think Michael was most surprised—and maybe most pleased—when Ted Kennedy phoned him one evening to say he'd found the book "so true it made me laugh and brought a tear of nostalgia to my eye." (I held my tongue as Michael recounted the conversation to me, not wanting to ruin the moment for him but pained by the effort not to say, "*Oh, I didn't realize the Kennedys once lived in the projects!*")

It made perfect sense to me that Michael's wonderful novel should be getting attention and even be up for the major book awards, but being outside the publishing world myself, it's likely I didn't have a real sense of just how far beyond the realm of expectation a Pulitzer nomination was. Michael liked to say that Frank McCourt and his copycat brother had paved the way for the stunning reception his novel was getting.

"Irish struggle is just in literary fashion right now," he said, but I thought that was too easy, too humble. *This Cold Heaven* was an amazing book—humorous, irreverent, brilliantly written, nostalgic without being sentimental, and more profoundly reflective of the spirit of America in our times than any recent book I'd read. He deserved everything, everything there was to give him.

Though I was delighted for Michael's success, the change it had wrought in the shape of his life was neither slow nor subtle, and I wasn't thrilled about some aspects of that. He was suddenly away a lot—more than he was in Boston, in fact. He said it was lucky he was in a sabbatical year, only teaching a Thursday evening class at Harvard Extension, a class he'd have liked to get out of now. "I'm very aware that it's not a great time to be away from you," he told me. "I know you're hurting, and I don't like leaving you here alone." He still phoned me each day from wherever he happened to be, and when he was in town he saw me regularly and was loving, humorous, and ardent. In fact he was bringing renewed vigor and creativity to our intimacies after the period of abstinance Dr. Vesta had advised following the miscarriage.

It would have been small of me to whine about his absences just when things were going so well, but there were other aspects of the situation about which I did *not* hold back.

Both the *Times* and the *Globe* had run profiles of Michael that made more than passing mention of his marriage, focusing on its longevity. The hardest thing for me to bear had been a detail in the *Globe*'s piece—a very nice article in which Michael was aptly described as "the humorous and unassuming son of blue-collar Irish immigrants, surprised by his sudden renown." Brenda had come into the house from work near the end of the interview, and the reporter had asked her a few questions. In response to a query about how life "might be changing in the Sullivan household these days," Brenda had mentioned her hope that they might soon buy a summer home where they could get away from the increasing demands of their professional lives.

I was stunned by this view of them as an operative couple and told Michael so. "This hurts me," I said. "I don't get it. I don't like it."

"Well, I can't blame you," Michael said, "but what else was Brenda supposed to say when the interviewer asked how all of this was going to change our life? She couldn't very well tell him her husband is now sleeping in his study and contemplating an escape from the marriage, could she? So she improvised—told the guy something we used to say we would do one day. Anyway, by then Bridget was home from school and right there taking it all in. If Brenda hadn't mentioned the summer house dream, I'm sure Bird would have piped up about it anyway."

Whatever he said, I felt the marriage was being celebrated, treated as a point of interest in any description of Michael's life. I was freshly tormented by questions, doubts, and jealousy. Was Michael no longer making his intentions clear to Brenda?

Worse, was he losing the will to change his life, to *leave* a life that was filling up beyond anyone's wildest imagining—especially to leave a marriage that was becoming more and more a part of the Michael Sullivan mythology?

Or was I just bitter and jealous?

"I wonder how you'd feel if the tables were turned," I said one morning when he came over for coffee. "This is not right, Michael."

"Believe me, both Brenda and I are aware of the irony in all this—to be seen as so happily and admirably married all of a sudden, just when we're more or less separated. But as long as I'm still officially married, it's just a part of what people are going to say about me."

"My point exactly," I said into my coffee cup, then waited for him to speak.

"I know it's terrible for you, but I wish you'd try to put yourself in my place for a minute, Norrie. What would it look like for me to up and leave my wife the minute fame and fortune start to come my way?" I could hear the South Boston cadences in his speech. "I'll be universally reviled as a monster." At least he'd said *I'll*, rather than *I'd*, I thought. Talk about grasping at straws for reassurance—verb conjugation today, split infinitives tomorrow.

"Well, you sure seem to have Brenda by your side a lot in public these days, and I . . . I just think I've got a right to ask if you're back on an intimate basis with her."

"You do have a right, and I'm absolutely not," he said. "But I can't believe you thought you needed to ask that question. Do you really think I would trick you that way?"

"Of course I didn't think you would *trick* me. I guess I thought you might've slid back into some kind of familiar intimacy . . . and then just . . . not had the heart to tell me."

"Norrie, when I got back from London I promised you that I wouldn't be sleeping with Brenda if you and I were to resume our intimacies. And we did resume intimacies, so I don't see where that question came from."

"Yeah, I know what you're saying. But it seems like you're not really looking at things from my side. I see your life getting fuller and more interesting every day. And, and more *comfortable,* too. It's only natural for me to wonder if you might be losing the urgency about making a life with me."

He pulled me into his arms then and talked into the top of my head. I could feel the buzz of his voice vibrating in my scalp, could smell his skin through the blue workshirt he wore, could feel his muscular, street-boy arms around me.

"*Nothing* could make my life better than your real presence in it, Norrie. I'm trying to make that happen." When I nodded I felt his chin rub back and forth against the top of my head. "Things are just a lot more complicated all of a sudden." He pushed me gently at arms' length to look into my face earnestly. His eyes were worried and his voice had taken on an uncertain tone. "I know you're frustrated. I can even see how you might just want to chuck this whole messy situation and just . . . *get on with your life,* as they say—maybe find someone else—"

"That's not what I'm saying," I tried to cut in, but he went on talking and pulled me back against his chest as he spoke. I felt his heart knocking against my clavicle.

"—but I haven't wobbled at all in my desire to make a life with you, Norrie, and I . . . I'm just hoping you'll wait a bit for me. Everything's crazy right now."

I sighed against his shirt pocket. I couldn't believe he had a pen in it. "I know," I said. When my voice came out unnaturally small, I amplified it to show a strength I didn't feel just then and added, "But would you just promise you'll tell me immediately if you find yourself having a change of heart about . . . me, us? And please . . . try not to forget how hard this is."

"No change of heart," he said, and then held me so close I could hardly breathe. "Ah, fuck, Norrie," he finally said, "I know it has to be awful for you. And here I am, getting all this glory while you're going through hell—by yourself most of the time."

"I have Devi now, and that's been helping a lot. I don't feel so isolated with her around. And I hope you know that I'm *glad* for all the good things that are happening to you." I *was*. Wasn't I? Sometimes I wasn't sure I was 100 percent sincere on this point, because his success seemed to be taking him away from me. In one sense, I was truly glad; in another, I felt threatened. "I'm thrilled for you," I insisted to us both, even as I wondered if by summer Michael would be out on the sailboat with Teddy and the clan, or barbecuing at Hyannis. I just hoped he wouldn't bring Brenda along to the Kennedy compound.

"Yeah, I know—you're happy for me even when my life seems to be saying you don't exist. But please believe me, I'm still trying to get to the other side of the river."

"I believe you," I said. My eyes fell on the empty canvases lined up against my bedroom wall. "I do believe you," I repeated.

It was myself I doubted most these days.

And then there were the holidays to contend with. If I'd had the money to fly to Santa Monica, I think I might actually have gone home to spend Christmas with Mother, despite all the inevitable anxiety such a visit would inspire in both of us. But she always had tons of plans for the holidays anyway, with the women from her Church Widows' Club. (That was what I called them; the group was actually called Our Lady's Ladies. Which is goofier?) This year my mother and her buddies were putting on a Christmas play in which they themselves played all the parts except that of the infant Jesus, who was being played by someone's daughter's old Cabbage Patch doll. It was good, I felt, that Mother was busy because when she wasn't she tended to worry. She'd recently been "bothered by these asteroids," she told me. At first I'd thought she meant hemorrhoids.

"No," she said, "*asteroids*. I saw in *Reader's Digest* where ninety percent of all near-earth asteroids are not yet identified. Meaning no one knows they're there! The article said that if just *one* of them hit us, it could wipe out one-fourth of the earth's population." She paused so I could absorb the impact of that. "One-fourth of the earth's population," she repeated, "—and of course, it would make things difficult for all the rest."

Liz was in Denver with her mother, who was recuperating from a mastectomy, and she would be there until after the New Year. She and I were back to talking on the phone several times a week, and I was very glad of her company, even if it was just phone company. It was such a relief finally to be able to talk openly with her about Michael. She was, of course, thrilled for his great reviews and the leak about the Pulitzer. "I do think he's got a shot at the NBCC next year," she said, "though it's definitely a long shot. But I just don't see the Pulitzer happening, not for a first novel. Especially from a house like Aperçu."

"Aperçu is an excellent publishing house," I said defensively. "It may be small, but they're very particular about who and what they publish, Liz. It's a high-quality place."

"Hey, they published my first novel, remember? I'm not attacking your employer. I'm just saying that's how the literary world works, you know?" I supposed she was right, but I couldn't imagine any other book edging out *This Cold Heaven* for any award. Its voice was too original; its story too powerful. "Remember," Liz said, "you're a painter. You get to be the expert on art. I get to be the boss of all literary opinions."

"Fine," I said, "I guess you have to start somewhere."

Just then I heard her mother calling, "Elizabeth!"

"Coming," Liz hollered back.

"Sounds like you've got to go . . . *Elizabeth*."

"Yeah yeah. She had such hopes of a regal aspect developing in me that she named me after two British monarchs—Elizabeth Victoria. Ain't that royal? Poor Mom. As it turns out, I'm just Liz. She hates that—says it 'sounds like a charwoman.' Yesterday she asked me, 'Couldn't you at least be *Beth,* like in *Little Women?*' I reminded her that Beth died."

"I thought your mother was Irish. Why'd she name you after two queens of England?"

"No, my dad was the Doyle, remember? He's the Irish one in the mix. Mom's a Bowles, and about as Brit as she could be, considering she's been stateside all her life." Just then her mother called again. "Gotta go," Liz said. "She's fixed us a lunch—can you believe it? I come all the way here to take care of her, and *she's* fixing *me* lunch. Fat chance she'd ever let anyone take care of her."

"Lots of women are like that," I said. "Maybe it makes her feel safer if she knows she can take care of things herself."

Clara had gone to Los Angeles for a UCLA journalism conference at which she was to be one of a panel of speakers from the foreign press. She had a distant cousin who lived in San Diego, so she would spend the holidays there with relatives.

The day she left, she'd told me she didn't want to go. And she didn't look well, it seemed to me—her eyes had circles around them, and her face was drawn. I knew she'd been working hard to reconstruct the lost chapters of her book. I wanted to ask her if she was getting enough sleep, but I decided she might take offense.

"If I had not agreed to do this conference a year ago, I would not be leaving," she said. "At least I wanted to be sure you and I had some time together before I left." She'd come over to give me a Christmas present—a five-CD set of all Maria Callas's recordings—and I thought her hands seemed shaky as she handed the package to me. I felt bad. I knew her gift to me had been fairly expensive, and it was such a thoughtful one—she knew I loved Callas and didn't have the whole collection on CD. I felt embarrassed that all I'd bought her was a small postcard book with reproductions of the works of contemporary American painters.

When I left her in my living room and went to get her gift from the bedroom, I stopped in the kitchen and grabbed a bottle of good wine from the rack to add to the postcard book. Actually, I'd not have bought her a gift at all but for the fact that I knew she would buy me one and I didn't want to hurt her feelings.

As she was leaving, she said, "I really do hate going, Norrie. It would have been nice to share Christmas festivities with you." Then, just when I thought she was going to envelop me in one of her embraces, she stood on tip-toe and kissed my cheek lightly. "Be well," she told me, and then her voice took on a bit of an edge. "I suppose you and Devi will have many pleasant adventures while I am gone." If she'd only managed not to say that, it would have been one jealousy-free visit from Clara.

"But Devi won't be back till the New Year," I said. "I thought you knew that."

"Devi tells me nothing of her plans." Devi had gone to London two weeks before Christmas to speak with her publisher and then to meet her parents and younger brother there for a holiday that would last right up to New Years. I missed her. Hers was the only face I looked forward to seeing in the apartment building. It always calmed me.

Finn was on break from college, and Michael was mostly at home with the family these days, though there seemed to be endless book signings, reading engagements, and parties, sometimes with Brenda by his side.

"It's our last Christmas together as a family," he'd told me, "and for Brenda I guess it's a chance to share in the glory a little, after all my lean years." They would have their Christmas.

Me? Honora Blume, attractive, highly sexed spinster and blocked artist, was spending the holidays in solitude at home on Brattle Street, thank you very much.

At first I thought that solitude might be a good thing—I could try to come to terms with my painting project, which had stalled in the weeks since the miscarriage. Depression, maybe, or distraction. Inertia brought on by physical and emotional fatigue. Who knew? Whatever.

All I could be sure of was that each time I tried to begin painting another of the nude self-portraits I'd sketched out long ago on newsprint, I would look at myself and feel a kind of revulsion. *La nausée,* as Sartre would say. *Did* say. Nothing I said, did, or thought was original anymore. Or of any intrinsic value. What a drag.

What else? Well, two more apartments had been burglarized—both of them on the first floor this time, and both leased by tenants who'd gone away for the holidays.

In the middle of all this, I'd had a call from Ed Hershorn at Aperçu. Word was out that *This Cold Heaven* was being nominated for the National Book Critics' Circle Award, just as Liz had predicted. This, in addition to the rumors of a Pulitzer. Everyone at Aperçu was "absolutely stoked," Ed told me, and he was making plans for a huge celebration party in Michael's honor if he won either award (*"When he wins,"* was actually what Ed said).

The NBCC awards ceremonies were always held in March, and the Pulitzer announcement would come sometime in April. Either way, Aperçu would stage a huge blowout, a party I'd be expected to attend. Even Liz would be invited. The party was still months away, if indeed it was going to happen in the first place—after all, we didn't know Michael would win anything—but I was full of dread at the thought of spending an evening in a room where he and Brenda were together, and I was trying desperately to contrive in advance a legitimate excuse to give Hershorn.

Such sticky situations were coming up more and more often lately, and all of them tended to push me to the peripheries of Michael's life—and beyond. How was it possible, for example, that last week several people I knew had gone to a book party for my lover, and I was not there? People who barely knew Michael were celebrating his success with him, while I was at home eating Cheetos and watching *Love Connection*. I could have gone to most any of these parties, of course, but neither of us could bear what Michael called "the doubleness" of such occasions; and really, beyond the psychic discomfort of seeing him with Brenda, I'd have felt like a shit being chummy with her, chatting her up, when I was in love with her husband and wanted him to leave her. Michael often phoned me from the restaurants or homes where such events took place, but those furtive, hurried conversations only dramatized for me the fact that I was on the outside of his life.

Furtive. That was the word for all of it and I hated it. *Furtive.* It sounded so rodentlike.

The fall and winter holidays had always been my favorites, but for the most part this year they were dismal. I'd spent Thanksgiving afternoon at the nursing home with Ida, and I felt guilty thinking of the occasion as *dismal,* since I adored Ida, but it *was* dismal. The spunky old lady I knew was gone; Ida had grown weaker, more jaundiced looking, and the whole time I was there she drifted in and out of sleep as I held her hand. It was tragic to see her like that. Marge was on duty at the Manor that day, and I felt a little better when she told me that Ida was just especially tired because she'd had dialysis that morning. "She's not always like this," Marge reassured me, "but you should be prepared . . . she probably doesn't have a lot of time left."

If Thanksgiving was hard, Christmas was worse. I actually sat in the bathtub and bawled for an hour in the middle of Christmas Eve day, thinking of the big bash Michael and Brenda were having for friends and family that night—their annual Christmas party. Several editors I knew at Aperçu were going, and when I'd stopped by my office that week to pick up an old portfolio in hope of getting some ideas to reenergize my Larkin project, two or three people had asked me if I was going to the party. When I said no, they'd asked why not.

"Busy," I'd said breezily, nodding at the portfolio.

Michael had invited Brit novelist Tom Beshears and his wife, Nicola, not only to the Sullivan Christmas Eve party, but also to the family Christmas dinner the next day. Both of the Beshearses got along well with Brenda and adored Finn and Bridget, so it would all be quite cozy. I could see it all now—just family and friends. The couple and their family and friends.

So I cried away Christmas Eve afternoon, and then that evening I discovered that Michael had done a sweet and surprising thing for me.

As we'd planned, he came over before the party so that we could exchange gifts. I was excited about my present to him—a signed first edition of *Ulysses*, which had cost me a chunk of my savings, but I wanted to give him something special and I knew Joyce was his literary hero and exemplar. I was happy when he got to my place a few minutes sooner than we'd planned, but he explained that his early arrival was because he had to run some preparty errands for Brenda and still manage to get back before the party began at seven-thirty. He wouldn't be able to stay long.

I felt a surge of disappointment that even this small allotment of time on Christmas Eve had to be shortened, but before I could express that, Michael handed me the gift he'd brought. It was a small box wrapped in red foil, and I guessed instantly by its size that it was jewelry. In fact it looked like a ring box, but I wasn't so pie-eyed as to believe that Michael would give me an engagement ring while he was still officially part of a now-famous marriage.

Carefully I opened the wrapping, trying not to tear into it madly the way I wanted to (my mother'd always said I had "a curiosity problem," and it's true I had a hard time waiting to see how anything at all was going to turn out—weather, basketball games, wars, relationships—and most particularly, gift exchanges).

It *was* a ring. I couldn't believe it. And that was not even the most significant aspect of the gift. It was a smooth, rather wide ring of brushed sterling silver, set with a fairly large, classically cut emerald. I knew instantly what he'd had in mind.

"My green glass ring!" I said, and my mouth went wobbly as I spoke. I was afraid I was going to cry. "I can't believe this," I said, "I really can't." He grinned his big lopsided Irish grin, the one where his eyes crinkled at the corners.

"You've said so many times that if you could just get back your green glass ring, everything would be all right, everything in your life." He brushed my hair off my forehead and kissed it right in the center. "So . . . you like?" he asked then, still grinning like an idiot.

"I love it, Michael. And just that you did this in the first place—it's the most loving, attention-paying thing any man has ever done for me, ever. I've been missing my green glass ring almost all my life—"

"—Well, I know this one's not *glass,*" he said mock humbly. "It's just an emerald. But it was the best I could do."

"I can't believe you found one that looks so much like my old green glass ring."

"Well, actually I didn't *find* it," he said. "What I found was a very good silversmith—when I was in New York a couple of months ago—and I told him what I wanted."

"You had it made? That must've cost a fortune."

"Didn't the etiquette doyenne ever teach you that it's bad manners to comment upon the cost of a gift, you little heathen?"

"I think she makes an exception to good manners where the price of jewelry is concerned," I said. "How'd you give specifications to the jeweler when you'd never seen the original?"

"Well, you've described it to me a couple of times, and for some reason I paid attention. So all I had to do was repeat your words. I wanted a kind of industrial-looking setting that would mimic the original expando ring without actually *being* an expando ring." He looked proud of his accomplishment. "Take it out of the box and turn it over," he said, then.

I did. The back of the band was formed with an overlap to make it look like an expando ring—it was a *faux* expando ring in sterling silver. With an emerald. It was stunning. And then I saw the engraving on the inside of the band. It read simply, TO HONORA MY LOVE—ALWAYS YOURS, MICHAEL. The words comforted me, soothed my recent doubt.

When he opened his package a minute later, he said, "My god—it's signed! Jesus, Honora, this must've set you back a few quid." He looked concerned and pleased at once.

I said, "Didn't anyone ever teach you not to comment on the price of a gift?"

"Nope," he said, "no one ever did." Then he pulled me to him and said, "Norrie, you're a brilliant wench."

"It's signed by the author," I said into his neck, though obviously he'd already commented on that. I was milking the occasion.

"You're amazing," he said. "I really can't believe you got hold of it."

"Well, when I was in New York a couple of months ago, I found a very good forger to duplicate the signature to my specifications," I joked, and then I was afraid he might think I meant it so I slugged his arm. "Hey," I said, "that was a joke. It's authentic."

"I never doubted it. Everything about you is authentic. It's absolutely the most wonderful Christmas gift I've ever had—in my life."

But nothing was as wonderful as the green glass ring, which was how I would think of it from then on. Maybe this meant my life would move in a wonderful direction.

I considered it confirmation of this when immediately we went into the bedroom and had sex—old-fashioned, missionary-style sex; fast, intense, utilitarian, and quite to the point. I came hard and had to muffle my voice to spare the neighbors. For a split second in the middle of things, as always happened lately when we had sex, I had a fleeting thought of the seed, accompanied by the now-familiar pang of loss, but otherwise it was just like our good old days.

* * *

At New Year's I had a wonderful surprise—Devi came back briefly with her brother, Sandeep. They were leaving for New York the next day, but she wanted me to go out with them that night to experience Boston's First Night celebrations. I'd lived in Boston for years and had done it before, but I was thrilled at the idea of spending New Year's Eve with her and relieved not to be spending it alone.

Devi looked glorious. She was wearing a long wool skirt of deep purple, a pair of black leather boots, and a big, vivid, handknit sweater in tones of violet, purple, lavender, and red. Her braid was bound with a red elastic strung with tiny purple glass beads. Sandeep—a slight, handsome, economics major in his first year at Oxford—was a real sweetheart. He said he'd never been to the United States and he seemed very excited about our outing—and about having Devi show him around New York City before he headed back to London in a couple of days.

I was moved to see the siblings together. Their affection was open and obviously heartfelt, their repartee easy and irreverently familial, as when she introduced him as "my little *bother*."

It was a freezing evening; we could see our breath like smoke in front of us as we walked to an Indian restaurant in the square for an early dinner. Then the three of us took the T into Boston and gawked at the splendid ice sculptures scattered over the Common. We sampled several of the First Night events, not staying for the length of any one of them. Devi was gripping our First Night program and walking just ahead of us on the sidewalk, enthusiastically directing us over her shoulder as she went. "Let's go and see the modern dancers now," she would say, or, "Oh, we must sample the sweets at this stand!" "We can't miss the Opera Sampler tonight," she said at one point, "they're doing Puccini arias!" We flitted around the city like mosquitoes.

At one point, as Sandeep and I walked behind her obeying her every directive, he nodded toward her back, rolled his eyes, and grinned, "The *queen*." We both began to giggle. It was so true, Devi was like royalty, so like it that you couldn't resent her rule!

"Come, we *must* stop in here for a nice cup of cocoa!" she shouted back at us then, and Sandeep and I lost it. "What's funny?" she asked, honestly baffled.

I hated the evening to end, but it had to rather early because Devi and Sandeep were catching an early commuter flight to New York. We took a T home at ten, and when we got back to Devi's apartment, Sandeep stayed in while Devi walked me upstairs. "I need a moment alone with my friend," she told him. No problem. He'd already switched on her small TV.

As we walked upstairs to the fourth floor, Devi said, "Isn't he a darling? I adore my little brother." Then she told me about the meeting with her publisher. Her book would be coming out in simultaneous hard and soft-cover editions in the fall.

"I asked them if you could do the cover art," she said. "At first they balked—they have their own artists, as they took the time to remind me. Then I showed them Marie Sarvosa's book, and they suggested you submit a design and they would think it over. I told them you'd not be able to waste your time without a contract. At last they admitted they thought you would do a wonderful job, and they agreed to commission your cover art. I hope you'll say yes!"

"Of course I'd be honored to do it, Devi—but when would they expect the completed artwork?"

"That's the rub," she said, "they would need it by June first, and I know you'll have just finished your Larkin project in May. Perhaps it's too much to ask."

"Not at all," I said. "I've planned all along to be done with my project well before May, if I can. And I love the idea of doing your cover. But I have to tell you, I'm having a hard time with my work—I can't seem to do anything these days."

"It's still a problem?" she asked sympathetically. "And only since the . . . since your . . ."

". . . miscarriage," I filled in for her. "I think I just can't bear to paint my*self* right now. I'm sure that's where the problem lies. I try, and end up hating everything I do."

"I'd be happy to sit for you if that would help," she said without hesitation, and the idea was so far beyond the reaches of my project concept that my first impulse was to say no. Then in the instantaneous way people say your life flashes before your eyes when you think you're dying, I saw the whole series in a flash, understood the way Devi's image would work with the rest of the paintings—how it would strengthen the project and make it more universal to have more than one female presence in the series. It would be about female desire, then, not simply about one woman's desire.

"Yes," I said. "Oh, Devi, thank you. Thank you."

She left shortly after that, giving me one of her quick, tidy embraces at the door. It made me think of Clara's huge, soupy hug on the night when Devi had offered to help her. I certainly wouldn't want Clara to know that Devi was sitting for me, I thought as I locked the door behind her. That would inspire enormous jealousy. This might be the time to use my Larkin studio.

It was eleven-fifteen when Devi left, and I saw in the New Year alone, not unhappily.

"Whoopee," I said quietly at midnight, "Wahoo." I could hear car horns honking in the street and somewhere the sound of fireworks.

Michael and Brenda had gone to a party at Tom and Nicola Beshears's rented house in Newton. At two minutes after midnight, Michael phoned me from the party. I couldn't believe he was taking a chance like that. But then he admitted he'd escaped the party by telling Brenda he was going to call and tell the kids Happy New Year, as well as sort of check up on things in case some of Finn's friends had dropped by.

"So I can't stay—I'm going to have to actually *call* them now, you see." We'd talked for about thirty seconds. To avoid saying anything snotty, I stared at the green glass ring on my finger. That was what I did now whenever I was tempted to be a bitch. I had my eye on the ring a lot.

On New Year's Day I fell into a kind of nameless, sodden gloom. It seemed especially quiet in contrast to the festivities with Devi and Sandeep the night before. But then I forced myself out of it. I wasn't going to start a whole year this way.

I phoned Ida and she asked me who I was; when I explained my identity to her and wished her a happy New Year, she asked me what year it was. Oddly then, she told me she loved me; I guess by then she'd figured out who Norrie was. Or anyway, I liked to think so.

Then I called Mother and she told me about several recent murders by decapitation in the Los Angeles area. Nothing seems to capture the Irish imagination like gruesome death, I thought. Fortunately Mother couldn't talk long because some of the church widows were coming over for dinner and cards.

Liz phoned me from her mother's after the two of them had eaten a dinner of roast beef and potatoes. "I actually *cooked*," Liz said proudly. "And fortunately we had a chainsaw to cut the meat." Liz was relieved that her mother was doing well, but she was also fearful. "She tries to hide it from me, but she's so tired," Liz said, "so little and frail. What if she doesn't make it? I don't think I could stand it." It may have been the first time I'd heard Liz say she doubted her ability to handle anything. I heard the vulnerability in her voice.

"I'm betting she'll be fine, Liz. The women in your family are among the stubbornest and most willful I've seen."

"Good point," she said, and actually sounded soothed.

"Do you ever wish you had someone to, to pray to?" she asked me then. It was something that had never once come up between us in all our years of friendship, and I was shocked into muteness for a moment. "Oh, never mind," she said hastily. "I can't believe I asked you that."

"No. No, I mean, of course I've wished . . . but to tell the truth, I *do,* I mean, I sort of do."

"What?"

"Have someone I pray to, I mean. Someone or . . . you know, Something. I do it sometimes at night, in a sort of extemporaneous way."

"Holy crap," she said. "How come you never told me?"

"I . . . I guess you never asked."

Michael called with felicitations just before the family sat down to dinner. He felt guilty.

"This isn't good for you," he said, "and I'm firmly resolving to have changed my life by the end of your Larkin term. We'll make this the year our dreams come true." Just then Brenda called him to the table for dinner. "Gotta go," he whispered, "love you."

It was in the teens and twenties all day and sleeting; I didn't feel like going out for a walk. At two o'clock I made a vegetable soup with a base of chicken stock, adding all the veggies I had in the house. While it simmered, I baked some biscuits.

At three I ate at the little dining table in a corner of my living room with "La Bohème" playing on the boom box, Mirella Freni singing the part of Mimi. Freni's voice was eerily beautiful and especially haunting in the fourth act when Mimi was dying. As I listened I saw myself in the role of Mimi, dying of tuberculosis or whatever it was she had, and having fallen onto hands and knees in the snow, looking beseechingly up at Michael's dining room window, while inside family and friends masticated their vulgar victuals, stroking their rounded holiday tummies with smug satisfaction. I felt tragic and noble until I reminded myself that I was not Mimi, I was just another Other Woman, apparently getting her just deserts.

It began to snow at about four, and I watched the flakes fall past my Brattle Street window, thickening for a while and then becoming sparse again. I wondered if Ida knew it was snowing—Ida loved snow.

At five I put on my painting clothes and started "La Bohème" again, this time in the bedroom. I was going to have to at least try to paint. If I didn't, I'd be setting a bad precedent for the new year. And then I would deserve not only lonely holidays but whatever else I got.

Even when I'd started mixing paints, I still had no idea what my subject would be. I mixed some vermilion with a tube called Old Rose and then I put in just a touch of whitened gray. The color was interesting—a warm but slightly faded red. I found myself turning away from the sketches I'd done before the miscarriage. Devi's offer to sit for me had given me the idea of having subjects other than myself in the paintings. Since I couldn't seem to get Ida off my mind, I decided I would try to paint her. I didn't have a photo of her, I suddenly realized with great shame—how could that be?—but yet her image was quite clear in my mind.

I mixed some flesh tones with white, yellow ochre, and gray, and as I worked I thought of Ida's life, how she'd loved her Harry. I knew from Henry that his parents had been quite passionately in love for all of their life together. Henry had told me of the many nights when, as a kid, he'd pressed the pillow around his ears to avoid having to hear them making love in the next room. He said his mother always had beautiful, sheer, long nightgowns, and there was usually a freshly handwashed one hanging to dry in the bathroom each day. I thought of how long Ida had been alone in her life by now with no one to touch her, and remembered how tightly she'd held my hand on Thanksgiving Day, though her face was slack and her eyes were closed. Sometimes the skin becomes lonely; I knew that. I began to make a sketch directly on the canvas.

By the fourth act, when Freni's voice was giving me shivers, I'd begun to apply the paint. I could see everything in my head.

In the room—again it's a red room, but dark red, like the color of old blood, the stain on my former mattress—the old woman is nude and viewed at a three-quarter angle as she sits upright, almost rigid, on a straight-backed wooden chair, looking out the window at the night sky. All around her are red objects of various hue—a long, sheer, cherry red nightgown on a hanger in the doorway; a woolly, brick red coat thrown over a chair; a pair of lipstick-red high-heeled shoes set side by side atop a bed stand, as if retired to the realm of decoration, having outlived their use as footwear. On the woman's lap is the red glass pitcher, her two veiny, bony hands clasped round it the way one might hold an overnight case while waiting for a train. The old woman's skin is white, tinged with yellow and gray, but her lips are red, brilliant red—obviously the result of lipstick. Her salt-and-pepper hair has come unwound from a bun, and a long wisp of it hangs over her left shoulder. There's a pale moon in the sky, so pale it almost seems translucent, as does the old woman's skin. It's as if slowly, by degrees, both may be disappearing.

I painted all evening and then most of the night, playing the CD over and over as I went, not wanting to take a chance that my mood would change. This would belong at the end of the series, I thought. Devi would come before this.

Sometime in the middle of it all, Michael called, but I didn't dare leave my work and chance breaking the mood. I kept painting as his voice, deep and very tender, spilled into the air of my bedroom.

"I'm sorry, my one," he said. "I'm sorry to leave you alone so much."

But I wasn't alone. That was the funny thing. I wasn't alone at all.

Every so often I stopped, brush poised midair, to watch the snow falling softly past my window in the night. I imagined the way it was making the world white, as if innocence were a season and could return one night without warning, long after you thought you'd lost it.

For months now, every time I've begun to feel this is all hopeless and foolish, every time I prepare myself for the thought of life without you, you come to me unexpectedly and waken my skin, you lubricate hope with desire. It was that way when I went to bed after the New Year's night I'd spent painting Ida. I dropped my paint clothes to the bathroom floor, stood under a full-blast shower, and then crawled naked into the sheets and fell into a stalwart sleep.

Sometime in the night I roused when my buzzer rang, and I stumbled to the hall intercom to see who it was, thinking blurrily it might be the burglar, which made no sense, of course, but I was too sleepy to see that at the time. I pushed the button and heard your voice:

It's me, love, out here in a blizzard. Can I come up?

I don't quite remember answering the door or walking with you back to my bed, and though I know we made love, I remember only a few details at the beginning. I may have drowsed eventually, exhausted as I was. But first I remember you slipped my kimono off me and laid me on my back, spreading my thighs and putting your lips on my belly, then sliding your tongue down and entering me. I remember the sensation of your tongue slipping in and out of me, running over me on the outside, then plunging back in. I remember that, and then I remember waking in the half light of sunup and seeing you'd gone.

Yes. I put my hand between my legs, testing, then bring my fingers to my nose and my tongue. Yes, you were here. It's not a dream. I breathe in your smell. I taste you.

I must have fallen back to sleep, and when I wake again it's midmorning and the winter sun is filling the room. The first thing I see when I open my eyes is myself on the canvas across the room, lying on the red blanket and looking sated, my arms spread as if to fly.

12

A couple of days later, Devi came to my studio at the Larkin on a day that was bright with silver winter light. We'd already prepared the room for her sitting. The previous day she and I had brought over some items in a cab, including objects of her own—some bedspread-size lengths of Indian gauze cloth with rich and intricate patterns, predominating reds and purples; some candles and pillows; and a long red velour robe that held the light almost as voluptuously as velvet does.

Today I'd brought my red blanket and a small boom box as well as the red glass pitcher, which I'd been reluctant to take from my bedroom because I liked looking at it each day, watching it reflect the changing light. I knew it would have to be here at my studio for the duration because I couldn't be carrying it back after each sitting, for fear of slipping on icy sidewalks and breaking it. And I wanted it in every painting of the series, because for me it was desire.

Devi brought some tapes and CDs today, including the sitar music she'd been listening to on the night of our first visit, and a tape of *Aida,* with Leontyne Price. As I locked the studio door to protect us from intrusion, I felt some trepidation for the first time. I had never used a friend as a nude model before, and Devi was a woman of a certain reserve and decorum; would there be an awkward moment when it was time for her to disrobe?

I was surprised when she simply stepped out of her clothes unself-consciously and carried the red robe over to the blanket I'd positioned in front of a window.

"Should I loosen my braid?" she asked, standing on the blanket. She was lovely, very fine-boned and small hipped, with surprisingly round breasts; her skin was both dark and luminous. I'd never seen skin like that. It would be a challenge to get that quality onto the canvas.

"What is it?" she asked, and I heard just a note of shyness then.

"I was thinking I'll have to work very hard to capture the lovely tone and texture of your skin—it's like there's light inside it." I remembered her question then and said, "I think we'll leave your hair in the braid, at least for this one. Maybe we'll let it down for the other paintings."

She looked down at the robe and asked, "May I use this, just for modesty's sake?"

"You want to wear the robe?"

"Oh no, I understand that wouldn't fit with the rest of the paintings . . . but I mean just perhaps to hold in front of me like this." She pressed the robe against her breasts then, letting it hang down in a narrow swath that covered her nipples and pubic region.

"Of course you can use it—but Devi, are you positive you're comfortable posing? I wouldn't want you to feel obligated to do this for friendship's sake."

"I'm fine," she said. "I feel completely comfortable here with you. But I don't think my family would be pleased about my posing totally nude in paintings that will be seen publicly." If Devi, at thirty-five, couldn't be with the man she honestly loved because it would displease her parents, I was certainly not going to ask her to risk their displeasure for me.

We set to work, the strains of *Aida* filling the air. I thought of how paranoid I'd been at first about painting here and realized I'd been selling short the other Larkin fellows. No one knocked on the door to chat, nor was there any noise out in the hall beyond the occasional pad of feet over the carpet whenever the music stopped. It was heavenly—a perfect studio. If it weren't for the fact that I liked to paint at home and found it helpful to live with my paintings-in-progress, this would have been an ideal studio for me.

I'd decided to make this a daylight scene, taking advantage of the studio's wonderful natural light. All the other paintings thus far were nighttime scenes, with the artificial light of lamps—no ceiling lights— and that was what I'd originally thought they all should be because night had seemed more erotic. But that was silly, I thought now, since desire doesn't only visit the body and mind at night.

As I worked, I was increasingly impressed by the way Devi was able to sit completely still for such a long time, I didn't think I'd ever seen anyone, even professional models in art classes, who could stay as still as she could—or who could *be* still in just the way Devi could. Although I have nothing against talking to someone while they pose for me, Devi and I had fallen into a comfortable silence. The only voices in the room were operatic.

When we took a break, I asked her about that capacity for stillness and she said, "Oh, but the stillness is all perceived from without! My mind is working furiously within." She laughed then, greatly amused. I didn't always understand the things Devi thought funny—that was part of her charm for me. And I'm certain she didn't always get my jokes either. But we laughed together a lot because there was so much we did see the same way.

"Do you mind saying what you were thinking of?" I asked then, "when you looked so still?"

"Not at all. Toward the last I was thinking about the function of the Swadhisthan chakra," she said. "I told you about it before—the sacral one?"

"That's the one that fuels creativity and female sexual energy, right?" Devi had talked to me quite a lot about chakras, but that one and the Third Eye were the two that had left the clearest imprint on me.

"Yes, that's the one. But when the system is unbalanced, the Swadhisthan chakra also feeds jealousy and possessiveness. I was mentally revising a poem about jealousy."

"I thought you told me the Third Eye had something to do with jealousy."

"Right, but very peripherally—the belief is that Third Eye problems are intensified when chakras are unclean, particularly in a romantic relationship, so if one person has an unclean power point, the other may experience jealousy."

"That more or less gives a ready justification for jealousy, doesn't it? If you're jealous you can just blame your lover for having unclean chakra." I tried to picture Michael with unclean chakra, but kept picturing chakra as a substance resembling tofu.

"Precisely. And that's just why I would rather concentrate on Swadhisthan as the focal origin of jealousy than think too much about the

Third Eye connection. Then one must be more honest, must take responsibility and admit that most jealousy comes from the same wellspring as does desire. The way to spiritual enlightenment is not to blame others for one's own feelings." That was Devi.

"Are you thinking of your lover in London?"

"My former lover," she corrected, and then sighed. "Yes, I suppose I might as well admit it. He's very witty and handsome, and I torment myself at times by thinking of all the women who would love to be with him." She shrugged, and her braid fell over her breast, which had come uncovered. She was truly the most beautiful creature I'd ever seen. "Sometimes I think his jealousy about me is worse," she went on. "When I left London, he knew I was struggling with my conscience and feeling that I should end the relationship for the sake of my family. He told me that sometimes he can't bear to think of me alive on the earth if I'm not going to be beside him. I asked him if that meant he would be relieved to have me dead, and he told me he'd thought of me dead sometimes and that if we can't be together, maybe it would be a relief. It hurt me very much."

"The thought of your beauty torments him," I said quietly. "It's no excuse, but there it is."

"Beauty is a mysterious and subjective quality," she said. "And to perceive beauty in another can be a kind of cruel judgment—even a curse—for the one who supposedly possesses that attribute. I really don't like to think of myself as beautiful. I find it bothering." Then she told me of a story she'd read in the paper some years ago about a Japanese man who had set fire to an ancient temple and then had turned himself in because he knew that what he'd done was wrong. When the police had asked him why he had done such a thing, he'd answered simply, "Because it was so beautiful."

"It's all about the need to possess," she said. "And the perception of unpossessable beauty is torment to some people. Maybe, in some measure, to everyone. And it breeds jealousy, which poisons the heart and the soul."

I thought of my bouts of jealousy about Michael and his wife. "Yes, I know," I said. "I've felt it, too." I found myself changing gears, maybe from discomfort. "Speaking of jealousy and possessiveness," I said, "I think it would be better if we didn't talk to anyone yet about what we're doing here. I'm afraid it would get back to Clara then, and if it does, it'll fire her jealousy again. She might even start pressuring me to paint her. I can hear her now: *Oh, but of course you would choose Devi, because she is so beautiful.* And you know, having you sit for me is not about beauty at all as it happens, though you are certainly beautiful. I'd want to paint you no matter what you looked like—for your interior qualities."

"Thank you, Norrie," she said. "That's a lovely compliment. And I wasn't planning to tell anyone because this is our business. But you know, she'll see the paintings at your colloquium exhibit here eventually."

"Yeah, but by then my project will be done. I just don't need that kind of distraction from my next-door neighbor while I'm trying to work. Besides, I'll have to move away from Brattle soon after that anyway— we all will, by the end of summer. I assume Clara will be going back to Santiago when the academic year ends in May."

And that was when it hit me—Devi would be going, too, home to Delhi. I guess my face fell then.

"What is it?" she asked.

"You," I said, "you'll be leaving, too, which means I can't be in a hurry for June. What an absurdity—as long as I have the great good fortune of your presence, I have to put up with Clara."

"The Gods don't like us to become complacent," she laughed. "They mean to keep us on our toes."

"But thinking of living next door to Clara made June sound so far away. Now when I think of you leaving, it seems so soon. Way too soon."

I had no idea then, of course, of *soon,* or of *a lifetime.* I didn't know how much would be lost to all of us.

In the painting the red blanket shades to purple in its folds, and Devi is kneeling on it in a pose she settled into without direction from me. She's holding the red velvet robe against her chest. I don't think it had occurred to either of us then that this partial covering would make the finished picture far more erotic and seductive than nudity could have done.

Devi's dark skin has a golden cast wherever the light falls on it; I worked very hard to reproduce that light within her skin on canvas, marveling inwardly at her beauty as I painted. Her warm, vivid colors were in powerful contrast with the sharp winter window light. I found myself experimenting constantly with the reds to make them hotter in that cool light. Devi is facing a window, and its light pulls the viewer's eye to her face and her two hands, which clutch the red robe against her breasts. Everything else falls back tonally from these focal points, and it's only after gazing awhile that you really take in the bareness of her skin where the robe doesn't cover, and then you begin to notice the patterned lengths of Indian cloth that lie on the blanket in deep folds, seeming to form a kind of nest around Devi.

Just past her bare hip you can see the red pitcher nestled in dim light on the floor, at first noticeable only where the light refracts along the edges of the red glass and around its curves. The body of the pitcher emerges subtly, its dark red filled with a whisper of light, the color I think of as the red of blood lit from within.

Devi's face is also lit from within, as is the skin of her hands, and even the more shaded skin of her body has a translucent quality. This wasn't a painter's device to add beauty or mystery to the subject on canvas; it was how she truly looked. And though later people would compliment me on the infusion of light into Devi's skin, I was never able to achieve on canvas the fullness of its luminosity.

The most extraordinary thing about the painting is the expression on Devi's face—an indefinable look that pulls you in even as it insists on its secrets.

For the next two weeks, Devi and I met at the Larkin every day except Wednesday, which was when we went to the colloquium presentations at the Larkin with Clara. I could feel that Clara sensed the growing closeness between Devi and me, though we had made no references to the afternoons we spent together while she was attending classes at Harvard.

One evening, after a surprisingly engaging colloquium presentation by geology fellow Georgina Brandt, Devi, Clara, and I walked back to Brattle Street together. I may have been somewhat quiet on the walk home because I was thinking about Georgi's description of accreted terrain— the way bodies of land drift together and fuse over time, becoming—or functioning as—one land mass. I was thinking of how that happened with people sometimes as they became important to one another. I thought of Michael and Devi, both of whom were important to me, but whose lives had origins and fidelities entirely separate from my own.

Devi said good-bye to us at the third floor, and then as the elevator continued its ascent to the next floor, Clara spoke. Her voice was grim.

"You think she's quite wonderful, of course." The elevator door slid open at our floor and we stepped out into the hall. "Tell me, do you see her often?"

"Devi?" I asked lamely, avoiding the question I was not about to answer. An image flitted through my mind of Devi in my studio, kneeling naked on the red blanket, the swell of her round breasts at each side of the long red robe. I hated Clara for making me feel the need to be furtive about something that was my own business; there was too much furtiveness in my life already.

"Yes, Devi. You are very drawn to her, aren't you?"

"There are lots of wonderful people at the Larkin," I told Clara. "We're all lucky to be there." I said good-bye and let myself into my apartment.

After two weeks of sittings, I'd not only finished the first painting of Devi, but had also roughed out the other two and was, in fact, fairly well along on the second of the trio. I'd never painted so much so quickly. Things were going better than I'd ever imagined they could, and the arrangement would have seemed perfect if not for an incident near the end of the two weeks.

All along it had seemed fortunate that Clara was auditing classes on weekdays and wouldn't be around to question my whereabouts or Devi's. During this period I'd made a point of having tea with Clara at her place now and then if she asked me. I did it to be cordial and maybe also to keep the questions down.

Then one afternoon when I left my studio shortly after Devi did, I dropped by the administrative office to get my mail. On my way back out, Serena Holwerda, the Peace Fellow, stopped me to say that Clara Brava had been looking for me earlier that day. "First she was looking for you," Serena related, "and then she asked if I knew where Devi Bhujander was. Without stopping to think, I told her that I'd seen the two of you together earlier, but that I didn't know where you might have gone." Serena seemed embarrassed. "Clara left rather quickly, without speaking another word to me. I— I hope I wasn't indiscreet to have told her that."

"Of course not," I assured Serena, at the same time wondering if she might have the idea that Devi and I were romantically involved. "It's fine," I said. "Clara just gets intense about things sometimes. She may have had something she wanted to talk to me about."

"Yes, probably that was all," Serena said kindly. She did not seem convinced.

I didn't like it. This was the first time Clara's possessiveness had followed me from Brattle Street to the Larkin Institute.

And now that I thought back, at one point in the afternoon Devi had told me she thought she'd heard a light knock at the studio door, but the music was loud—*Aida* again—and I'd told her not to worry about it. "I don't answer the door when I'm working." It may have been Clara, I realized now.

Clara's colloquium had been a week earlier, and she'd done well enough but had presented her writings on feminism in Chile in such a rote manner that it had been off-putting; she'd read the entire thing directly from the page, head bent over the podium. Her writing was graceful and cogent, but her ideas about feminist principle were by now rather hackneyed, and she failed to articulate ways in which Chilean feminism might have a different mandate than had the burgeoning women's movement of the '70s and '80s in the United States. The Larkies were very supportive, though, and the question-and-answer session following the presentation had gone well—better than had the lecture itself, actually.

That was one thing about the Larkin, I realized by now; you almost couldn't fail to do well in that setting because the women were so unquestioningly supportive of one another. I'd heard a lot of criticism on that count from the larger Harvard academic community, and in fact it was one of the issues that had led many to feel it would be better— more intellectually honest—for the Larkin to go coed if and when Radcliffe merged with Harvard. I could see the arguments on both sides. I didn't buy into the sentimental idea that anything a woman did was worthwhile; but on the other hand, perhaps if there'd been men at the Larkin, it mightn't feel quite so cozy and serene, conducive to work and contemplation. Wasn't it important to have a place where women could congregate to think, talk, study, and create? But whenever men wanted to do the same thing, their institutions were criticized for being exclusionary. All I knew for certain was that I was grateful to the Larkin

Institute for giving me a year to develop my art. I'd never had that before in my life and might never have it again.

During this period Michael was traveling a lot, and sometimes when he landed at Logan, he came straight to my apartment, day or night.

"I couldn't wait to see you," he'd say when he showed up, hair tousled and shirt rumpled from the plane. I was adjusting to his frequent absences better now than I had at first. Of course I missed him while he was away, but more in the abstract lately. I really was filled up with my painting.

After a lifetime of secluding myself in my work, painting in solitude, I had to wonder how much of this renewed creative vitality was the result of sharing my work process intimately with a friend. Inevitably, whatever Devi and I talked about, if we talked during her sitting, found its way into the painting. The end results were richer for this unforeseen collaboration. I had art on my mind again all day now, like a lover; I often dreamed of it at night.

Still, whenever I found Michael there in my doorway looking like a pile of laundry, I was his. And it became a kind of rousing erotic duel when we hit the sheets; unlike many men, Michael was a leisurely lover and could linger for hours over my body with his fingers, lips, and tongue if I would let him. But as much as I loved his ardent tending, my body often grew impatient for climax before long, the way men are reputed to be impatient. Especially when we hadn't slept together in a while, I wanted him to ravish me, wanted it to be hard and fast and explosive. And Michael knew just how far he could take me before I found the waiting unbearable. Invariably I was in agony before he finally put himself inside me, and sometimes my climax would come at the very moment he entered me. He knew exactly how to work me, and the erotic tension of our lovemaking was a good part of its explosiveness and, ultimately, its fulfillment. It was lucky I wasn't a man, though, I often thought. I would have made a terrible one—I'd have been an absolute *pig* of a lover, the sort most women hate, and with good reason.

*   *   *

Late one night in March Michael called me from Chicago, where he'd gone to give a reading at Borders Books.

"Norrie," he said excitedly, "are you sitting down?"

"What! Are you okay?"

"Sandy just phoned. You're not going to believe this." By the time I'd reminded myself that Sandy Brightbill was the name of Michael's agent, he'd gone on to the big news. "I won," he said. "The NBCC—I got it! Sandy phoned me from the awards ceremonies—I can't believe I didn't go. Honestly, I never thought I'd get it. Can you believe it?"

"Oh, my God! That's amazing! I mean not *amazing*—I always thought you *should* get it, but amazing because—"

"I know what you mean—no one thought I'd get it. It doesn't happen this way very often. God, I'm shaking."

"What did Brenda say?" I was trying to find out if he'd told her first.

"I'm just about to call her," he said. "I wanted to tell you first." I could have kissed the soles of his feet.

"Thank you," I said. "When will I see you so I can show you how happy I am?"

"Well, I'd planned to come in on the four-thirty flight tomorrow, but I'm going to try and get on an earlier one so we can have the afternoon together. If I do that I could be at your place by about one."

I was painting Devi tomorrow afternoon, and she'd arranged her calendar painstakingly for these sessions, even turning down a poetry reading to make tomorrow's schedule work out. Ordinarily I'd have canceled anything to see Michael—and, God knew, this was a big occasion—but I knew what I had to do, and I heard myself saying, "I'm painting Devi then, Michael. How about tomorrow evening instead?"

"Oh, but Norrie, the thing about that is, everyone I know will be calling and dropping by the house with congratulations by then and it'd be impossible for me to get away. If I come see you when I first get in, no one will even know I'm back in town yet. Surely you can put Devi off just this once," he said, and I thought I heard a little tension in his voice.

"Actually, I can't—I really can't, Michael. She moved heaven and earth to clear her schedule for this. Couldn't you just keep the flight plans you already have and come straight over here for an hour at four-thirty— please? No one will know you're back then either, if you don't tell them."

"All right," he said a little stiffly, just when I thought we were going to have a struggle over our split-screen lives. "I have lunch plans here tomorrow anyway, and I was going to have to cancel if I left early. Maybe this way is better anyway." He paused uncomfortably. "You know I . . . well . . . oh, never mind."

"No, what? Don't do that. What?"

"I don't know. It just seems odd. I mean, I think this is the first time you've put someone before the two of us, you know? Oh, fuck, it sounds so goddamned male, I know. Never mind. This is your work. Of course you should put it first."

"But, Michael, actually, it's not the work that I can't put aside for this occasion. I could easily bend my schedule if it only affected me—and I would. Surely you know that. It's really not the work."

"Then what are you saying? Are you saying it's Devi?"

"Yeah, I am. You have no idea how much she's sacrificed to do this for me. And she's literally pulled me out of the biggest creative desert I've ever been stranded in."

He blew out a puff of air. "Honora, are you sure it's only gratitude?"

"Only? What do you mean *only* gratitude?"

"Well, I don't know. Maybe I'm a little . . . just a little jealous. I know it sounds silly, but I have to ask—Are you sure it's nothing . . . you know, nothing *more?*"

I both knew and could not believe what he was implying, and I was going to make him say it right out explicitly. It was almost funny. Almost cute. Almost. "What do you mean, Michael. Just spit it out, would you?"

He sighed audibly. "All right," he said. "Sure. I guess I've just been wondering if Devi . . . well, if she's become important to you in a *different way*. I mean, the two of you spend a lot of time together over there in your studio . . ." he laughed, embarrassed. "In the altogether, actually! In that setting, anyone might discover they have, well, *feelings,* or whatever."

I couldn't speak for a moment. Maybe I should have just been amused or even flattered that he was jealous. But all I felt was pissed. "Michael? You must be hallucinating again. First of all, *I'm* not in the altogether while Devi poses for me, okay?"

"No, I—"

"—and no matter what private version of Every Man's Fantasy you've concocted, I'm *not* sleeping with Devi! Get a grip, will you?"

He seemed a little wounded, or embarrassed, or both. "Yeah, okay. I apologize. Let's just forget this conversation ever happened, huh? Obviously, I'm a dolt." I softened.

"How can I forget this conversation ever happened," I asked him, "when it began with such wonderful literary news? Listen, I'm sorry for getting so pissed off just now. It's just that men always think of two women that way, and it gets old, you know?"

"Well, shit, Honora," he said sorrowfully, "we're all of us such lumpy, foolish creatures and we entertain such lumpy, foolish thoughts about naked women. I feel more like an idiot than usual, and that can't be good."

"Sure it can," I laughed. "Let me count the ways."

"So, then . . . I'll see you at around five tomorrow?"

"Wonderful. I can't wait. And congratulations, love. I couldn't be happier for anyone about anything. The book deserves this and so do you."

"I don't know if either one of us deserves it at all," he said, clearly not yet having absorbed the good news. "I only know I'm happy—idiotic, but happy."

"Well, bring your idiotic self to me tomorrow evening and I'll make you very, very wise."

"It's a deal," he laughed. "Hey, I'm really sorry about . . . a little while ago. I was an imbecile."

"Only because you thought I might have been untrue to you. Jealousy makes us all crazy now and then."

Late the next afternoon before Michael arrived, Ed Hershorn called me to say that we would be having our celebration for Michael on the first of April, which also happened to be my birthday—and, of course, April Fool's Day. I clenched up inside at the thought of being in a room where, as I imagined it, Brenda would be sitting with Michael, her arm through his. "And if he wins the Pulitzer, too, we'll just damn well have another fucking party at the end of April!" Ed shouted into the phone gleefully.

For now, I couldn't allow myself to obsess over such abstractions. Devi's sittings had been very productive lately, and I was now finished with the second painting and working my way into the third. Sometimes I wondered how I could possibly repay her for all she'd given me.

One evening as we prepared to leave the studio after a sitting, I said as much. Devi smiled.

"Oh, but that's not necessary at all! The best purpose of a gift is to inspire more giving. I'm sure you'll give back to someone else whatever it is I may have given to you. And that will be a gift to me, you know, Norrie, for it will echo my name in the heavens!" That was Devi.

I was pleased with the second painting of her, a close-up in which she's larger than lifesize—only her head and shoulders and the upper swelling of her breasts can be seen. The lengths of Indian printed gauze cloth are hanging from the ceiling behind her this time—I'd had to borrow a ladder from maintenance to accomplish that—and Devi is looking directly out from the canvas, her hair down this time. At the bottom of the canvas, centered in front of Devi's chest, you can see the top half of the pitcher. Because it's meant to be dusk and the light is not strong, the deep red of the pitcher is muted and there isn't a lot of refraction.

Devi, too, is different in this painting, and there was a reason. She'd had a call from Paul, her former lover in London, that morning, and he'd been hurt and angry that she'd been in London in December and hadn't called him. He'd only found out about her visit after the fact from someone who'd seen her at a play with her parents and brother.

"You don't even treat me with the regard you would accord a casual friend," he'd said. "Maybe I need to face the fact that I'm *not* your friend."

The truth was, she told me, she'd been afraid that if she saw him, temptation would be too strong and she might lose her resolve. A "casual friend" would pose no such threat to her family beliefs and traditions.

"I must see you," Paul had insisted over the phone. "You must at least have the consideration to tell me face-to-face that it's over. We have been everything to each other. We can't allow such an important union to have ended by transatlantic telephone. I will come to Boston to talk to you. I must." This man certainly said "must" a lot, I thought but didn't say.

Devi told me she had decided to use some of her frequent-flyer miles to go and see Paul in London. "Because he's right that I owe him the respect of telling him face-to-face. And at least if *I* go *there,* I can end the visit when I need to. If he came here, he might stay and stay. I don't know how long I could sustain my resolve not to be with him anymore." At this, Devi blushed.

"But surely he would leave when you told him to," I protested. "Why interrupt your life that way?"

"First of all," Devi answered, "you don't know Paul. He's very intense, and he really might stay on just to persuade me not to leave him. To tell the truth, that's why I waited till I got to the United States to tell him of my decision, though I'd made up my mind before I left. But that was cowardly of me, and inappropriate. You need to understand how . . . again I use the word *intense* . . . how intense our love was, how all-enveloping—for both of us. I have never experienced anything like it." Again, Devi blushed. "Paul is right that for a time we were everything to each other, and I know that I must go to London and tell him face-to-face that it has to be over and try to help him to understand why. He deserves the respect of having it told to him that way, at least." She would go to London immediately, she said, and would return in a week.

It was clear that nothing anyone said would dissuade her, though I thought it seemed an extreme thing to do—and in that way, very unlike Devi, who was so measured in her actions, so in control of her own movements and decisions. Paul must still mean a lot to her, I thought. It was painful to think of her traveling so far on such a sad errand.

The weight of what she had to do was very much on her this afternoon when she sat for the second painting, in fact, her beautiful face was ravaged. Oddly, she looked even more beautiful with the play of such pain on her face, a look of vulnerability and unfulfilled longing.

I used finer detail in this painting than in the others—every hair of her brow is clear, every lash of her eyes. She is so close that the pores on her face can be seen. I strained to capture the expression in her eyes— it was the closest to crying I'd ever seen anyone without the actual presence of tears in the eyes.

When Devi and I finished our sitting that afternoon, she went home to pack for London. We embraced at the top of the stairs outside my studio, and I watched her disappear down the stairway.

I wanted to be done with all three of her portraits—or at least to finish everything for which I needed her present—as soon as possible, for in addition to her week in London, she had mentioned that she had a six-week commitment to work with a community poets' group on Sunday nights beginning in a couple of weeks, and I knew that she would have a lot of manuscripts to read, in addition to running the two-hour workshops themselves. It seemed to me our sessions should come to a natural end when the workshops started. Devi needed time for her own work, and she'd given enough to me. Her colloquium reading was scheduled for the week before my own presentation at the Larkin, and she needed to concentrate on that.

After she'd gone, I noticed that the first painting—the one in which she'd knelt with the robe clutched in front of her—was dry. I would take it to my usual framer on Mass Ave tomorrow and see what sort of frame I might find that would work for the entire series. Since all the *Hunger* paintings were the same size, this would be very helpful. I could order all the frames ahead, to save prep time at the end, which could prove to be very important if I was running close to deadline for my colloquium exhibit. I would bring the second one home as well—though it wasn't yet dry, I could lay it faceup in the cab trunk.

And maybe tomorrow, I thought, I'd bring the newly started third painting home that same way—in the trunk of a cab. I could easily finish it at home, and Devi would find it convenient just to come upstairs and sit for me there after she got back. It was set in a night room anyway.

The cabbie waited for me while I ran into The Frame-Up to leave off the first painting and choose a frame; then as I left the store, I saw Clara walking toward me on the sidewalk. The one person I didn't want to run into right now.

"Norrie!" she called, smiling brightly. "What luck to run into you like this!" She caught up to me and then took note of my nearness to the cab door. "Are you taking a cab home?" Oh God, what would I say if she asked to ride back with me? I couldn't let her see the portrait of Devi without first having prepared Devi. As always when I found myself caught in a predicament, I began to babble.

"Oh, Clara! Yeah, what a coincidence. I just took a painting in there to be framed . . . " I nodded toward The Frame-Up. ". . . and now I'm just . . . where are you headed?"

"Me? Oh, I have an appointment to have my teeth cleaned, just up the block here."

A swell of relief washed over me. "Too bad, or you could have gone back with me in my cab."

"Yes," she agreed. "But why spend money on a cab when the day is so beautiful for walking?"

How could I explain the cab, when I was now only a couple of blocks from home? *I have a nude oil painting of Devi in the trunk?* In desperation I grinned and said, "Just another example of American profligacy, I guess."

"Oh no, here I go again. I am so sorry. I would never judge you, Norrie. You must be tired or something."

"Yeah, actually I am. I've been painting like mad." It was a relief to be able to tell Clara the truth about something, for once.

I got into the cab and headed back to Brattle with the other painting in the trunk. Michael was due at my place very soon to celebrate his award. I was thankful when I didn't have to worry about running into Clara as I carried the painting up in the elevator. I put it on an easel in my bedroom and felt pleased to have it there in the company of the paintings of myself and Ida. Then, remembering Michael's nervous query about the state of things between Devi and me, I turned the easel to the wall before he arrived. I didn't want to distract him from his celebratory duties.

When Michael got to the apartment, I had a good Spanish champagne chilling, and I was wearing the red silk kimono over some *Coco* by Chanel.

"Behold, the time is upon us for the Red Silk Commingling," I told him solemnly as he walked in and I shut the door behind him. He grinned like an Irishman as I led him to the bedroom by the arm. "In his time of triumph," I announced into the air as I guided him, "Michael Sullivan shall speak to the masses of his plans for the betterment of man."

"I feel like a beauty queen. But I'm pretty sure man is too hopeless for betterment."

"You're a beauty, but you're no queen. And you may be right on your last point, if *you're* any example of man."

We had our red silk fuck then, sweetly and slowly. He led this time, and I let him browse for as long as he wished. It was the least I could do. He came into me after great attention to detail and moved with slow intensity and impressive heft. When he came, he let out a booming laugh of release. God, I loved him.

While Devi was away in London, I worked on the background of the third painting, which I'd brought home. I was happy to be painting at home again where I could work at any hour I pleased, day or night. If I got enough done now, I'd have only the figure to work on when Devi returned. It had been a simple matter to reconstruct the scene I'd started with at the studio, and since it was a night scene, the lamplight was also easy to recreate.

Twice that week, I got together with Clara. On Monday we went out to dinner at Casablanca, and on Wednesday we walked to the Larkin together for a colloquium presented by Mira Berg, a literary fellow from Michigan who talked about the "unconventional" relationship between Jean Paul Sartre and Simone de Beauvoir. Clara was friendly and calm, I thought, not so desperately attentive as she'd been other times recently. Actually, we had a good time.

On the evening Devi got back, she phoned me and asked if I could come down to her place to have a chat. "Actually, I rather need to talk with you," she added. I could hear some urgency in her voice, so I went right down.

She answered the door in the old pink chenille robe I'd first seen her in the day I met her in the laundry room. As we embraced, I smelled her spicy scent. I took off my shoes and followed her into the living room, where she already had a teapot and two cups waiting, but this time there was no music. Devi looked both tense and in some way excited. I noticed that her color was heightened, and she smiled a lot—but nervously.

"It's wonderful to see you, Norrie. I can't tell you how glad I am to look into your face."

"I've missed you," I said truthfully. "I was a little worried, to tell you the truth." .

"Worried? But about what?"

"I don't know. Just how difficult it would be to get through your mission. I mean, having to tell Paul that you were ending the relationship permanently. It must have been very painful."

Her cheeks took on a deeper level of pink, which, over her olive skin, was quite lovely.

"I have a lot to tell you," she said, stirring her tea and then testing it gingerly at her lips. I watched her closely, and suddenly I knew. I knew but was stunned by how absolutely my intuitive knowledge did not correspond with the image of my composed, restrained, and always wise friend.

"Oh, Devi, you . . ."

"Yes," she said, smiling shyly and looking down in embarrassment. "I was with Paul again, as before."

"But I thought you were so firmly resolved not to be with him anymore. What happened?"

"When I told him that it had to be over, he asked me to make love with him one last time. And although at a distance I might have told any of my women friends that such an act would be pure foolishness, I can't begin to explain how fiercely I was drawn to him. And I'd been feeling angry at my father for his rigid beliefs that make no allowance for human need or emotion. All of a sudden, I felt I had a right to share myself with the man I love, and I have never wanted anything so acutely in my life. I could feel it in all the skin of my body, the way one feels fear."

"Yeah, desire and fear have that in common. And other things, too, I guess." She seemed not to hear me, almost not to know I was there. She was inside the memory now and unreeling it like film for us both.

I sat back, forgot my tea, and just listened. I'd never seen Devi like this.

"From the moment he put his arms around me after so long a time, I could not have found it in me to reject him. I consider myself a strong person, but I was overwhelmed by the need to be with him, to . . . I must say it this way, Norrie . . . to *have* him. And the moment he . . ." The blush was back. ". . . when he came into me, I felt a kind of blessed relief and then overwhelming release. Instantly we were back, Paul and I, fully back, as ever. Days went by, and we did nothing but make love."

I was reeling, trying to reconcile this image of a lustful Devi with my idea of her as a woman always in command of herself and certain of what to do in any situation, and above all, unutterably *pure*. But did I feel that erotic desire was *impure,* dirty? I was as confounded by my own response to Devi's revelations as by the revelations themselves. After all, I reasoned, she was a woman as I was. If I was capable of such appetites, why shouldn't she be as well? I heard her voice as if from a great distance. "Do you know tantra, Norrie?"

Now it was my turn to blush. I thought that tantric sex had something to do with the *Kama Sutra,* that compendium of sexual positions. But I was still tongue tied—not only by the notion that Devi was as subject to the desires of the flesh as I was, but also by the idea that those desires could overwhelm her will, her long-held sense of right and wrong, as my own desires had done. "I know it's got something to do with inti-macy," I said at last, sounding to my own ears as prim as my mother.

"Yes!" She smiled, apparently pleased that I'd said *intimacy* rather than *sex.* "So many people think it has only to do with sexual matters, but it's so much more. It's based, you know, on the sexual and spiritual union of Shiva and Shakti, and it has to do with a balance achieved in the union of opposites, making possible the deepest sort of union between a man and a woman.

"Oddly enough, when I met Paul, it was he, a non-Indian, who had knowledge of tantra! I had, actually, no sexual experience—I'd only dated one man in Delhi—Ajay, who was the man my parents had long hoped I would marry. Ajay and I had kissed and embraced a bit, but that was all." So Devi had remained a virgin into her thirties; that was less shocking to me than her erotic nature was. "But with Paul, although I was afraid at first—terrified, if you must know—when he began to touch me in a . . . in a more intimate way, I found suddenly that I was filled with a need I'd never experienced, a need to know a man intimately." Devi paused here, as if reminiscing, and I couldn't take my eyes from her face. "In the early days of our love," she said at last, "he taught me how to extend and expand the peak of sexual communion, to prolong that ecstasy. It becomes, then, a transcendent thing, a moment when all boundaries between two people simply dissolve." She paused, and I leaned forward. "Nothing is forbidden in tantric love," she said. "The tantric vision embraces every ecstatic and pleasurable possibility as an opportu-nity for learning."

"I don't know tantra," I said, "but I think I do understand the ecstatic power and intensity you're talking about." I wanted more than anything to tell her all about Michael but held back, remembering my promise.

"It's nearly impossible to turn away from it," I added, "once you've reached that level of sexual intensity."

"Yes," she agreed, "and that's why I've come back from London with the intention of telling my father that I want to marry Paul. If it's to be this way between Paul and me, the right thing for us is to marry. My family must try to understand, and I realize I'll have to speak to my father first of all." Suddenly Devi's eyes filled with tears, and when she brought the cup to her lips, I thought I saw her hand tremble slightly. "To say it plainly, I'm terrified," she went on. "I've never once stood up to my father, never. I love him so much, and I've always tried to be the good daughter and obey our family traditions. I fell in with Paul shortly after I arrived in London and was ravaged by guilt from the outset. Finally, it just seemed easier to stop—easier than to pull down the monolith of family tradition."

"But now you feel differently about that."

"No! I feel the same about it, but I feel . . . I feel so much desire, a desire I can't speak of separate from love. It's all one and the same."

I reached out and covered her hand with my own. "Do you want me to stay here while you call your father?"

"Oh no," she laughed as tears spilled down her cheeks. "I must do this on my own if I'm so right about it. I must be strong. I'll call my father on the weekend when I've had time to rest a bit." She stood then and put her hands out to take mine. "Let's go upstairs and work on the painting," she said. I was stunned.

"God, no, Devi! You've just returned from a long trip by air, and you've got to be jet lagged. No way we're returning to work till you've had some rest."

"Really, I'm hungry to do it," she insisted. "All I'll have to do is lie there like a queen—I may even allow myself to doze—I'm just tired enough to feel a kind of enticing ease. And I think my present mood may be exactly the right one. Honestly, Norrie, I love the idea that what I'm still feeling in my flesh will make its way to the canvas. I love the thought of having you paint what I'm feeling for Paul. Maybe that will even help me to understand it better myself."

"But can't it wait till tomorrow when you've rested?"

"No, honestly. Because by tomorrow I'll already be preparing my heart and mind for what I have to say to my father. Tonight I'm still feeling Paul's touch. I haven't slept, even on the plane, since I was last with him."

Now I could see the same flush in her cheeks and radiance in her gaze that I'd seen before she'd mentioned her father. I realized that Devi was afraid of losing this feeling, of losing what she had with Paul, and that she saw my painting it on canvas as a sort of hedge against such loss. I could see that even now she wasn't certain of her ability to stand up to her father. And it seemed to me she wasn't taking into account the larger difficulty of going against her own convictions, which I'd heard her express so often and so passionately.

Together we went back to my apartment, keeping mum as we passed Clara's door. Clara had called me earlier that day to see if I wanted to go to a movie, and I'd let the machine take the call because I knew it was the day Devi was coming home and I wanted to be there when she got back. Anyway, twice in one week was enough, considering Clara's tendency to be possessive.

I put on some music—some Chopin concertos this time, because they were quiet and wouldn't carry out into the hall. Devi disrobed quickly and with her usual grace. I couldn't help watching, freshly surprised by her beauty. There was a new ease to her movements. The calm of sexual satiety, it seemed. She caught my glance and smiled beatifically. "I'm so happy," she said as she settled onto the blanket.

All I wanted in that moment was for my friend to find a way to make her happiness last.

On the night Devi came back from London all aglow with sex, she'd drowsed once or twice during the sitting, and I'd found myself fascinated by the way that even in sleep her face retained the glow of erotic fulfillment—it was the first time I'd seen such ecstasy in repose. I wondered if I had ever looked so filled up. Then, thinking of your lovemaking, I imagined I must have and I wondered if you might ever have seen such a look on my face in sleep.

You'd been gone for a week to do some readings on the California circuit, and I felt your absence powerfully that night in the empty apartment as I prepared for bed. As I stepped out of my clothes in the bedroom, preparing to go into the bathroom where I had the tub filling, I caught sight of myself in the full-length mirror behind the bedroom door and though I tend not to engage with my own reflection in a mirror unless I'm painting—more the opposite, most of the time— now I watched myself moving out of my clothes. I watched the woman in the mirror moving her long limbs, her strong body, moving with ease like a woman who has someone to love her in bed each night.

In the bathroom I put some oil into the bathwater. When I stepped into the tub, my skin instantly awoke to the warm, oily water and I slid slowly down into it, not even bothering to twist my hair up on top of my head to keep it from the oily water. I lay there for a long time, eyes closed, letting the warm water cover me, my hair floating atop the surface of the water like Ophelia's. And I felt like Ophelia then, disappearing into the water past the pain of wakefulness.

And I knew in that moment that I would never end my life as Ophelia had because then I wouldn't get to find out what happens. I want to be alive. I want to make my own choices. I don't intend to live my life pining away for any man, even you, as much as I love you—even you. I slid my hand down my belly to where you like to go, and let myself feel what it must be like for you to feel me there, warm and oily under bathwater the way it must feel when you've lubricated me with desire. I spread myself open and slid my middle finger in, moving it slowly up and down over my clitoris till my body went rigid, urgent, and then I pushed two fingers hard into myself, hard, hard, hard, until I came arching up from the water like a dolphin, again and again.

That's who I am, please remember that. I want you, but I won't give up my life for you.

13

Devi was glad to be working closer to home now, and I was happy to be using my own place again. We were putting in long sessions each night in my apartment in hopes of wrapping up our collaboration before her poetry workshops began.

At one point she mentioned that if we were going to have the rest of our sittings here in my apartment, Clara was likely to run into us as we entered and left, and we both agreed (I, reluctantly) that it was time to tell her about the paintings if it should come to that.

"I don't want to tell her unless I have to, though," I said, "because I want to paint without anything disrupting my concentration."

"Oh, I agree," Devi said, "but I'm glad you're ready to tell her if you must. I've never really felt we should have to hide from her."

"I'm not sure you see her the way I do then," I said.

On Saturday night Devi was planning to call home to Delhi and tell her father the news—what the family would consider very *bad* news— that she wanted to marry a non-Indian, non-Hindu man. "I'm more and more scared," she confided when she called me to say that she would come up after she and her father had talked.

I worked on the painting while I waited for her, and listened to *Aida*. In the time we'd had to work on this painting since her return from London, I'd concentrated almost wholly on the face, trying to capture the essence of Devi's erotic fulfillment. The skin of her cheeks was rosy, glowing, even her lips seemed fuller and rosier, as if the blood of desire remained there even now.

When she rapped on my door nearly two hours later I found her shaken, her eyes puffy from weeping. "Devi! What happened?" I led her to the couch. "What happened?" I asked again.

"It's no good," she said, "How could I have ever dreamed it would be possible to change my father?" And then she began to weep again. It was unsettling to see Devi, the embodiment of calm and self-possession, so distraught. In going back on her vow to end the love affair with Paul, in breaking her own resolve, had she fatally compromised her capacity to be strong and certain, at ease in her body and soul? I put my arm across her back and patted her shoulder, careful with my physical reassurances because I knew Devi was not the demonstrative type.

Then, thinking of her native reserve, I was struck anew by the thought of how much power the sexual union with Paul must have over her—how, after years and years of restraint and self-control, the uninhibited expression of physical desire and that desire fulfilled—what a potent effect it had to have on her constitution. I was quiet, waiting for her to feel ready to speak.

After a time she blotted her eyes on a tissue I handed her, and she shook her head, seeming to muster resolve.

"It was a long phone conversation. I tried to start out with calm conviction, but as I spoke into my father's silence and distance, I could feel my calm weakening, not to say my conviction. From the moment I told him about Paul, my father was very . . . I can't think what word to use. *Adamant* is not nearly enough to describe it. He was nearly violent in his tone, his speech. He said everything ten times. He told me he would disown me. He said that my mother would die of shame. He said that I would single-handedly destroy everything he and my mother had worked and sacrificed for—everything *their* parents had worked for. After hundreds of years, I would be the one to destroy our family line, he told me." Devi began to weep silently, her face buried in the tissue. "It was like being beaten," she said. "The truth he spoke was that brutal. How can I argue with hundreds of years?"

I thought of the Kipling quote Michael had repeated to me when some of the Irish in South Boston were down on him for telling the truth about their lives. I couldn't recall it entirely, but I remembered it was an admonition not to "think with the blood." I repeated this to Devi now and said, "That's what your father is doing—thinking with his blood. You don't have to think with the blood, Devi, just because he does. You have a right to think for yourself."

"Thank you, Norrie. I know you're trying to help. But one could as rightfully apply that quote to my desires as to my father's beliefs—after all, 'thinking with the blood' could refer as much to passion as to family loyalty. In saying that I want to be with Paul no matter what the damage, am I not thinking with the blood?"

"But you've a right to think with whatever you want, Devi—that's my point."

"You can't really understand how it is, though. Your cultural traditions are so very different from mine, Norrie. More to the point might be what Empedocles said—'The blood around men's hearts is their thinking.' How can we *not* think with the blood, Norrie? Whether we're referring to passion or to family loyalty?"

"Yeah, I guess Empedocles predates Kipling by a few years!" Actually, I had no idea when Empedocles had lived. I was in over my head.

"Yes," she said, "by well over two thousand years. But I think that the final arbiter of what's right must be the good of the many, not the selfish desire of one family member." Now she sighed. "I have to go and telephone Paul. I can't bear to tell him. And again by telephone, just as I did before. It's awful. He'll be so upset and angry, I know it. I want to sit for you when I get done talking to him. I need to come back up here and work with you, to keep myself in control. Posing helps me to discipline my moods."

When she did come back an hour later, it was with the news that she had talked to Paul, and he had "first broken down, then exploded."

"He is so terribly angry at me," she said, her face quiet. "I've never heard Paul sound this way. Then after we hung up, I went into the bathroom to wash my face so that I could come back and sit for you, and when I came out of the bathroom I found a disturbing new message he had left on my answering machine while I was in the bathroom. He started by begging me to pick up the phone—'I know you are listening to me,' he said. Clearly, he imagined I was sitting there hearing him and not answering the phone! I would never do that to him. He apologized for losing his temper before, and when he tried to explain how he felt, how his grief had taken the form of anger, he . . . he began to cry." Devi looked away, her eyes brimming with tears. "I have never heard Paul cry before. I know you may find this surprising, but until tonight, I had never seen any man cry, never in my life." At this, Devi put her face into her hands and wept.

"It was after that point that he began to be angry again," she went on. "Maybe it was his hurt pride at the thought of my witnessing his tears, or maybe his tears simply washed away his self-control." Devi wiped her eyes on a tissue, blew her nose, and continued speaking, her voice gravelly. "He began to say, 'Pick up, please, Devi, you must! How can you be so cruel to raise my hopes and then kill them again? This is crazy, after we were just together last week and so happy. It means nothing, then, how much I love you? You can do this after all the pleasure we have given to each other, despite all that we mean to each other?' " She shook her head in shame.

"And he's right," she said quietly. "We were completely happy together. I've transgressed terribly, Norrie—not only my family traditions and beliefs, but also Paul's humanity, his heart." She looked down a long time before she began to speak again. "It became very bad," she said, "Paul spoke to me in a way I've never heard him speak to anyone. 'But *no,* you won't pick up the phone and speak to me,' he said. 'Fine, then, I hope you have enjoyed my little moment of agony. You are . . . ' Oh, Norrie, I can't say his words, can't bear to think them, even. He called me a bitch, and then he elaborated by using a profanity. 'Fucking bitch,' he said. That's what he called me. And then he slammed down the phone."

I couldn't imagine anyone speaking to Devi so crudely and disrespectfully under any circumstances. "Devi, I'm so sorry—"

"No," she said, "*I'm* sorry. I deformed his heart with my selfish desire. I thought of nothing but that hunger while I was with him. He was wrong to speak to me that way, I agree, but I'm the one responsible for his state. I know that."

"But you can't be responsible for his bad behavior," I said hotly. But even as I said it, I realized that although I hated Paul for speaking to Devi that way, I knew how it felt to have hope continually raised and then dashed by one person. I knew he was filled with the kind of helpless anger I'd felt but not expressed when Michael had let me down profoundly in a similar way.

"You can't understand, Norrie, because you don't know Paul. He has always been so loving with me," Devi said now, "so protective and respectful. He is never crude, never would he speak to me this way, when he's himself. To tell the truth, I have never heard him curse or use foul language of any sort to anyone, ever. It's very disturbing. He was suddenly a stranger as he spoke to me that way."

"Love pushes people to the reaches of their endurance sometimes," I finally said, because it seemed wrong not to share the other side of my thinking with her. "I'm not excusing Paul's awful outburst, but I think you might see such uncharacteristic extremes in any lover who's been pushed to the edge of longing."

How ironic, really, that in my situation with Michael, I was in the position of Paul, while Michael, like Devi, was holding fast to family values. I couldn't excuse Paul for how he'd spoken to Devi, but I could understand his torment, especially when she had allowed him to hope again. I'd been where Paul was now, I'd just not expressed my frustration and hurt the way he did. "That seems to be the power of love. For better or worse," I added.

"Well, then, love is a dangerous state, because what you're saying is that we never can truly know the one we love—nor can we know ourselves—until we've reached love's extremities."

I had no answer all of a sudden.

"Let's work, Norrie," she said then, *"please."* I could hear that she meant it, that she needed it. She disrobed and resumed her pose on the blanket, and I began to paint. It was odd, surreal—I thought a casual viewer might have found the whole scene strange indeed. Devi and I remained quiet for most of our session.

When she left later, I said, "Maybe we should take some time off, Devi. In fact we could almost just quit at this point. I'm nearly to a place in the paintings where I don't need you to be here. And your workshop begins next weekend. You've got to get some rest. You're absolutely worn out."

"No," she said almost ferociously. "This is what we planned, and I need for something in my life to be the way I've planned it. I'll be here each night this week as I promised you I would. Please. We're stopping soon enough. For now, we'll work on as we said we would."

"Sure. Okay."

*   *   *

On Wednesday afternoon Clara and I went to the Larkin colloquium without Devi, who had stayed home pleading fatigue. The presentation, by Larkin fellow and Boston businesswoman Ricci Lott Swift, was called "The Contemporary Woman's Mandate in the World of Commerce." I found it self-conscious and of little interest, but Clara was riveted, which surprised me.

Afterward, as we joined the other fellows at The Bombay Club for dinner, I asked her what she'd thought of the presentation.

"Although I am not at all a materialist," she answered, "I respect Ricci Swift's point of view. I see in my own life how economic independence would give me choices I do not have. The choice to write a novel, perhaps, instead of being a slave to my newspaper job." I thought of Clara's colloquium presentation then, remembering the beauty of the prose she'd read in such a robotic way. Even the poor presentation had not obscured the excellence of Clara's writing.

"I wish you could do that," I told her. "You have such talent. But the idea of shaping your life around a business strategy, making money, as Ricci has—that's just not you, is it? Why were you so interested?"

She thought a moment. "Maybe it is the idea of any self-liberating endeavor I admire," she answered. "I especially like the idea of a woman taking action to liberate herself economically. Economics is the *heart* of liberty in a postindustrial world."

Later, as Clara and I walked back to Brattle Street in the dark, she said, "Don't you know that this is how it was always meant to be?"

"What?" I asked.

"You and I," she said, "the two of us. Surely you feel it, too."

"I—Clara, I'm not sure what you mean. It was a nice evening. I enjoyed our conversation very much."

She sighed. "Maybe it will just take time for you to understand all of this," she told me, "or maybe it is more to the point to say that you need to learn to *accept* it." There was something in her tone that put me off even more than did the words, which were unsettling enough in themselves.

"Learn to accept what?" I finally asked.

"Destiny," she said, and I felt in that moment as if the night air had become something solid and was closing in around the two of us, immovable, not to be reckoned with.

Clara called on Friday night while Devi was sitting for me, and again on Saturday afternoon when I was alone, and I didn't pick up the phone either time. Her Saturday message said that she had "been trying to reach Devi, too," but that neither of us had "seemed to be around." I didn't return Clara's calls because I didn't want to tell her I was at home—it was too likely she would come knocking that night during Devi's sitting. But at least, I thought, her message meant she hadn't seen Devi arriving at my place, which helped me to relax as I worked.

"I don't know why you give her such power, Norrie," Devi commented on Saturday evening as I was mixing some Crimson Lake with Prussian blue, black, and just a touch of ochre, for the blanket shadows.

"How can I explain," I said, thinking of Clara's words the other night. "The weight of her expectation smothers me. I anticipate it; I dread it."

"You hide from her."

"Well, I didn't at first. I guess now I do find it easier to avoid her sometimes."

"Poor thing," Devi said then, and I wasn't sure which of us she meant. I hoped it was Clara, but I feared she was talking about me.

By late Saturday night I had a lot of the third painting finished, and I was definitely getting near the point where I could do the rest alone. Devi had been wonderful to work with—even now, in her distress about Paul, she was focused, quiet, and undemanding. I knew she had needed to prove to herself that she could keep her word to sit for me despite her emotional state. I wanted to tell her it didn't matter if we quit now, and that her weeks of sitting for me had already been a supreme act of friendship. But I knew that Devi didn't want to hear any of that right now. She was absorbed in disapproval of herself. No matter how she looked at recent events, she'd hurt and disappointed someone who mattered to her, and she'd lost her father's respect, she was sure of that. Now she was proceeding by force of will alone.

The face I'd painted the first few nights after Devi's return from London was a wholly different face from the one I was looking at now. There was no longer a trace of the ecstatic days and nights in London with

Paul, the mood of voluptuous pleasure satisfied had been replaced by grief, loss, and self-recrimination. It was hard to look at her in this state, but for both our sakes I kept going, as she did, and as I worked I reminded myself that she'd wanted her pleasure with Paul ritualized in paint as a hedge against losing it entirely. And now she'd lost it and had only this, and memory.

We worked so late Saturday night that it became Sunday morning, and we were both ready to drop. I told Devi she could crash on my sofa if she wanted, and she was tired enough to find that a good alternative to dragging herself back down to the third floor at 3:00 A.M.

On Sunday morning I made us pancakes and after we ate, Devi had to go home to prepare for her workshop. I was planning to go and see Ida this afternoon. As we said good-bye, Devi promised to stop back after her workshop tonight just to see if I needed her anymore.

"You're welcome to stop by for a cup of tea tonight," I told her, "but absolutely *no more* sittings. We're done. You'll have the workshops every Sunday evening now, and all that manuscript reading for the next six weeks—and you need time for your own writing, too. I honestly think we've got it to a point now where I can do the rest alone."

"Well, if you're sure," she said.

"I'm sure. But come on up after your workshop if you're not too tired. I'd love to hear how it went."

Devi said she would. As I watched her walk to the elevator, I saw fatigue in her gait. I'd taken a lot of her energy for my own work, and even though it had been her idea to pose, I felt guilty about it. I would find a way to return the favor.

That afternoon I went to see Ida, who slept through my whole visit, rousing once to say, oddly since it was late February, "Happy New Year, Dear." Marge wasn't there today and the charge nurse was hopeless. I could get no information out of her but that Ida was "tired today."

On the way back from Brookline on the T, I began to feel the effects of painting nonstop the last few days and nights, and by the time I disembarked in Harvard Square I had the sensation of dragging my legs behind me up the sidewalk. In front of the Coop, the highwire guy was all set up for Sunday crowds; as I passed him he was balanced on his rope holding two flaming torches and yelling, "Heeelllp! A whole bunch of people are staring at me and I don't know whyyyyyy!" I didn't bother to acknowledge him. "Hey!" he hollered, "SMILE, lady!" I wanted to deck him.

When I got inside my apartment I went straight to the bedroom and turned off the phone, kicked off my shoes, and threw myself onto the bed fully clothed. It was four-thirty. I didn't wake until nearly nine o'clock that night, and when I checked the phone machine I had calls from Liz, Clara, Mother, Michael, and Ed Hershorn. I called no one back. I was blasted.

Devi stopped by at about ten-thirty to tell me about her workshop. She said there were some bright poets in her group "and a couple of 'noodges' "—a word she'd gotten from me. She was really tired, she said, and wouldn't stay long.

At that moment someone knocked at my door. I opened it to Clara, who was looking grim.

"Oh," I said, "hi, Clara." She looked from Devi to me, then back to Devi.

"Hello," Devi said, smiling genuinely. "How are you, Clara?"

"How would you expect me to be?" Clara asked. "I was not born yesterday, you know."

"Clara, what do you mean?" I asked her, already dreading the answer.

"What I mean is, all weekend I've called both of you and neither one of you returned my calls. This morning I heard you leaving Norrie's apartment, Devi. And now I realize that the two of you were probably together the entire weekend." She had tears in her eyes, and I felt awful.

"But, Clara—" I began, and she cut me off.

"Why do you hide from me? *Why?* Don't you think I know the two of you meet for hours in your studio?" Her voice trembled. It was heart-breaking. I took over immediately, in a desperate move to dispel the tension.

"The secret can now be told," I announced. "Devi and I have been *working* together." This was as good a time as any to tell her, I thought— in fact, it was necessary.

"What do you mean?" Clara asked, looking from one of us to the other again.

"Come in," I said, "and I'll show you."

"Would you two mind," Devi interjected, "if I just go on home? I'm very tired."

"Of course," I said, and I wished her good night. Clara said nothing. It occurred to me that perhaps Devi felt shy of being in the room when Clara saw her nude portraits, and that made me reluctant to show them. But Devi had already agreed that I should let Clara know about our collaboration, and clearly it was time to remove the mystery from the proceedings.

I led Clara into my living room and seated her on the couch. I would bring one of the two paintings out to her here, I decided, rather than have her come into my bedroom and see both of them. I was trying to limit things, I guess, some sort of damage control.

"Let me show you one," I said brightly, "just to give you an idea of what I'm doing." Clara just sat there, mute, hands clutching the edge of the sofa at each side of her, face still grim.

In my bedroom I immediately wished I had the first painting of Devi here instead of at the frame shop. That pose with the red velvet robe clasped against her front would be the best one to show Clara, I thought, though certainly none of them would soothe my jealous neighbor. But my choices were between the current painting, of Devi nude and recumbent on a blanket in shadows, and the previous one, the close-up in which one could see that she was nude, though not much of her body was shown since the picture ended at the upper swell of her breasts. But that portrait revealed so much inner turmoil that it felt crude to show it to Clara just then; I couldn't bear to violate Devi's privacy by exposing her vulnerability that way before Clara's angry eyes.

I stood nervously debating while Clara waited in the living room. Finally, though later I might wonder if I'd made the right decision, it seemed the lesser of two violations to show more of Devi's skin, rather than to expose her heart and soul in a fragile moment, her eyes filled with sorrow and loss above those delicate bare shoulders.

When I brought out the painting of Devi on the blanket, Clara's face went pale. She stood quickly and then froze on the spot, her gaze fixed on the painting. "The one I'd have liked to show you is still at the frame shop," I said, trying to see what she was seeing. Oddly then, when I looked through Clara's eyes, I saw the painting more clearly than I'd seen it yet.

Devi is lying across the red blanket on her back, her eyes half open as if during a sleepless night. There's only the light of some small candles in the room—in this sequence of three paintings, light is gradually abandoning the room. In general the tones are muted, but whatever the candlelight touches comes to life. All the reds and purples are dark. I'd mixed colors I thought of as *boysenberry, currant, claret,* and *garnet;* there was also a brownish red I kept thinking of as *day-old blood*—I couldn't rid myself of the image of my bloody mattress, though it was long gone from the apartment and a new one in its place. I could still see that color when I closed my eyes.

At the front of the picture plane, the pitcher is tipped onto its side and partially nestled in a piece of red-and-purple print fabric. The other lengths of fabric are folded in a tidy stack beside Devi, and her left hand, which faces outward from the canvas, is resting on the bowl of the overturned pitcher. Her right hand covers her genital area, and her breasts are bare, their nipples small and dark brown. Devi had decided that this pose called for that degree of exposure and had insisted that she didn't mind, especially since the lighting was dim.

And she was right that one has to really look in order to see the details of her body in the painting, though a thin ridge of lambent light illuminates the upper outline of her body all along the length of her. The refracting red lights of the pitcher are brilliant against the muted tones behind it, and being so prominent an aspect of the picture's composition, the pitcher seems to dwarf Devi, making her look particularly fragile. Her face has caught the dim light and her eyes are half shut, her lips parted, as if in an erotic reverie. It's the most beautiful of the three pictures, I saw suddenly, because of the fullness of desire on Devi's face.

Clara shook her head violently, features working, and started toward the door.

"I knew it," she said as she turned to face me. "I knew that you and Devi were lovers."

"Clara—" I began. She was starting to cry. "We're most certainly *not* lovers. She's my *friend.*"

"And what am *I?*" Clara sobbed. "What am *I?*" I felt a swell of compassion for her in that moment, and in response to it, I kind of lied.

"You're my friend, too," I said, though I didn't feel it, and realized in that moment that I hadn't felt it at all for some time. I gave her a one-armed squeeze around the shoulders. She let me.

God, I thought, I'll never be able to keep my resolution to stop lying.

"Stay," I said, "we can talk." I was surprised when she declined. Clara never declined.

"No," she said, "I am very tired." I stood in my doorway as she walked next door, her back oddly rigid and her face down. I called good night as she opened her door, but she disappeared inside without another word.

All night it rained, and I lay in bed awake. I felt guilty, full of sorrow for the pain I'd seen on Clara's face. I asked myself over and over again how I might have been nicer to her all these months, which day I could have tried to be different, more yielding, which moment I could have chosen to let her into my life more generously. But I couldn't have, I thought, I couldn't have done it differently. I shuddered under the sheets, thinking of Clara's need, her unending expectation.

Her suspicion. I couldn't believe I'd been accused of sleeping with Devi *again*. What could they be thinking of, Michael and Clara?

How odd it seemed then to have paired the two of them in my thoughts.

Finally I got up and went back to work on the painting. I worked all night adjusting the light, trying to show it as both muted and somehow invasive, as if what Devi felt in that moment was not meant to be seen nor to be shared with anyone. It was odd, I thought, how the invasiveness of Clara's gaze had brought the emotional subtext of the painting into clearer focus for me. And though I regretted Clara having seen it at all, the experience reminded me of something Michael had often said about the completion of art's process—that a painting is brought to fruition under the gaze of a viewer, just as a book comes to completion beneath the eye of a reader. "*We* don't finish the work," he'd said. "All we can do is put the elements in and hope that we've accomplished what Ezra Pound called 'a sort of inspired mathematics, an equation for human emotion.' "

I guessed that if he were right, that meant that the painting of Devi was good, though it had inspired an uncomfortable depth of emotion in its first viewer.

The next morning I rapped on Clara's door and she answered, her eyes puffy from crying.

"Let's go for a walk," I said. "This is silly. We've got to try and get past all this bad feeling." I believed what I was saying.

"All right," she said, sounding surprisingly docile after last night's anger. "Are you going to ask Devi to go with us?" I thought that by asking me this Clara was trying to show equanimity about my friendship with Devi, which seemed a good sign.

"No," I said, "Devi started that six-week Sunday night workshop at her Larkin office last night, and I'm sure she must be pretty tired this morning since she was already pooped from all the hours she's been sitting for me." I thought it better just to talk openly on the subject so that Clara would see it wasn't some deep, dark secret.

We walked around the square where life was gearing up for the business week; the florist said hello as he set potted plants and buckets of cut flowers out on the sidewalk in front of his store. Over coffee and muffins at Warburton's, Clara said she knew Devi disliked her.

"I have really tried to be her friend," Clara said, "but I guess she found you first. Or you found her."

"But I wasn't looking for her," I said, "the friendship just developed naturally—maybe because we're both involved in the arts." With this remark I was trying to find a way to soothe Clara's hurt feelings and hurt pride; it was a bad call.

"Oh yes," she said bitterly, "the *arts*. We all know that artists are *special*, don't we. People like me—newspaper writers—we are *nothing*."

"I didn't mean anything of the kind," I said rather hotly. I wasn't going to let Clara get me on the defense again. She heard the unaccustomed anger in my tone and immediately backed off.

"Oh, I'm sorry, Norrie, I really am. It's just that I know Devi thinks I'm some sort of lowly creature compared with you."

"That's ridiculous," I said. "Devi isn't that kind of person."

"Oh, I'm sure you believe that," she said, "but I have been on the receiving end of her elitism and disdain."

"Clara, she gave you several thousand dollars when you were in a jam. How can you talk about her that way?"

"I don't know," she said, looking down. "I do like her very much. I'm sorry." And after that she stopped talking about Devi and seemed to relax as we walked up and down Mass Ave, around Harvard Yard, and finally through Radcliffe Yard, where we stopped at a bench to watch squirrels and birds. It was a clear morning, but the ground was still soft and moist from last night's heavy rain, and in the air there was a rich smell of dampened earth.

"She is very beautiful," Clara said then, out of the blue. "Devi is very beautiful."

I didn't answer her; I pretended to be watching two squirrels fighting over an acorn.

On Tuesday I called The Frame-Up to see if my first portrait of Devi was ready to pick up, and the owner's assistant, Lin-le went to check. When she finally returned, after fully six or seven minutes of searching, I had a nervous sensation in my belly before she even began to speak.

"You did not pick up already?" Lin-le asked.

My heart began to pound, but I kept my tone modulated. "No, I sure didn't. Is it ready?"

"Is ready. Was ready, Wendy tell me, but is not there—is not where she think it was."

"Let me talk to Wendy," I said abruptly. Wendy came to the phone quickly.

"Honora," she said breathlessly, "just hold the fort a minute longer. We're looking, and I know it's here because I did this job myself! It looks lovely in the marbled black, by the way. What, Lin-le? Did you find it? No, she didn't find it. Well now this is ridiculous, I must say. I *know* it's here . . ." Her voice trailed off.

I felt like vomiting. The painting of Devi was gone? If so, I'd lost my work—one of the paintings I needed for my colloquium exhibit—and Devi had lost some essential measure of privacy. But who would take a painting? My painting? I wasn't a famous artist. Who would do such a thing?

"You need to find it," I said to Wendy. "This is serious. . . . Wendy, you *have* to find it!"

"I know it's here somewhere," she said. "Well, anyway, it *was*."

After we hung up, I began to shake. Never in all my life as a painter had a piece of my work gone missing. That night I didn't sleep a minute. The sense of invasion was powerful.

I called Liz. I called Michael. I called Ed Hershorn. Why I bothered to call Ed I don't know. Never a sentimentalist, always a pragmatist, he just said, "Well, so you're going to really have to hump it now if you want to get that show of yours ready, huh?"

Finally, I even called my mother. And oddly, as upset as Michael and Liz were about the loss of a painting I'd worked on for weeks, only my mother offered what felt like the proper level of hysteria. And even though her hysteria was misplaced, it kept my own hysteria company—perverse company.

"Oh boy, I don't like this. I don't like this," she said over and over. "I think you're in danger."

"Mother, I don't think my safety is at issue here—and it's not the point."

"What the point is I don't think you're capable of ascertaining right now, little lady. Because you are an artist, and you have to be concerned about the artistic consequences to yourself. But I am a mother, and I am thinking about the safety of my daughter."

"How do you feel this has anything to do with safety?"

"Someone is watching you." A chill ran over me. Even though it was my mother talking, a chill ran over me and stayed.

In the next few days Boston was hit with a surprise snowstorm, and I stayed in until Wednesday's colloquium, very glad to be working at home. My stomach was bothering me, and I knew it was nerves, anxiety, my mother's daily call to tell me I was in danger. I took some small comfort in the fact that I'd brought the red glass pitcher home from the studio before the storm hit—I liked having it nearby when I was working. I tried not to think about the missing painting every minute, but it was always there, and I called Wendy each day to check on it.

Forcing myself to work, I was putting finishing touches on the other two paintings of Devi I'd done at my Larkin studio, but now without benefit of her presence. Still clearly despondent over Paul, she'd been immersing herself in her own poetry whenever she wasn't reading workshop manuscripts. I was sad to see her so worn down by recent events. I couldn't ignore the thought that she'd used so much time for my work instead of her own.

I couldn't bear to tell her my unpleasant news about the painting right now; Devi was going through enough. Yet I knew I had to tell her soon. But maybe Wendy would find it.

Then days went by, and Wendy seemed to be nowhere nearer to finding it.

Finally, when Devi phoned to beg off our weekly trip to the Larkin because she was swamped with workshop reading, I took the opportunity to tell her, very gently, that the painting was missing. I was surprised to find her oddly passive about the idea of her nude image being exposed to unknown eyes. But no, she insisted, it was my loss that bothered her more because she knew it would be impossible to recreate it. As for her own emotions, she said she was in such a state of numbness already that she couldn't find it in her to care who saw the painting.

She told me Paul had called and apologized for how he'd spoken to her on the phone, and when she in turn had apologized for having let him down yet again, he'd said he had forgiven her. Then he'd told her he couldn't talk to her again—*ever* again—because it was too painful for him.

"There's nothing to replace him in my life," she told me sadly, "and I know there never will be. But I seem to be caught in a web of righteousness, and I will stay with my word this time. I've learned a hard lesson about desire and the human will—and about my own limitations." Whenever I saw her now—and it was less often since we weren't working together—she looked tinier than ever, as if the finality of losing what she'd found with Paul had reduced her.

On Wednesday Clara and I went together to the colloquium, which was presented by a science fellow who was studying the effects of paternal drug use on fetuses. The fellows went to dinner at The Bombay Club afterward, and Clara sat beside me and spoke to no one else. She hadn't really made many friends during her year at the Larkin—in fact, I wasn't sure she'd made any but me and Devi—*if* you could count Devi. If you could count me. Poor Clara. As we walked home together after the dinner, it began to drizzle and Clara put her head back and let the light rain catch her face.

"This is nice," she said. "I like the rain when it falls so kindly on the skin." She turned and faced me as we walked back into Brattle Street. "It's nicer this way," she said, "with the two of us. *You* are always kind. Not *everyone* is as kind as you are."

I felt the weight of her words as we walked into our building.

In the night I dreamed the snow falling onto me, falling and falling until I was buried deep inside it, and when I looked around me in the blue-white light, I saw Devi lying there asleep. Her skin was golden brown against the cold whiteness and her long hair fanned out around her on the snow like a black veil. I had a sudden awareness that I was the one who'd put her there, just so I could see how her skin would look encased in snow.

Someone called to me then, I heard the voice and knew I had to leave. I would come back for Devi. I burrowed through the snow above me until I reached the air, and when I stepped out into the bright white day and looked around, I found there was nothing there, no one calling, but in my hand was a tiny red glass stone, smooth and oval shaped. It warmed my hand in the winter air.

It was clear I had to return for Devi soon or she'd suffocate. I slipped the stone under my tongue to protect it and began digging and digging in the snow. Finally I reached the hollow beneath the surface where I'd seen her just minutes before, but now only the imprint of her body remained. I called her name, and as I called, the stone that had been beneath my tongue dropped into the snow and turned to silvery white, invisible among the countless microcrystals on the ground before me.

I returned to the world of air unaccompanied.

14

March was ending and the painting had still not turned up. Wendy called and told me she thought we might have to consider the possibility that it had been stolen. She'd gone so far as to telephone the Cambridge police and tell them she thought a painting was missing, but they seemed to feel that she would need more facts before they could write a formal report. There were a few obvious gaps in the idea, they informed her, motive being a big one. Was the painter famous? Were her works of great monetary value? "Do a spring cleaning," the policeman advised her, "and get back to us when you've done it. I'll bet you find it."

"The little pissant," Wendy sputtered.

Only when I was with Michael did I manage to stop thinking about the missing painting. He came over the day before the big Aperçu party to celebrate our birthdays—his had been the previous day, March 30, and mine would be the next day, April 1. We'd settled on the thirty-first, a Saturday afternoon, for our private birthday celebration because it was the day between the two, and also because there wasn't much chance we'd get to spend a minute of the Fool's day together.

We'd spent a couple of hours at midday looking at apartments, but everything we liked had a ridiculously high asking price or else was just too far outside Boston and Cambridge.

"Time's racing by," Michael said. "It's just two months till June, and it's not getting any easier." I knew he wasn't only making reference to our difficulty in finding somewhere to live, but also to his struggle in keeping to the resolve to make a clean break by the end of my Larkin year.

"Let's not turn it into some grim deadline," I told him. I didn't want to ruin the day with hard reality—there was always time for that. "We'll find something just right before long. Let's open our presents."

Michael and I had agreed to buy each other something to wear for our birthdays. He said he liked the idea that clothing each other was an intimacy; I said I liked that it was clothes.

I'd bought him an Armani shirt at a men's shop on Newbury Street. It was a sort of grayed-celadon with a supple hand and just the slightest sheen, one of those wonderful miracle-fiber blends the Italians have created. I liked it so much I would've been pleased to have one like it for myself. But Armani shirts aren't something you buy in multiples—at least not if you were in my income bracket. I figured after we lived together, I might borrow it sometimes.

"Tomorrow night I'll wear it to the party," he said. "Then, in some dumb, private way we'll be together—maybe that'll help both of us to cope."

It was easy to see Michael was nervous about the party, though we really hadn't talked yet about how hard it was going to be—probably because we knew that we both had to be there, so what was the point? But the tone of his comment about "coping" reminded me that Michael was as leery of our two lives colliding at this event as I was. To make everything all the harder, *Boston Alive* would be filming the proceedings to air later; Ed Hershorn had set that up and was proud of his publicity coup. He had no idea how much anxiety his little accomplishment was producing in his guest of honor. I knew Michael was unnerved by the idea of having the whole thing filmed, his wife and I both in attendance, and all the world watching. It can be painful to see your own life through the unforgiving eye of a television camera.

He'd bought me a lovely white silk robe for my birthday—it was a soft, heavy silk with a wonderful drape and a delicate, just-discernable pattern of satin swans in the weave.

When I tried it on for him, he said, "God, you look like an angel in that white silk. I'd like to fuck you in it."

"Every man wants to fuck an angel," I observed.

"Oh, is that right?" he said, "I thought that was a *nun*."

Very shortly thereafter we adjourned to my bedroom, and as he was undressing I said, "First, I want you to fuck me like a husband." I'd never said anything like that to him before—had never even thought about it before. And although I knew what I meant, I didn't want to examine what had inspired it. It just sounded lovely to me—like something I had no idea of and wanted to experience. It was, in some way, the unaccustomed quotidian become exotic.

"What?" he asked, an uncertain grin on his face. "What do you mean, *like a husband?*"

"I mean I'd like a husbandly, utilitarian fuck—nothing kinky or creative this time, no costume, and hardly any foreplay or kissing—just calm, ordinary, no-frills sex like a husband and wife have." I wanted so much to sample that mysterious marital coupling. I imagined it must be missionary style, very straightforward, nothing fancy. I wanted him to love me that way just once. "That's the birthday fuck I'd like," I told him. "Please?"

" 'Calm' and 'ordinary'," he laughed. "Norrie, I don't feel the least bit calm about you, and fucking you couldn't possibly be ordinary under any circumstances. I'm not sure I'd be able to achieve the proper *affect,* much less *effect.*"

"Ah, come on, can't you at least try?"

"We'll give it a shot. But don't blame me if I'm not calm enough to suit you, darling."

"Deal," I agreed. "And afterward if you still want to fuck me in the swan robe, you can."

"Very kind of you," he said.

We made love very simply then—a couple of tender kisses and a little touching (I had to make him stop that part of it)—and then penetration and the inevitable. Interestingly, we came simultaneously and very, very hard.

Just afterward, when we looked into each other's face, we began to laugh. I'm not sure either of us could have said why we were laughing, but it seemed we couldn't stop. We held each other and rolled around on the bed, laughing.

The next thing I knew, he was hard again. Then he was in me again. Then we came again.

Afterward I said, "Hey, what about the swan robe fuck?"

"What do you think I am," he asked, "Hercules?" My own mother had recently compared *me* to Hercules, but I didn't suppose it was feminine to mention that.

"Well, just remember you had your chance," I said primly.

"You know what I've always wanted to do, but have never in my life done?"

"Been impotent? Admitted you were wrong? I give up."

"Played strip poker."

"Oh, please—you're forty-eight as of yesterday, and you've never played strip poker?"

"Never," he said. "Remember, I'm Irish. The Irish don't like sexy card games. Actually, they don't like *sex*."

"Yes, I've heard that," I said.

I found a deck of cards and let him shuffle because if he'd seen my lightning-fast card-shark shuffle it might have unmanned him, and that wasn't in my best interest. I'd got back into all my clothes, of course, or what was the point?

To cut to the chase, I let him win. I wanted to lose every item of clothing so we could make love again.

If he saw me naked, I knew he'd want to. So I did, he did, and we did.

"I just want you to know," he said afterward, "that I know you let me win."

"What's your point?" I asked, shuffling the deck in my blindingly fast "magic carpet" style.

In all, it was a most delightful birthday celebration. And we still hadn't had the swan robe fuck. "All in good time," he told me at the door.

"Good." I kissed him. "I promise to keep the swan robe at the ready."

"I'll remember that, ma'am," he grinned.

As I observed his graceful, long-legged lope down the hall to the elevator, it occurred to me that the next time I saw him, he'd be with Brenda, not me.

My dread of the Aperçu party grew as I lay in bed trying to fall asleep that night. It was less than twenty-four hours away, and I couldn't imagine how I'd be able to act normal when Michael and Brenda would be standing around nearby, looking for all the world like the happy couple. Liz had been invited but had decided that she wouldn't come out from

San Francisco for the occasion unless I really wanted or needed her to be there.

"It's just I've been traveling so much, and I've missed so many classes," she'd said. "I've had more substitutes this semester than anyone else in the department. Yesterday that weasel Dan Bryant asked me if I used a stunt double." Then she added, "If it'd make it easier for you to have me there, though, I'll find a way to come."

I told her I actually thought it might make things worse to have her there because it's easier to fake equanimity if not too many people in the room know you're in the eighth circle of hell. She decided to send Michael a note and a bottle of champagne.

"Anyway, I'd rather see the two of you together in one place when his wife isn't there, too," she told me. "I'll be coming to Boston in a few weeks on my whirlwind book tour, so maybe the three of us can have dinner together then, or something."

On Sunday I got so nervous about the party that I called Liz and told her I didn't know if I could go through with it.

"Let's cut to the serious stuff," she said. "What're you planning to wear?" Liz was way into fashion, and though I liked clothes a lot, I hadn't had the luxury of buying many in recent years. Canvases and oil paints were pretty expensive.

"Just something I already had," I told her.

"That tells me nothing. Describe."

"A black silk wraparound skirt, kind of longish, with a split," I told her. "It's cut on the bias so it hugs the tush." Michael loved me in that skirt, but now I kept thinking about the fact that I'd been wearing it in the jazz club the night we'd conceived. That association made me sad, and yet in an odd way it also made me feel more a part of Michael's life. "I bought a new top to wear with it," I told Liz. "Actually, I just went back to Jasmine and bought the top that went with it in the first place—black silk-satin, short and loose, with a mandarin collar. The front closes with little loop-and-knot things, and it's sleeveless with cut-away armholes. Kind of sexy in a less-is-more sort of way." Which was the opposite of Brenda, I thought, who seemed always to feel that more was more.

"Well, good," Liz said, "if you're not going to show off your killer legs, at least show those buff upper arms." She knew how to be girlie at just the right moments, and this helped because I knew I was going to need confidence to get through tonight.

"There's a split," I reminded her, in reference to the legs comment. "What?"

"A split in the skirt—so when you walk or sit with your legs crossed, you know, they show just enough."

"All the better," she said. "What shoes are you wearing?" She was trying to keep me occupied in nonanxiety-producing conversation. I knew what she was doing, but I submitted like a lamb. There was nothing like superficiality to soothe the savage breast, and this was profoundly superficial.

"My black faille high heels with the ankle strap."

"Your fuck-me shoes? Good girl," she said, and I laughed. "How are you wearing your hair?" she asked me.

"I'm just wearing it down," I said. Michael liked it down.

"Jewelry?"

"Just a thick silver band on my wrist, the ring Michael gave me for Christmas, and some fake emerald studs I happened on at a street vendor's stall the other day. They look so real and they match fairly well, if you don't look too close, though they'll probably turn my ears green."

"It all sounds perfect," she said. "So, good. Go, and just know the whole time how beautiful you are, sweetie. Don't let anything make you feel sad or . . . well, marginal." Liz knew just what it was going to be like.

I'd thought of making an appointment at the Charles to have my hair and nails done, but when it came right down to it, I felt that if I put too much into my preparations I might be building myself up for a letdown. Expectations could be lethal tonight.

After I'd washed my hair I took a long bath; then I filed my nails and put some clear polish on them. My hair was shiny tonight, but I felt that maybe I should wear it up to look more elegant. Maybe it was tacky to wear it down. But finally I just ran a brush though it and let it go; expectations, I reminded myself, would ruin my evening. Just at that moment, as in a bad movie, the phone rang. It was Michael, of course.

"Norrie," he said, "shit. I don't know what to do. Those damned *Boston Alive* people have been all over us here at the house this afternoon—that fucking Hershorn and his big publicity grab—and I just . . . I'm not sure you should go tonight. I'm really not."

"What?" I couldn't believe Michael was saying this. He knew I was expected to go. Even on leave as I was, there was no escaping the fact that I was his book designer, head of Aperçu's design staff. Sure, I'd been having cold feet today, too, but I didn't want him telling me not to go!

"It was already going to be hard for both of us tonight," he said. "You know that. And now with these goddamn TV types hanging around, it's just going to be that much more stressful." He paused, and I said nothing. "Maybe you could just say you're indisposed. There's an intestinal bug going around right now—I just don't know if either one of us wants to go through this."

"Look, Michael, I'm all dressed and ready to go. And since I just talked to Ed Hershorn a few minutes ago, there's no way I can play sick. I can't believe you're saying all this. Now."

"Norrie, you know I'm thinking of you, too. I can just foresee a terrible occasion tonight, if . . ." He faltered.

"If I'm there?"

"Well, yeah, terrible for both of us. It's inevitable, isn't it? I'm afraid you're going to be very upset by all of it. No doubt Brenda will be beside me all evening—she and that tubby interviewer are getting along like a house afire."

That Brenda, I thought. She was a clever one.

"I can take care of myself," I said huffily. Clearly, I would have to. "I have a professional life, too, you know. Don't forget, my employer's throwing this party."

"Right," he said, his voice suddenly deflated of its nervous energy. "Okay. But don't be mad at me if I'm not able to talk to you."

"Are you saying this to a *lot* of your friends?" I didn't wait for him to answer; I just hung up. Then waited beside the phone for him to call back and tell me how sorry he was for being a schmuck. He didn't.

I grabbed my black trench coat and left the apartment, glad not to have to worry about running into Clara. She'd told me she was going out tonight to do some research on her book at the Widener Library.

On the way down, the elevator stopped at the third floor and Devi got on.

"Norrie," she said, "how nice to see you! You look beautiful! Where are you going?"

"To that party my employer's having for one of our authors," I said. "Michael Sullivan, who just won the National Book Critics Circle Award for his novel, *This Cold Heaven*."

"Oh yes," she said, "I hear it's a wonderful book. Do you know him well?"

I've heard that during a tornado a strand of straw can pierce a rock. Sometimes an unexpected question penetrates your defenses that way and strikes you dumb. I couldn't lie to Devi, could not, yet neither could I tell her that Michael Sullivan was my married lover. I guess I paused for too long before answering. "Yes," I finally said, "I do." Devi looked at me intensely then, and I felt some acknowledgment passing between us. I knew she'd figured it out, and after a momentary stomach pang, I found I was glad. We wouldn't speak of it—we wouldn't need to—but it was a comfort to think it possible that finally she knew the rest of the secret that had isolated me from almost everyone for so long.

"Well, I hope the evening goes well for you." She squeezed my arm, dozens of thin wrist bangles jingling on her own arm with the movement.

"Thanks," I said. "I hope so, too. Where are you headed?"

"To the final night of my poetry workshop. To tell the truth, I'll be glad to have it behind me—I really must concentrate on my own writing." She'd taken on this unpaid workshop series for a group of unaffiliated poets in the community in the first place because, she'd told me, she believed in "contributing something to the community you live in." I knew I was much more selfish in the pursuit of my art than Devi was—or had become so, of late. I resolved to find some kind of community work to do again. I remembered the volunteer painting workshops I used to do for a group of formerly homeless women who had been given rooms at the Y downtown. And I'd done painting classes at Ida's retirement home a few times. It was only in the last couple of years, really, that I'd pulled away from the world so thoroughly.

I looked at Devi. "Hey, you look pretty wonderful yourself," I told her. Though she seemed a little tired, she did look lovely tonight, in a loose, yellow silk tunic with a long, tan gabardine skirt and brown leather boots. "I keep forgetting that your group meets on Sunday nights. That seems such an awful night to have to go out for something like that."

"Oh well," she said, "which night of the week it is makes no difference to me while I'm at the Larkin and have no other job. So many of the poets in my group are graduate students or academics, and they find it easier to do these kinds of things on a weekend."

As we got off the elevator in the lobby, she put her hand on my arm briefly, then removed it. "Norrie," she said, "I wonder, could you come down to my place when you get back from your party? I think I need to talk a bit." Devi so rarely asked for any kind of help or counsel that I couldn't help feeling something must be wrong.

"Sure," I said, "though I don't think I'll be back before eleven-thirty or twelve."

"But what's midnight to two veteran nightowls!" She smiled. "My workshop ends at ten. I'll be back home by ten-thirty or so and will probably be at work on my poem. By the time you get to my door, I'll undoubtedly be dying for a break. And really, I need your advice."

"Of course, Devi . . . are you okay?"

"Oh, we'll talk later," she smiled, but I saw fatigue mingling on her face with something else—something like uncertainty or unease. Quickly she covered the look and grinned her old grin. "Have a wonderful party," she said, "and I'll tell you everything tonight—I promise!"

We walked out to the street together in the crisp spring air and bid each other good-bye outside the entrance to the courtyard, Devi giving me one of her tidy, brief hugs. She headed off to her Larkin office, and I headed down to the Charles Hotel for Michael's party.

It was nearly eight o'clock, and the streets were still fairly busy; they would be practically deserted by the time I came home. I was really dreading the party now. How could Michael pull such a last minute fink-out on me? We'd known all along that the evening was going to be hard for both of us; now it would be even worse—at least for me—because I'd have to know all evening that he didn't want me there.

The first thing I saw when I entered the party was Brenda standing with Michael, her arm through his, both of them talking on camera to Bob Brock, the *Boston Alive* interviewer Michael had complained about earlier. She was wearing a knee-length skirt suit of power red, buttoned up with large gold buttons, a triple strand of pearls at her neck. Her hair seemed to have been bleached even blonder than before, and it was that kind of helmet hair, but except for that I had to admit she looked nice.

She was even smiling for once, diamond-and-pearl earrings glinting in the light, her long nails the same red as her suit. She looked for all the world like the wife of a presidential candidate.

I was pleased to note that her legs were skinny and chickenlike. Thank the Lord for small favors, as my mother would say.

Michael was wearing my shirt, I noticed, with a beautifully cut charcoal suit. His wavy hair was slightly tousled, as usual. He looked pretty sensational.

The on-camera segment seemed to be just winding up, and people were approaching Michael and Brenda to talk. I saw his eyes flicker toward me and away again as if he hadn't seen me. Couldn't he just say hi? Well, fine, I thought, two can play at this game. As I ambled past, looking everywhere but at them, I felt both intense pain and a manic, snotty sort of liberation. Fine, I told myself again, I could enjoy this party without Michael.

I went directly to the hors d'oeuvre table and began plowing into the canapés, starting with crab rolls and moving right along to stuffed mushrooms, caviar, artichoke hearts with melted lemon butter, and miniature spinach tarts. I wound up with chocolate-covered strawberries and apricots. When I felt the immediate chocolate rush, I wolfed some Godiva chocolates nearby, and then some obscene truffles. When finally I could eat no more, there was nothing to do but socialize.

Ed Hershorn was standing near the table, so I went directly to him. Ed was easy to talk to. And anyway, if I had to be here tonight because he expected it, I wanted to be sure he saw me.

"Wow," Ed said. "Look at you!" I thought I might've dropped some food on myself so I looked down at my blouse. "I didn't mean literally to look at yourself," he said, "I just meant you look pretty good for a lumpen prole chick who spends all her time locked up with an easel."

"Shut up," I said. "Where'd you rent the suit?"

He laughed and I realized he wasn't alone when he turned to a pale, nice-looking man and rather pretty red-haired woman who were standing beside him. Imagine my surprise when they turned out to be Michael's pal Tom Beshears and his wife, Nicola. When Ed introduced us, he explained to them that I was "a real artist" whose day job was doing art for Aperçu.

"She did the cover for Michael's book!" he said, jerking a stubby thumb at me.

Both Tom and Nicola exclaimed over how wonderful the cover was, and I could have killed Ed for bringing it up as if we were fishing for praise. Before long the four of us got into an animated conversation about the difficulty of pursuing careers in the arts today. I thought both Tom and Nicola were wonderful. Even after Ed migrated to another part of the room, the three of us went on trading wild riffs on politics, poetry, and theater. They'd been to see Anna Deveare Smith's new one-woman theater piece and had been very moved by it.

Just as I was musing aloud that Anna Deveare Smith and Anna Nicole Smith might be nonidentical twins, Michael passed by and saw us laughing; he looked the other way and called out to someone on the other side of the room. What a schmo he was tonight. What in the world was happening to him?

A little later, during Michael's brief acknowledgment of gratitude to Aperçu for the party and for "believing in the work when no one knew my name," people gathered around the podium with their drinks, and Brenda happened to stand beside me with Bob Brock on the other side of her, putting the two of us together in Michael's field of vision. I was sure that two or three times as he spoke, he took in the contrast between his brittle, power-suited wife and the woman beside her in black silk, the woman he truly loved (anyway, that was how I was scripting his thoughts).

As he finished talking there was wild applause, and when he walked back to Brenda afterward she embraced him, letting her carefully manicured hand linger on the shoulder of the shirt I'd given him just yesterday. I willed a message to her: *Don't touch my shirt!* And to Michael: *You were inside me yesterday—three times.* I wanted to leave the party right then, but it was only 8:30 and my own pride and stubbornness wouldn't allow me to run.

I'll probably always wonder if things might have been different if I'd only left when I first had the impulse to go. I think of it all the time. But at that moment, my worst problem was witnessing Michael playing the role of devoted husband to his estranged wife.

At around nine, when Brenda was head-to-head with the TV interviewer on camera, I approached Michael and said hello. This was ridiculous, and I wasn't going home without the two of us speaking. Michael said hello back to me and even smiled, but he sounded forced and stiff as if he were speaking to an insurance salesman who might pin him down with some schtick about term life. "Good to see you!" he said heartily.

"Michael," I said in a low voice, "stop this right now!" He looked at me then as if a fog were lifting, and the next thing I knew he was leading me off to a quieter corner.

"Norrie, I'm going nuts here. I hate this. I'll come over late tonight after I leave this bloody burlesque show. I need to be alone with you." My heart flopped.

"Oh, Michael, I can't. I promised Devi I'd go down to her place later."

"Devi. Great."

"Don't be that way," I protested. "She's feeling upset about something, and she asked me to come over. I know something's wrong."

"Okay, look," he said, brightening, "I've got an idea. This damned party is no fun for you anyway, and you've put in an appearance now, so your publicity-mongering boss is satisfied. Why don't you just leave now to go and see Devi, and I'll pop over to your place as soon as it's decent to leave the party—it might be eleven-thirty or twelve, but no later, I promise. Brenda came in her own car tonight because she has to leave early, so it'll be easy for me to stop and see you on my way home."

"Michael, I'm so sorry but I just can't. Devi won't be getting home till at least ten-thirty herself—she's teaching a workshop. And I really have to go because she needs me. I promised."

"I need you, too, Norrie," he said. "Does that matter?"

"Of course it matters, but Devi—"

"Right," he said. "Go see your Devi." He turned and walked away from me. I couldn't believe it. I stood there for a minute just looking witless.

I wandered around the goddamn party then, lumbering into people and saying excuse me, feeling alone and stupid and sad. I wanted Michael to talk to me again, to make things normal, but he was in demand tonight and there was always someone talking animatedly into his face.

At nine-thirty I saw Brenda leave, and I thought Michael might calm down then and approach me again, but now he seemed to be in deep conversation with Bob Brock. I spent some time talking to Bebe Rust—

she was Michael's editor—but afterward I had no idea what we'd talked about. It was just a matter of filling time for me. When I looked over next, Michael was gone. I walked around the room but couldn't see him anywhere.

"Where'd our guest of honor go?" I heard Ed Hershorn saying to his bilious ex-wife a few minutes later. "It's barely ten-thirty. Did he wimp out on us or what?"

Could he really have left without saying good-bye to me—after our sad little encounter? It just wasn't like Michael to be this way.

I hung around for a while then, thinking Michael might come back, but he didn't. Finally I decided to leave, but then I kept getting caught in meaningless conversations with people I barely knew. Where were all these people a little while ago when I felt like a lonely loser? I managed to make my escape at a little past eleven, feeling very low.

Maybe I should have just left after my ridiculous exchange with Michael, but I know there's no point in making hypothetical calculations about time. It wouldn't change anything now.

I walked down the wide steps at the entrance to the Charles, noting that it was almost eleven-thirty, and I was glad I'd warned Devi how late I might be. She'd said it wouldn't matter what time it was, and I knew she worked into the night the way I did.

As I walked toward home, the streets were quiet except for a siren in the distance. Then as I felt the chill of an ocean breeze, it occurred to me that I'd forgotten my trench coat. Damn. I headed briskly back to the Charles to retrieve it.

A few minutes later as I was heading through the lobby again, coat over my shoulders, I ran into Delia Hershorn, Ed's bridge-playing ex-wife, who pinned me there for ten minutes yakking in her shrill voice about a friend of hers who'd also been a Larkin fellow sometime back in the seventies. She didn't ask a single question about my Larkin year, which was just how Delia was—all output, no intake. It was easy to see why Ed had never married again—post-traumatic stress disorder obviously.

By the time I was finally walking up Brattle, it was after midnight and I was tired; if it weren't for the fact that Devi needed me tonight, I thought, I'd just phone her and beg off.

As I neared our building, I was startled to see an ambulance and two police cars parked at the curb. There were four other cars parked at odd angles in the street: one was a police cruiser and the three others looked like unmarked police cars. There was a small crowd of people standing off to each side of some temporary barricades, and as I got closer I recognized a couple of people as tenants in our building.

Above the barricades that blocked the sidewalk all the way to the curb, there was yellow crime tape, which extended at each side to the courtyard archway. Between the lengths of tape I saw something dark like motor oil tracing a path across the sidewalk and into the courtyard, where several policemen had gathered, most of them with clear plastic booties over their shoes. People were crowding close to the iron fence in an effort to see what was going on.

There was a short policeman standing just outside the barricades telling people they couldn't go in; I saw another policeman on the steps at the front of our building, apparently barring anyone from coming out across the crime scene. I heard two officers asking people where they'd been and who or what they might have seen between ten and eleven tonight.

"What happened?" I asked a blond girl I recognized as another fourth-floor resident.

"I'm not sure, we just got here, but I think someone was raped or something," she told me. "They're with her in there." She pointed to the courtyard. "She's on the ground." My God, I thought, it might be Devi or Clara, both of whom had gone out tonight.

"No, Jen," the man in front of us turned to her and said, "that's not it. I heard them say someone's dead. Three people over there were coming home and found the body. It's a woman."

I pushed my way through the crowd, heedless of everyone in my path; a man said *Hey* as I pushed past, but I kept burrowing through till I got to the front. Through the wrought-iron fence grating I could see the backs of three detectives with plastic booties on their shoes; they were bending over the weathered bricks of our courtyard looking at something I couldn't see—it had to be the body. Then one of them opened a white blanket and bent forward with it to lay it over the body. I moved farther down along the fence past the men to where I could see the blanket-covered body; there was blood puddling around it and already beginning to soak through the blanket. Then I saw the dark and slender arm extending from beneath the blanket, the dozens of bangles on it.

226

"Devi!" I screamed. "Devi!" I began to shake all over and just then a uniformed policeman made his way though the crowd to me.

"Ma'am?" he said, taking my elbow, "do you think you might know the victim?"

"It's Devi," I said, "Devi Bhujander."

As I said the name I heard someone behind me say, "God, that's the Indian poet—she's really well known."

"Devi's my friend," I said to the cop. "Is she, is she—" I knew the answer but couldn't stop the words from coming out.

"I'm sorry, ma'am," he said. "The victim had already expired when we arrived on the scene half an hour ago. Could we go over to the patrol car and talk? I'd like to ask you a few questions. But first I'm going to need you to make an identification."

"Oh, God," I said. "Oh, God, I can't." But he led me into the court-yard, instructing me to step carefully wherever he stepped, to be certain my feet wouldn't make contact with any blood evidence. Here and there the deep red of spilled blood shone in the light from the lampposts at either side of the front doors.

He uncovered the body slowly, starting at the head, as if he knew better than to show me all of the mayhem at once. The dead woman's face was turned away, but I saw that this was a short-haired woman!

"Oh, thank God," I blurted. "I'm sorry—I just mean thank God it's not . . ." My voice trailed off as he continued to pull the blanket back, and now I saw the blood-soaked yellow silk tunic and tan skirt Devi had been wearing when we parted this evening. He moved me (literally moved me like a doll because I seemed to be paralyzed on the spot) around to the other side of the body so that I could see the face.

God, oh God, it was Devi, her beautiful eyes open, mouth agape as if to cry for help, a look of terror on her dear face. Her throat was cut deeply—it gaped, a long bloody gash—and there were stab wounds over her breasts and thighs.

"I'm sure she didn't suffer at all once her throat was cut," the officer said, seeing my face. "The rest was just . . ." His voice trailed away, and one of his hands gestured lamely.

"Devi has long hair!" I cried, "Where's her braid?" I felt frissons of panic.

"She had a braid?" He walked around to the back of Devi's head and examined it. "Yeah," he muttered, "looks like it was hacked off here." He stood and looked at me. "Well, it's nowhere around here. The braid's gone. Perpetrator must've taken it for a souvenir."

Everything around me suddenly became a scene viewed through the distant end of a telescope—nothing here was real or connected to me. I remember that I did not resist the police officer when he led me by the elbow to one of the police cruisers in the street. He sat me in front on the passenger side and stood on the street beside the door, leaning his clipboard on the doorframe. After recording my name and address, he began asking me things about Devi—where she'd been tonight, what time she'd been expected back, things like that. I couldn't seem to make my lips work at first, and he gave me a Dixie cup of water from a thermos that was lying on the seat. The water tasted stale, like water from a puddle. I answered every question I could; *due home at ten-thirty, was leading a poetry workshop,* all that.

"She got any family around here you know about?" the officer asked.

"No. She has a brother in London and parents and a sister in Delhi." He looked blank. "India," I added, just in case.

"And you're a close friend?"

"Yeah, I guess I'm the only one she knows really well here—she's a very private person. I can't imagine anyone wanting to hurt her. Why would someone do this? *The fucker,*" I blurted, "The fucker." And then I began to cry again. He waited patiently for me to compose myself and then began questioning me again.

"Have you seen any suspicious characters around the neighborhood lately?"

"Sure," I said, "lots of them, depending on what you mean by suspicious. I mean, there's a druggie called Mutton who sits on the bench down by Radcliffe Yard and offers a toke to every woman who passes by. But I think he's basically harmless . . . except for that."

"Well, this could have been a random act of violence, so any street person is a potential suspect," the officer was telling me.

I nodded numbly. I couldn't bear this. I wanted it not to be true, Devi's death, I wanted it just to be another one of my stupid dreams. But I realized she had no one here but me to be her advocate, so I had to be strong for her. I tried to muster my feeble forces.

"It wasn't a robbery," the skinny officer was saying, "we're pretty sure of that because we found the victim's undisturbed purse. We weren't sure it was hers before you ID'd her because there was no photo identification inside, just a Harvard ID card. The purse had a fair amount of cash in it and was found in plain sight on the street—right near the curb, like it was thrown away deliberately—probably by the victim herself, as a way of—"

"—getting the attacker to run after it," I interrupted. "I know. The Harvard Police taught us about that in a self-defense class at the Larkin."

"Larkin?"

"Institute," I said. "At Radcliffe. It's a research and study center for women."

"Okay, yeah, over on Concord Street. Well look, I have to ask you this, ma'am. Did the victim use any kind of street narcotics?"

"Jesus," I said, "of course not."

"Remember," he said, "this is nothing personal. We have to ask these things or our detectives won't know where to start the investigation. Do you understand?"

"Yeah," I said. I couldn't look at him. *Street narcotics.*

"Do you know anyone who might want the victim dead?" he continued.

"God, *no!*" I said sharply, and then I remembered Devi telling me once that Paul had said he sometimes felt it would be a relief if she were dead, if she couldn't be by his side—or something like that. "Oh, God," I said in a small voice.

"What?" he asked. "D'you know of an enemy she might've had?"

"Not an enemy," I mumbled. "I mean, he was her former lover, and there was kind of a bitter argument a few weeks ago—then he called her once and left kind of a creepy message. But he apologized later. Would someone really come from so far away to commit a crime of passion?"

"Anything in a case like this has to be looked at," the officer said, "but we'll let our homicide squad decide what needs to be checked out."

At that moment a burly detective in a tan polyester suit came over to the car with his own clipboard, and the officer I'd been talking to instructed me to tell Detective Burns everything I knew "about this ex-boyfriend of the victim." I struggled to remember everything Devi had told me.

"His name is Paul Monnard," I told Detective Burns, "M-O-N-N-A-R-D,

I think, and he lives in London." Burns was writing down what I said in that laborious policeman's printing, and I felt I should talk more slowly so he could keep up with me but it was hard to slow the words down in my state of stress. At that moment I couldn't recall whether Paul was an Englishman of French derivation or still a French citizen, I told the detective; I remembered Devi telling me that Paul was the longtime friend of a poet she knew, which was how she'd met him. That was all I could remember. That and that he taught somewhere in London— philosophy, I thought.

Suddenly I thought of the missing painting, and at the thought of it I took in my breath sharply.

"What is it?" the officer asked me.

I shook my head. "It . . . it probably has nothing to do with anything, but a painting I did of Devi—a . . . a nude—was stolen from The Frame-Up last month."

"Frame up?"

"It's a picture framing shop. Over on Mass Ave."

"Whereabouts on Mass Ave?"

"Just down from Au Bon Pain." He was writing and nodding.

"So you're telling me that someone stole a painting you did of the victim." Victim. I hated him to call her that.

"Of Devi," I said quietly. "Yes. You should go and talk to the proprietor, Wendy. She can fill you in on the details better than I could." He wrote something again.

Just then, past the detective's shoulder, I saw Devi's body being rolled away on a gurney, strapped down and covered with the white blanket, its center gone red with blood. Devi was so tiny beneath the sheet, her body like a child's body; it was the saddest sight I'd ever seen. I began to cry quietly and couldn't seem to stop. Detective Burns gave me a handkerchief and his card.

"I'm going to call you tomorrow," he told me, "to do some follow-up when you might be feeling a little clearer about things, might remember something you couldn't think of tonight. And you can call me anytime if you think of anything else." He pointed to the card. "I have e-mail, too, see there?—and voice mail. And there's my fax number there."

Altogether I was out in the street for two hours. Finally the police conferred with the super, Joe O'Connor, who'd been called back to

Brattle at some point, and it was decided that everyone would use the back door until the investigators had finished with the crime scene. Our keys would also work in that lock, so we could let ourselves in and out the back way till further notice.

It was after 2:00 A.M. when I marched with the other tenants in a somber queue around to the back door of the building. No one was talking now. Once inside, most of them hurried to the elevator. They would have to go up in shifts, I knew, and it might take two or three trips to accommodate all of them in the small elevator. I took the stairs rather than stand there, and there were three others who took the stairs with me, including the blond woman I'd spoken to earlier and her companion, but no one spoke. There'd been a lot of buzz earlier out on the street, but now it was as if the reality of the killing had settled in: Everyone was now inside the apartment building the murdered woman had been trying to come home to tonight when someone stopped her.

When I got to the fourth floor and was heading toward my door, I thought of Clara. Oh, God, she'd have to be told about Devi—and I guessed I would have to be the one to tell her—but I couldn't bear to talk to anyone right now, especially Clara.

I could hear opera music playing full blast inside her apartment as I passed her door. I recognized *Aida* then, the same Leontyne Price recording I'd been listening to so often lately. With it playing so loud in there, Clara had probably heard nothing going on in the street four stories down. She was probably at work on her book, and I could imagine how the sounds of the sirens had merged with the strains of *Aida,* Price's unearthly soprano. It may well have been playing up here while someone in the courtyard below slashed my friend to death.

Shivering, I stood just outside Clara's door for a full five minutes, and almost knocked several times, but finally could not bear to deal with her tonight. I hoped I'd be forgiven for waiting till morning to tell her that our beautiful Indian poet was dead. If this was wrong of me, I'd take my lumps tomorrow. Nothing mattered, suddenly, but that Devi was gone out of the world.

When I closed my apartment door, I could still hear Clara's music. I would never be able to listen to *Aida* again.

I sat at the foot of my bed, limp and unable to think what to do next. My restless eyes stopped at the easel, which held the painting of Devi

231

lying on the red blanket, eyes half shut. I couldn't bear to look at it. I sat there for a long time then, seeing nothing. After a while I noticed that my answering machine was blinking the signal for two calls. Numbly I pushed the button, and my heart crashed against my ribs as I heard Devi's voice.

"Norrie, this is Devi. I imagine you may still be at your party, but on the possibility you might have come home early, I just wanted to let you know that I'm leaving my office a bit later than I'd planned. I've had a marvelous idea for my poem about the connection between the Swadhisthan chakra and jealousy! I'm thinking I'll include a reference to the Third Eye after all—but I'll explain later. It's kind of an interesting twist about where jealousy originates. I was jotting down some notes for it after my students left, and I'm just leaving now. I hope you'll still want to stop by tonight . . . I'm feeling the need of some counsel. It's ten-thirty now, I think [a pause, as if she were checking her watch]. Yes, ten-thirty. So I hope I'll see you later, my dear! We'll have a fine chat, if you still feel like it! Bye bye." My eyes filled.

I knew I was going to have to turn this tape over to the police, and it pained me to part with it. I would copy it on my boom box recorder before I called Detective Burns. I played the whole message a second time—the voice I would never hear again any other way—before listening to the other call, which turned out to be from Michael.

His voice filled the air of my bedroom, and it actually took me a minute to recognize it. It sounded both familiar and oddly foreign to my ears. I listened as the message went on and on.

"Norrie," he said, "Norrie, are you there? I don't know where you could be at this hour . . . *surely* you're home by now, it's nearly 1:00 A.M." He sighed, then blew out that puff of air. "Maybe you're mad at me and just not picking up—and, and I can't really blame you. I was an asshole tonight. I'm sorry. God, I'm sorry. I don't know what came over me. I've been driving around for hours, feeling ashamed and confused and . . . I don't know . . . I guess I just, just couldn't handle being on TV tonight with one foot in each world at the same time. It just sort of freaked me out. Please try to understand. You looked so beautiful. I saw you standing beside Brenda when I was up there talking, and my voice caught in my throat. So are you there? Please pick up if you are, Norrie, for *Chrissakes*." He sighed again, and when he spoke this time it was with a slightly formal tone. "All right . . . I can only ask you to forgive me. What more can I say? Good night. Good night . . . I guess that's what more I can say."

I lay on my bed then, fully clothed, and closed my eyes. I couldn't call Michael at home this late anyway, but the truth was I didn't want to talk to him. Or anyone. Somewhere in the distance I heard a siren and wondered who else might have their lives shattered tonight. I didn't sleep at all, didn't want to. It didn't seem right to have the comfort of sleep right then. I tried to think of Devi alive, Devi laughing at something too obscurely funny for me, Devi eating *dhal* with her fingers, Devi pouring tea into chipped cups in her beautiful red room. But every living image slid away; I couldn't hold a single one in my mind.

All night I saw Devi lying in the courtyard in a pool of blood that spread dark and glistening like port wine, her beautiful black hair hacked away. All night my eyes cried of their own accord though I tried to stop them. Sometimes eyes will do that, and there's not a thing you can do about it.

In dreams I see her asleep on my red blanket, her eyes straining to open, but she can't muster the strength it would take to rouse. As in a fairy tale, I know that if I kiss her she'll waken, but I can't. In the dream I can't. I'm afraid to kiss a woman.

I watch her for hours. She doesn't stir. I see her lips, blood red, her eyes closed.

Clara comes into the darkened room then and gazes at Devi, then looks at me as I stand beside the blanket where our friend lies.

All it would have taken was a kiss, Clara tells me, I would have done that for her. But now it's too late, she says. You let her die.

15

The world's an indifferent place; it eats its own young and doesn't think twice. Nothing really matters, or not for very long. Devi was dead and yet day turned into night turned into day, car alarms shrieked each night, and the back-up beeps of trash trucks sang me awake in the morning.

Everything went on as usual in Harvard Square—traffic, shopping, the tightrope walker in front of the Coop. Several times I'd seen people laughing and talking right next to the bloodstain on the sidewalk, a stain that could still be clearly seen despite a hosing down the super had given it. Devi's blood. The police called that stain the "product of the killer's first blow." It was shaped like nothing. I couldn't assign the contour of any quotidian object to it—flower, seashell, bird, face, foot, boat. It was amorphous; it looked like nothing so much as a bruise.

Michael told me that for a brief time on the morning after the crime, he'd been afraid I was the victim. Over breakfast he'd read in the *Globe* that there had been a killing at around 11:00 P.M. in front of 82 Brattle, and that the victim was a Larkin fellow. Identification was being withheld pending notification of next of kin. The *Globe* had managed to get that brief mention of the killing into the morning edition before the police had given out an identity for the victim. Michael put two and two together: I'd not been home when he phoned late Sunday night; he knew I'd walked home alone from the party sometime after he left. He threw the newspaper down and ran to the phone, sure it was me.

When I answered his call at seven-thirty that Monday morning, Michael's voice was thin and cracking. "Oh, God," he said. "Thank God you're all right. I thought you were the one—I thought you were dead."

"Only in spirit," I said grimly. I really didn't feel much like talking to him, and I didn't know how to explain it. So I told him I had to go over to the Larkin, which I did. "And first I have to go and tell Clara that Devi's dead." As I said it, I realized it was my first mention of *who* had been killed. "Sorry," I said, "my head is a mess. It was Devi who was killed."

"Oh, no," he said. "Oh, Jesus, Norrie, I'm so sorry. What happened? Do you know?"

The last thing I wanted to do was rehearse the known details of Devi's death over the phone.

"I really can't talk right now, Michael. But I'm sure it'll all be on the evening news tonight. You can find out then." I knew I sounded curt.

"All right," he said, and I heard the uncertainty in his voice, but I couldn't find it in me to reassure him. *Now you don't have to be jealous of Devi anymore*, I thought bitterly.

"Talk to you some other time," I said, trying to wrap up this phone call.

"Maybe tonight?"

"I don't think so."

"Norrie, I'm so terribly sorry about Devi. God, and I'm sorry, too, for how I acted about the plans you had with her last night. I was such a shit. I know how upset you are about Devi, but is this also about that— how I treated you last night? Because I want to talk to you about that. I was an ass, and I'm just so sorry." I couldn't believe it. How pathetic. My voice was cold when I spoke.

"My friend was murdered last night, Michael. Believe it or not, that's enough to account for my mood—even without factoring *you* in."

"What an ass I am," he said again. "I'm sorry."

"Forget it. I just really don't feel like talking, I just don't. Maybe you can try me tonight. Or tomorrow."

I wasn't sure I would answer, though. "I just don't feel like talking," I said again.

When I knocked at Clara's door on my way to the Larkin, I was filled with dread of the grim duty ahead of me—telling the histrionic Clara that Devi had been killed. I waited in the hall but there was no answer. Then I remembered that Clara audited a 7:30 A.M. class at Harvard on Mondays, and I realized this meant she'd be finding out about Devi's

236

grisly death from strangers before I could talk to her. I felt ashamed of myself for avoiding this unpleasant moment last night, for taking the easy way out and walking right past her door when I could hear her music playing and knew she was home.

I'd told Michael I didn't feel like talking to anyone, but the truth was I did want to talk to the women at the Larkin; I felt that distinctly as I walked the eight blocks there that morning, blinking away tears and looking over my shoulder all the way. It seemed as if no one else could possibly understand what I was feeling—the grief and the fear and the shock. When I got to the Larkin administration building, I found most of the fellows and staff in the common room; it was very still, a tableau of grief. Then I saw Clara near the edge of one small group, crying her eyes out. I felt guilty again for not having told her last night.

Later, walking home with her, I didn't say anything about my omission, and she didn't ask me when or how I'd found out about the murder. We were both quiet, and I found that a relief. I was surprised to feel Clara's presence beside me a comfort.

As we walked up Garden Street, suddenly Clara said, "It's my fault. I put my bad feelings out into the air. Now she is dead. I will never forgive myself."

"Clara," I said, "that makes no sense. Of course it's not your fault. But I know how you feel. I keep thinking of things I could have done differently, too. I could have left that damned party earlier, for one thing. Why did I stay? Maybe Devi would still be alive if I'd come home earlier."

"The world is ruined," she said, and she looked at the ground all the rest of the way home; we spoke no more. We hugged briefly outside our doors, and I heard her night lock go on as soon as she was inside. I followed suit.

I got three phone calls from other parts of the United States in the days after Devi died, all of the callers casual acquaintances who'd seen news accounts of the slaying in the national press and knew I was at the Larkin, so I guess they figured I might have the inside scoop. One of them, a friend of my mother's in Los Angeles, called to ask me if I thought Devi "had done anything to bring it on herself."

It was bad enough to hear such things from three thousand miles away, but even in Cambridge the rumor mill was starting. Within the Harvard community and Cambridge in general, people who'd never met Devi were speculating and making innuendos about her "secret life," possible drug connections, romantic intrigue, all sorts of things that were based on absolutely nothing real—other than the newspaper's assertion that Devi was "a very private woman, a fabled international beauty."

Three or four times I heard Cambridge people asking, nearly verbatim, the question my mother's friend had asked: *Do you think she did anything to bring it on herself?*

Devi was such a gentle, ethical person. I couldn't imagine anyone thinking anything smutty or bad about her. But then neither could I imagine anyone being motivated to harm her, and someone had. Some of the Larkies began saying that it was possible we were all in danger. After all, Devi had been coming from her Larkin office when she was killed, possibly by someone who'd followed her home from there. What if someone was systematically going after Larkin fellows? It was possible, some of the women asserted, because the institute had a feminist orientation and maybe some disgruntled man was out to get "uppity women."

In the days following Devi's murder there seemed nowhere to be but the Larkin, because it wasn't "the world." I didn't want to be alone in my apartment during the day; it was bad enough at night when I lay in bed awake, straining to identify every creak and settling of the walls, every knock of the pipes inside them.

And until they'd found the killer, I was scared going out after dark, even just to walk around Harvard Square, *especially* to walk around the square. After all the years I'd felt safe alone on those streets at all hours, suddenly I was terrified. I wouldn't go anywhere after nightfall unless I had a ride. Even in daytime I found myself looking over my shoulder. I wouldn't meet the eyes of anyone coming my way on the sidewalk. Devi's murder was the end of feeling safe. Walking the eight blocks to the Larkin in broad daylight, if I heard footsteps behind me I'd turn quickly and look; if it was a man, any man at all, I'd cross the street even if it took me out of my way. One evening on the way home, twilight deepened toward night more quickly than I'd estimated and I ran, actually ran, all the way back to Brattle.

Whenever I was home, I paced my apartment floors. Sometimes now in the rhythm of my footsteps I heard the echo of my mother's words, "Someone is watching you. Someone is watching you." The idea didn't seem so crazy anymore. And of course, it was impossible not to concede the likelihood that the missing painting was tied to Devi's death. Someone had killed her, someone had taken a painting of her—how could the two events not be related? And yet, how would the killer know about the painting's whereabouts? In my mind now, the painting's worth was no longer tied to the time and work I'd put into it; now its value lay in its relation to Devi and in whatever clue its disappearance might offer in the solution of the crime. The Cambridge police had finally taken their written report about the missing painting from Wendy at The Frame-Up, so it was clear they, too, saw a connection.

The Larkies left fresh flowers every day in the courtyard on the spot where Devi had died, and they planted a flowering plum tree in her memory at the edge of the Larkin green. They staged three "Take Back the Night" marches around Cambridge, though some of us were afraid to attend. Well, *I* was afraid to attend, and I took some paltry comfort in the suspicion that others might be, too. I never liked admitting fear, maybe because I'd watched the way my mother gave into it after Daddy died, and I knew from that how fear bred bigger fear, more invasive fear. So I told no one how scared I was, at first, and I learned that fear can be a lonely state to hide in.

Many of my fellow Larkies came over to console me when they saw me at the Larkin in the days after Devi's death; I probably hadn't been hugged by that many women, combined, in my entire life. Everyone at the Larkin seemed to know that Devi and I had been close. Clearly my colleagues had paid more attention to me than I had to them; I wasn't too far gone to be a little ashamed of that.

One evening at the Larkin shortly after the murder, a few of us had stayed around talking or making photocopies—anything to put off leaving our comfort zone. Somehow the sky had gone dark without my noticing, so I phoned for a cab; no way I was walking home alone. I saw another of the Larkies (a Canadian playwright whose name I could never remember) heading to the door at the same time and it occurred to me that she might want to share the cab, for safety's sake, if she was going in the same direction. Right behind her, I tapped her shoulder, and I swear to God she fainted to the floor. She was out cold. Georgi Brandt, the geology fellow who'd impressed me with her energetic talk about accreted terrain, ran over with a Dixie cup of water and a wet paper towel, which she began to apply to the woman's forehead. That was Georgi—like the Boy Scouts—always prepared.

After a few minutes, the woman opened her eyes and looked from my face to Georgi's and then all around the room that loomed above her. "I'm scared," she said, "to leave."

"I'm scared, too, honey, all the time," I heard myself telling her. Larkin women didn't call one another "honey," I realized as I said it, but it had just popped out and in the moment it felt right. As I spoke, the woman's eyes settled on mine, filling with tears, and immediately I began to cry. Georgi put her face in her hands, and before long a couple of other Larkies who were still there were looking down at the woman, tears running down their faces, too. Even cool and collected Jane Coleman teared up when she saw us all huddled there sobbing. It was, I suppose, like a funeral scene from a bad Italian movie, and as pathetic as it might have looked to any outsider, it was my first real experience of shared fear, and I'll never forget how it felt. Nor will I forget how it clarified for me my own foolish pride, my refusal to acknowledge my own fear until someone else collapsed.

Clara went to the Larkin with me most days now, though in the first day or two after the murder she'd stayed in her apartment a lot, crying and blaming herself for "treating Devi badly," and wondering if the killer would now be looking for us. If she'd been needy before, she was impossible now. But I was rather needy myself these days, and actually I felt less afraid if Clara was with me when I went out. She'd never be what Devi had been to me, or what Liz was, but she and I were growing closer, it seemed, of necessity.

A certain amount of crime scene information had somehow gotten out to the Boston and Cambridge press. An unidentified police source told the *Globe* that Devi had been attacked from behind, probably just as she walked through the entrance to the courtyard. The attacker might have been concealed in shrubbery at the entrance, either inside or outside the courtyard, or he might have followed her home from the Larkin—or from some point in between—and grabbed her from behind as she walked through the archway. One thing was sure, the *Globe*'s source had said: The attacker had meant to kill.

"He cut her throat from behind in what we have come to think of as 'OJ-style,' right in or near the archway entrance," the source was quoted as saying, "which accounts for the blood that ran across the sidewalk and over the curb. So much blood," he said, going on to explain that the victim had fallen just inside the entrance, right at the edge of the courtyard, and then the perpetrator had continued to slice at her, again and again. Devi would have no doubt been near death at this point, if she was not already dead, according to the source, but the killer had just kept slashing. The detectives on the case found it "hard to account for the 'overkill' style of this crime," he said, "and I would have to wonder at the extreme violence—especially considering the locations of the stab wounds, which were in the, you might say the *personal female* areas of her body—the breasts and the lower abdomen and thighs."

So many people had been comparing the style of this killing to the O. J. Simpson case that I'd begun thinking about that murder again for the first time in years. Nicole Simpson, the beautiful blond wife. Was Nicole Simpson murdered because O. J. wanted her but couldn't have her, I wondered, because he couldn't bear the thought of anyone else having her? Could it become so painful, so unbearable, to see the unattainable object of your desire walking the earth without you, perhaps beside someone else, that it might be more bearable to kill than to witness that betrayal?

Suddenly I remembered that night—it seemed so long ago now—when I'd seen Michael and Brenda together at a poetry reading just hours after he and I had been in bed together, happy as puppies. I remembered a fleeting but fervent wish I'd had as I sat behind them in the audience that night, a wish that both of them would disappear from the earth right then, that I wouldn't ever again have to see Michael with someone else. Of course, it was not news to me that jealousy was the progeny of desire; it was just terrifying to think that such jealousy could lead to murder.

And of course thinking of the O. J. case that way made me think that Devi's former lover, Paul Monnard, might actually have come across the Atlantic to erase her from the earth.

But it could even be some deranged street person who'd admired the beautiful Indian woman and made an overture on the street one day, been rebuffed, and then been overcome with the urge to destroy her. Intimacy was not a prerequisite to desire, I thought, nor to the possessiveness born of desire. All that took, really, was imagination, and sexual imagination is a potent force. I remembered how, before we were involved, Michael had

241

said, "I think we'd better try to control our imaginations." He was afraid of that power and of what it could do to his life.

And now, when I thought of what it had done to both of our lives, how it had strained or torn long-held relationships, isolated both of us in different ways, taught us to lie with ease, I could understand that fear more acutely than I had then.

There had been gatherings at the Larkin every day the week after the murder. Security meetings, counseling sessions, informal brown bags in the fellows' lounge where many of the women wanted to talk about Devi—even those who hadn't known her. And I was surprised, actually, at the number of Larkin fellows Devi had gotten to know in some way. Clearly she had made more of an effort than I had, despite her feelings that she'd not done enough.

On Wednesday before the colloquium presentation, the Harvard Police and the Cambridge Police held a two-hour meeting about security with the Larkin fellows and institute staff. They gave us blue-and-white plastic whistles that said "Harvard Police" on the side. Whistles, when we wanted mace; some of us went out and bought it, and also body alarms. (I wondered, though, if no one paid attention to the car alarms going off around the city night and day, who was going to find the scream of a body alarm occasion for a heads-up?) At the security meeting, many of the fellows wanted to know more details of Devi's murder, and several asked whether the details in the *Globe* were accurate. The questions seemed to me like morbid curiosity at first, and as such it offended me because I knew how private Devi had been. But then Georgi Brandt, who saw my upset, pointed out that the questions were just attempts by the fellows to understand this horrible crime in any way they could because of the fear they felt for their own safety.

One of the Cambridge cops stood in front of the assembled women and told us what he could about the circumstances of the crime and then gave us what he called "a fact-based hypothetical scenario."

"The victim had adjourned her poetry workshop at ten o'clock that night," he told us, "and apparently stayed in her office doing paperwork. At around ten-thirty she made a phone call to one of her neighbors at Eighty-two Brattle, Larkin fellow Honora Blume, in which she said she would be back later than she'd thought but hoped they could still have a late visit, as planned. Ms. Bhujander was seen by Harvard Security leaving her Larkin office at just past ten-thirty and walking toward Harvard Square. It would have taken her fifteen minutes—twenty at most—to get to Eighty-two Brattle, which would put the crime at sometime between ten forty-five and eleven-ten, when the body was found by three tenants of the building who were returning from a movie on Church Street in the square."

Detective Burns took over when it got to this point. First, he nodded at the assembled women and cleared his throat as if to sing; then he told us that "many details of the murder have been let out that shouldn't have been, but that doesn't mean I'm going to stand up here and do the same thing." He pulled at his collar and looked around uncomfortably. "Some of us feel that the nature of this killing indicates some sort of personal vendetta," he told the assembled women, "and that's where all of you come in. We'd be grateful for any information any of you may have about the life and habits of Devi Bhujander. We understand she was a very private person, so there may have been things in her life that she didn't want people to know about."

All of a sudden it seemed Devi's life was on trial. Wasn't it enough that she was dead?

"Devi Bhujander was a quiet poet who rarely went out," I spoke up. "Just because someone is private doesn't mean they're keeping secrets."

"I don't mean to offend anyone, Ms. Blume," Burns said, "but this is a normal direction to take in a homicide investigation like this one. If you want the killer to be found and brought to justice, you need to accept this." He went on to ask if anyone present knew of anything in Devi Bhujander's life that might have put her in such peril. The implication was clearly drugs, I thought, and I was pissed.

After the meeting Clara said, "I feel sick. I can't bear to hear any more of this." She did look terrible—almost green—and so I followed her into the restroom outside the meeting area, where I heard her throw up inside one of the toilet cubicles. She was crying when she came out.

"I feel like I made it happen." She sobbed. "I spoke badly about Devi and now she's dead. I should not have put those thoughts out into the air."

There was no doubt Clara genuinely felt bad, but I was tired of her mournful self-blame. I felt tempted to say, "Not everything is about you, Clara." But I didn't. There was too much hurt all around us already. Even the brisk spring air of Cambridge felt harsh against my skin this year.

During this time a sort of bunker mentality began to prevail among the Larkies. Many of us spent more waking hours at the Larkin than at home, just for the company. I got to know some of my Larkin colleagues better, in particular Georgi Brant, and one day over lunch at the Larkin I mentioned to her how the imagery of her presentation had made me think of human relationship and isolation. It was the first time since Devi's death that I'd really felt like talking to anyone, and maybe it was partly that the subject was one I'd discussed with Devi during her sittings for the second painting—right after that first unhappy phone call from Paul Monnard. Once again Clara had begun attending the Harvard classes she'd been auditing before, or else I might not have had the opportunity to talk to Georgi that way. My next-door neighbor on Brattle was getting more and more dependent, more possessive than ever.

There was a special service at The Memorial Church in Harvard Yard a week and a half after the murder; I was surprised to see how many of Devi's family and friends had come in from Delhi and London, since the official memorial gathering had been held in India. Maybe it was a way of having her with them for a little longer, feeling connected with her in this world.

Sandeep was there, as were Devi's beautiful sister, Rina, and their parents, a dignified older couple who broke down and sobbed when Sandeep talked lovingly from the pulpit about his sister.

"My sister believed in living every day to the fullest," he said, "but in her own quiet way. To her, living life fully meant caring about others, especially the less fortunate, it meant living in her art, it meant being awake to the beauties of the world. Sometimes I teased her"—he looked at me—"about being 'queenly,' and she honestly didn't know what I was talking about. But it was true. Small as she was physically, she had a kind of inner confidence that made her seem regal, like a queen. She'll always be a queen to me."

Several well-known poets had flown in from London to talk about

Devi, too. They spoke of her brilliance as a poet and her generosity as a teacher of student poets. Some of them read her poems; one read John Donne's "Holy Sonnet Number 10," which begins, "Death be not proud . . ."

I was asked to say a few words, too, as Devi's closest Larkin friend, and I did. Afterward I couldn't remember exactly what I'd said, though I remember I spoke of her kindness, her gentle wisdom, her spiritual side, her sense of beauty, and her intense love of, and respect for, her family, which I had seen so clearly when her brother was visiting at the New Year and all she wanted was to share with him the wonders and curiosities she'd found in our part of the world, as many as possible in that one night we had together. Sandeep lowered his head then, putting his fingers and thumb to his brow to shield his eyes, Devi's "little bother." It was a struggle to keep talking. After the ceremony, Devi's parents embraced me, as did Rina and Sandeep. I wanted to stay in their embrace, for it felt like my last earthly connection to Devi.

Georgi Brandt had invited me to her apartment for dinner one night not long after the murder, but I was afraid to go out at night by myself so I'd begged off, saying I was busy. (Even to take a taxi to her place would have terrified me; the murderer might even have been a cab driver— who knew? I thought of the surly cabby who'd left me alone in the middle of the street at 3:30 in the morning.) Georgi approached me the next time we were at the Larkin and apologized for having been "insensitive."

"It was thoughtless of me to just ask you to come over to my place," she said. "It was only later that I thought about the fact that you might feel leery of going out alone at night. I never really think about that because I have a car. Next time I invite you, I'll just come over and pick you up."

I thanked her and we promised to get together soon.

Emotionally I was frozen. I didn't cry about Devi anymore, hadn't since the memorial service. But neither did I paint. I'd gone to see Ida as usual the last two Sundays. The fact that she was so out of it lately was upsetting, but it excused me from conversation. I watched TV when I was alone at home; sometimes I went next door and had tea or wine with Clara. I talked on the phone to Mother and Liz fairly often, letting them lead the conversation.

Mother was in full tilt Irish about the killing, and she'd said to me at one point, "You could be next! Don't you know that? I want you to come home *right now.*"

I hadn't lived in Santa Monica or called it home since I went off to RISD at eighteen, so it was funny that she was calling it my home again all of a sudden. I was surprised to find that in this situation my mother's concern actually comforted me. Not because it *was* concern—more because it had been a normal and familiar part of my life before the murder. And lately I'd found myself thinking of my life as Before and After the murder, feeling nostalgic for everything I could count as Before. I guessed it was like the way some men speak of "before the war" and "after the war." We humans seemed to use traumas as life markers. Maybe because that was what they did—they marked our lives in indelible and irrefutable ways.

Though I spoke with Liz and Mother fairly often and saw Clara every day, most of the time since Devi's death I hadn't been calling Michael back, and if I was home when he called, I rarely picked up. I wasn't really still mad at him; it was more that I was afraid to feel anything intensely. And with Michael everything had always been intense—sex, laughter, anger, joy, jealousy. It seemed as if one real emotion, just one extreme feeling allowed inside me, would open up the way for all the rest. Michael and I hadn't seen each other since the night of the murder, and he kept calling to ask if he could come over and see me.

"Just to look into each other's eyes for half an hour," he kept saying, "I don't care if we talk, and I certainly don't expect us to make love. I just want to see your face. I need to know how you really *are,* Norrie." Finally I agreed he could come over one afternoon and pick me up for a drive. I didn't want to be in my apartment with him.

"Maybe we can go out for a meal somewhere," he suggested. "Would you like that?"

"Okay," I said. I didn't tell him there was nothing I would "like" right now.

I took a fast shower, dressed carelessly in an old pair of jeans and a loose, white linen sweater that had stretched out of shape, and slid my feet into some beat-up clogs. I didn't particularly care how I looked to

Michael right now. My hair was washed—that was the most I could say for my personal grooming—but I had pulled it back into a clasp so it wouldn't look "sexy," as Michael always said it did when I left it loose. I didn't want to look seductive. I didn't feel seductive. I might have put my hair into a braid, but it made me think of Devi's braid, which someone had hacked off and taken as a macabre souvenir.

When I saw Michael standing in my living room, long and lanky, a look of concern in his blue eyes, uncertainty all over his face, I felt tears springing into my eyes for the first time since I'd hugged Sandeep at the funeral. "Oh, God, Norrie," he said into my hair, "I've missed you so much."

We ended up staying in the apartment, but not making love. I couldn't have. In fact, for the first half of the visit I was wary of Michael, afraid he would try talking me into bed. I thought that if he did anything in the least sexual, I might get hysterical and lose the self-control I'd worked so hard to sustain since the murder. But he didn't. He sat beside me in the living room and talked quietly about work, about what he'd been reading lately, and about his kids. Bridget was becoming a little moody and defiant lately, and he joked that he never should have told her that her name meant "the High One." Finn had won an important poetry award at NYU and talked about scrapping plans to go on for an MFA so that he could devote all his time to "just getting a book out right away." Michael rolled his eyes at this, grinning. "Apparently all the years of his father's struggle to break into print have taught him nothing."

"Maybe he just feels he's more talented than you are," I teased. It was the first time I'd said anything in fun since Devi's death, and immediately I felt guilty. Michael cocked his head at me, and the corners of his eyes announced the smile on its way to his lips.

"Well, well," he said, stroking my hair, "so the mischief is still there, thank God."

His talk of paternal exemplars led Michael to the subject of what he'd learned by seeing how hard his parents had worked to support the family. After they'd arrived in the United States from County Kerry and taken up residence in the projects of Southie, he said, his father had worked two jobs—policeman and janitor—and his mother had clerked at Woolworth's Five-and-Dime and Filene's Basement in Boston, in addition to taking in laundry and ironing on the side. "We didn't have much, but I was one of the lucky few in the projects who *had* a father," he said. "Not that we got to see the man very often!"

I think he knew I liked hearing him talk, despite the fact that I wasn't adding much to the conversation. My silence would have likely sent many of my friends and former lovers running to the door. I liked that Michael simply talked to me today without expecting any return, quietly weaving a story about his Irish family, taking me away from my own pain for a little while.

At some point I fixed us oatmeal—that was about all I had on hand— and we sat on the couch together, bowls in one hand, spoons in the other, eating warm, lumpy oatmeal with brown sugar but no milk, saying little.

"I feel like one of the Three Bears," Michael said as we spooned porridge into our mouths. I just nodded and smiled faintly. I guess normally I'd have asked him which one.

After the oatmeal and without making a big deal of it, Michael held me close to him as we sat side by side on the couch, and I let him. As I felt his familiar embrace and smelled the skin I knew so well, I felt something inside me soften and maybe unknot a little. We sat together like that for a while, and after he left the apartment my skin felt cold where his arms had been, as if some necessary insulation had been re-moved from my body.

About an hour later, I was surprised when Michael came back with bags and bags of groceries for me from the big Star Market. I'd had no idea he was going to do that.

"Somehow I don't enjoy the idea of your eating nothing but milkless oatmeal three times a day," he said, then tipped an imaginary hat the way courtly men did in old black-and-white movies, "—not that it wasn't delicious, ma'am."

"It sucked," I said. "And I don't eat it three times a day. Does instant macaroni and cheese ring a bell? Have you heard of Top Ramen?"

"How could I have underestimated your culinary skills?" he said, and I actually grinned.

As we said our good-byes at the door, I wondered if Clara might be able to hear us talking there. Then I just didn't care. It was way too late to worry about her now.

A few days later Michael came over again, and this time he led me into the bedroom and made love to me very gently. It was hard to feel anything at first. And though finally he aroused me physically, I had tears in my eyes the whole time, even when he made me come with his tongue, and again later, when he was inside me. He looked down at me while I was coming, and I closed my eyes rather than engage his gaze. I didn't feel like showing anyone my feelings, even him. I'd turned all of my recent paintings to the walls of the bedroom except for the not-quite-finished painting of Devi, which was still on the easel, covered with one of her Indian print bedspreads that we'd used during the sittings. I'd started to put a sheet over the canvas, and that had brought back the image of the body being carried off, strapped to the gurney, the blood-stained white blanket covering it. I couldn't bear to work on the painting yet.

When Michael was leaving, he stopped in the doorway and looked at me for a long time. "I love you so much," he said. "I've felt like some kind of cardboard character without you." Ordinarily I guess I'd have been moved to reply in kind, but I was a big scaredy cat right now, shaky nearly all the time, and at that moment love felt like a responsibility I couldn't handle. Even though I felt exactly the same way—as if I'd been made incarnate again by making love to him.

I just returned his embrace.

The next morning I got two unexpected phone calls. The first one was from Devi's brother. Sandeep had gone directly back to London after the Harvard memorial service because he'd had finals. Now he was returning to get Devi's things in order. He'd called to say he was meeting the movers at our building tomorrow to pack and ship Devi's belongings. He asked me if I would talk to the super and let him know, which I did as soon as we hung up.

"Awful sad, all that," Joe O'Connor said when I called him, "Such a beautiful girl." Did everyone think it was sadder to be murdered if you were beautiful, or was it just men?

The second call was from Marge at Brookline Manor.

"I think you'd better get over here, Honora," was all she said. I dressed quickly and called a cab.

When I got there, I pretty much burst through the doors of the Manor.

Marge was at the desk, and when she saw me, she said, "Have you been sick again, honey? You look kind of pale."

"A friend died," was all I said. I didn't want to go into it. "I've just been kind of out of it."

"Well then, this is bad timing for you, dear. Doctor thinks Ida won't last the night." She led me into Ida's room, which had been darkened to keep out the unseasonal heat and glare. Ida's eyes were almost shut, but I could see she wasn't actually asleep, just terribly weak. She seemed to breathe with effort, and her skin had discolored in places and was sunken in around her bones. I sat down beside the bed.

"I'll bring you a cup of tea in a bit," Marge whispered from the doorway, and then she left me alone with Ida.

"Hi, Ida," I said softly, and her eyelids trembled and stretched, as if she were trying to open them but couldn't summon the strength. I stood and walked around to the head of her bed and leaned over. "It's me— Norrie," I whispered into her ear.

"Yes," she whispered, and then seemed to lapse back into silence. Just as I'd decided she was going to say no more, she spoke in a weakened version of her natural voice. "It's so crazy," she said. "It's just so crazy. The pain."

"Oh, Ida, I'm so sorry." I held her hand and could feel her returning the pressure a little. "I hate you to be in pain."

"It's okay," she said. "It's how you get to the other end." I wasn't sure if she was talking about death, but it seemed she was. Then, for just a moment, the old Ida came through. "You buy your ticket," she said in a crackly voice, "and you take the ride."

That was the last thing she said for a while; she seemed to lapse into sleep. I checked to see if she was breathing; she was. Marge brought in some tea on a tray, Earl Grey, with a little pitcher of milk. She actually remembered how I liked my tea.

Now and then she came back to check Ida's vital signs, but she never intruded.

A couple of hours later, Ida suddenly opened her eyes and spoke. I'd let my thoughts wander to Devi, so Ida's voice startled me—not least because it suddenly sounded normal, completely normal.

"Well, honey," she said, "what are you doing here? Is it Sunday?"

"No, it's Tuesday," I told her. "I just wanted to see you."

"Oh, I know," she said, and made a kind of feeble chuckle. "I think I'm about done for."

"No, Ida, don't say that. You sound perfectly normal now."

"Harry always said I was never 'normal,' and that was why he liked me—because he thought normal was boring. He felt I was a little eccentric, though I don't know why." She coughed, trying to clear her throat. "Is there a drink of water handy?" she asked.

I got her glass and filled it from the plastic pitcher on the bed tray. When I put the glass to her lips, she drank greedily, placing her own hand over mine to hold the glass along with me.

"You're a good girl," she said to me after she'd finished. "You've been a wonderful daughter." For a moment I thought it was dementia speaking, but then Ida went on, her voice weak but clear and not faltering. "I always wanted a daughter of my own," she said. "And when Henry was killed in that car accident, all I had left was you. It felt like he gave me you to take his place. Henry was like that, so considerate." She seemed tired after saying so much, and a few minutes later she lapsed back into sleep. I took the opportunity to go and find Marge.

"Marge, Ida seems much better," I said. "She's been talking up a storm. Her eyes were wide open just now." Marge looked worried and put her hand on my shoulder.

"Honey," she said, "that often happens just before the end. I don't know why. But you mustn't get your hopes up. I have to be honest. Doctor says it's probably a matter of hours."

"I'm staying, then."

"Yeah, I think you should, if you can. I'll come in every now and then to check on her, and you can call me if . . . if there's a change."

Before I went back to Ida's room, I called Michael on Marge's phone. I knew it was okay to call, since he was alone at the house. I told him what was happening, and that I'd not be home when he called tonight. "I didn't want you to worry, with everything that's been going on," I said.

"Norrie, I don't feel comfortable with the idea of you going back alone to Cambridge tonight," he said. "I'll come and get you."

"But how will you know when Ida's—when I'm ready to leave? I can't call you at night."

"Yes, you can," he said. "I don't care. I'm not letting you come home alone late at night. We don't know who's out there, Norrie." For a change I welcomed Michael's protectiveness—it made me feel safer, made me feel loved—not that I'd have admitted it. I wondered how much I'd crippled my entire adult life by being afraid to admit to my own fears and insecurities, by never letting anyone look after me. Maybe it was time I learned how to trust a man, to believe he wouldn't go away. But I knew I had to hold on to my defenses in this relationship for now.

At eleven o'clock that night Ida opened her eyes once, said, *"Oh,"* and stopped breathing. I sat with her awhile, and whispered what I could remember of John Donne's "Holy Sonnet Number 10," from Devi's memorial service:

> One short sleep past, we wake eternally
> And death shall be no more; Death, thou shalt die.

I couldn't bear to leave yet; once I had, Ida would be gone forever. I kept looking at her features in their eternal repose. The expression was one I'd never seen on her face before, and I tried to read it, as if that might give me some idea of what she had seen at that moment when she stepped into the hereafter and said, *Oh!*

The room was completely silent except for the big round clock on the wall. I'd never noticed its ticking before. I thought about how Ida had spoken to me just a while ago, and now though I could still see her body, her face, though I could see the mouth that had spoken to me, I couldn't see her. She was gone. She was not inside her body. She'd shed it like a cocoon.

When I finally left Ida's room, that expression on her face was etched in my mind. I found Marge sitting on a chair in the hall with her purse. I knew her shift was long over.

"She's gone," I said. "Thank you for staying, Marge. I know your shift must have ended a while ago."

"Ida would want me to be here for her girl," she said. "We'd better go and tell the new charge nurse. She'll have to make a couple of calls." Marge went into Ida's room briefly then, and I knew it was to confirm her death and say good-bye, so I stayed out in the hall.

"I almost forgot," Marge said when she came out of Ida's room. "You have company. He's waiting in the lobby."

252

Of course it was Michael. He stood as I entered the lobby, and walked over to me quickly, took me in his arms.

"Norrie," he said into the top of my head, "Oh, baby, you've been through too damned much." All the way back to Cambridge in Michael's car I let myself lean into him, my head on his shoulder. We didn't talk, but he held my hand. When we pulled up in front of my building, he said, "I wish I could come in with you and stay for a while, but I really have to get back. I'll walk you to the door, though."

I couldn't complain—though I hadn't realized it earlier, Michael had been at the nursing home for about four hours, waiting for me to come out. When I stepped out of the car and onto the curb below the street-light, I saw the stain. Devi's blood. It had soaked into the concrete and set, which mystified and unsettled me. Management had hosed it down the day after the crime and rain had fallen on Cambridge a couple of times, yet though the stain had faded it didn't seem to wash away from a concave spot where the concrete was worn and rough, and there was an especially dark place at its center where the blood had pooled. I stepped around it, feeling my body clench like an overused muscle. Maybe Michael noticed it, too; at that moment he decided to accompany me all the way up to my apartment.

"How can I just leave you on the front step," he said. "What if someone was waiting inside?" That scared the hell out of me. Since we didn't know who—or where—the killer was, I knew Michael could be right; and as it turned out, it was a very good thing he came along. He punched the button and we went up in the elevator together. When we got off and walked toward my apartment, I realized something was not right, but I couldn't think what it was at first. Then I noticed that the hall carpet was gray; on my floor it was blue. The third floor's hall carpet was gray. Suddenly I knew we'd gotten off on Devi's floor.

"Oh God," I said, "Michael, you pushed the wrong button. Oh God." I hadn't been on the third floor since Devi's death. Could not bear to.

"Shit," he said. He must have realized where we were then. "Oh, Jesus," he said. "Oh, no. I'm so sorry."

"That's Devi's door," I said, "right there. Her brother Sandeep is coming tomorrow to pack her things and ship them to Delhi."

Michael and I stood in the hall for a moment, looking at the door.

Then we walked back to the elevator, and as we were waiting by it we heard a door unlock. We turned around. Devi's door. It was opening; then it stood still. My heart clenched, and I grabbed Michael's arm.

"No one's supposed to be in there," I said. "Sandeep is coming in tomorrow at ten. The movers are coming at noon."

We heard someone say, "Get that goddamn cord that's dragging on the floor, willya?"

Then I saw Joe coming out the door with another man, a younger man. Joe was carrying Devi's computer; the other man was carrying her printer, with a telephone on top. They stopped to lock Devi's door, and the elevator opened at just that moment, and Michael pushed me in— rather roughly, I might add.

"What the hell are you doing?" I said when the doors closed.

"I didn't want them to know we saw them," he said. "We know they're not supposed to be there taking Devi's things tonight, so obviously those guys are your burglars—but what if one of them is also the killer? Do you want them to know you saw them?" That hadn't occurred to me.

"God," I said, "what if Joe recognized us?"

"He doesn't know me, and I don't think he could have recognized you," Michael said. "I tried to block you with my body as I pushed you into the elevator."

"Thanks," I said as we got off on the fourth floor. "How did you think so fast?"

"I have no idea," Michael said. "I just had the feeling I had to hide you."

"They must be taking the utility elevator," I said. The minute we got into my apartment we called 911, and within minutes Detective Burns was there, along with three patrol cars. In short order they found Joe and the other man filling a small truck with Devi's belongings. They'd apparently already loaded her microwave, stereo, and television, along with a mahogany box that held some gold coins. Joe and the other man were taken away separately in two cruisers, and then Detective Burns came up to the apartment to talk to me.

Michael had stayed, though he looked nervous and twitchy. I knew he was wondering what he would tell Brenda.

"I'm okay now," I assured him. "You can go. Really."

"Are you sure?" He looked at Burns dubiously.

"I'm sure," I said, and took his arm, led him to the door. "And thank you, Michael, for everything tonight."

"Nice to meet you," Detective Burns shouted, as if he'd just remembered his manners, and from out in the hall, Michael called out, "Yeah—same here." That was when Clara peeked out to see what was going on. My head was spinning. Burns was hovering near my doorway, and at first it seemed Clara might have been distracted enough by the sight of him not to take in Michael's presence. But then I saw her eye on Michael for just a beat too long as he walked to the elevator. She looked at me then, and I'd have been hard put to define the expression on her face.

"Wait till you hear what happened," I told her, to deflect possible questions about Michael. But I knew Clara well enough to be sure the subject was not dead.

As she walked into the apartment with me to talk to Detective Burns, I told her about Joe's theft of Devi's things. Before we even sat down in the living room, she told Burns she'd been suspecting Joe of Devi's murder for some time.

"He was always repairing things for her," Clara said, "attending to her more than was appropriate." She frowned, looked at me, then addressed Detective Burns again, her voice shaking. "This more or less proves he . . . *did it* . . . doesn't it?"

"Oh no," Burns said, "it just proves that some people are vultures. But you know, of course, we're going to look into the possibility that these guys are connected to the murder."

I asked him if they'd pursued the angle of Paul, Devi's former boyfriend. I saw Clara's expression intensify, and I remembered she'd known nothing about Paul—or really, about any aspect of Devi's personal life. I knew this new information had probably revived her jealousy over my closeness to Devi by reminding her of that fact. It didn't seem a stretch to imagine that Clara could even feel jealous of someone who was in the ground.

"We've located some people in London who know the gentleman," the detective said, "but he seems to have been away for a couple of weeks on some kind of trip."

"Pretty big coincidence, isn't it," I said. "It does sound . . ." I didn't go on.

"Suspicious," he finished. "Yeah, maybe, I know what you mean. But maybe not. He's on leave this semester and has been going off on climbing trips—apparently quite the outdoorsman, this guy. His friends and co-workers at the university thought he might even be on Everest—the Big One! So it could be pretty hard to locate him. If he's somewhere like that—and if he's innocent—he's got no clue she's dead."

"Do you consider this man a likely suspect then?" Clara asked.

"*Oh* yeah," Detective Burns said. "*No* doubt about that one." He paused. "Look," he said to me, "I know you were Miss Bhujander's good friend," he nodded at Clara then, "and maybe you were, too. I just want you both to know we're working on this twenty-four/seven." Clara looked confused at the expression *twenty-four/seven.* "We're gonna find this guy."

When the detective left, Clara turned to me and said, "I still think Joe is the one. I have suspected him the whole time." It was true she'd said as much to me once or twice before, but I didn't think it was a good idea to confuse a burglar with a murderer—then we might never find Devi's killer.

"I don't think that's necessarily a good assumption," I said. "One crime has little to do with the other. There's been a burglary series here for a long time—Joe must have been behind it all along. But that doesn't mean he killed Devi."

"Why are you defending him?" Clara was angry. "If he killed Devi, I want him dead, too."

"Jesus, Clara," I said, "I'm not defending him! How can you talk like that? I just want to be sure we find the *right* guy. If the wrong man is accused, it'll take even longer to find the real killer." The phrase *find the real killer* made me think of O. J. Simpson again, how many times on TV they'd played a clip of him vowing to "find the real killer," his face all earnestness. I shuddered. "Look," I said to Clara, "we need to be sure we're blaming the right guy."

She began to cry then. "We are not safe," she said, "until we find out what is going on. I am afraid to walk outside by myself."

"Well, what if the killer was some guy out there on the street who could kill us, *too*? All the more reason we want to be sure they get the right guy."

For about the twentieth time since the murder, I thought of Mutton.

Devi'd told me once that he'd often called out to her, too. That once he'd said, "Pretty India Lady, I'm going to marry you."

"I know," Clara sobbed now. "It's just that I'm so worn out from all of this. I can't even work on my book, I can't think, I can't do anything." I knew exactly how she felt, and I put an arm around her.

"Let's try to go somewhere one afternoon this weekend," I said to her. "Maybe we could go to a movie—get our minds off all this fear and grief."

"That would be wonderful," Clara was saying, "I would like that." But I was already drifting. The word *grief* had reminded me of Ida. Ida had died tonight. It didn't feel real. I tried out the thought: *Ida's dead.* I'd never go to Brookline to visit her again. Of course, with Ida, death wasn't so "untimely" as with Devi; I knew it had been a release from pain for Ida.

Still, I suddenly felt overwhelmed with all the loss, the death.

"I need to go to bed," I said to Clara then. "I'm about ready to pass out." No way I was telling Clara about Ida's death. I didn't feel like sharing something so personal with her.

As Clara was leaving my apartment, she turned to me with a kind of deliberate movement and said, "Perhaps you can bring your *friend* over for a glass of wine some evening. I would love to talk to him about his wonderful book." The sickening sweet smile on her lips, almost coy, was belied by the insinuating tone of her words. She was saying she recognized the celebrated Irish-American novelist. "He has such an interesting life," she added, and by this I felt she was also saying she knew about him, knew he was married, and had figured out that we were lovers.

Caught off guard, almost dizzy, I unintentionally shut the door at the same second I said, "Good night." Alone in my apartment at last, I went straight to bed, but once again I couldn't sleep. Now I had something entirely new to add to my roster of worries and cares. I was sure Clara somehow knew that Michael was my lover. For all I knew, she might have been suspicious for some time, might have observed more than I'd realized, more of his visits, more of our arrivals and departures together. Was she warning me subtly that if I didn't tend to her she would tell the world about us? Or was paranoia taking over my brain?

At some point Michael called to see if I was all right, but he had to whisper the whole time for fear Brenda would hear him on the phone at that hour, so we didn't talk for long. I couldn't bring myself to tell him of my new anxieties about Clara.

I lay back down and continued trying to sleep, but after an hour or so I gave up, got out of bed, and began pacing around the apartment. I turned on CNN; I don't know why. Maybe to hear about wars, as if in the hope that the routine global mayhem might dwarf my private sorrow. There was a short segment with a septuagenarian Brooklyn woman who, they said, had "won the Pulitzer for her novel on April 9th, after a relatively obscure literary career." My God, I'd forgotten all about the fact that the Pulitzer was to be announced in April, and Michael hadn't mentioned it even once since the murder. He'd been too busy watching over me. I switched off the television then, feeling sad for Michael, sad for everyone. Just sad.

Ida. I could see her in my head so clearly, lying back on the pillow and breathing her last breath. The expression on her face in death had stayed with me, as I'd known it would. Now I tried to read that expression from the image of her face in my memory. If only I could see it again with my eyes, maybe I'd understand it.

In a minute my fatigue disappeared—creative adrenalin does that, and you always know that when you collude with it in hope of a new work of art, you're taking your health into your hands because you will be absolutely unaware of your body's warning signals then, for the duration.

I thought of the painting I'd done of Ida a few weeks back. I turned it around so that it faced into the room. Then I got out a fresh canvas and sketched a design on it. I wanted to paint Ida sleeping, her body emptied of earthly desire.

The room is cooled down, and the reds have faded to rust, brick, and the old-blood color I'd mixed for Devi's last portrait. Ida is seen from above, lying against the white sheets, her face calm yet somehow curious, eyes closed, her hands clasped across her middle over the red blanket. The tone of her flesh is cool and slightly blued in the lines and shadows, but it has a kind of luminosity as well, as if filled with a living spirit about to fly to the heavens.

On the bedstand beside her stands the red pitcher, a cooler red now, nearly a dusty rose. Seen from above for the first time, the glass pitcher seems less a vessel than a globe, round and shining, but without the capacity to hold anything inside. Viewed from overhead, it might be simply a bubble or a figment of the imagination.

I wish I could be freed of desire like Ida, but without dying, wish I could feel this way when I think of you. I wish I didn't need you, wish my flesh didn't waken at the thought of you. But one day I'll be ready for what Ida has met—the moment when all earthly desire empties from the body and the spirit rises to ascendancy over the flesh.

And in the meantime I have to accept two things: that part of being alive is to desire; and that desire is, by nature, not containable.

I lie on my bed in the pose I painted for Ida, hands clasped across my middle. I empty my mind of all thought of you. But still my body hungers for you, because the flesh can only tell the truth. A truth, in our case, that leads us to live a lie, a life that isn't any realer or more durable than a bubble.

16

It was a rainy spring and every night thunder boomed in the air and lightning flashed. There was a great, rich aroma of rain coming in the open windows of my apartment, the sound of traffic hissing on the wet street below. I could remember loving spring rainstorms. I could remember almost everything about being alive in the world.

Down the street at the American Repertory, F. Murray Abraham was playing King Lear nightly to a sold-out house despite the *Globe*'s review, which called him a "too, too human" Lear with not a hint of kingliness, depriving the play, the reviewer said, of much of its tension and shock. Devi and I had talked about going to see it when it got to the ART, but that was a lifetime ago and everything was different now.

It had been three weeks since her murder, and no one had been taken into custody yet. Joe had been cleared of any involvement in the killing, as had his accomplice in the burglaries (it was reported that Joe had been "the mastermind and driving force" behind the burglary series from the beginning); it turned out Mutton had been in jail for the entire week of the killing after being picked up for smoking weed on the street, so he had an alibi; Paul Monnard had still not been located, and an Interpol search was now underway. Some had settled on him as the most likely suspect.

"We're gonna find the guy," Detective Burns said, "unless he's gone to Mars or something. If he's on this particular planet, we'll find him." I kind of liked Detective Burns, his innocent optimism. Give him a few more years, I thought, and that'll be gone.

The painting had still not been found. Everyone was taking its disappearance seriously by now, and that brought an unpleasant focus on me, as the painter who had done the portrait of Devi. I was getting phone calls from newspaper reporters, and someone had even called from *Vanity Fair*. I began screening my calls.

I wasn't sleeping at night. I began hearing sounds I was sure I'd never heard in our building before: knocks, thumps, hissing, scraping. Several times I was sure I heard footsteps in the hall coming close to my front door. I feared I had become like Mother had been all those years ago, floating around the house nightly in her swath of flannel, her features frozen in a despairing kind of fear, as if she knew there was no way out of the terror because it was part of her now.

One night a tremendous wind hit Cambridge, causing branches to scratch and bump against my bedroom windows. I woke to the sound at 2:00 A.M., gripped by fear as the scratching and bumping sounded increasingly like an intruder trying to get in. I reached to turn on my bedside lamp, then realized such a move would allow a prowler the advantage. After a time the wind died down, but by then I was clenched like a fist and I knew there was no hope of sleep. As I lay in bed trying to calm down, I heard footsteps in the hall again, as I thought I had on several other nights. Now I *knew* I heard them. Grabbing a heavy flashlight for a weapon, I stole into my hallway and stared at the door. Why had I forgotten to tell Harvard Housing to put a peephole in my door? My heart literally stopped as I saw the shadow of two feet in the crack beneath my door, backlit by the light out in the hall. I pulled in my breath so abruptly that it felt like a punch to the chest.

"WHO IS IT!" I yelled. There was no answer. I saw the feet shifting. "Who's out there?"

I heard her voice then, Clara's voice.

"It is me," she said with a sob. "I am scared. Please let me in."

What could I do? I had to let Clara into my apartment at 3:00 A.M. I settled her on the couch with a glass of wine and told her as gently as I could manage that we must not allow ourselves to get fixed in the habit of fear because then we would lose our independence and our humanity. I didn't tell her how terrified I'd been at the shadows of her feet in the crack below my door. She stayed until sunup, when I locked the door behind her, feeling trapped, a prisoner.

It was at that moment that I found myself hating Clara for the relief

I knew she must feel sometimes now, despite her histrionic grieving, relief at not having to wonder all the time if Devi and I were together, at not having to be jealous anymore.

I'd felt myself growing more bitter and fearful by the day. And though I knew there was no circumstance under which Devi's death would *not* have been devastating to me, I couldn't help wondering if the life I'd been living for two years prior to the murder—the secrecy and isolation of my relationship with Michael, the jealousy, the resentment, the un-natural highs and lows of illicit love—had made me more vulnerable, had made it that much harder to face life in its aftermath.

"You don't sound good," my mother had pointed out helpfully one evening. "You need to find a counselor before you have a nervous break-down."

"Gotta go, Mother. Someone's at my door."

"Don't answer it!"

"Mother, stop it. And I'm fine."

"You've got a problem, Norrie. You can't admit you're falling apart at the seams."

Yes, I might well be falling apart—and why not? My dear friend had been murdered in the courtyard I had to walk through each day to enter and leave this very building! I'd been isolated in an illicit romance for nearly two years. My old friend Ida had died. One of the paintings for my colloquium series had disappeared. And all the traumas of late were exacerbated by Clara's constant presence in my life, which was stifling.

I thought of what she had said one afternoon as we walked to the movies together.

"We need each other now. Neither one of us would be going out to the movies right now if we did not have each other. We really shouldn't go anywhere alone. It's too dangerous until they catch the killer."

It occurred to me that Clara was going alone to audit her day classes at Harvard, but I decided it wasn't worth it to point that out. Still, that fact told me that in a way Clara was using this whole scare to keep me by her side whenever possible, and I resented her selective nervousness.

The thing that bothered me most about what she'd said, though, was that in a way she was right. I wouldn't have gone alone to a late afternoon movie like the one we were headed to, because I'd have been afraid to walk home when the movie ended after dark. When I wanted to go out,

I often invited Clara just for the added safety of someone walking beside me. And now it seemed she expected to go everywhere I went. I felt caught in the ever-widening web of her expectations.

On one particularly frustrating day I complained to Georgi about Clara's clinginess. We were at the Larkin after one of the brown-bag lunches I'd been attending since Devi's death.

"I don't think I can take much more," I told Georgi, "everywhere I look, there she is."

"You know, some of the Larkies think Clara's a bit . . . well, *unstable*." Georgi told me. "Did you know she talks about you all the time? People say she's in love with you—"

"What?"

"I'm serious. And you ought to know that some of the Larkies think you two might have been a couple before Devi came along."

"Jesus Christ," I sputtered. "That's ridiculous. Why should they think that?"

"I'm not sure . . . I think because at the very beginning of the year you were seen with Clara around the Larkin, and then after a while it seemed like you were always in your studio with Devi, and Clara would sometimes ask people if they'd seen you. No one ever wanted to tell her you were with Devi because I think they weren't sure what was going on."

"What was going on! I was painting Devi. Jesus." I remembered the day Serena Holwerda had said Clara was asking for me, and how I'd wondered if Serena had the wrong idea about us.

"Yeah, I know that. But I think it was just because of how obsessed Clara is with you that the idea sort of germinated among some of the fellows that . . . that maybe this was a romantic triangle or something." At the look on my face she hastily added, "I don't mean *menage à trois!* I mean, you know, triangle. And now with Devi . . . gone . . . you're often seen around here with Clara again."

One more bit of damage Clara has caused, I thought. "I can't believe any woman here would pass along that kind of sexual innuendo," I said hotly.

"It wasn't like that, Norrie. Be fair. No one at the Larkin thought they were saying something *bad* by asking if you and Clara—or you and Devi—were a couple. After all, several of the women here *are* lesbians, and the Larkies are sophisticated enough not to be shocked by two women together. It was Clara's obsession with you that made some of them talk in the first place."

"I guess. What if the police get hold of these rumors? Life's going to be hell for Clara and for me—it could make the murder look like something it isn't."

"Hey, Norrie, you're borrowing trouble, you know."

"Yeah . . . I guess." That was what my mother did—borrow trouble. Was I turning into her?

"Are you still up for dinner at my place tonight? I bought a beautiful piece of salmon."

"Sure," I said, "as long as we don't talk about any of this, okay? I'm fried."

"I didn't mean to upset you, Norrie, I really didn't."

"No, I'd rather know what people are saying about me—really. It's just . . . it may sound funny to say this, but it's not the idea that some of the Larkies think I might be gay that bothers me . . . it's the idea that anyone might think I was involved with *Clara*."

When I got back to Brattle I ran into Clara in the elevator and we exchanged pleasantries, but I kept thinking about what Georgi had told me and feeling repulsed. I didn't tell Clara I'd be going to Georgi's that night; I felt it was time to liberate myself from the joined-at-the-hip aspect our friendship had taken on.

Georgi picked me up in front of the building in her zippy black VW Jetta with a sunroof and drove us to her apartment on Francis Street. She served a salmon dinner with broccoli and red potatoes and some perfect chardonnay, and we enjoyed an easy conversation afterward. We didn't discuss the murder at all, which was a relief. Georgi and I didn't have a lot in common, but even so we seemed to have no problem coming up with things to talk about. After a cup of coffee and some cheesecake for dessert, Georgi drove me home and waited in her Jetta at the curb while I walked into the building. It was about ten o'clock.

As I was unlocking my apartment door, Clara opened her door and I heard her voice behind me, shrill with anger. "Where have you been? I have been so worried that I was ready to call the police." When I turned to answer, I saw that she was crying.

"Clara—" I began, and she interrupted.

"Where *were* you!" she demanded again.

"I went to dinner at a friend's house. What's going on?"

"How could you do this to me," she cried. "You knew I would worry about you. We could be killed anytime we turn our backs out there on the street. How could you do it?"

"Calm down. I didn't walk, I had a ride. But, but look, Clara, you can't do this. I mean . . . I can't live like this, I just can't. We're both adults—we're not supposed to be answerable to each other for every little thing we do!"

"You should have let me know you were going out," she said, "in light of the current dangerous situation. You should have known that I would worry about you."

"Maybe I *should* have known you would worry," I said coldly; I was getting mad. "So let's make an understanding right now. You don't have to tell me when you go out, okay? And I don't have to tell you when I go out."

She began to cry again. "I thought you were dead," she said bitterly. "I thought he got you, too. Then I was in my bed shaking, thinking I would be the next one, it would be part of his plan because the three of us were such friends." I let that delusion pass unremarked. Poor Clara.

"Look, I'm sorry you were worried, Clara. I really am. But I can't live this way, feeling watched all the time. Can you understand that?"

"We owe each other the consideration of saying that we are going out when we are going out," she said. "That is the least we can do after Devi's murder." I couldn't accept that. It was too much for me, murder or not. I'd never given any *lover* the power over my life that Clara wanted.

"I'm sorry, Clara. I don't want to cause you worry or upset, but I can't agree to that. I've had to fight my mother most of my life about this same thing. I'm not going through all that again. Not with anyone."

"You are *selfish* then," Clara said angrily. "Like so many others I have known, you have no idea *how* to be a friend. And you are *not* my friend." She turned and went into her apartment, slamming the door behind her. *You are not my friend.* I thought of Paul Monnard's similar words to Devi. My God, what a chilling comparison to make.

Inside my own apartment I saw the phone machine blinking and steeled myself for what I knew I'd find. Aside from a message from Michael and one from Liz, who was calling from a hotel in Portland, I found three messages from Clara on my machine, each call more agitated than the last. I sighed, erased the messages, and went into the bathroom, where I washed my face and brushed my teeth.

Just as I was getting into my pajamas, the phone rang again; I let the machine pick up, and I heard Clara's voice. "Norrie, I am so sorry I yelled at you," she was saying. "Please pick up the phone so that I can apologize."

I did pick up the phone—just to preclude further calls from her. I was expecting Michael to phone me sometime tonight so I couldn't turn off the ringer, as much as I'd have liked to do so for my peace of mind.

"Clara, I'm tired. I understand you were upset, and I'm not mad at you. But I am *not* changing my mind about anything." She said not a word at first, so I went on firmly but in a quieter voice, "I meant what I said."

"You are so harsh," she said. "I wish you would try to understand how I feel."

"I think I do understand how you feel—you've made that pretty clear. But I'm not going to change how *I* feel. And I really have to go now."

"But I just wanted to say I'm sorry. I really am sorry that I lost control of myself out in the hall just now. That was so unlike me."

"It's okay. Don't worry about it." I sighed.

"I was wondering," she began, and her voice became sweet all of a sudden, "did you have a good time tonight?"

"Sure," I said, offering no details.

"So . . . who did you have dinner with? Maybe your good friend Michael Sullivan?" My heart literally stopped. To hear his name spoken so casually by Clara conferred a degree of false and inappropriate familiarity to the question.

"No," I said slowly, trying to think how to handle this. "No, I wasn't with Michael."

"Maybe one of the Larkin fellows then?"

"Yes," I said. "That's right. Now, Clara, I really have to get to bed."

"But why is it such a secret?"

"Why is *what* such a secret?"

"The identity of your dinner companion," she said, and it sounded so funny, so police-interrogation style, I almost laughed.

"Jesus, Clara, it's not a *secret*. I just don't feel I should have to explain everything I do."

"That's fine," she said primly. "I certainly will try to understand this from now on and will not invade your sacred privacy." I knew she wanted me to protest.

"Okay," I said, "thanks. I'll see you Wednesday for the colloquium, if you're still planning to go—but I have to hang up now." And then I just said good-bye and hung up. That seemed to be the only way I was getting off the phone.

By the time Wednesday rolled around, Clara seemed to be over her pout. But I was more leery of her than ever, so I kept my distance conversationally even as we walked over to the Larkin together, and I made a point of talking to other Larkies at the dinner afterward. It was getting dark when Clara and I walked home from the restaurant, and even now I had to admit to myself that I felt glad not to be alone. We said good night cordially enough at our doors.

A day or two later a stunning, never-dreamed-of thing happened. I received notification from Ida's lawyers that she'd left me an inheritance. The letter had been forwarded from my Watertown address, so I knew Ida must have made out the will some time ago. I couldn't believe it. I'd thought she was practically penniless after selling her apartment to pay for Brookline Manor. I went for a meeting at her lawyers' offices, and they told me Ida had left all that remained of her estate to me, as she had no other living relations.

"To Honora Blume, to help you in the pursuit of your art," Ida's will said. I was very moved and grateful—though too frazzled by recent events to have any idea what I wanted to do with it. The lawyers suggested I hire an accountant, and they gave me the names of two good ones.

It wasn't enough money to make me independently wealthy—I would still have to work—but it was enough to change my life. Not in a lot of ways, but in one way or another. For example, I could use it to buy a very nice house in a good area—and pay cash, thus eliminating monthly rent expense. *Or* I could invest it for my old age. *Or* I could invest it and use the interest to augment my income each year. *Or* I could put it into a savings account, let it draw interest, and use a portion of it to take time off annually from my paying job—maybe a month or two each year—and just concentrate on painting. I would have enough to do any one of these things, but not more than one of them, it seemed to me. The main thing was, I wanted to use it as Ida had intended me to—to help me pursue my art.

For the time being I put all of the money into my regular savings account. It was kind of a lot of money to keep in a straight savings account, and the interest rate was much lower than if I'd bought CDs or government bonds, but for right now I wanted the money where I'd have access to it. Having it available made me feel secure, at least economically. Everything else in my life these days felt—and was, I guessed—uncertain. I'd lost two people who meant a lot to me, and I was beginning to wonder if I was going to lose Michael, too.

It occurred to me that I hadn't factored in a future with Michael when making my financial projections, and it seemed less an oversight than realism. It had been nearly seven months since he'd stopped sleeping with Brenda, yet they were still living in the same house. He'd been loving and protective of me throughout the recent troubles, he'd even begun taking me to do my grocery shopping. Our lovemaking was as intense as ever and had moved into explorer mode again.

But everything on the outside of our lives was a lie, and there seemed to be no end in sight. Increasingly I found the furtiveness and secrecy untenable. There was so much already to worry about and feel insecure about.

One morning I told Michael I didn't think I could go on much longer in this "Dark End of the Street" relationship. "We don't even know what we're turning into as a result of all this lying," I said. "If every day we live is a lie, maybe we're becoming so used to lying that one day we'll actually be comfortable with it."

"I know," he said. "And it's not a life, anyway—not for you or Brenda—or me. I promised to make a break by the end of your Larkin year, and it's nearly here. I guess I've been having trouble finding the right moment to make the final break—it's just felt like bad timing since all the good news started coming in. But I want us to have our life, you and me—I want it more than anything. I've just got to try harder. Could you bear with me a little longer?"

"I don't know, Michael. I don't know how long I can hold on at this point."

"I don't blame you for losing faith, Norrie—I've made you wait too long, and lately you've had good reason to feel left out of my life. I know that. I think I need to show you I mean what I'm saying. Listen, I know Liz is coming to Boston soon. Let's go together to hear her read. We'll take her out to dinner or something, meet her like the couple we are."

"Well, I guess that would make the relationship feel less like a fairy tale," I finally said.

"I'd really like to go with you. I've never had the chance to see you and Liz together—two of the funniest women I know."

You've never had the chance to see me with anyone, I thought—*anyone but you.*

Liz was on her whirlwind "two cities a day" book tour to promote *Never Trust a Woman With a Brain,* a witty novel about contemporary sexual politics in academe (it was sort of a sequel to 1998's *Never Let a Man See You Dead,* which had gone into multiple printings, and she was being hailed as "a female David Lodge"). She was coming into Boston from an afternoon bookstore event in New York City and would be around just long enough to give a reading at the Boston Public Library, after which she'd have to race to the airport to catch a redeye to Seattle.

"My publicist has just fucked me up so badly here," she complained one night when she called me from Cleveland. "The idiot doesn't know which way is up. He practically has me in two places at once! I've got to do an early morning live TV show in Seattle the day after my evening reading in Boston! And this isn't even the worst example of how my life has gone this week, thanks to him." She sounded manic and tense, and I could hear her exhaling smoke over the phone—I couldn't believe she was smoking again, after the health problems smoking had caused her mother. "So that means we're not even going to get to have dinner together! Shit." Again I could hear a hasty, nervous breath of smoke.

"Well, at least we'll get to see each other face-to-face," I said. "And guess what—Michael is coming with me to your reading." It occurred to me just then that Devi had planned to go with me to see Liz. I pushed the memory away. What was the point in such thoughts? I knew that for a time everything I did would have some connection to Devi. If I allowed myself to, I could just cry all the time. "The man himself will be there," I said, "incarnate."

"No shit, he's actually coming out in the world with you in front of God and everybody? Well, that's some kind of progress anyway." Liz was worried about me, afraid I was ruining my life. She hadn't said as much, but I could tell. She liked Michael, but I knew she thought he would never leave Brenda. He was so "traditional," she'd said once— only once—not the type to rebel against convention. She would not say that if she'd ever seen him in bed.

"He's trying to change his life," I told her, feeling a little defensive of Michael and of myself. "That's why he's promised to go and see you with me."

"Uh huh, that's good. I'm not saying it's not good."

"It'll be kind of a relief to be with someone who knows about us."

"Hey, I'm looking forward to seeing the two of you together. Maybe it'll help me to understand it all better. I just worry about you, I can't help it."

"Well, don't. You don't need to. If it weren't for Michael, I don't know how I'd have gotten through the last month, with Devi murdered and then Ida dying so soon after. He's been tender and protective and wonderful in every way."

"Exactly," she said.

"*What*—now you're saying that's *bad?*"

"Oh, never mind," Liz muttered. I heard her lighting up again. "Just forget it," she said.

"No—*what?*" I was trying hard not to get riled at my friend.

She sighed, then spoke with audible reluctance. "It's just, you know, that mensch compulsion. It makes it very hard to let anyone down. And in this situation Michael's gonna have to let *someone* down."

We were both quiet for a minute, letting the implications sink in.

"And that's compounded," Liz went on, exhaling, "by the first-time felon thing."

"What?" I was starting to wish I smoked.

"He told you he'd never stepped out on Brenda before you, right?"

"Yeah, but it's *true,* Liz. I know it is."

"Right. And that's just the problem. He has no *idea*—NONE—what he's capable or incapable of doing in this situation. *Of course* you believe him—he's sincere when he says he wants to make a life with you. But he's got no way of knowing what he'll finally be able to do. And his history says volumes—he's been married about a million years."

"Twenty-five."

"Same difference."

"You're getting me upset," I told her. "I wish you'd try to shut up. *You* don't have any idea what he's capable of either."

"Sorry. I'll stop the sermonizing. But remember, I'm older than you and I know more."

"You're eight years older than me, but you're three years younger than Michael. So apparently, by your own measuring stick, *he* knows more than *you*."

"Jesus, that's right. You're eleven years younger than this guy," Liz said, ignoring my point altogether.

"Don't even go there," I said.

"I hate when people say, 'Don't go there.' It's canned repartée."

"You need a good night's sleep, Liz. You're a bloody pissant tonight. And I notice you're smoking again, by the way."

"Don't even go there," she said.

On the afternoon before Liz's reading, I was just figuring out what I'd wear that night when the phone rang. I went to answer it with a kind of intuitive dread. I knew it was Michael.

"Shit," he said, "I don't know what to do. Brenda just now called from her office and told me she'd like the two of us to go out to dinner tonight because she's tired and stressed—she had some sort of problem with an account today, an unexpected loss—and a big corporate client is steamed. I don't know what to say to her about tonight."

I overcame the temptation to say, Tell her that "the two of us" *will* be going to dinner tonight. I was trying to rein in my tendency to sarcasm these days.

"Tell her you're going to a reading," I said instead.

"I did. She said she'd go *with* me. Lately she wants to go everywhere I go, even when I go out to mail a letter. It's like she knows something."

"Well, Michael, I think any woman would 'know something' when you haven't been sleeping with her for seven months. Don't tell me she's never asked if there was someone else."

"No, she hasn't asked me once. Actually, that's surprised me, too."

"Well then, she doesn't want to know. I would know. Anyone would know. She knows."

Michael blew out a puff of nervous air. "That doesn't help tonight. Look, Norrie, I think I'm stuck. I'm just going to have to tell her I'll go to dinner with her and that I'll skip the reading because she's feeling rough. What else can I do?"

"Obviously you've already decided what you have to do," I told him. Then I clammed up. No way I was making this easier for him. Maybe Liz had been onto something after all about the mensch compulsion. Not to mention the first-time felon syndrome.

"You're probably right," he admitted, and then sighed. "Okay. I'm sorry, honey, but I just can't go."

So what would I do now? I wasn't about to take Clara with me to see Liz, and I'd not gone out alone after dark even once since Devi's death.

Michael seemed to think about this at the same moment I did.

"Look," he said, "I'm coming to get you right now. It'll be a little early when you get over there, but you can have a cappuccino at Starbucks and then walk over to the BPL—it's right down the block. Then you won't have to take a taxi over or go on the T by yourself."

I knew driving me to the library was the only thing that would make Michael feel better about finking out on me, so I let him do it even though it meant I'd be downtown about ninety minutes before the reading. And it didn't address the problem of coming home alone.

He picked me up about thirty minutes later, and we drove into Boston listening to some jazz station he'd no doubt turned on so we wouldn't have to talk about what was happening. He pressed twenty dollars on me for cab fare home. "I'm not letting you take the T that late," he said, "and you never have any money."

"I'm solvent now, thanks to Ida—remember?"

"Right, well, take this anyway because it's my fault you have to take a cab."

He looked glum as he waved good-bye from his car. I felt pretty glum myself. This turn of events did not bode well for a future together, and I knew it. Michael was more worried about what Brenda would find out than he should be if he was going to leave at any point in this lifetime.

I sat in Starbucks for a long time, nursing a frappuccino and a muffin, and then went over to the BPL at 7:20, ten minutes before the reading was to start. Liz wasn't there yet when I found a seat, and she wasn't there ten minutes later either. She came rushing into the room at 7:35, five minutes after the reading was to have started, so we didn't get to talk first. She grinned at me from the podium as soon as she saw me, but then during the reading I saw her looking over to where I was sitting as she read, and knew she was taking note of the fact that I was alone and wondering what had happened to my plans to come with Michael. I was mortified. The one person in the world who knew about us *would* have to witness the fact that he'd more or less stood me up.

After the reading I waited for Liz to sign copies of *Never Trust a Woman* and then when she'd finished I stepped forward. We hugged and I told her she'd been brilliant tonight (she had) and looked wonderful (her *clothes* looked great—Liz's funky-elegant style always did—so it wasn't a lie exactly, but she looked exhausted and stressed). She told me I looked great (I didn't; I was too pissed to look great, so clearly she was lying). I thought it a shame that women had to begin every conversation with commentary about how one another looked, because that usually meant we got every visit started off with lies. After a decent interval of nearly half a minute, Liz asked me what had happened to Michael's plan to come with me. I explained briefly and then saw her admirably resisting the "I told you so" impulse. For Liz that was no small thing, but in this case I knew she took no pleasure in being right.

"I'm going to have to talk to him," I said grimly. "I know that." She just leaned forward and kissed me on the cheek.

"What's that," I asked her, "the kiss of death?"

It was sad to see Liz leaving for the airport so quickly. But at least she had someone driving her, which was more than I could say. I caught a taxi at the stand in front of the Westin Hotel down the street and became madder and madder as I rode back to Cambridge in the backseat while my French-speaking cabdriver yelled at his French-speaking girlfriend who was somehow, against all the rules, riding along in the front passenger seat. They were both smoking, too, which was also against the rules. I decided right then and there that one of the things I would do with Ida's money was buy a car—and take driving lessons.

"*Tout de suite! Tout de suite!*" he yelled, raising the heel of his hand at her. The guy was an asshole, but still I would blame everything he did on Michael, and that was that. He turned the cab into Brattle Street at eleven—exactly the hour the police believed Devi had been murdered in that spot. I shivered.

As I got out of the cab in front of the apartment building, I saw a thin, dark-haired man standing just outside the entry to the courtyard. I froze, sure it was him. Paul Monnard. No one else was around, and the cab had pulled away. I didn't know what to do.

"Eh, pardon me," he called across the sidewalk, moving toward me. I heard the accent. It had to be Monnard.

"No!" I barked and ran up the street. I wasn't even half a block up when a skinny blond girl coming in my direction waved at someone behind me and called out, "Serge! Sorry I'm late!" I realized she was calling out to the man I'd thought was Devi's killer. I felt like a fool and kept walking to cover my embarrassment. But then there I was, alone, late at night, walking past Radcliffe Yard. I stopped near the sidewalk bench Mutton used to sit on. I turned then, just to be sure the happy couple were gone, and slowly made my way back to the building.

Without warning something brushed my ankles and I let out a yell, then saw a cat racing into some shrubbery. Dear God, please just get me safely inside the building, my apartment. I had my keys in hand before I entered the courtyard. The courtyard. Dear God. I was not going to be able to stand much more. Something had to give; the killer had to be found and locked up.

Throughout everything, I was not unmindful that Michael had let this happen tonight.

Walking into the courtyard tonight, suddenly it was as if I were her. Devi, on that terrible night. It must have been the fear, the displacement I suddenly felt, as if I didn't belong where I was and could not survive the walk across those bricks. I wanted to turn and run, but watched my legs as they carried me step by step over the weathered bricks, my feet her feet, my legs her legs, sound of my breath the sound of her breath. With each step I felt it pumping in my chest, her heart.

Then I see them, the hands, reaching out for me, in one of them a knife, and I think, My God, I've seen those hands before, I know those hands. Yet I can't think whose they are. It's as if they're so familiar to me I can't name them. Am I awake? Am I asleep?

No one, no one is safe. No one is innocent. Everywhere I look I see guilt and pain. Wake me, wake me.

17

The next day I woke in damp and tangled sheets, my hands shaking, mouth dry. The night had been filled with horrible dreams, nightmares, waking images—I could hardly separate one from another.

I showered under a full blast of hot water, trying to purge my flesh of a crawling sensation, and afterward I dressed quickly and went in to the little eating table in my living room with a strong cup of coffee, which I didn't usually drink and only kept in the house for Michael.

Then I forced myself to sit quietly and take stock.

When I felt myself drifting back to bad thoughts, I got up and put on a tape of piano concertos, thinking Chopin might calm me. But piano music only put me in mind of the hands in my dreams.

I had to stop. I knew I had to stop. Had to ask myself what was important, what needed to be done.

All right, then. I would talk to Michael. I wouldn't live this way any longer. That was one thing I knew for certain. I would not do it anymore.

I stood up from the table.

But wait. What else? I sat back down.

The colloquium. It was coming up soon, and I needed to finish the paintings in time for my colloquium presentation, had to find my way back to my work. *But the lost painting . . .*

Never mind the lost painting. Now the police would worry about it. What else?

All that entered my mind then was *I want to go home.* And though I've heard those words in my head for most of my life, this time when I heard them I saw the little house I'd grown up in, the little frame bungalow on Orange Avenue in Santa Monica. *I want to go home.* Good God, I was slipping badly. I shook my head, stood up again, and went to call Michael. He would probably be home alone at this hour. *Furtive.* I was fucking tired of being furtive.

I called him several times, and there was no answer. Each time the machine came on I hung up and went back into the living room with a fresh cup of coffee. I was getting wired.

Finally, after an hour or two—I'd lost all sense of time—he answered the phone. His voice sounded tired, though it warmed immediately, as always, when he heard me on the other end.

"Norrie! God, I'm glad it's you." And then, at the same time and exactly in sync we both said the same thing:

"We need to talk." Yes, I thought, I was sure he'd worked out an apology, excuses.

"Come over," I said. I would tell him it was over. It was time, no matter what he said, and I knew that. Obviously, this was the day I'd long dreaded, put off. Now it was on us. That was that.

"Yeah," he said, "I'll be there in fifteen minutes." He sounded somber.

When he arrived I was waiting by the curb. I didn't want the temptation of him upstairs in my apartment with me. Not that I felt temptable today, but I wasn't taking any chances.

As we drove, Michael put his hand on my knee, patted it, left it there. He had no idea, I knew, of the nightmares in my head. It was odd, I thought, how we can be within inches of someone we know so well, love so much, and not have the slightest mental image of their interior landscape. The sight of his hand on my knee so companionably filled me with grief and with dread of what I had to say.

"Maybe this isn't an indoor day," I suggested uneasily. "Will we have enough privacy in a restaurant?"

"Yeah," he said, "you've got a point, I guess."

We decided to buy take-out sandwiches and drinks and eat them at our old meeting spot, Mount Auburn Cemetery. I didn't like the symbolism of a cemetery—the feeling of how appropriate it was for what was about to happen—but there was nowhere else to be private. It was too late to suggest going back to my apartment, and anyway Clara was home today and might see us.

When we settled on a bench inside Mount Auburn with our lunch bags, neither of us said anything at first. I knew that if I opened my mouth, the sentences would fly out of their own accord. Was I really ready for this?

Finally Michael spoke. "I want to make a life with you, Norrie. Last night at dinner I told Brenda I want a divorce." His words, so much the opposite of what I was prepared to tell him, left me utterly at a loss. "I felt awful leaving you alone last night, making you come home in the dark by yourself. I knew then it was just time for me to act." He sighed. "It's going to be hard, you know, telling Bridget and Finn . . . all that. But it's time, and I know it."

I was so unprepared for this that I didn't know how to feel, what to say. We sat wordless for a time. I felt a faint afternoon breeze skim my face as I read a nearby tombstone silently: *Harold Moore, Beloved Husband of Rita, 1909–1969.*

"Norrie?"

"Yes?"

"Please say you'll have me." A dove landed on Harold Moore's tombstone; flew off. Still I couldn't speak aloud, even though inside I was saying, *yes, yes,* like Molly Bloom, *yes,* while Michael waited for me to speak into the afternoon air that suddenly seemed to be crammed with redbirds, bluebirds, doves, and robins. Oh God, I was so afraid to believe this. I looked at Michael.

"Are you sure?" I asked him. He didn't hesitate for a second.

"I'm absolutely sure." He pulled me into his arms and spoke into the top of my head. "I know I've let you down, kept you waiting for too long. But please say yes. Please say yes so that we can start living." He was holding me so close I could hear his heart beating, could feel it pounding hard against my cheek. *Yes, I said inside, yes, yes.* But when finally I found my voice, it came out more hesitant than Molly Bloom's.

"I want to say yes, but I—I think I'm afraid of joy, Michael, afraid to trust it."

"Look at me," he said, tilting my chin with his fingers till my face looked directly up into his. "Look at me, Norrie. I love you completely. I want to be with you for all the rest of my fallible, living days. I want to sleep beside you when our surfaces have gone all shriveled. I'll love you just as passionately then."

"I don't intend to shrivel," I said. I always make stupid remarks when

I'm about to cry but can't afford to. The truth was, I knew this was it, right now on the earth, my one real chance to be happy with a man. "Yes," I heard myself saying then, "yes."

There didn't seem to be any comprehensible way to expand on that, so I let him fold me up in his arms again. "Yes," I said over and over into his chest, into his thumping heart; I had to make it hear me and remember, had to speak directly into that refuge of want and love, grief and joy. *Listen to me, listen: Yes, I said, yes.*

We sat in each other's arms on the bench for a while without talking. I realized I'd never felt so perfectly happy in my life. It was as if I'd finally given in to something I'd always wanted but had been afraid of. After a long time Michael spoke.

"Will you make an honest man out of me?" He nuzzled my neck.

"I'll try, but I can't promise any miracles," I said.

"That's all I ask."

"Will you help me to stop telling fibs?"

"I'm only one man, Honora."

"Good point."

We hadn't eaten a bite of our lunch. When we tore up the bread and fed it to the birds, they gathered around us like disciples, heads bobbing at our feet.

"The two of us are going to be together," Michael told them. "We're going to make a life."

Back at my apartment, I led him to my bed and said, "May I choreograph this one, sir?"

"I'd be honored," he said, and when I unzipped his pants and found him already hard, suddenly more than anything I wanted to swallow his desire, to incorporate it with my own, and so I took him in my hand and put my lips just against the tip of him and murmured into his cock *yes, yes* like a lullaby sung close into a microphone *yes yes yes,* my tongue darting then along his wet and rigid cock, and when finally I took him fully into my mouth, I heard his voice come deep—*Oh, oh,* he said, *Oh,* and filled my mouth with his sweet liquid, and I drank it all, didn't let a drop slip away, and then he pulled me up toward him and kissed my face all over. Just as we were falling toward a peaceful slumber, I noticed the early afternoon light at the window, the way it fell into the red glass pitcher and rested securely there in its bowl.

When we woke it was two-thirty and Michael pulled me close to him again. "I had no idea I was going to fall asleep," he said, stroking my shoulder.

"No, I don't think you've ever done that before." Maybe it was the relief, I thought.

"I love the smell of your hair," he said, "it's like ginger." I was pretty sure that was the cheap conditioning shampoo I always bought at CVS, but I didn't say so.

Michael looked at the clock and jumped up. He had to go watch Bridget play softball at three-thirty, he said. "Brenda's been on her about her weight all year, even trying to put her on a diet, and I hate it when she does that to Bird. So I got the idea that joining a team might help the kid to get some healthy exercise that has nothing to do with weight loss—and that would get Brenda off her back. I told Bird I'd go to all her games if she signed up, and we'd make that time each week *our* time, hers and mine. She's so proud she made it to third base last week in her first game ever—she's not the most athletic kid." He smiled, shook his head. "She swears she's going to make it to home plate today, and I want to be there."

"Of course you do. You *have* to be there."

He put his arms around me. "Next time I see you, we'll start planning the rest of our life."

Our *life.* Not our *lives.* All I could do was grin at the sound of it.

For the rest of the day after he left, I went around in a daze, and I fell asleep on the couch before 9:00 P.M., lulled by the steady, muffled hum of traffic on Brattle. When I woke it was nearly 4:00 A.M., and I realized that Michael had never called me last night. He'd said he would and he hadn't. I wondered if there'd been more fireworks with Brenda.

I tried to go back to sleep, but now I felt uneasy. Where was Michael? What had happened?

At 8:00 A.M., when I knew Brenda would have left the house, I tried phoning him and got no answer. I hung up when the machine came on. What did this mean? Now, during the hours when he usually stayed home to write, he wasn't there either. Could he be avoiding me? Did he have a case of "buyer's remorse"?

I went distractedly about my day then, taking my laundry down to the basement facility and then running a couple of errands in the square. Every so often I rang Michael, but got no answer.

*   *   *

It was later that day that I found out Clara had been sick. I'd noticed she hadn't phoned me in a couple of days, but I didn't tend to question such bounty. There'd been a lot of flu going around Boston and Cambridge most of the academic year, but you didn't expect it so much in midspring. She called me that afternoon to say she couldn't go to the colloquium; I could hear in her voice that she was pretty sick. Remembering how she'd helped me when I had flu a while back, I went over to check on her. It took her fully five minutes to get to the door after I knocked.

When I saw her it scared me—her face looked greenish pale, and the whites of her eyes looked pink. The little love seat was opened into a bed and the sheets were disheveled. I led her back to it and helped her to lie down. Then I went and got her a glass of water.

"Clara, I can't believe you didn't call me and ask for some help!"

"I thought you wanted me to leave you alone," she said in a tone of self-pity.

Her forehead was damp and very hot to my touch. She closed her eyes.

"She used to do that," Clara murmured, eyes still closed, "when I was sick."

"Your mother?"

"Yes. You reminded me." She breathed shallowly. "Your touch." Poor Clara. I felt sorry for her. It seemed she might never get over the feeling that her mother had abandoned her.

"I'm sure she loved you very much, Clara."

Her eyes opened then, though her face did not move, and she fixed her gaze on me. I felt those angry dark eyes riveted on mine. "Don't tell me," she said, "don't try to tell me what you cannot know." I had no idea what to say. I guessed my comment might have been facile or even presumptuous, but I'd only been trying to comfort her.

"Do you have a thermometer?" I asked, changing the subject. She lay there with her eyes closed then and didn't answer. I hadn't seen my own thermometer since I was sick, and I had no idea what had happened to it. I might have thrown it away in a pile of tissues for all I knew.

Again I asked Clara if she had a thermometer, and this time she motioned feebly toward the bathroom. It was hard to tell if she was just

281

being testy now, or if she was getting weaker. I went into her small bathroom and found nothing in the medicine cabinet but some bottles of prescription pills—one of them was Prozac—and the usual toiletries. There was nothing but some little soaps in the brightly woven basket atop the back of her toilet.

Then I remembered the storage closet next to the bathroom. That must have been what she was directing me to. She seemed to have slipped into sleep when I emerged from the bathroom and went toward the closet.

"Clara?" I said softly, "is it in here? The closet?" She didn't answer and I could hear her breathing the long, heavy rhythms of sleep. Her face had cleared of its discontent and was strangely like the face of an infant, unlined and free of the patina of personal history.

In the closet I rooted through several plastic storage boxes and looked into the built-in drawers that went up the wall just inside the doorway. I found a hot water bottle in the second drawer and decided I must be getting close. But as I went through the third and fourth drawers I still found no thermometer. I knelt on the closet floor to reach the two bottom drawers.

It was in the very last drawer that I found it. Not the thermometer, but the object that would change life's landscape for a long time to come. On a piece of plastic wrap lay a long, black braid with a yellow glass-beaded elastic at the end. I recoiled. I couldn't touch it. Devi's braid. Was there a slight odor in the air of the closet, or did I imagine that?

I stood with effort, and then stayed in the closet for what seemed a long time, weaving on my feet, terrified.

The possibility had never crossed my mind! Never for a moment. Now, suddenly, it seemed the inescapable truth: Clara had killed Devi. I thought of all the times she had told me Joe must have killed Devi, all the times she'd cried and claimed to be afraid to go out for fear the killer would get her next. All the times she had claimed to be worried about me when I went out without her. Carefully I closed the drawer and hoped nothing would give away the fact that I'd been in the closet.

I was frightened now, and I felt my entire body shaking when finally I walked out into the living room where Clara lay, feverish and sleeping. I didn't know what to do. Could not think rationally. Very simply, this didn't seem real.

Immediately I began to doubt myself. It couldn't have been Devi's braid. I'd had the image of it in my mind since the murder, so it was natural that any black braid would seem to be Devi's. Maybe Clara had once had long hair herself and had kept it—her hair was as black as Devi's. Lots of women keep their hair to use as a hairpiece after it's been cut, especially if it was very long. And Devi couldn't have been the only woman in the world who had those beaded hair elastics, I was sure, though I'd never seen them on anyone but her and had always assumed she'd brought them from India. For now, while Clara was sick, I decided I had to believe she was innocent. I had to *not believe* my own instincts.

I put cold cloths on Clara's forehead and sat beside her, grateful that she was too out of it to talk to me. I didn't know how I could carry on a normal conversation with her right then. My eyes kept sliding to her muscular arms and sturdy hands, thinking what they might have done. Clara roused and asked for more water. I held the glass to her lips, feeling as close to hatred in that moment as I ever have, for in some way, despite my resolve to hold off judgment, I knew it must be true. Clara had killed Devi out of jealousy.

Suddenly it hit me. Clara's jealousy of Devi—the missing painting. Was it possible Clara had somehow taken it? Stop, I told myself, don't get carried away here.

Back at home later, I found myself trembling, feeling as if I might vomit. I couldn't eat dinner. The longer I was in my apartment, away from Clara, the more unreal it all seemed, the more I began to doubt what I'd found there. Lots of women had false braids and "switches" of hair; they kept them in their closets and bedroom drawers. Maybe that was what it was, though Clara didn't seem at all the type for such artifice.

And I couldn't actually recall seeing that particular yellow beaded elastic on Devi's braid that last night, though it was the exact hair accessory she used and yellow was the color she'd been wearing.

Still, how could Clara have done it? Hadn't she been home on the night of the killing when I passed her door and heard the music? *Aida?* The sound of it had made me believe she was at home, but couldn't she have planned it that way? I didn't recall Clara's music ever being as loud as it was that night. Had she turned it up to suggest her presence inside, and then left—maybe with the CD set to repeat play? But if she'd done that, wouldn't she think I might come knocking on her door to tell her Devi had been killed? And wouldn't I think it odd to find her gone?

Then I remembered all the times Clara had knocked on my door while my own music was blaring—sometimes that very recording—and later I'd told her I couldn't leave my work to answer the door. She could have planned to say that. I could imagine her enjoying the thought of telling me that.

One thing for sure, there was no way she'd have been able to come back into the bright lights of our building after the bloody murder out front. She'd have had to run away from the scene quickly, maybe around to the back of the building and out onto Mason Street. It was late, very dark. If she'd worn dark clothes, no one would have seen the blood on her. But where would she go at that hour?

Then I knew. The Larkin. It would have been eleven-thirty or even close to midnight by the time she got there, and no one would have been working in their offices at that hour. She could have spent the night in her office after showering in the bathroom that was provided on each floor of every Larkin building. She might have kept a clean change of clothes in her office for that purpose.

I would be going back into Clara's apartment later to check on her and bring her some kind of nourishment. I could go into the closet again then if she was asleep. I would have to look, no matter how dreadful the prospect of seeing it again. The braid. I had to be sure of what I had seen.

Then I thought of her face, innocent just now in sleep.

Later I fixed some thin broth to bring her. She had let me take her key so she wouldn't have to get up to let me in, and I discarded a random thought about having it copied so I could sneak in later and look in the closet when she wasn't home. I wasn't the type for such gumshoe antics. I carried the bowl of broth over on a tray, along with some hot chamomile tea and some toast with honey. I knew she couldn't eat much, but she had to have some nourishment—in a corner of my mind I was thinking, *so she can be brought to justice.*

As I spoon-fed Clara the beef broth, I was repelled by her nearness and at the same time mindful that I couldn't be certain of her guilt until somehow I confirmed my discovery with a clear head. I would look for my painting in the closet, too—maybe wrapped up in something.

Though I waited around for her to go back to sleep, more and more she seemed to revive. She was pleased to have me there tending her, I could see that. I fixed another pot of tea in her kitchen and decided to do some conversational fishing.

"I like your hair," I told her. "It has beautiful highlights. Did you ever wear it long?"

"Oh no," Clara said. "This is the longest I have ever worn it—just to the collar." My stomach tightened. "My mother always kept my hair short," Clara continued. "She hadn't the patience for a daughter with long hair. She had short hair herself, and she cut mine every month with a pair of big sewing scissors." She looked at me with what seemed a kind of cautionary gaze, though I knew I was reading dark intention into everything now. "One of my most distinct memories of my mother," she said, "is the feeling of those cold blades against the back of my neck as she took my hair away from me." I felt the hairs stand up on the back of my own neck—the same physical response a cat has to danger, that lifting of hairs along the spine.

Not meeting her gaze, I got up and went into the kitchen and began washing dishes in the sink. Now and then my eyes slid to the Crate and Barrel knife block with its assortment of sharp carving and paring knives. My hands were shaking so badly I could scarcely keep hold of a dish. I heard Clara turn on the television from her bed with the remote. An old *I Love Lucy* rerun. It would be funny if it weren't so grotesque, I thought, this injection of wacky '50s humor into my blooming terror. Done with the dishes, I stood in the doorway and watched along with Clara as Lucy and Ethel stuffed chocolates into their mouths and down their blouses, trying to keep up with the pace of the candy factory. Occasionally I slid my eyes sideways to catch a glimpse of Clara, who seemed to be steadily rousing from her former fevered state.

"Come sit here," she said once, patting the mattress beside her. "You can't stand up all evening." There was nothing else to sit on in the apartment. I hesitated, then sat on the floor.

"I'm fine," I said rather abruptly. She looked hurt. I couldn't help that. There was only so far I could go with this sister act.

At some point in the evening, Clara mentioned that she'd left a couple of research books in her office at the Larkin, and she needed them in order to work on her book about feminism in Chile.

"I brought them over to the Larkin right after Devi died because I was there so much. I was just writing by hand in my office then. Now I am at a point where I need them again at home. I should be working even if I am sick," she said. "I wish I had them here."

"Maybe I could go over and get them for you," I offered. I'd like to look around her office when she wasn't there, I thought. "If you want to lend me your key."

"No," she said quickly, "I really don't like anyone to go through my research papers and books. I have it all arranged just so, and I'd be afraid something would get mixed up."

"Let me know if you change your mind." I was relieved and disappointed at once.

I stayed as long as I could bear to, and Clara never fell back to sleep, which meant I was unable to enter the closet and look at the braid again—or to look for the painting. At nine-thirty, when she said she was feeling a bit stronger, I decided I might as well leave. She got up and locked the door behind me when I left. I wished for a moment I hadn't put her key back on the kitchen counter.

At home I paced and paced. If Clara had never had long hair, then the braid had to be Devi's. It had Devi's hair elastic on it. And what about that faint smell, like old blood or some sort of rot? It could have come from something else in the closet, I guessed, but how likely was that? Or had there actually been a smell at all? Had I imagined it? Had I supplied the sensory accompaniment to what I'd thought I was looking at? The imagination was a powerful suggestive force.

Realistically, did I believe Clara could have lain in wait to hack Devi to death?

A person can pace until a rhythm takes over, and then thinking becomes clearer. That was what happened to me. I must have paced for at least an hour, thinking of all that had happened in the last few months—Clara's jealousy, her shock at seeing Devi's nude portrait, her suspicion that Devi and I were lovers. The more I walked, the more certain I felt. Clara had killed Devi.

I thought of calling Michael, but I couldn't call him at night, especially this late, not now when his household was coming apart. But where was he? Why hadn't he called? I had to push the thought of him out of my head if I was going to focus on the problem of Clara.

Late as it was, I decided to phone Georgi. Her voice was soft and slurry when she answered, as if she'd been asleep. I didn't bother to ask if I'd wakened her, didn't mess with niceties at all.

"I found the braid," I blurted into the phone.

"Who is this?"

"Norrie. I found the braid. Devi's braid."

"Oh God." She was wide awake. "Oh God. Where? Outside?"

I sucked in a big gulp of air. "It was in Clara's closet. I was looking for a thermometer—she's sick tonight—and I found it in a drawer. There was an elastic on it with glass beads—"

"—like Devi's," she finished in a small voice.

"Yellow. The color Devi was wearing the night she—"

"Oh God. Oh God. This is too horrible to be real. Tell me I'm still asleep."

"What am I supposed to do?" I asked, feeling panicky. "I don't know what to do!"

"Call the police? I don't know either."

"How can I call the police? What if I'm wrong?"

"But how can you be wrong, Norrie?"

"Okay, but I think I need to find a more, a more neutral alternative, just in case. I can't just have the cops come and haul her away in leg chains."

"Oh God."

"Right. So what do I do?"

"You know, that Australian science fellow, Jana Conger, made a crack the other day when Clara left the common room after talking about you nonstop. Jana joked that Clara had probably killed Devi to get rid of the competition."

"Oh my God. What did you say?"

"Well, she didn't say it to me directly. She said it to Kila Dotubu—you know, that beautiful African AIDS doctor? And Kila really put Jana in her place for saying such a thing, even in jest. 'This is not a matter for joking,' Kila said, 'I am ashamed of you.' "

Even as I murmured, "Good for Kila," it was hitting me that if Clara had killed Devi, it probably *was* because of me. I couldn't bear the thought that I might be in any way connected to the death of dear Devi. "Look, Georgi," I said then, "I need some help here. Just tell me what you think I should do now—*please.*"

"Well, you *have* to turn her in, I guess."

"But what if I'm wrong about this?" I said again, "How can I do that?"

"Yeah, I know," Georgi mused. "Like you said, you can't just have her hauled away in leg chains. Norrie, I have no idea how things like this are done."

"That's because there *are* no things like this," I said. This was a grotesque occurrence, a hideous anomaly.

"I have an idea," Georgi said then, "how about the Larkin? It would be a safe place to confront Clara, maybe in Jane Coleman's office—with Jane there, I mean. That would be, as you say, *civilized,* wouldn't it?"

"Yeah," I said slowly, mulling it over. "So I'd have to call Jane and tell her—*convince* her—about what I found. The braid." I stopped. "She'll never believe me, Georgi, I know it. It's just too weird, too messy. She's such a tidy WASP."

"Well, you have to try," Georgi said reasonably. "If Clara is the killer, none of us is safe. It could be you next. Or me." Georgi's words reminded me that if Clara had murdered Devi out of jealousy, Georgi herself could indeed be the next victim, as another possible contender for my affection. But wasn't this all crazy? Could it be true? I felt a chill run through me as I realized that it sounded unmistakably true.

"I'd have to call Jane in the morning," I said, working it out aloud, "and then she could call the police. And we'd all go to Clara's to examine the braid."

"Well, I don't know if it would work that way," Georgi said. "Anyway, Jane probably wouldn't call the police until you'd both finished questioning Clara about the braid." We were both quiet, and then she said, "We'd better get some sleep, don't you think?"

"Sure," I agreed. *As if,* I thought.

All night I ruminated. I didn't want to do anything ill-considered or panicky. I kept reminding myself that there was always the possibility I was wrong about the braid.

Again I thought of the missing painting. I didn't want to blame Clara for everything in the world, but it made an awful kind of sense: I recalled the day Clara saw me coming out of the frame shop. And I was pretty sure I'd also mentioned to her, on the night I brought out Devi's portrait to show her, that the one I'd have liked to show her was at the frame shop.

At some point I found Detective Burns's card in my desk and put it beside the bed. For a moment I thought I should just call him now. He'd even given me his home phone number. But then I pictured the cops swooping in and pulling Clara away, handcuffed and crying. I thought of Devi—her dignity—and I knew she would prefer to have things handled with as much decorum as possible. Even if Clara was guilty, I didn't want there to be sensational photos of Devi's killer being dragged away by burly policemen. Devi's poetry was her legacy; it would be an injustice for her to be remembered for being a murder victim. Maybe if I could find a seemly way to handle this thing, it wouldn't become such a big story in the press. I wouldn't call Burns until after Jane Coleman and I had confronted Clara at the Larkin. It would be an easy matter to call him from there, and it seemed more discreet somehow.

Clara's quandary about the books gave me the perfect opening to suggest a cab ride over there together as soon as she was well. *If* Jane Coleman could be convinced that I wasn't insane when I told her I'd found Devi's braid in Clara's closet. Even thinking the words through like that, I began to doubt myself again.

I drank three glasses of dry sherry to help me sleep. I would need all the strength I had in order to get through the next few days. Where was Michael?

The next morning I woke early and went directly over to Clara's to check on her. I kept fearing she'd get rid of the braid, which might be the only physical evidence that would positively link her to the murder.

But of course that was silly, since she didn't know I'd found it.

Unless, of course, she'd seen me go into the closet yesterday but had said nothing.

I felt nervous as I knocked on her door. I realized again I was actually fearful of Clara now. If she'd killed Devi, she could kill me. Clara wasn't tall, but she was powerfully built. And certainly she was considerably taller than poor little Devi had been. And immeasurably stronger.

Clara answered the door still in her pajamas and a little pale, but looking better.

"After three days of sickness, I am getting better," she smiled as she waved me in. "I have even had a light breakfast."

"Oh," I said, trying to hide my relief about the breakfast, "I was going to fix you something to eat—I came over to take your order."

"Thank you anyway, Norrie. You are so good to me." Her appreciation made me freshly uncomfortable in my duplicity, but I had to forge ahead, for Devi.

"I've been thinking about your books over at the Larkin," I told her. "I know you need them. Would you feel up to going over there with me tomorrow? I told Jane Coleman I'd pop in to say hello, and I'm sure she'd love to see you at the same time." I felt like a spy. It wasn't a pleasant feeling, whatever the justification.

"Oh, I would love that," Clara said, flushing with pleasure, "I like Jane very much and have hardly had the chance to know her. But I don't think I will feel quite up to walking all that way by tomorrow. Maybe we could do it on the weekend when I am stronger."

"But then you won't have your books," I pointed out. I didn't know how many days I could stand being locked inside this horrible secret. "How about a taxi? We could split the cost."

"Oh yes," Clara said. "That would be much better. I would like that. What time tomorrow would you like to go?"

"I don't know yet," I told her, and my heart was beginning to race at the thought of the confrontation that would have to happen then. "Let me call you when I've got the time all figured out." What if Jane Coleman wasn't going to be there tomorrow? Or what if she thought I was crazy and refused to participate?

As soon as I got back to my apartment, I called Jane and told her secretary, Mimi, that I had an emergency. Jane was in a meeting at the moment, Mimi said, could she call me back? No, I told her—this was too serious. Mimi put me through.

Jane answered, sounding disgruntled. "Mimi says you have to talk to me now, but can't this wait, Honora?"

"No—it's urgent," I told her. She shooed someone out of her office and came back to the phone, sounding rather cool.

"Now what is this all about?" she asked me, the unspoken *It had better be good* afloat in the telephone air between us.

I told her I'd found what seemed to be Devi's braid in Clara's closet, but that I couldn't be sure until I confronted Clara and let her try to explain it. As I heard my own words coming out into the air, I knew they sounded farfetched, even loony.

Jane was flabbergasted and extremely dubious. I didn't blame her a bit. She wanted to know why I thought Clara would do "such an unthinkable thing." I told her it was a fact that *someone* had done that unthinkable thing, and then I went down the list of odd or jealous behaviors I'd noted in Clara, especially in regard to Devi or me. I told her how several other Larkies had noticed this behavior in Clara and thought of her as unstable. I mentioned my suspicion about the missing painting. I even told Jane about Clara's bitter and irrational words concerning her mother's death. Finally, I think I had Jane convinced that at least we should talk to Clara.

"This is . . . it's just shocking," Jane said. "What if she didn't do it, Honora? Are you prepared to live with that eventuality?"

"I guess I'll have to if she didn't do it," I said. I'd thought of that again and again, and I knew it would be a nightmare. "But I saw the braid, Jane. It had one of those elastics with glass beads attached, just like Devi wore. The beads were yellow. That was the color Devi was wearing the night she was killed. And it had a . . ." I could hardly bear to say it—it seemed an indelicate reference to Devi's mortal remains—"an unpleasant smell."

"Oh, my Lord," Jane sputtered. Then she sighed. "All right, but we will not *accuse*. We will *confront*. We will give her a chance to explain."

"That's all I want," I said. "I'll bring her over tomorrow at about eleven." My stomach was churning.

Jane sighed again. "Dear God, I thought Devi Bhujander's murder was the worst thing I'd ever encountered in all my professional life. If this is possibly true, it makes everything so much worse."

I phoned Clara to tell her what time we were going to the Larkin the next day, but her phone rang and rang until the machine picked up. Where could she have gone? Thinking she might be sick again, I hung up without leaving a message and went back next door. I was at her door knocking when she came out of the elevator. She'd put on some chinos with her pajama top.

"Clara! Where were you?" Immediately I thought I sounded just like her. She seemed oblivious to the irony of the role reversal and answered willingly.

"I had to take my trash downstairs to the Dumpster," she said. "They are picking up today, and I have not taken it down since I got sick—it was piling up."

"But you should've told me. I'd have gladly taken it down for you."

"You are right, for I feel very tired again suddenly, just from this little exertion."

The rest of the day was tense for me. I brought Clara some soup for lunch, and then she napped for hours. At dinnertime I brought her macaroni and cheese—the only thing I had on hand—and I was surprised when she was thrilled by it.

Clara retired early, thank God, and I went home to call Liz. When she wasn't home, I hung up without leaving a message because there was no way to tell a machine what I had to say tonight.

I hadn't heard from Michael since he'd told me he was leaving Brenda. Not a single call in two days, which had never happened before. Even allowing for chaos and sorrow at his house, it was strange. I couldn't imagine what was going on that would keep him from phoning. I reflected, not for the first time, that if he was sick, no one would know to call me. If he'd been hurt in a traffic accident—ditto. I paced. Wrung my hands.

Finally, I forced myself to go to bed, taking a glass of wine with me to induce sleep. But I lay atop the mattress as if levitating, my body rigid with wakefulness and worry.

At 10:45 the next morning, Clara and I took a cab to the Larkin. It was a hot day, and there was very little breeze; I found myself sweating profusely in the backseat of the cab beside her, and I wasn't sure if this was due to weather or nerves. I kept putting my hand into my pocket to feel the card I'd put into it before I left the apartment—Detective Burns's card.

"Do you want to go to see Jane now," Clara asked as we drove up Concord, "or should we first go to our offices—I mean your studio and my office—and take care of our own things first?"

"Let's go and see Jane first," I said, feeling a little underhanded; Jane would be waiting for us in her office at eleven, so there was no choice. Again, I asked myself, what if I was wrong?

I will never forget that meeting as long as I live. Jane ushered us in with a strained smile playing over her lips. It was a large and elegant mahogany-paneled office with an enormous antique Oriental rug, and floor-to-ceiling shelves filled with leather-bound books. Not the sort of place at all for such goings-on as I was planning, and I suddenly felt all the more the riskiness of what I was about to say.

After we were seated and had exchanged pleasantries, at some point there was a sort of pause, and it felt as if the air in the room had crystallized. Jane was looking at me, Clara was looking at Jane, and then at me.

When I finally spoke, I did so with the counterfeit forcefulness that characterizes any act of will in the middle of fear. "There's something I need to ask you about," I told Clara. She looked surprised and quizzical; glanced again from Jane to me. Suddenly I felt her helplessness, and my self-doubt grew, but that had become a familiar feeling in the last two days and I knew I had to keep on. "When I came over to help you the other day," I began, my lips quivering as I spoke, "I was looking for a thermometer to take your temperature. Do you remember that?"

"A little bit," Clara said. "What is this about?" Rather than answer that question, I moved forward with my line of inquiry. Jane looked as if she'd swallowed something bad.

"When I asked you where your thermometer was, you indicated the west wall, where your bathroom is."

"I don't know," Clara said. "I don't remember much about that day—I was still pretty sick." She was frowning now steadily. "I don't feel that well even yet, today." Indeed, she did look unusually pale.

"There was no thermometer in your bathroom," I went on, ignoring the reference to the state of her health. "And then it occurred to me that your storage closet is also on that wall."

Her face changed now. I can't define the new expression other than to say it was as if she had switched herself off. She said nothing. Nothing at all.

"Clara . . . I found the braid."

"What? What do you mean?"

"I found the braid in your closet."

"But you are wrong. I have no *braid!*" She spat out the last word angrily. "I don't know what you are talking about."

"You *do* know what I'm talking about," I said, taking a chance. "I found Devi's braid."

"Devi's braid? I cannot imagine what you mean!"

"In the drawer. I found Devi's braid in your closet drawer."

"But I do not have a braid!" Clara expelled a sharp, hysterical laugh as she stared at me. "My *God!* What is going on here?" she shrieked. "What are you saying? Are you saying I killed *Devi?*" Her voice lowered a bit. "My God, I cannot believe you have tricked me in this way just to humiliate me in front of Jane. I cannot believe you would think I could do such a horrible thing as kill someone. Especially a person I loved and admired." There was a tear rolling down one of her cheeks. She began to weep aloud, in big gulping sobs. But she was lying about the braid, and that seemed to confirm my worst fears.

"I saw the braid, Clara. You know it was in your closet drawer."

Jane cut in. "Clara, why don't you just tell us about the braid and then we can all go home. Maybe there's a perfectly good explanation."

"Why are you interrogating me?" Clara nearly screamed, "it is like Chile under Pinochet! Why don't you question *her!*" She glared at me.

"Fine," Jane said calmly and reasonably. "I want you both to tell me where you were that night—the night Devi died." That was Jane's way— to soften everything. *Died.*

"The night Devi was murdered I was at Aperçu Archive's party for Michael Sullivan," I said, then saw Clara's eyes sharpen at the mention of Michael. Before she could say anything embarrassing on the subject, I went on, "Lots of people saw me. And there were television cameras filming it."

"Clara?" Jane's voice was quietly commanding.

"What?" Clara was sullen now, deeply angry.

"Where were you that night?" Jane was keeping her cool.

"I was at the Widener Library."

"The Widener closes at eight on Sunday evenings," Jane said.

"Yes, I came home then to work. I played music, an opera. I fell asleep with the music on."

"Did you talk to anyone on the phone that night? See anyone you know?"

"No. *NO!* What *is* this? Who do you both think you are? I refuse to say another word."

Jane looked at me levelly. "You're sure about the braid?"

"I saw a black braid," I said carefully. "It had a glass beaded band on it, the kind Devi always wore on her braid. The beads were yellow— the color Devi was wearing that night."

"It is *not* Devi's braid," Clara said now.

"I thought there *was* no braid," Jane said.

"Tell me about the braid," I demanded at nearly the same moment Jane spoke.

"I bought it," Clara said. "It is not Devi's. It is not even human hair. I bought it because I wanted to be like Devi. I thought you might then want to paint me, too."

"It had a beaded elastic on it," I said again, "like the ones that Devi wore."

"Yes, I . . . I had had that for some time. I found it on the floor of the colloquium room one day and I knew it was Devi's, but I kept it. I am *so* sorry," she said with mock contrition, "for the crime of stealing a hair elastic. My God! I cannot believe this is happening to me. What did I do to deserve such treatment? For the last time, it is *not Devi's braid!*"

"Take us to see it then," Jane said, and I hoped she was bluffing. Clara could be a killer, and there was no way I was going to her apartment without the police.

"It is gone," Clara said. "I took it out to the Dumpster yesterday morning. It was just a reminder of . . . of my foolishness."

"Isn't that a bit of a coincidence?" Jane said to Clara. "Throwing the braid away just after Honora found it? Are you sure it's gone?"

"Yes! It is gone. I told you."

"The trash was collected before noon yesterday," I informed Jane. "If it really was thrown out, it's gone—they'll never find it now."

"Well, they'll surely have to try," Jane Coleman said, and then she turned to Clara with an almost courtly gentleness. "You know I've got to phone the police, Clara."

I got up and handed Jane Detective Burns's card, and she picked up the receiver. Clara began to cry out loud in a thin, pathetic wail, almost a howl. Someone knocked on the door.

"Everyone okay in there?" came Mimi's nervous voice. After all that had happened lately, of course the sound of a woman's cries were utterly terrifying in the halls of the Larkin.

I went to the door and opened it to tell Mimi that things were under control. When I looked out past her shoulder, I saw several Larkies in the foyer, looking frightened. "It's okay," I said to everyone. "Just an emotional moment in here." I didn't want to say what was actually going on—for what if Clara was not the murderer? Even now, after her suspicious responses to our questions, I found myself waffling in my conviction that she was.

A few minutes later when I opened Jane's office door to Detective Burns's leathery, tanned face and bright blue eyes, I was surprised to feel safe suddenly, for the first time in weeks. The first time since Devi's death.

"Thank God," I said, and was startled when he patted my shoulder quickly and awkwardly, then looked past me at Jane and Clara. I waved him by me, and then as I turned to shut the door, I saw two uniformed officers and three plainclothes detectives come into the foyer. One of the detectives stopped at Mimi's desk, and she gestured toward the doorway where I was standing. I moved aside to let the man in, and Detective Burns introduced him to all of us as Detective Polk. Courtesy was comforting on this occasion, I realized, for it gave it an oddly sane and normal feel.

Clara sat scrunched down in the velvet chair next to Jane's desk, her cheap, vinyl purse on her lap and her eyes cast down. I looked away from her and out into the foyer again before I shut the door.

Counting Burns, that made four detectives and two uniformed cops. I thought. They must have brought at least three cars, more likely four—or even five. I could imagine what people were thinking. I wondered if anyone knew that Clara was the one crying in Jane's office. I hoped not. Soon enough people would hear, but it would be best to protect her from that for as long as possible—just in case.

While Detective Polk questioned Clara with two uniformed officers nearby, Detective Burns asked me to go over to Clara's apartment to show him where I'd seen the braid. Then he turned to Clara.

"Excuse me, I'm going to need your key please, ma'am," he said quietly.

"I will not give anyone my key," she said angrily. "This is an invasion of my privacy!"

"Ma'am, I'm very sorry," he said courteously, "but we have to look in your apartment. It's better if we go in with your permission, isn't it, than if we go in on a warrant? We don't want to have to go to Harvard Housing for a key and rouse a lot of curiosity around the building." Clara dug in her purse and gave him the key. She looked at me sorrowfully then, and I felt embarrassed.

"I'll be there the whole time," I said, to reassure her.

"That is a great comfort," she said acidly. "We all know how well I can trust *you*."

At this point I couldn't dispute the sentiment. All the way out to the street beside the burly detective and followed by two others, I wondered if my colleagues thought I was being arrested. If so, there was nothing I could do about it for now. They'd know the truth soon enough.

I rode up Concord Street beside Detective Burns, who said something into his radio once or twice. Two other detectives followed in a car to the rear of us. The reality of the occasion hit me with such force I felt faint. I put my hand to my brow and squeezed, to make my head work better.

"You okay, ma'am?" Detective Burns asked. "You look a little peaked."

Bad as I felt—*peaked* as I felt—the word made me laugh weakly. Maybe it was hysteria.

"What?" he asked, clearly baffled.

"Oh, nothing. Just that word. 'Peaked.' "

"Peaked? What's wrong with that? It's a real word. Even my mother and my grandmother used to say it."

"Yeah, I know," I said, "that's kind of my point, I guess."

"*Huh!*" he said, as if he'd learned something useful for the future. We said nothing else till we got to the building, and then after I led the three detectives to Clara's apartment, we all put latex gloves on out in the hall and I led them inside to where I'd found the braid. We found the drawer empty but for some old socks. So she *had* thrown the braid out. But why? Why *now?*

There was a sort of antiseptic aroma in the closet, as if she had sprayed Lysol or something.

"The smell," I said to Burns.

"Beg your pardon?"

297

"The smell is gone." No braid, no smell. I shuddered. He wrote something down.

"I wonder if she saw me go into the closet the night I found the braid," I said.

He shrugged. "Yeah, could be."

"You should look around in here for the painting," I told him. "I don't know where else Clara might have stashed it. I guess maybe in her office, if it's not here."

"Yeah, okay, we'll check it out," Burns said.

"Would you mind if I go next door to my own place? I don't feel right being here."

"Actually, that'd be better. You don't need to be here now. Probably shouldn't be."

The phone machine was blinking in my apartment. It was a message from Michael, who sounded shaken.

"Things have been harrowing here or I'd have called you." His voice low, a tremulous rush of words. "It's Bridget—she was hit with a bat at the game the other afternoon—some stupid kid got mad after striking out and just mindlessly flung it—right into Bird, who was next up to bat. Got her full force in the side of the head. Aw, God. She's been in a coma, Norrie. Brenda . . . Brenda and I stayed at the hospital, and Finn flew in from New York yesterday. We played Bird her Britney Spears CD over and over, but what finally brought her out of it early this morning was when I said, 'Birdie, come on, let's go, you can make it to home plate!' All of a sudden she just opened her eyes and said, 'Daddy, I was looking for you everywhere.' " I heard him pull in a ragged breath. "So now they're going to watch her closely for a couple of days, and then if she's okay she'll be going home with us. I need to talk to you, Norrie. We're going to have to talk. I—"

The phone machine cut him off right there, just like in a B-movie. But I knew what he was going to say. And all I could think was, of course, it was how it had to be.

I had no time to absorb my feelings because a minute later Detective Burns rapped at my door and told me they'd found nothing and were leaving. I was numb, and it was only with effort that I remembered what he was talking about. Of course it all came back to me in a swoop, the way nightmares do. Clara, the braid, the painting.

"Does that mean you're not going to arrest her?" I asked him, panic rising in me.

"Not unless the boys back at the Larkin office have found something out. We can't arrest anyone without something solid to bring charges on." My God, I thought, and what if she *is* the killer? I could just imagine trying to sleep at night with her next door. It seemed as if Detective Burns had read my mind.

"Do you have somewhere you could go for a few days," he asked me, "just while we do some investigating? We want to be sure you're . . . comfortable." I was pretty sure he meant *safe*.

As soon as he left, I called Michael back, hoping he'd still be at home. He answered the phone on the first ring.

"Oh God, Norrie," he said, "I'm so glad you called back. I can't talk long, though, I'm on my way back to the hospital. God, it was awful. I've never been so afraid in my life. I thought she was going to die. I even started thinking that maybe——" He stopped.

"You thought God was punishing you for your decision to leave Brenda and be with me."

He sighed. "Something like that, I guess. I'm too Irish not to think of the Wrath of God at a time like that—or imagine some kind of curse I've invited down on my household. Whatever."

"I know. Look, I know what you want to talk to me about," I told him. "I know what you want to say." *don't say it don't say it just please don't say the words.*

"Norrie, let's not do this now, on the phone. It's awful. I want to talk to you face-to-face." I thought fleetingly how angry Paul had been because Devi had broken off with him by phone.

"Michael, there's no time now to meet face-to-face. Look, I really want you to go and be with your little girl." I did.

"I can't seem to imagine now, just the idea of not being there when she needs me, Norrie."

At that I knew I just had to go ahead and say the words and have done with it, as much for me as for him. "If staying in the marriage is what you have to do, how could I argue with you about it, Michael? And *why* would I?" I heard the tremble in my voice and prayed he hadn't. "I just, I just really don't feel up to hearing the . . . the actual words of it right now, okay? Out of your mouth. You know?"

"Jesus," he said. "I'm crumbling."

"No, yeah, really, just get back to the hospital. We'll catch up soon. Please don't worry."

"Norrie, I love you."

"Yeah, I know that, Michael. This has nothing to do with that."

"Are you okay?"

How could I begin to answer that question? He didn't even know yet about Clara, the braid.

"I'm trying," I said. "Just call me when you can." I hung up then, because he couldn't seem to. I looked at the bed I was sitting on, thought of our happy nap the other day. Thought of the seed, the blood. I got up and went into the bathroom, sat down on the toilet lid.

"Don't leave me," I said out the little window beside the toilet, "Please don't leave me."

Four flights down I could see two people walking across the alley behind the building, holding hands as if love were all it took, as if anyone had a right to be unafraid.

After a while I got up and phoned Georgi, and she came to get me, solemn faced and with shadows under her eyes—she'd probably slept no more than I had since the night I called to tell her about having found the braid at Clara's.

"I was at the Larkin, but I had to leave," she said. "I couldn't bear to see all those police descending on us. I know they're there to help out, but it just felt so macabre, so unreal."

"Yeah, I know." I didn't feel chatty. She didn't have a clue what was going on inside my head and heart. I held my overnight case on my lap, pressed up against me like armor. I thought of my painting of Ida, the red glass pitcher held on her lap in this same way. It seemed as if it had been in another lifetime that I'd been a painter. I thought of Michael, and my eyes filled up. I looked out the car window for privacy.

We drove in silence. I was full of dread and gloom. I couldn't imagine ever sleeping again. Or smiling. Especially that.

I see it in dreams where it's always dark and moonless. Devi's walking into the courtyard, small and birdlike. In bushes beside the archway, Clara's waiting. As Devi passes the spot where Clara hides, Clara grabs her and then holds her from behind, a knife at the front of Devi's delicate neck. Always I wake, shaking and drenched in sweat, when the dream has unreeled to the part where Clara is about to bring the knife across Devi's throat. After so many nights, the dream has taken on a documentary quality, as if I've actually seen the murder replayed. I can't go to sleep without seeing it again and again, in horrifying slow motion. Afterward I lie awake in damp sheets, wishing nothing, desiring nothing, for in that moment it seems there is nothing left to desire.

18

In the days that followed, the world seemed to be waking to spring—
lilacs were blooming along Brattle Street, grass was turning green after
the long, gray winter, and children in sunsuits and shorts were swinging
and shouting in the yard at the nursery school I passed each day on the
way to the Larkin. But while the world was waking, I seemed to have
gone to sleep inside: I couldn't feel anything most of the time, and when
the blankness did give way, I only felt grief, fear, anger, or dread.
Clearly, I couldn't afford to feel. I began to understand how necessary
emotion is to identity—I felt nothing, therefore I was no one. Simple
as that.

Worse, in the absence of *felt* emotion, there was only thought. And
why not? There was everything to think about. Even exhausted as I was,
I couldn't seem to shut my mind down for a minute, couldn't stop trying
to understand what had happened, as if anyone *could* understand what
might fuel such an unthinkable act as the murder of Devi Bhujander.

Michael had no idea I'd gone to stay at Georgi's—indeed, he had no
idea Clara was a suspect in Devi's murder. He'd begun calling again,
late, "just to say good night and let you know Bridget's doing better,"
but when I retrieved these messages I couldn't return them because I
couldn't ring his house at night. I found myself not calling back the next
day either because I was afraid of depending on his presence now. I had
to get over Michael. There was no other choice.

Finally one morning I returned his calls. My hand trembled as I
punched in the number.

"Norrie! Oh God, I miss you," he said. "How would I live my life without talking to you?"

"I don't know," I said dully. We both knew his decision was made, so why belabor it? I missed him terribly, too, but didn't tell him so. What would be the point in describing how acutely I missed his jokes, his sense of the world, his ardent eyes, his kindness, his fingers and lips on all the skin of my body?

Instead I brought him up to date on events at the Larkin and on Brattle Street.

Michael was shocked. "My God," he said, "you could be in real danger, Norrie. You've got to stay away from that Clara."

"That's why I'm at Georgi Brandt's apartment," I said.

"You shouldn't even be going over to the Larkin right now—not until they've charged Clara and taken her out of circulation."

No one seemed to understand why the Larkin fellows were congregating at the institute when the murderer had not yet been arrested. It was hard to justify the feeling that we were somehow "safer" there or to explain why suddenly we felt more comfortable there than out in the world. I'd got to the point where I was tired of trying to explain it to Liz or my mother, and I didn't bother arguing the point with Michael now.

"I'm certainly avoiding Clara," was all I said. I didn't mention her oddly inappropriate response to the suspicion swirling around her. The problem seemed to be that she didn't have a realistic sense of the situation. She'd actually gone to the Larkin the day after she became an official suspect! I couldn't believe she would do that under the circumstances. It was awful for everyone. How did we know what to do with her presence? No one spoke to her; we were all afraid of her now, repulsed by her. It was so like Clara, I thought, to insinuate her presence into even the most unthinkable circumstance.

Despite the fact that no one I knew was talking about it publicly or irresponsibly, everyone did seem to have confided in someone about what was going on at the Larkin. I'd talked to Liz and Michael about it—how could I not? But the trouble was, if everyone spoke to just one or two people, it was inevitable that someone in the press would get hold of it eventually.

And of course that was exactly what happened, with the end result that a reporter at the *Boston Herald* wrote a smutty, speculative, little front-page article about the possibility that Devi's killing had been, as he so delicately put it, "a female-on-female crime." The headline blared "Murder at Radcliffe a Jealousy Crime?" Would the next step be broad hints about Clara's identity, and then, finally, would they print her name?

I went to Jane Coleman with my concerns about the press picking up Larkin gossip, and she called a meeting of the fellows to say that she knew word had gotten round the Larkin that one of the fellows was being questioned as a possible suspect.

"And it's actually premature to put it that way," Jane said, "so although I realize you can't help talking to one another about Devi's death, no one should discuss the subject outside the walls of the Larkin for the time being, *period.*" She didn't mention Clara's name, but everyone knew who she was talking about. How could they not? Quite a few people had seen Clara come out of Jane's office crying that day, after hearing her shrill cries earlier inside.

Clearly I'd put something in motion over which I no longer had an iota of control. Sometimes a chill would run down my back as I considered the possibility that Clara was *not* the murderer. I confided this thought to Liz one night on the phone when she asked me why I'd not mentioned the matter lately.

"What if she's innocent?" I asked Liz. "My God, think what I've done."

"I'd say it's pretty obvious she did it. If I were you, Norrie, I'd be worrying about my safety. You should be watching your back!" Liz wasn't a panic artist, and I knew she felt legitimately worried about me. "Jesus," she added, "I hope you haven't told dear old Mom that your neighbor is the principal suspect."

"Good God, no. If she knew Clara was a suspect, she'd go nuts. She's been up in arms since Devi's murder. Anyway, I'd be afraid she might tell someone. But to clarify a point, no one in the police department has called Clara the *principal* suspect. They've just told her not to leave Boston."

"No *doubt,*" Liz said. "I really think you should stay away from the Larkin for now. Honestly. You know, that's the first place she might look for you if she's feeling particularly vindictive about all this one day."

"I keep telling you, Liz, I *have* to go there. It's the only place that feels comfortable these days. God, I can't even go to my own apartment! And as much as I like Georgi, bunking in someone else's place is beginning to drive me mad."

"Well, sure. It's awful not to have access to your own things."

"It's been four days since the meeting in Jane's office. Wouldn't you think the cops would've found the braid by now if they were really looking?"

"A black braid? In a landfill? Jesus, Norrie, I doubt they'll ever find it. Even if it isn't hidden in a bag or wrapped up in something—and you know it must be—it wouldn't show up to the naked eye, anyway. And it's not metal, so they can't look for it with detectors."

"I'm too depressed to paint, but I feel I've got to try," I said. "I have to finish my colloquium project sometime in the next few weeks. But where? I can't bear to go into my studio at the Larkin, where I spent so much time with Devi. I couldn't work there now. I need to get back to my apartment." Georgi had surprised me the previous day by offering to let me paint in the guest bedroom I was using at her place. Most people don't like the mess and fumes of oil painting inside their houses, and though I warned her about that, she insisted.

"And if I should happen to come into the room to call you for supper or something," she'd added, "I promise I won't look at your work unless you invite me to." I was gratified and kind of surprised—I'd not said a word to her about privacy. Interesting how she could understand such a need without it being mentioned, while Clara would never have learned, no matter how many times I'd told her.

The problem was, I didn't know if I could paint at all. If you can't feel, how can you paint? But I had to try, and for that I needed my supplies, which were in the apartment.

"I definitely wouldn't advise going over to your building," Liz said, "not before they've arrested Clara. My God, you can't go back before then."

"Well, I guess I have to," I said. "My work is there, my supplies are there. I didn't think it'd be this long. I thought she'd be arrested in a day or two. I have to try to get back to my work."

"Then call that detective on the case and ask him to send a police escort. Believe me, under the circumstances, they'll do it if you ask."

For some reason, I hadn't thought of that. I phoned Burns and told him my problem. "Could you send someone over just to walk me into and out of my apartment?" I asked, hastening to add, "but, please, no one in uniform. I don't want to make a spectacle of myself over there."

"Sure, I'll just come and get you right now," he said. I was surprised that he would do it himself instead of sending someone. I gave him Georgi's address, and within ten minutes he was rapping at the door. We drove to my place without much conversation. Burns wasn't a big talker and neither was I at present. I did feel safe with him, and I appreciated that. Feeling safe was the most I could hope for right now.

"I have to carry a few things down," I told him as we turned onto Brattle, "there's kind of a lot." I was thinking of bringing some of the paintings back with me.

"Hey, no problem," he said, "I can help you with that. Glad to do it." He turned and smiled at me then, a quick flash that softened his sun-weathered face, and then he turned back to the traffic. In that moment I thought of all the times Michael had turned to me in just that way and smiled as he drove us somewhere, and for the first time the full reality of the loss hit me: Michael was not mine anymore. Michael and I wouldn't be driving together anymore; we wouldn't be going anywhere together at all, in any sense. Right then I resented Detective Burns for not being Michael beside me with his hands on the wheel. I looked at Burns's freckly hands as he parallel parked in front of 82 Brattle and thought of Michael's sinewy hands, the springy auburn hairs at his wrists.

I let us into the lobby. "Nice place," Burns said, looking around, though he'd been there several times before. Save the chitchat, I thought, but I tried to smile and nod as if the place still delighted me, as if it weren't overlooking the scene of Devi's murder.

Then inside my apartment I felt a fresh bloat of grief at the sight of all my familiar things; not so long ago this apartment had symbolized hope and anticipation, a fresh start. I kept my face averted so Burns wouldn't see it. In the bedroom, oh God, the red glass pitcher by the window and beside it the last painting of Devi, which faced out into the room on its easel. Burns let out a breath when he saw Devi, and I felt bad to have invaded her privacy by letting him into the room, but he had to be there if he was going to help me carry things out to the car.

"That's Devi," I said quietly, flatly.

"She was a beautiful lady," he observed. "What a shame she had to die the way she did."

"At *all*," I amended tartly, and he nodded. Then we stopped talking, thank God.

The trunk of his car could hold a surprising amount, I saw on our first trip down, and I thought of just bringing all the paintings back with me right then. In the end, though, I left them in my apartment where they'd be safer from people's scrutiny. I didn't want people looking at Devi, and who knew who might see them at Georgi's? I ended up just bringing two fresh canvases, an easel, and a large box of paints and supplies, as well as some fresh clothing and shoes. I'd brought little with me to Georgi's when I left my place in such a hurry the other day.

As we were walking to the elevator with our last load, we ran into Clara in the hall, a basket of laundry in her arms. Somehow it seemed grotesque that she should be occupied with such quotidian activity in light of her suspected crime. *Murderer doing laundry,* I thought. I expected her to avoid my eyes and look past me, but she spoke.

"Hello, Norrie." Her voice was clipped, but I was shocked that she was speaking at all.

"Hi," I said carefully. Burns stopped by my side, and then Clara recognized him. She turned to me, eyes flashing.

"So it has come to this?" she said. "You must have a police escort to walk past the apartment of the dangerous Clara Brava? I cannot believe this!"

"Okay now, ma'am, that's enough," Burns said. "Let's just keep things neutral here."

She turned to him, enraged. "Shut your mouth!" she said. "I do not need you to tell me how to speak to my friend." She looked back at me. "Does that word surprise you, Honora—*friend*? I should imagine it would."

"Clara—I don't know how to talk about this. I—"

"Good-bye," she said. "You should be looking for a message from me at the Larkin." She slammed the door of her apartment, and Burns and I looked at each other.

"I'd be a little careful for now, if I were you," he said, "just till we get all this figured out." When we got to his car, he called on his cell phone to ask Polk to meet him at the office in half an hour. "We need to come up with some answers ASAP," he said.

That night at Georgi's I didn't sleep at all. I kept thinking of Clara's words, which seemed a veiled threat. Or not-so-veiled, depending on whom I was talking to. Michael and Liz both told me again to stay away from the Larkin until Clara was arrested. ("She's dangerous," both of them said.) Georgi, on the other hand, felt we shouldn't allow anyone to make us prisoners. "You already can't go home," she said. "Don't let her take away the Larkin, too. Our year's nearly over." I heard the ring of Devi's philosophy in Georgi's words and decided to lean that way.

There was a black notebook waiting for me in my Larkin mailbox when Georgi and I arrived for the colloquium presentation the next afternoon. Clara's note atop it was chilling. "You can give this to the police if you wish," it read, "but first I would like you to read it yourself so that you will understand about Devi and about me. There are things you do not know."

"What should I do?" I asked Georgi.

"Don't touch the notebook," she advised. "Call Burns right away." I knew she was right about that: Clara was a suspect, and in case the notebook held something pertinent to the murder, I would have to leave it there and let Burns and his team see it first. When I rang him, though, I got a voice-mail recording saying he was off today. It was the first time it had occurred to me that Burns had a life separate from this crime investigation. I hung up without leaving a message. I had no way of knowing who might follow up on my call in Burns's absence, and the idea of adjusting to yet another police personality was distressing somehow. I'd try him tomorrow.

Today's presenting fellow was Sarah Berg of Michigan, who was writing a book on the domestic life of Hasidic Jews, with a focus on women of the Hasidim. Sarah had just stepped up to the podium and was saying, "For those unfamiliar with the subject, Hasidism is a Jewish mystical sect that had its beginnings in Poland in the middle of the eighteenth century. This sect was founded in opposition to the prevailing rationalism of the time and in response to what was perceived as a growing laxity in Jewish ritual during that period . . ." Sarah's voice hesitated for the barest fraction of a moment, but her eyes were now focused on the door to the colloquium room and remained riveted there, even as she struggled to continue.

I looked over to the door just as an audible gasp ran through the audience. I'm sure everyone in the room saw Clara at the same moment I did. She stood in the doorway, hesitant and pale, her hair cut close to her head like a boy's. It occurred to me that she bore an odd resemblance to Jeanne d'Arc, and I thought she may well have cut her hair this way to put people in mind of historic witch hunts—a symbol she might feel favored her in the present situation. That would be like Clara, I thought, but maybe I was fantasizing again. She took a seat at the end of the second row and sat there in a rigid posture, seeming to feign attentiveness to Sarah's remarks on the Hasidim. Poor Sarah, I don't think anyone heard a word she said after Clara arrived.

Georgi leaned close and whispered into my ear, "I heard they've been searching the dumps all week and haven't found it yet." I didn't answer. I could hear others whispering around me, and I couldn't bear to take part. I just wanted out of here. I wished I hadn't come. The audience was astir, twitchy.

Whenever I glanced at Clara across the room, alone and shorn, my heart contracted with pity of its own volition. Then I thought of Devi lying on the courtyard bricks, neck slashed, eyes open, her lifeblood running across the sidewalk and puddling at the curb. I looked away from Clara then, and later I refused to meet her eyes when she sat across the table from me at the Indian restaurant the fellows adjourned to. I honestly couldn't believe she had come along under the circumstances. It was a cinch she had no conventional sense of boundaries, but had she no pride? Even now, I thought, she doesn't know when to let go.

"She has no right to be here," Georgi whispered angrily.

"Well, but what if she didn't do it?" I whispered. "I mean, just for a moment put yourself in her position, if she didn't."

Georgi was silent for a moment, then said, "God, what a thought."

Still, I wouldn't meet Clara's gaze, though I felt her looking at me intensely. Some of the other fellows noticed it, too, and were looking from Clara to me and back to Clara. I remembered that some of them assumed we'd been a couple.

Dinner was nearly over when Clara spoke, and she did so in a voice that carried round the table. "Did you get my package, Norrie?"

"The notebook? Sure."

"Where is it?"

"Back at the Larkin. I didn't want to carry it over here."

"I would like to know what you think after you've read it." Then she stood and breathed deeply, as if preparing for some difficult challenge, and left the restaurant.

"She didn't pay," Georgi whispered, "she didn't leave her share on the table."

"It's okay," I said. "She knows someone'll pick up the slack for her." It sounded petty to me as I said it; still it seemed true.

"I don't like this," I heard Sarah Berg say to Serena Holwerda. "It doesn't seem right that we should have to break bread with someone who may well have killed one of our sister fellows."

"But what if she didn't do it?" Serena said. "Innocent till proven guilty."

I went home with Georgi, thinking about the notebook Clara had left for me. I knew it had to be some kind of personal journal, and I was not eager to read it. In fact, I had no intention of doing so, period. Clara had no right to expect that of me. Her need for attention was all-consuming, even now, when she knew I thought her a murderer.

The phone rang at Georgi's just before ten, and I started at the sound. Georgi jumped up from a nearby living room chair and answered it. It was Detective Burns for me, she said, holding the phone out. I thought this was his night off.

"Everything all right?" he asked.

"Yeah, for a train wreck, it's just fine."

He chuckled. "What's up?" For an instant I wasn't sure if this was a personal call or a professional one. "On the Clara front," he added, and I realized with relief that it was business.

"She put a notebook in my mailbox at the Larkin today. I left it there, if you want to see it."

"Thanks," he said. "I'll need to go on over there first thing tomorrow and bring it to the station to let the team look it over."

"Oh," I said. "Okay."

"*Okay,* then," he said cheerfully, "sleep tight, bedbugs bite, all that good stuff." The phone clicked in my ear.

When I checked my messages at home, I found one from Michael, one from my mother, and one—I couldn't believe this—from Clara. Suffice to say the first two messages were essentially the same: *Are you all right? Be careful. Let me know how you are.*

Clara's message was brief: "I miss you, Norrie," I heard her voice say haltingly. "I felt very left out tonight. I do not like feeling that way." Then she hung up. My hands and feet went cold.

All night I tossed around on the little futon in Georgi's spare room and kept wondering what Clara would do next. I'm pretty sure I never closed my eyes.

The next morning I found that Detective Burns had taken the notebook away with him before I arrived. He'd left a note in my box promising to return it. No thank you, I thought.

Over the next few days, I found more messages on my phone machine from Clara, all of them brief, usually saying things like, "You are misunderstanding who I am," or "I have done nothing wrong." Once, she said, "I miss our friendship." I kept wondering what was in the journal—did it connect her to the crime? Or had she possibly concocted a fake diary to exonerate herself? I waited each day to see if she'd be arrested, but nothing happened.

To keep from losing my mind, I fiddled with watercolors one night in Georgi's guestroom, thinking that at least I could be trying to work out an idea for the cover art I'd promised to do for Devi's next book, which she'd titled *After Love*. Her last book. My artwork was due at the publisher's by June first. And maybe because it was for Devi—because it was the only thing on earth I could do for my friend now—I found myself able to focus on this one thing so completely that by the end of the night I thought I might have finished the artwork for her book cover.

It was a soft, cloudy wash of blue sky tinged with violet and gradually paling till it was pure white at the top. If you looked carefully, you could make out the figure of a woman in the clouds, running or dancing, free. At the far right bottom of the picture plane was a small hand, finely detailed and colored in flesh tones, reaching up—maybe in greeting, possibly in supplication, or perhaps only to touch the ethereal, disembodied figure whose flesh had become clouds. It seemed to work for the title, and also for what I was feeling, how I was missing my friend. I hoped it wasn't too sentimental, and I would have to put it aside for a week or two, just to be certain it was not.

The idea for it had come to me as I worked and happened to think of her words to me the time I tried to thank her for how much time she'd given to posing for me, which had saved my Larkin project. Devi'd said to me, "The best purpose of a gift is to inspire more giving. I'm sure you'll give back to someone else whatever it is I may have given you. And that will be a gift to me, you know, Norrie, for it will echo my name in the heavens!" I hoped I would live up to her prediction and do her gift justice one day, but right now I was just imagining her name echoing in the heavens.

Days after the confrontation with Clara, there was still no arrest, and I was a wreck. I didn't feel like talking to anyone, and was still not regularly returning Michael's calls, but I felt I had to phone him today because a message he'd left the previous night had sounded so urgent. "Please, Honora," he'd said, "I have to talk to you." I had to dial his number three times because my nervous hands kept messing up the sequence of numbers.

The phone only rang once, and Michael still sounded urgent when he answered it. "I need to see you," he said. "Have to." I wondered what was going on. "Tell me how to get to Georgi's apartment, and I'll be there in twenty minutes." Before I could think how to respond, he added, "Please, Norrie."

I gave him directions.

"Make that thirty minutes," he said, "I'll stop and get us something for lunch."

"But you can't pick me up here," I reminded him, "Georgi might see us."

"Meet me at the corner," he said. I thought then how like criminal activity the movements of adulterous lovers are—even when they're no longer lovers.

Thirty-five minutes later I was sitting in the car beside him on the way to Marblehead, trying not to look at his hands on the steering wheel. It was a gray day, and windy.

"I missed your face," he said once, turning to me as he drove. I wanted to ask him what was going on; I wondered if he was having second thoughts about his decision to stay in the marriage. But then I told myself to grow up. If I began to hope again, I was asking for whatever pain I got. I only hoped he wasn't going to suggest we start up our affair again.

"You're very quiet," he said at one point.

"I know. That's okay, isn't it?"

312

"Of course," he said. And we drove for a long time in silence, letting the clouds move past us, watching the world go by outside the car. The ordinary, out-in-the-open world, I thought, the world that doesn't have to hide itself from the eyes of people it knows. I wanted to be part of that world, and there was no way I was going back to the dark end of the street with Michael, no matter how much I loved him.

When we got to Marblehead, it was cold and gusty. We ate our lunch on a stone bench overlooking the ocean. Or, I should say, we tried to eat our lunch. Neither of us could seem to chew and swallow—we were too nervous, too awake to each other's physical presence. We sat close to each other in the chilly wind, and at some point, Michael began to stroke my hand, nothing more, and we sat wordless, the physical sensation of our two hands touching having arrested conversation and thought. After what may or may not have been a long time, he spoke.

"It's hard. I seem to be having a struggle getting back into my old life," he said. "Life doesn't feel real when you're not in it with me."

I couldn't answer him, I was afraid to let myself say how badly I wanted him back when I didn't know for sure what he was leading up to. I couldn't afford to nurse romantic hope anymore.

"Bridget has been having panic attacks since the injury, and she follows me around the house whenever I'm at home," he said then, and I knew that was no non sequitur. I knew exactly what it meant. I thought of the last time we'd sat together on a bench, so happy and filled up, imagining a shared future. Oh God, I missed our future.

A seabird flew overhead and shrieked once, twice, like a crone. Hah. Hah. Nearby, a pregnant young woman—she couldn't have been more than nineteen or twenty—pushed her blond baby boy in a blue stroller. I was acutely aware of Michael's hand around mine, I felt the answering warmth of his skin blocking the cold, damp air of the world, and I knew like a fist in my chest that this had been the right man for me and that there might never be another so right.

As if reading my thoughts, Michael said, "I made a promise a long time ago, and a family was built on it—I'm trying to honor that promise. But I need to be sure you know that I'll always believe you and I were right for each other. I wish to God I'd met you before I made that promise." I didn't remind him that I was only ten when he made it, because I knew what he meant. He put his arms around me before I saw it happening and pulled me close to him on the bench. It was the first time I'd been in Michael's arms in a while, and everything, everything, was still there. He spoke into my hair. "I have to try to stay in the marriage, Norrie. I have to, especially for Bridget's sake. But I needed to tell you that I love you, and I know I always will."

When he let go of me, he had tears in his eyes but he ducked his head and pinched the bridge of his nose to surreptitiously wipe them away.

"Michael," I said, "I think it's going to be all the more painful for both of us now, after today. Everything's all opened up again." My voice wobbled, in spite of me.

"Yeah, I know. It was a dumb idea doing this. I wanted to ask you if we could keep the *friend* part going, but seeing you now I know I can't do it. I could never be this close to you and not want to make love with you." We both looked at the bulge in his jeans at the same time, and he said, "It's hell being a man—how can you keep your dignity with a boner?" We both laughed a little awkwardly, and then he said, "Maybe in time we'll get over the desire part." I looked at his jeans again just as he said, "Who am I kidding?" He sighed. "Well, I guess we can still talk to each other on the phone. That way we'll still have one another in our lives."

"Sure, we can still talk on the phone. But you know, sometimes I don't want to talk to you, Michael."

"You think I haven't known that? That's one of the reasons I wanted us to talk today—so we could work on that."

"Michael, it's not something we can work on. There's nothing to fix. I love you, okay? I want to make love with you every day of my life. Whatever needs fixing, it's not *here*. It's all working only too well here. When I don't return your calls, it's because I can't afford to let myself feel all this. If I can't be with you, I don't *want* to feel it!"

"I shouldn't have asked you to come today," he said.

"Probably not," I agreed. I wasn't going to lie. I'd lied enough to everyone.

Several gulls were on the ground near our feet, waiting for the food neither of us could eat. I broke my bread into tiny pieces and tossed the crumbs to them while Michael followed suit; before we knew it, we were aswarm in gulls. The young woman with the baby in the stroller came past us in the other direction, and the baby put out his plump hand to the feasting birds and called, "Ba! Ba!"

314

"Birdie? Birdie? Wait till your daddy hears that you tried to say *birdie*," the girl said proudly—more for our benefit, I thought, than the baby's.

"Bah!" the child called out all the way down the beachwalk with his mother, and I could see his tiny hand waving out the side of the stroller. I couldn't take my eyes off the two of them till they were out of sight. Then I turned to Michael and said, "I need to go home now, please."

All night I dreamed I was making love with you. I woke several times, hot and wet as if you'd been inside me. I haven't felt such overwhelming desire in a long time, and it isn't good for me to feel it now.

Can you understand that I need to forget wanting, need to eradicate hunger from my skin?

Why did you do it? Why did you come back for a moment when you knew you would have to leave again? As we sat on the bench above the ocean, I felt your body close beside mine, felt it acutely, the way one always feels love or danger.

And now you're inside me again, just as before, only now you're not mine. There is no harder feeling to live with than the awareness of an unattainable presence residing in your heart, as if it had the right.

19

The next day everything happened.

At just before nine I woke to the clatter and beep of Cambridge trash collection trucks and stared at the ceiling, trying to remember where I was. Reorientation to my surroundings brought with it the memory of why I was at Georgi's, and all the rest of the bad stuff followed. God, what a way to wake up.

Georgi and I walked over to the Larkin after breakfast, and just as we arrived we saw Detective Burns pulling up out front. Though he called out, "Mornin', Ladies," his face was serious, nearly grave, as if he had some enormity to deliver up. That would not be an understatement as it turned out.

As the three of us walked into the administration building, Burns continued on to Jane Coleman's office. He didn't even ask Mimi if Jane was in. Maybe he'd already phoned her to say he was coming. About fifteen minutes later, Jane and Detective Burns came out of her office, and Jane asked Mimi to call all the fellows in their offices or at home and have everyone assembled there in one hour.

At eleven that morning, nearly all the fellows were gathered in the colloquium room. In fact, the only one I could think of for sure who wasn't there was Clara Brava.

Detective Burns walked up to the podium, cutting a rather bulky and comic figure in the spot where we were accustomed to seeing female scholars and artists speaking passionately about their life's work. Beside me, Georgi began snapping her fountain pen nervously; when she saw me looking, she stopped.

"Good morning, Ladies," Burns said, and looked around at the faces. "We've had some important developments in the Bhujander case. I wanted you all to be the first to hear about this, since you're the ones who've been the most affected by what happened—except for the Bhujander family, of course, and we've called Delhi already. But what I meant was, you are the ones most affected by it here in the States. We'll be having a news briefing with local media immediately after I finish here." He stopped and concentrated, as if this were a great ordeal for him. "Let me start at the beginning," he said, though no one was going to stop him from starting wherever he wanted.

"A while back it was learned that several phone calls had been made to Ms. Bhujander on the afternoon of the murder from a public pay phone in Harvard Square at a phone stand right in front of the Coop." I recalled how worried Devi had been when I saw her that evening in the elevator. A chill entered my blood right then. I felt it coursing through my limbs. Somehow I knew what was coming—or rather, what was *not*.

"Of course," Burns went on, "it can be hard to get good fingerprints after the fact from a pay phone in a busy place like Harvard Square, but we did get one complete handprint that came out pretty clear. And now we have confirmed the fingerprints belong to Paul Monnard, a Frenchman Ms. Bhujander used to date when she lived in London." He cleared his throat. "Now this in itself didn't necessarily inculpate Mr. Monnard, and in fact I wouldn't be telling you this much except for what happened after that point. Our investigators learned that Paul Monnard had been in the Boston area on the night of the murder—had flown in, in fact, a day before the murder. On the morning following the crime, he took a plane back to London and then dropped out of sight for a few weeks. We have no indication of where he was, but he had to be lying low, or we'd have found him. Then three days ago he went by rail to Lyon, France, where his family lives. That's where we caught up with him.

"We found that Mr. Monnard was staying at the family home in Lyon—in fact, his mother told our investigators he was sleeping in the same room he'd slept in as a boy. Mr. Monnard was out at the time our people arrived with the Lyon police—his mother said he hadn't come home the night before—but we'd obtained a warrant, so our guys went ahead and searched Mr. Monnard's room."

He cleared his throat. "In a clarinet case in Paul Monnard's bedroom, wrapped in a blood-stained black T-shirt, we found Ms. Bhujander's, eh, braid." There was an intake of breath throughout the room. Detective Burns raised both hands, palms out, like a bishop about to confer a blessing on the masses. "No weapon has been found. We have to assume he discarded it somewhere before he got on the plane back to London. Now, I have to tell you, we couldn't be releasing all of this information if there was going to be a trial. But you see, Mr. Monnard, as it turns out, has taken his own life. And he left a note—pretty much a confession, though the contents can't be made public. Our men found him expired in a stable at the far southern foot of his parents' property. The note was with him there, a little damaged by a rain but still readable."

The colloquium room was still. It was dawning on everyone at once that Clara was innocent. I felt the air go out of me, and then it seemed as if there was no breathable reservoir of air left in the room.

"Are there any questions?" Burns asked, and no one said a word. What was there to ask? A lot, maybe, but of ourselves more than of him. "Well then, thank you, Ladies," he said, and he stepped away from the podium. Immediately the room was abuzz.

As the women stood and walked out in twos and threes, talking quietly, Jane Coleman stood at the door and patted each one who stopped to talk to her. It was distinctly un-Janelike behavior, but nothing was usual around here anymore. I was still in my chair beside Georgi, immobilized by the thought of what I'd done to Clara. Georgi was quiet.

Detective Burns approached me. "Could you spare a minute or two?" he asked.

I just nodded. My head was whirling. Georgi made her excuses and left us alone.

Burns touched my shoulder. "You all right?" I nodded again, feebly. What had I done to Clara? What had I done? I saw her in memory, standing in the doorway of that very room, shorn and pale, hesitating before us. *And she was blameless. Irritating, maddening, but blameless. She'd done nothing.*

Detective Burns sat on the chair beside me and began rummaging in his satchel. I looked down at my hands folded on my lap like a schoolgirl's hands. Except I was not a schoolgirl; I was a grown-up woman who had ruined someone's life.

"This is yours, I guess," he said, "there's no reason for us to keep it now." He was holding Clara's notebook.

"Oh God," I said. I couldn't seem to reach out my hand to take it.

"I think I know how you might be feeling right about now," Burns said. "I mean, you're the one who—"

"—who started all this," I said for him. "I'm the one who thought I'd found Devi's braid in her apartment. I'm the one who ruined things for Clara at the Larkin. I—"

He broke in. "I think you should read this," he said somberly.

"You mean it's the *least* I can do?" I said acidly.

"No, no, I don't mean it like that. It's just I think you'll feel a little better if you read it."

"Better? I'm sure."

"No, *really*. After I read it I understood even more why you'd suspected her in the first place. In fact if we'd found this in her apartment that day we searched, I think we'd have taken her in. I don't know where she was keeping it."

"What do you mean?" I looked up at him quizzically.

"I mean maybe it was in her office files or—"

"No—I mean about what's in the journal."

"Honora," Detective Burns said, and it startled me because he'd never before used my first name, "she thought she had a claim on you."

"What?"

"Really. Her mother was a painter like you. Also named Honora, Honora Brava. Clara thought that meeting you was some kind of, like, restitution, you know? Like you were sent to make up for her losing her mother." His face was very earnest and he spoke with great emphasis, as if it were of supreme importance that he make me listen and comprehend his words.

"Her mother was a painter? But Clara hated . . ." I didn't finish. My God. Her mother was a painter. A painter named Honora B.

"You'll see what I mean about all this when you read it," Burns said, "but I'll say this one thing more—she wrote more than once that she wished Devi Bhujander was dead. 'Gone from the earth' is, I believe, how she put it one of the times. Between her own writings and your statement to the police about seeing the braid in that closet of hers, I think we could have brought charges, though I'm not sure we could have made them stick."

"But she didn't do it," I cried. "That's the point!"

"Right. But after reading this, seeing how fixated she was on you and how jealous she was of Ms. Bhujander, I understand why you thought she had." I knew he was trying very hard to ease my feelings of guilt. I looked at him and smiled as well as I could.

"Thank you, Detective Burns," I said. "I know what you're trying to do."

"What?" He put his big hands up as if to fend off some assault. "No, really, I'm not trying to do anything. Honest."

"Right," I said. I took the notebook in one hand and put out my other hand to shake his big mitt. "Thanks anyway."

"You bet," he said. "Anytime."

"There's just one thing more," I said hesitantly.

"Sure," Burns said, "you name it."

"I need to know what Paul Monnard said in his note. I have to know why my friend was murdered." Burns took a deep breath and lifted his shoulders, looking up. I knew he was not supposed to tell me. I kept quiet while he struggled with himself. Finally he let out a long breath, as if relieved to have made a decision.

"Okay," he said, "I'll tell you some of it if you'll promise not to tell anyone—and I mean *anyone at all,* okay? 'Cause it could be my heinie if you do."

"I promise. I just need to know so I can . . . so I can . . ."

"—have some closure?" he said. I hated that term, *closure*, but in a way he was right, so I nodded.

"It was a long letter to his family, so I don't need to tell you all the personal parts for them. But when he got to the section about Devi Bhujander, it was like suddenly he was writing the note directly to her. 'I can't go on living without you in my life,' was one thing I remember he wrote, and I think the next thing was about how she had 'destroyed' him by refusing to be with him anymore. He said he couldn't stand the thought of her with someone else, and he described how his jealousy had started to feel 'like rage,' even though it was all based on his imagination of what she 'might do in the future.' And then he said something like 'but now I'm finding I can't live in a world you're not alive in' or something like that. 'Course, it was a lot more poetic than I'm making it sound. And you've gotta understand, this letter was in French, and we had a lady at the department translate it for us. But those were the main parts about your friend. It sounded to me like he really loved her."

"How can you say that? He murdered her. Viciously. Overkill, remember?"

"Yeah, I agree about that. Of *course*. I think the letter said something about how he couldn't understand 'the power of desire,' how it could 'begin to feel like hate' when it was refused or taken away, something like that. Look, I'm not saying this guy was playing with a full deck, but most of the people our guys talked to said he was very smart and serious and had a good character. Well-liked guy, but no social butterfly—kind of intense, and he kept to himself a lot. But not one person had a bad word to say about him, so I can only say I guess something snapped in him when he couldn't have her anymore." He shrugged. "I don't really know how to explain it."

"Thanks for telling me about the letter," I said. I was truly grateful. I don't think I could've stood not knowing.

"Hey—sure. Listen, I'll check in on you sometime and see how you're getting along."

I didn't know what to say. Was this personal or professional? I thought I knew, but I didn't want to hurt his feelings. I could always make myself clear in the event I needed to later.

Georgi had waited for me in the outer office, and we were quiet as we departed the Larkin.

At home we found a message on the phone machine from Wendy at The Frame-Up. I punched in the phone number she'd left, filled with dread for what she might say, or might not.

Lin-le answered the phone, and when she heard who was calling she got nervous. "Oh oh," she said, "I get her for you. Please wait. I hurry."

"Oy, I'm so embarrassed," Wendy said, instead of hello. "Look, I need to just tell you this whole thing in sequence, if you'll bear with me." Even in ordinary circumstances, Wendy had a rather brisk, staccato kind of speech, but today her delivery was cranked up beyond staccato, and I knew the mystery of the missing painting had been solved somehow. I had a fleeting inclination to hang up on her then and there—she was about to give me some urgent information, and these days I greeted all information with dread.

"About three months ago," Wendy began—I rolled my eyes and sat down beside Georgi's telephone stand—"a very good customer of mine came in to have me frame an oil portrait of her daughter, a portrait this customer had painted herself, from a photo of the daughter that had been taken when the girl was thirteen. This daughter is thirty-five now—in fact, this was a gift for her thirty-fifth birthday. I know you wonder where I'm going with this, but you'll see in a minute.

"So when the woman came in to get the portrait framed, she warned me that her daughter would hate any frame that was ornate. She said her daughter was just hugely hugely *minimal*. So I recommended the marbled black cherry because it's the kind of thin frame that will go nicely around a canvas that's stretched over a frame . . . *exactly* the same framing material you ordered, is my point." Now she was beginning to make sense. "The woman had asked if we would just package the painting for shipping and send it to her daughter from here at the shop whenever it was ready. This is a service I often extend to my good customers. Anyway, when it came time to package and mail the framed oil painting to the daughter, poor Lin-le somehow packed up your lovely oil of the woman in the red room and mailed it to the daughter of my customer—in Hastings, Nebraska. Remember, it was in the same frame."

"My God," I said.

"Right, I know. So here's the thing. All this time, no one knew this had happened. The daughter just thought this was her birthday gift and thanked her mother over the phone—told her it was an amazing painting. The mother was so proud to think her daughter liked her work so much—between you and me, she's not what you'd call a real *pro* at painting, but that's neither here nor there. So anyway, life went on. But then the other day I saw the oil painting the woman had done of her daughter, all nicely framed in the marbled black and stuck behind another picture I was getting ready to work on. My God, I thought, something is very weird here.

"At that point I called Lin-le into the framing room and said, 'I thought you mailed this to the woman in Hastings, Nebraska. But here it is.' Her face went pale, I have to say. Before long, the two of us had solved the riddle, and I'd called my customer and she'd called her daughter, and . . . well, to make a long story short, it's all sorted out. Your painting is on the way back via FedEx, and the daughter's painting is on its way to her in Nebraska."

"I'm stunned. I mean, I'm so relieved, but also just stunned."

"Well, I can certainly see how you would be, and I'm so sorry you had to go through all this. But the painting is fine. The daughter says nothing has happened to it, and you should have it back in a couple of days. Lin-le sends her abject apologies, believe me!"

"Tell her it all turned out okay, and that's all that matters."

"She wants me to explain to you that when I said to go and pack the oil portrait in the marbled black frame, she just went to the *wrong* oil portrait in the marbled black frame."

"Yeah, I can see how that could happen."

"Uh huh, I know. And the daughter of this woman, she was just puzzling and puzzling over why her mother would send her a nude oil painting of a beautiful woman for her thirty-fifth birthday. 'I thought you thought I was gay,' she finally told her mother when this all came to light. Isn't that just a kick?" All I was thinking right then was that Clara hadn't stolen the painting.

"Right," I said.

After I hung up, I told Georgi the news; then without waiting for comment or chitchat, I went straight to my room. She knew me well enough to let me be.

In bed I wrapped myself in sheets and blankets, feeling inexplicably cold over the length of my body. I lay still as a mummy for a long time, but finally I had to accept the fact that I wasn't going to sleep, and after a while I sat up, turned on my lamp, and began to read Clara's journal. Might as well get it over with, I thought. I could consider it a kind of penance.

The journal's opening entry was dated just after our Larkin year began, and though it hadn't occurred to me before, as I read it did seem odd that Clara had written in English, rather than in her native Spanish, as if expecting other eyes to see it eventually—mine, perhaps, as her recent actions seemed to bear out. Had she planned all along to show it to me? Or had she just written in English as a way of sharpening her writing skills for publication in the United States?

On the first page of the journal, Clara fretted about how the Prozac her Santiago psychiatrist had prescribed was "killing" her "intellectual acuity." I remembered the half-filled bottle in her medicine cabinet the night I found the braid. She wrote that she had to go off it so she'd "be brilliant enough to keep up with the other women at the Larkin Institute."

The rest of that first entry was a long, bitter diatribe against her mother, and it was there that I found the information Detective Burns had passed along to me—Clara's mother, Honora Brava, had been an artist, a painter. But why had Clara never told me? All those times we talked about our early lives, she'd not said a word. In fact, she'd once even claimed to have "never known a painter" before meeting me. I should have realized then how unlikely such a statement was—Clara was a journalist, after all, in a large city. I'd not paid enough attention, clearly.

Clara had written ecstatically the night she met me, which was only the second entry in the journal. "An artist named Honora B!" she wrote. "This cannot be mere coincidence! Clearly, after so much disappointment in my life, so much loss, this is the karmic restitution I have long awaited. I can hope that Honara Blume will be with me now for the rest of my travels on life's road. Finally then, I have family again. I will no longer be alone in the world." I felt a chill as I read. She'd written as if she had a legitimate claim on me. I suddenly understood why Clara was so possessive and had so many expectations of me and also why, having turned bitterly against her mother, she'd so often made snide comments about art. ("Oh, *art*. Yes, you artists are so *special*.")

"My mother had no heart for anything but her art after Papa died," she'd written. "Day after day, year after year, she buried herself in painting, as if she could find consolation nowhere else but there. She would close her door and paint for hours, and I would stand outside that door sometimes, a little girl afraid to knock, afraid to upset her. Sometimes I did knock anyway, and if I needed something she would tell me to go and ask my grandmother. She didn't seem to understand that I needed *her*." I thought of my own closed door then, of course, and of all the times Clara had knocked, feeling I'd been put there expressly for her, to make up for her painful exclusion from her mother's thoughts.

She had first written lyrically about Devi, I found, referring to her as "a universal female literary hero" and "so beautiful it pains the heart." I thought, as I had so often since Devi's murder, of the Japanese man who'd burned down the temple because he couldn't bear its beauty. The journal narrated Clara's growing resentment of Devi, and her suspicion that Devi and I were more than friends. "This is not right," she wrote ominously at one point. "I have been given this blessing of friendship and a second chance to have a family, and now the Indian poet who has so much already is trying to take it away from me. I will not let this happen." The references, as Burns had warned me, became darker, uglier.

"I wish her to be taken out of this world," Clara had written. "I have had enough taken from me, and it is not right that she should take anything from me when she has everything already—beauty, renown, success, family. She does not need Honora. I do. It is no accident that I found Honora living next door to me. This was fate's way of telling me something, and when I heard her name, and that she was an artist, I knew what fate was saying. I have lost too much. I will not lose her, too."

And finally I learned about the braid. "I am so ashamed," Clara had written, "to have stooped to buying an artificial braid after seeing the painting of Devi that Norrie did. I was consumed by a need to show Norrie that I, too, was a worthy subject for a painting. But now, after the way she has watched over me in my sickness, I see that Norrie does care for me, and that she cared for me all along. I am embarrassed to think of my foolish attempts to be like Devi. Today when I knew Norrie was coming back to care for me, I hid another sack of garbage in the closet so that my apartment would be presentable, and when I went inside the closet I thought how appropriate that it was beginning to smell like rot—the rot of my former insecurity, which is symbolized by my foolish purchase of the braid. In that moment I pulled the braid from its drawer and put it into the bag with the garbage, and tomorrow I will take it to the dumpster so that I may never again have to look at it and remember my former desperation. To the garbage, then, silly braid! That is where you belong."

So the braid was in a trash bag at the dump—in one of thousands and thousands of bags just like it.

It was interesting, I thought, how the braid's only unpleasant association for Clara seemed to be her own feeling of humiliation rather than the murder of Devi Bhujander, whose own braid had been hacked off by the killer. Not so odd, though, when taking the whole diary into account, for as I read, it became clearer and clearer that Clara saw her self as the center of everything. Even Devi's death was about Clara herself: "I feel this is one more punishment directed at me for trying to win someone's love. Whenever I allow myself to love, I am knocked down in the dirt. Now I am supposed to suffer guilt for being alive when she is dead and for having Norrie to myself, no longer having to share her with Devi Bhujander."

I fell asleep with the journal across my middle and woke up late the next morning, the book having slid to the floor. When I went into the kitchen for some orange juice, I found a note from Georgi saying she was going to the Larkin and would see me there if I decided to come over. "But I know how fried you feel, so don't worry about it if you just want to crash at home all day."

Suddenly I remembered that I hadn't checked my messages last night, so I went to the phone and dialed my home number. I listened to messages from the usual people—Michael, Liz, and Mother—and then was surprised to find another one from Clara.

"I am going home, Norrie," she said, "now that I am *allowed* by the police to leave. Before I go I just want to tell you that it was always only you I loved. And that I have forgiven you for what you thought I did."

It wasn't hard to figure out what I had to do. Immediately I rang Clara—I found I still knew her phone number, or my fingers did. I had to apologize to her before she left, maybe even convince her not to leave her Larkin year prematurely. The phone rang and rang, and not even a phone machine answered.

On the way out I grabbed my anorak, for it was raining lightly, and I left Georgi's apartment to walk back to Brattle, suddenly aware that there was no murderer loose on the streets. Cambridge was benign again. As I crossed the brick courtyard leading to the front doors, I tried not to look at the spot where Devi had died. Just this once, I owed my thoughts to Clara for, imperfect as she was, maddening as she was, even hateful as she was in her private journal, she had not done the awful thing I'd accused her of doing, and I owed her my deepest apology.

I knocked on her door, knocked and knocked. No answer. Then I went into my own apartment and phoned Jane Coleman to see if she'd had any word from Clara.

"Clara's on her way back to Chile," Jane said matter-of-factly. "She pho-ned me early this morning from the airport to say she'd found space on a plane and was departing for Santiago in half an hour. She said she'd packed days ago in anticipation of being cleared to leave the United States."

"Oh my God," I said, "this is all my fault."

"That's not true," Jane argued, "you started events in motion, but I was with you in the act of accusing Clara. I thought she'd done it, too, Honora, after the discrepancies in her answers and how labile she was under questioning. And many Larkin fellows have come to my office to tell me they'd noticed odd behavior in Clara. You can't take all this on yourself."

"But what can we do to make it up to her? Maybe she could be given another Larkin year."

"I doubt she'd want *that*," Jane said. "The last thing she said to me was that she never wanted to see Cambridge again."

"But I have to find a way to make it up to her," I insisted.

"Don't start obsessing, Honora. It's unhealthy. And in a way—if you'll forgive me for saying so—it's a form of self-indulgence anyway. A way to make *yourself* feel better."

I was stung. But even if Jane was right in her WASPy philosophy of stoicism, I knew I owed Clara, and I'd find a way to give back to her what I'd taken. I just wouldn't talk about it. *That* was the self-indulgence—talking about it.

As I left my apartment to walk back to Georgi's, my heart lurched as I saw two men in coveralls carrying Clara's flower–power love seat out of her apartment, as if it weighed what a normal piece of furniture of its size would. I wanted to tell them that Clara had carried it here by herself from a store more than a block away. When I got out front, I saw the men loading the love seat and two plastic shelf units into a Salvation Army truck. I stood and watched as the truck drove away.

Over the days that followed, the guilt hovered, as did the ghosts. Back in my own apartment, more and more I was isolating myself.

Michael had been calling me every day and sounding worried, but I'd been refusing to see him—he was just one more loss now, one more grief. One day he came over without calling and rang the downstairs bell. I didn't know if I could really bear to see him, but he'd come all the way over, so I buzzed him up.

When I first saw him we didn't speak; we just looked into each other's face for a while. Then Michael stepped forward and pulled me into his arms, where I stayed for a long time, just inside the entry hall.

"Oh God," he said, "I hate being apart from you." He kissed me—softly at first and then with gathering urgency. I let him. Suddenly I had no willpower. "Lately I've felt like a robot," he told me. "I go through the motions at home, and no one notices that they're talking to a mechanical replacement of me."

We stood together in each other's arms, kissing until I felt myself go limp with desire. When I was with Michael, desire was always possible, even now when I thought I'd become deadened to everything. But I knew we had to stop. I knew I had to stop because Michael's life was moving full speed ahead without me.

Bridget had her cousin Deirdre staying for the summer because Michael and Brenda felt she needed the company. Michael was going to coach the girls' softball team for the summer, and Dierdre would also be on the team, which had convinced Bridget to sign up again, though she'd been resisting since her injury, saying she would never play again. Finn, home from school, had decided to come out of the closet and had brought his witty and adorable new boyfriend, Xavier, with him. I knew Michael would not change his decision to stay with Brenda now, and I couldn't let myself make love with him. As he held me I felt him hard against me, felt my skin responding to his hands as they ran over my body. God, I wanted him.

"Wait—I can't," I said when he began to walk me backward toward my bedroom. "Michael, I can't. Everything's changed."

"We love each other the same as always," he said, then sighed in resignation. "Oh, I know, we shouldn't make love if it isn't going to mean anything in our real lives anymore." I knew what he meant, but still it hurt me to hear it put that way. Much as I wanted him, I was glad I'd told him no. *If it isn't going to mean anything in our real lives anymore.*

I stood in the doorway after he left, looking out at the empty hall and thinking of all the times I'd worried about Clara seeing Michael leave my place. Now she was gone. Michael was gone. Everyone was gone. I closed my door against the emptiness.

What's harder now than the dreams is absences so real they take up space. Devi and Ida—I'll never see their faces again except in my mind—and, imperfectly, in the paintings. Thoughts of Devi are compounded by a bitter sense of waste—the waste of a young life, a rare and shining talent not allowed to fulfill its promise.

Clara's face is more problematic when it comes to me in memory or dreams because the guilt her image conjures is fraught with a kind of revulsion I can't flush from my heart.

But Devi's philosophy of giving—that the real purpose of a gift is to inspire more giving—seems to have provided me with the answer to my guilt about Clara. I know what I have to do about her now, and I can thank Devi—and Ida, of course—for the solution to that problem.

I'll do it, and then I'll tell no one—especially not Clara.

Devi's voice—I can hear it so clearly in my mind: And that will be a gift to me, Norrie, for it will echo my name in the heavens!

20

The next morning I woke from a fitful sleep in a fog that felt as real to me as any fog I'd ever driven through along the Pacific Coast. I could barely lift my head from the pillow, and it was only by an act of will that I got up to go to the bathroom. Then I just went back into the bedroom and curled up in bed, devoid of energy, hope, curiosity. This depression had been coming on for weeks and weeks, I knew. I'd just finally allowed myself to slide over the verge and into it, letting it swallow me up. Now it was as if I wasn't here anymore to witness my own life.

I stayed in bed day and night for two, maybe three, days, I'm not sure. I'd lost all sense of time. But I'm pretty sure I never once went to sleep. I couldn't let myself because my dreams were too scary. I saw Devi in dreams, walking up Brattle in the dark, and I saw a shadowy figure lying in wait for her. Sometimes, even now, it was Clara. On other nights I dreamed I was awake and the figures of the dead were walking toward me through the dark bedroom, their hands outstretched. One night I dreamed I'd killed Clara, and my hands were dripping with her blood.

In my waking hours now, my thoughts often wandered to my mother, how she'd been left alone a long time ago and I'd judged her for feeling like this.

Devi's lost painting had arrived via FedEx, but I still hadn't opened it. I didn't have the constitution to look at it.

Georgi came by once, and I told her I needed to be alone for a couple of weeks. Liz would never have accepted my word as compliantly as Georgi did, I thought, and though I appreciated that, a part of me felt let down by her willingness to just walk away. What was wrong with me? Was I never satisfied? Was I losing my mind?

I kept thinking of how it might feel to die—and each time I thought about it, it sounded like relief, but it terrified me at the same time. Nothing made sense inside my head anymore.

After a while, I stopped screening my phone calls; now whenever the phone rang, I just didn't answer at all. My answering machine tape was filled up and I left it that way, didn't erase, so no one could leave any more messages. There was nothing I wanted to hear.

I drank water but had no appetite for food. Sometimes I watched TV, though later I remembered none of it—all I made sure of was that it wasn't the news. And I'd stopped going down to get my morning *Boston Globe* and my mail.

Three days passed and I could feel my body getting weaker, but I couldn't summon up the energy to care. Michael came over once, and I answered the buzzer only so he'd know I was alive, but I didn't let him come up.

I phoned my mother once but didn't stay on the line; I just wanted to let her know I was all right, for my own selfish peace of mind.

Whenever I got out of bed to pee—I rarely had to do more than that, since I'd eaten almost nothing—I saw my face in the mirror and flinched; my skin looked like tapioca and I had deep circles under my eyes.

Then on Saturday Liz showed up without warning. It turned out she'd gotten alarmed and called Michael—I couldn't believe she'd done that—and he'd told her I was in scary shape. I wondered how he knew that, and then I thought, *of course*. Michael and I always knew each other's state of mind.

Liz had caught the first plane to Boston with space available, landing at Logan in the early afternoon. When I heard her voice coming through the intercom from downstairs, I was standing in my hall barefoot and in my old shrunken sweats, my hair a bird's nest and my face particularly gaunt. I'm a tall woman, and I never had a lot of meat on my bones—except for my ridiculous ass—and I seemed to have lost a lot of weight in the last few weeks. If I'd had a scale, I probably could have scared the hell out of myself; I was afraid if Liz saw me it would scare the hell out of her.

"What?" I said into the intercom.

"Excuse me? What do you mean *What?*" Liz said. "I just flew here all the way from San Francisco and that's all you can say? *What?*"

"Sorry," I told the intercom.

"So do you think we should just communicate through this thing for a couple of days while I camp out here on the front steps, and then I'll fly home? Because if so, I guess I could have just stayed in San Francisco and phoned. If you ever answered your phone."

"Okay," I said, and buzzed her up. When she saw me she didn't gawk as I'd thought she would, she didn't make me feel like a psycho or a freak.

"All right, now, what's going on, sweetie?" she said as she swept me into her arms. "Oh, honey, I can't believe what you've been through."

"I think I may be having some kind of breakdown," I said into the shoulder of her jacket.

"No shit, Sherlock." She led me to the bed and sat me down by pushing on my shoulders. "Now why haven't you answered my calls?" she demanded. "I must have called you thirty times and left messages till your machine stopped taking them."

"I turned the ringer off," I said. "I didn't know you'd called. Well, I knew you called a couple of times. But I probably wouldn't have called you back anyway even if I'd known you called thirty times."

"Great," she said, looking at my answering machine. "Do you realize you have a filled-up message tape?"

"No. Well, yeah."

"Yeah you do."

I shrugged.

"Well, I'm turning your phone back on," she said. "Right now."

Then she told me to go into the living room while she listened to my messages and wrote them down. Liz was smart; she often understood things without being told. "We can call them back later," she said, "the ones you know, anyway. There were a couple of reporters on there— the one from the *Herald* is really persistent, isn't he?"

She sat down with me then and made me tell her everything. Everything. And I did. I talked about Devi's death, about all that had happened with Michael, I told her about Ida dying, told her how I'd publicly misjudged Clara ("Jeezo, girl, who wouldn't have thought she did it?" Liz said), and I ended with the fact that my Larkin colloquium was next

Wednesday—just four days away—and I wasn't finished with my *Hunger* series; worse, I hadn't yet figured out what I was going to say at the presentation itself.

"I am so fucked," I told Liz.

So then she made me show her all of the paintings, every one of them, including the one I hadn't yet unpacked from its FedEx wrappings. I opened it up in front of her, my mouth in a tight line to keep from crying. It was stunning now, after so long, to see Devi kneeling, the red robe held up against her, her beautiful skin filled with light. When I set it beside Devi's other two portraits, Liz gazed for the longest time, and I saw tears in her eyes.

"It's so sad," she said, a little embarrassed by her tears—Liz liked to think she never cried. "But they're amazing," she added, looking then at the two of Ida. "What power! These may be the paintings of a lifetime."

I didn't believe that. Already I didn't feel they worked together as a series, and I couldn't bear to look at any of them. All of them, including the three of myself, were pictures of dead people. The mistake I made was in saying that to Liz. She shook me by the shoulders hard and put her face against mine.

"STOP IT!" she said. "You stop this right now." She had tears in her eyes again, so I told her I was sorry I'd said it, told her I didn't mean it. There went another lie. The truth was, it was how I saw myself. A dead woman.

Liz stayed with me. She wouldn't leave my side. She cooked for me, she gave me the first bath I'd had in days, and she slept in my bed with me at night. (The bath was a prerequisite to that, she informed me.) I lay awake that first night, as always, afraid to go to sleep. When I cried, Liz held me and patted me. At first that made me cry more, but then, after a while, it began to calm me. I even fell asleep once, sometime before dawn; but then I woke in a sweat and found Liz looking down at me in a panic, just as the room was beginning to lighten.

"My God," she said, "what was that? You were yelling at someone in your sleep."

I told her about the dreams. That was the one thing I hadn't talked about yet.

"Those aren't dreams, honey, those are fucking Quentin Tarantino nightmares." She got us both up out of bed and said, "Okay, now what are we gonna do about this?" I didn't answer her and she didn't wait. She went to my racks of tapes and CDs and found "Aretha Sings the Blues."

"Oh, *please.*" I said, "not *that* right now—are you nuts?"

"Sure," she said, "that's a foregone conclusion. But I think you've just got to work your way through this stuff, and at least Aretha's brand of blues will remind you of Michael—someone who's still *alive.* To some extent, anyway, even though he's a loser and a weasel."

"He is not," I said.

"Whatever," she answered, and the next thing I knew Aretha was singing "I'm Drinking Again." Somehow that struck me funny, made me laugh a little. It was just so *out there.* "Good girl," Liz said, and then she went and found a blank canvas from the stack against my wall.

"Okay," she said, "I'm the Pope and you're Michelangelo suspended on your back below the ceiling of the Sistine Chapel. So, you know . . . *paint* already. If you can't sleep, you may as well paint."

"I can't, Liz," I said. "I just can't."

"Well, so then just tell me what the last painting was going to be about." That was so like a story writer, I thought, to ask what a painting was "about."

I sighed a long, deep sigh and shrugged, threw up my hands, shook my head, buried my face. I felt like a psychotic mime.

"Come on, Norrie," Liz said. "I'm trying to help you save your life."

"No thanks," I said. She slapped my shoulder, hard.

"Next time it'll be your face," she said, but she didn't sound so tough.

"Ow," I pointed out, and then she kissed my shoulder where she'd hit it.

"Let's face it, I've got no innate authority." She sighed. "I'm inconsistent, undignified, and I send mixed messages. I'd be a lousy fucking parent." She was talking in a kidding style, as always, but I could tell she was miserable.

So miserable that I began telling her about my painting, just to help her out. And as I stumbled through it, I could remember how it had felt to want to paint. But I didn't feel it now. I had no desire to paint. I thought of trying, though, just to please Liz—and I remembered how Michael had said that inspiration comes during work, not before it. Liz interjected questions as I talked, smart questions like how would I mix the color for a particular object or element of the painting, and where would the central weight of the composition be.

"I know what you're doing," I told her at some point.

"Well, shit, little girl, I should hope so."

"You're using psychology on me."

"I'm trying," she said.

She sounded so tired just then, I felt awful. She'd been running all over hell for two months to promote her new book, and now just a week or two after all that was finally finished, here she was in Cambridge trying to save my ass.

"I'm thinking," I told Liz. She didn't ask about what.

Finally I just went and got my old painting clothes and put them on. Then I got out another easel—I couldn't bear to take Devi's unfinished portrait out of its place on my other easel as if I'd given up on it. I figured I could go through the motions of painting, just to give Liz some comfort, and it didn't matter if I came up with anything worth keeping. *Process, not product.*

Aretha was singing "Natural Woman" when I started to mix the paint, and the smell of the oils made me cry. Smell is, I believe, the foremost vehicle of remembrance, and what I was feeling as I mixed my oils was maybe a kind of nostalgia for myself, the self I used to be. I kept on mixing paint, sobbing and cursing as I went, wiping snot onto the sleeve of my painting shirt. Somewhere in there, the sobs turned to muttering: This one would have to have much different tones than the others had. Seeing the faded light of early morning falling across the room, I realized the tones of the last painting would have to be a lot like that.

Liz sat down beside me on a kitchen chair she'd dragged in, and watched. No one but Devi had watched me paint since my college art classes.

This final painting is set in the same bedroom, nearly empty now, its window bare of the red curtains. There's a moonless sky outside, fading to morning light. The red blanket on the floor is noticeably darker in hue, though that perception may be a trick of the eye in the absence of full light. Across the surface of the rumpled blanket there may or may not be the impression of a formerly reclining figure, and nearby on the floor is the red satin kimono in a heap, as if thrown off carelessly in passion, anger, or despair. Those two items provide most of the color in the painting, and they are at the center of its composition though they seem to take up less room now than they did in the other paintings of the series—but maybe it's the absence of a human form that leaves them so reduced. In this emptied-out scene, it becomes clear that the "red" room was always a sallow, dulled eggshell color. The room is still and dim in the early light. On the floor below the window lies a shard of red glass; caught in weak rays of early sun, it's distractingly bright, jarring against the subdued tones that make up the rest of the scene.

When at last I ran out of energy and paused, the picture was probably half done and midday light was streaming through my windows. I turned to look at Liz and said, "I have to stop for a while, your holiness." I cleaned my hands with some turpenoid and reached for the dirty brushes, but at that moment Liz came over to me and put her arms around me and led me to the bathroom, where she ordered me to get into the shower.

"I'll do the paint cleanup this time," she said, "because you've been a good puppy. But never again, my friend!"

And so I showered, I let the hot water hit me for a long time, and then I washed my hair, which I hadn't done in days—maybe a week. I stood under the hot, driving water after my hair was shampooed, and I felt almost alive.

Over the next two days I did nothing but paint and, in my off time, talk to Liz. She called The Frame-Up and arranged for all the frames I'd ordered to be delivered to Brattle so we could just put them on the canvases ourselves in some quick, makeshift way. Wendy could do it properly later, Liz said, and I knew that was true.

She also listened to my phone messages for me and returned all but my mother's calls, which she told me I had to return myself, and a few media calls, which we both ignored. As it turned out, reporters from the *Herald* and the *Globe* were still ringing me from time to time.

At one point I heard Liz return a call she hadn't told me about, from Jane Coleman who was apparently wondering if I'd be able to go through with my colloquium.

"You're right, Jane, it would be a shame," I heard Liz say, "but our girl is not about to get the vapors. Oh no, that's no problem, either— it's all taken care of. I've ordered a truck to deliver the paintings in time to set them up for the exhibit." I didn't know she'd done that.

Later that same evening she even called Michael, which amazed me. I'd never been able to do that, because Brenda would be suspicious. Apparently if you weren't an actual Other Woman, it was not a suspicious call. I left the room while she was talking to him because listening made me miss him too much. I was almost jealous of Liz that she could call him openly and talk unfettered. Almost. But not. I was never again going to be jealous of anyone for anything.

By Monday night the new painting was finished, and I was putting the final touches to Devi's last portrait, forcing myself not to cry as I went over her beautiful skin, smoothing and burnishing. I wouldn't let tears penetrate this painting. I would not allow that to happen. I turned around once and saw Liz wiping her own tears away with the hem of her T-shirt; I turned away quickly so she wouldn't know I'd seen her.

"You would really have loved her," I said as I worked with a fine brush.

"Yeah, I know," she answered. "Would you like some of these Cheetos?"

On Tuesday afternoon the series was ready, but then I got nervous. What if reporters got into the gallery and took photos of the paintings? Devi wouldn't have wanted those pictures in newspapers for the purpose of illustrating a story about her as murder victim. I couldn't do it.

"I can't do it," I told Liz.

"Can't do what?"

"Have my exhibit. Or at least can't have the pictures of Devi in it."

"My God," she said, "those are essential to what you're doing here, even I know that—without them the series would feel incomplete! It would *be* incomplete."

"Well, I can't do it. That's that."

Liz went to the phone and called Jane Coleman at the Larkin. Liz herself had been a Larkin fellow once upon a time when Jane was only assistant director. I heard her telling Jane what was going on. "Absolutely no one allowed in there but Larkin fellows and staff, that's right," she said. I imagined Jane was then reminding Liz that people from the larger community were always at these presentations; it was a Larkin tradition.

"Well," I heard Liz say, "this is different. They can all come in and listen to Norrie talk about her series. They can see one or two of the paintings then, during that part of the event. But only Larkin people can get in to the exhibit itself or Norrie can't do it . . . I know it will, but that's the best we can do under the circumstances." There was a silence, and then Liz said, "Well, for one thing she's naked in them—yeah, naked—Right, uh huh . . . Okay. Okie dokey. No, I don't think she's up to going out to dinner afterward." She hung up and turned to face me. "Say *naked* and these New England ladies capitulate in a trice."

"What *is* a trice?" I asked. I'd always wondered that but kept forgetting to look it up. Liz didn't answer. Maybe she didn't know either. Instead she stood up and clapped her hands.

"Okay," she said, "that's done. Now let's figure out what you're gonna wear tomorrow."

"That's not all," I said. "I just realized—the paintings can't be hung on the walls after tomorrow. In fact, I have to be able to get them back immediately—at least the ones of Devi—so they're going to just be leaning against the walls of the gallery."

"Should I call Jane back and see if this is going to be a huge problem?" Liz asked, and then answered herself. "Nah, she can deal with it. It's actually kind of interesting to present them that way. She wanted us to go over in the morning and show the gallery person how to hang them, but I'll just call and tell her about the leaning exhibit tomorrow when it's too late for her to say no."

We went to my closet then, and after a few minutes of staring, Liz pronounced it pathetic. She was right, of course. Even at Aperçu I'd never dressed for success. Larkies always wore good clothes when they gave their presentations, and the only halfway appropriate thing I had was the black wraparound skirt. Its history weighed on me, but Liz told me to get over it. She found the black silk-and-lycra T-shirt with elbow-length sleeves that I'd worn with it the night Michael and I went dancing and made the seed. "Perfect outfit for an artist's colloquium at Radcliffe," she said. She found the sandals I'd worn that night. She went to the little wood jewelry box on my dresser and dug out the ring, the green glass ring. I had taken it off after Michael and I broke up.

"After all, it wasn't an *engagement* ring," Liz said. "This is your GREEN GLASS RING, for God's sake, what's the matter with you!" Then she found my fake emerald ear studs. "You're damn lucky you're so good looking, because you don't take care of yourself for shit," she told me as she washed and conditioned my hair at the kitchen sink with some of her own expensive hair stuff. "You are the worst-groomed person I know," she added cheerfully. From Liz, verbal abuse was a kind of affection; she didn't bother with it if she didn't like you.

On Wednesday we went over to the Larkin together in a cab, and the truck followed us. All the way there I was worried about the new painting, which was still very wet.

"Relax," Liz said, "they *know*. And they promised they'd put it in the truck in a way that will ensure nothing can happen to it."

By the time we'd finished bringing in the paintings and arranging them, it was three-thirty and I still had to write the notes for my presentation. Usually art fellows gave their presentations inside the gallery, but this time, because of the sensitive nature of the paintings, I was going to give my talk in the regular colloquium room so that we could allow the larger community in there but keep them out of the gallery.

Liz, Jane, and I brought three paintings into the colloquium room: the first one I'd done of myself (the one that had bothered Michael so much); the one of Ida where she's sitting in the chair, nude, holding the red glass pitcher on her lap like a small suitcase; and the one of the empty room. It was interesting to see how just the three of them together made a kind of intimate narrative, since they were all set in the same room—it could have been the passage of time. Of course, I hoped the series had a larger meaning when all of the paintings were together.

I'd just tested the microphone and prepared myself for the audience before me when Michael walked in, and I sucked in my breath so fast you could hear the sound all over the room. I tried not to look at him as I began talking about the articulation of desire in color, form, texture, and composition, and about the narrative progression of feeling from one picture to the next within this series; how the two nudes differed in terms of desire's role in the two women's lives, and how I'd used the red glass pitcher to embody desire, which was why it was in every picture of the series except the last one, in which only a shard is left.

After my presentation there was the usual question-and-answer session, and a bad moment occurred when that creepy reporter from the *Herald* asked me about Devi's murder. Jane stood and asked him to leave, but he just sat down and got quiet. When I finished with the questions, the Larkin fellows stayed on as they'd been told to before the public session.

Michael came up to speak to me then, and I told him, "Wait—don't

leave yet—I want to ask Jane to let you into the gallery, too." His face—
I can't describe the look on his face when I said that. I guess after how
much I'd held myself away from him in recent weeks, he was glad that
I wanted to share my work with him now. And I did, of course I did,
but I had another reason, too, for wanting him to come in and look at
the paintings—I wanted him to see the cumulative power of all that
desire. I wanted him to understand what he had taken out of our lives
by leaving.

I didn't look at him while he was in the gallery. In fact, I stayed in
the doorway and didn't look at anyone. I'd seen the paintings lined up
all around the walls once already, and the impact of all nine together had
been like a punch to the gut. When he came out of the room he didn't
look at me at first, and I was nervous to look at him anyway, so I went
into the restroom and stood just inside the door waiting to get my courage back. When I came out, Michael was waiting for me.

"It's the best work you've ever done," he said, "and it kills me to look
at it."

"I don't think I want to talk about that," I said, but I smiled at him.

He put his arm through mine, right there in front of everyone, and I
found my arm electric at his touch, my entire body tuning up. He walked
me back to the door of the gallery so that the Larkies could talk to me
about the paintings. But I don't remember anything anyone said about
the work because I really couldn't let myself think about what it meant.
At least Michael was tortured by it; what more could I ask?

The gallery was locked before we left, and the truck would come back
this evening to fetch the paintings when the reporters weren't around.
Mimi would let them in. Liz and I were to meet the truck at the apartment, so we couldn't stay out for long, but when Michael suggested the
three of us at least stop for a drink somewhere, she looked to me for
silent direction and I nodded.

We went to the little lounge behind the Sheraton Commander, and
after we'd been there for ten or fifteen minutes Liz very thoughtfully
went to use the restroom for a long time.

Michael put his hand over mine as soon as we were alone and I noticed
how his hand covered mine entirely, as if sheltering it from something
dangerous. I remembered how it had felt to know I was safe with a
man—or to think I was. We sat there mute, skin to skin for the first

341

time in a while, and finally he said, "I know what I had, Norrie, and I know what I've lost. I'm going to spend the rest of my life thinking about how things could have been if you were with me."

"I know," I said. "So am I. But here's the thing—you're the one who gave it all up. I have to live the rest of my life knowing you left me."

"So do I, Norrie. So do I."

Just then Liz came back and led the two of us into a raucous discussion of recent movies, most of which we'd all seen. I could feel Michael's eyes on me, but suddenly I was having trouble looking at him. It was too sad.

Liz and I decided to walk home; it wasn't dangerous anymore. When we all parted, Michael gave Liz a little hug first—to save ours for last, I knew. Liz walked out to the curb while Michael and I said good-bye. When he put his arms around me, the world tilted. I held my breath.

"It never stops," he said, "all this longing. What are we going to do, Norrie?"

You know at certain moments in your life that you're standing in an unprotected space, rooted on the single spot of terra firma that holds your entire world in balance. What you do in that moment, which way you move, determines everything to follow. Very simply, it's up to you.

"I guess we're going to have to respect your decision," I said. I could smell his familiar skin through the thin, white linen dress shirt he wore today, could feel the heat of him beneath it. "But I can't stay this close to you for long, or there's no telling what I might do." I pulled myself gently from his embrace, had to, even though it seemed I was turning my back on home. When I momentarily lost my balance, Michael took my elbow. His voice was gravelly with feeling.

"Norrie, I love you. I've never loved any other woman the way I love you."

"That's funny," I said, "I've never loved another man this way either."

"Oh God," he said, shaking his head and looking straight ahead at nothing, "I feel like I've sold my soul."

"By loving me?"

"No, you idiot—" he sighed and put his arms around me again. "—I mean by *leaving* . . . by leaving *us*." He looked into my face and ran the backs of his knuckles gently down my right cheek and jawline. I shivered.

"Is it going to stay like this forever?" he asked. "Will I just lurch around missing you every waking minute for the rest of my life?"

"I hope so," I said. "It's the least you can do." I kissed his lips quickly and walked back to Liz, letting a breeze blow my hair over my eyes to keep them private. I heard him call out something softly, but the wind took it away.

Liz and I strolled up Garden Street toward Harvard Square. Michael's little VW made a racket when he passed us and waved. It came to a clattering stop at a traffic light a block up.

"Will no amount of success convince that man to buy a new car?" Liz laughed.

"Success doesn't phase him," I told her. "He's just . . . he's just Michael." I watched him drive on when the light turned green and then disappear around a corner.

The next day Liz was set to leave. But first she did a very nervy goddamn thing. She phoned my mother and told her I was depressed and shouldn't be alone. I couldn't believe she would do that to me. And I really couldn't believe the cockamamie idea she'd cooked up with my mother. I not only resisted going along with it; I flatout refused.

"Just once in your stubborn life you can do as I say," Liz told me.

"Like hell," I said.

"Pack," she ordered. "I'm not leaving till you do."

I packed, but it was just to get rid of her.

"You're the only person I know," she said caustically, "whose entire wardrobe fits in a carry-on bag." I didn't say a word. I would let her feel important. But no way was I going.

Still, somehow, three days later I was on a plane lifting off from Logan and headed to LAX. What the hell, I thought. What have I got to lose at this point?

A few hours later my first glimpse of the Pacific Ocean blue and sparkling far below us constricted my heart. You can sing about your Old Man River till you're blue in the face, but nothing keeps on rolling like the blue blue Pacific, the endless rhythm of saltwater, those bracelets of foam across the tops of breakers that hurl themselves onto the shore like heedless love.

I stepped out into the sunshine with my carry-on bag. I was upright and back in the land of my childhood, where surf was always up.

Four times I drove by my mother's house before I could bring myself to stop. Finally, I parked in front of the little white two-bedroom bungalow I'd grown up in. I sat and stared at it. This was the first time in two or three years I'd laid eyes on it, the first time in ten years I would actually be staying there. The intestinal trouble I inevitably got on any visit with my mother announced itself in the form of abdominal pain accompanied by an overwhelming urge to break wind. I looked at my watch. Forty-five minutes till my mother-induced headache would hit, that was a given. You could set your watch by it.

The corny, twinned wooden hearts that bore the house's street address—4353—were still there. I'd made that fucking heart thing in a ninth-grade woodworking shop—a class Mother had vehemently opposed because she'd thought it "unladylike" and afterward had begun buying me frilly dresses and questioning me about what she called my "gender confusion." She didn't understand that I wanted to take the class for two reasons: I wanted to make things with my hands, and I wanted to meet boys. But there was not much doubt I'd have been better off following the lesbian route my mother so feared, I reflected. Except for my mother, women had understood me better all my life, and had had more staying power.

But God help me, I still loved men. I still loved Michael.

I walked up the little brick-lined cement walk to the front of the house, my legs suddenly all noodly and my eyes dripping a couple of tears for no reason at all. It was one of those perfect Southern California days I always think of as having "no discernable temperature."

Five, four, three, two, one, *boom:* As I reached the end of the walk and lifted my foot to the bottom step, she opened the door and came out onto the porch. It's like clockwork, I swear. I'd never once made it all the way to my mother's door before she opened it and came out— never even made it onto the porch.

I bent to hug her, smelled that soap smell I guess all mothers have. She was even littler now than she used to be, I saw that right away, and her hair, once auburn, was now dyed a soft, golden blonde. She had the same big blue Irish eyes as always, though, and the same smile. I'd rather not mention this, but in the interest of accuracy I'll just have to say it: As we let go of each other and headed toward the front door, I burst into tears and had to be escorted into the house by a crazy little Irishwoman who seemed to come up only to my knees or thereabouts. It was mortifying.

"Let me get you some cocoa," she said. *Cocoa.* I began to laugh. I laughed and cried so hard I had to squeeze my sphincter shut in an effort not to pass gas in my mother's house just yet. "You're hysterical," she said sweetly.

For the next ten days I stayed in the sunny yellow bedroom that had been mine in childhood, when I still had a father and Mother still had a husband, long before the fear of loss made her resolve to keep her world small and always the same, letting no new man into it, and long before that same fear had made me strive to keep my own life in flux for years and years, never settling long enough in love to lose, until I met Michael Sullivan.

During those days and nights with my mother, I ate more meat loaf, pot roast, and pork loin than any quasivegetarian has ever eaten. I made my bed. I took the Dumpster out to the curb both Mondays I was there. I set the supper table in the evenings while Mother stood at the stove stirring a pot and smiling at Dan Rather on the little counter TV, a look of heaven on her face. I sat stoically in the passenger seat of the old Buick while Mother threw on the brakes each time a car stopped two blocks ahead. I ate like a stevedore, slept like the dead, let my mother brush my bangs off my forehead eighty times a day without once rolling my eyes. I was, in short, the daughter I never was. She was, in short, the mother she always was. It was no day at the beach, that's for sure.

Somehow I became myself again in that little bungalow with my mother. I remembered what it means to be a blood relation and to have one, just one, on the entire earth. A clan of two.

Which is not to say it was altogether pleasant. But I found that the two of us were actually alike in many ways, though I'd always preferred to think I was wholly my father's daughter. Mother and I both enjoyed our independence, we needed order in our daily lives, we were not social butterflies, we liked to read, we had a habit of stashing a box of candy in the bedroom so that we could indulge in a covert piece of dark chocolate now and then. It made me wonder if Mother might ever have appreciated sex the way I did, but it was not a thought I particularly wanted to entertain.

Often during those nights in my mother's house, I would lie awake in my old twin bed and try to transport myself back in time to when Daddy was asleep beside Mother in the next room, but usually all I could summon up—inadvertently—were the nights after his death when I would wake to find my little mother clinging to that very doorway like a wraith, afraid she'd heard "a burglar."

In a made-for-TV movie, this would be the visit where I'd break down and tell my mother everything I'd been hiding from her all these years. Like hell, I say. Not once did we talk about men, love, or sex the whole time I was there, except for a cryptic—but stunning—revelation she made one evening over an ornate needlework pillow she was making for a friend, embroidered with the legend, THE GOLDEN YEARS SUCK. She said, "You know, I understood your father."

"What?" I asked, feeling the dread that comes with impending disclosure from a heretofore silent source. "What?" I asked again, then realized I'd already said it.

"Men have needs," my mother informed me, and suddenly I knew she meant Betty, the woman upon whom my father had died in flagrante delicto. My throat caught in a swallow that held till she went on. "He didn't want to compromise my relationship with the Church."

"What?" I sounded like my old Chatty Kathy doll, but with a one word repertoire.

"He wasn't Catholic, you know. After you were born, we . . . I . . . used the rhythm method but it, it didn't work. I . . . got pregnant again when you were a baby. Had a late-term miscarriage and nearly bled to death. After that, well, we just had to stop. It would have been a sin to use birth control. Well, a sin for *me*." She bent over the *K* to make a final cross-stitch, letting the words sink in. My God. She seemed to be saying she'd known all along about my father's infidelities, and that she understood, maybe even had an *understanding* with him. But how could they bear it? I imagined my parents all those nights in the bedroom next to mine, holding each other chastely in their maple bed with the eagle headboard, but never . . . *never again having sex!* I realized my mother was looking at me to be sure I understood. When I struggled for something, *anything*, to say in reply, her face made clear that she didn't want to discuss it. "We had a good marriage," she said, and then stood and laid her handwork on the chair. "Well, get some sleep." And she left the room.

The subject did not come up again. I heard no other long-held secrets about my dead father. We did not discuss what my mother calls "intimacies." I did not, in short, have a *Roots* experience in Santa Monica. More of a *blood* experience, I guess. But those nights spent lying in a bed shorter than I was, my toes extending over the end, I had a lot of time to think—surprisingly peaceful time. And I came to realize that it had taken stamina, heart, and courage for my mother to stay on alone in that little house after Daddy died, to make new friends at the church—Our Lady's Ladies—and to go back to teaching, spending years and years as a demonically cheerful home ec teacher when she herself had no one left to cook for.

I figured out something else, too: Whenever my mother was afraid of something close to home—a sound in the dark, a lump in her breast, loneliness—she found a sort of surrogate fear she could relate to at a more comfortable and generalized distance—asteroids, rabies, botulism, continental drift—and in that way, she managed to go on without acknowledging fear too close at hand. I'm not saying my mother was brave, exactly, just that she found a way to survive alone and be happy. And that was, I finally realized, why I'd been thinking of my mother so much in recent weeks, and why I'd given in and gone home to Santa Monica. Because I wanted to see how she'd done it. I wanted to know how to go on when you've lost the only man you ever loved.

And ten days later, armed with the kind of answers only example can provide, I boarded a plane for Boston while my little mother watched me go, her eyes stretched big with tears and her mouth flattened into a huge and wobbly pretend smile. She was sad I was leaving, she said, and very glad I'd finally come home. Ditto.

"Don't be a stranger," she sang out jauntily through her tears.

"Never again," I called back. And I headed back home to Cambridge.

I looked out the window of the plane as it taxied down the runway and then accelerated upward, making for the sky.

As always, when I felt the thrill of lift-off, I thought of you. But then my thoughts ranged beyond you, beyond earthly love, and as I felt myself moving through the sky I thought only this: that I will make myself ready for the next step, the next stage, I'll just go on toward what we're all heading for—that ultimate moment when, bodiless, and without intent or scheme, we find ourselves ascending, mute, alight.

Epilogue

Anyone who believes that an artist's best work springs directly from the belly of grief and trauma is just romanticizing the place of pain in art's creation—that old "starving artist suffering in a garret" cliché. I don't believe the most enduring art happens that way. In the weeks and months following the deaths of Devi and Ida, and Clara's departure—and the end of my love affair with Michael Sullivan—I didn't have it in me to make a single painting but the little watercolor I did for Devi's book and the last oil painting I did for my Larkin exhibit, of an emptied room.

I've come to feel that the most lasting and affecting art probably grows out of constancy and order rather than out of violent emotions, and that violence should be saved for the work itself. Though risk and danger are essential elements of any serious work of art, when the artist's life is too risky and dangerous, too full of grief, all that can result is sentimentalism and chaos.

Maybe something similar can be said about human sensibility and emotion: A profusion of overblown passions can only lead to a kind of inflationary standard, I think, one which inevitably reduces the value and impact of moderate feeling and expression, of self-control. In such an environment, sensation becomes more important than emotion.

Knowing that doesn't change anything, though, does it. In a normal life, it's not possible to control events that bring grief, rage, jealousy, or humiliation. And a person living fully can't repeatedly stifle desire without becoming less human. So what's the answer?

I only know what the answer is for me—That time must pass after passion or emotional chaos before the experience becomes truly useful to art or informative to life. Because only time can give experience the necessary context and meaning.

My *Hunger* series, painted in the midst of the most awful pain and turmoil, will probably always have meaning to me—it would have to, since it represents a time that changed me forever, changed my life. But I don't think it's great art. For me its failure is that I never got far enough outside the subject matter to achieve the kind of restraint that would have allowed the work to transcend *me*. Even the paintings of Ida and Devi are, in some way I don't admire, all about me.

I sold the three paintings of myself in the red room to a collector, and I used the money to buy a secondhand Volvo. I kind of enjoyed the idea of that—swapping my own image for a used car. But I've kept the paintings of Devi and Ida, and I don't show them in galleries, nor do I allow them to be photographed for any publications except legitimate art journals. In my dining room I've hung the painting of Ida sitting on a chair with the red glass pitcher on her lap, and in my studio I have the one of Devi holding the kimono against her front. Maybe someday I'll change my mind about exhibiting the paintings of Ida, but I don't know if I could ever show the ones of Devi. Even when the scandal is long past, it may feel as if I would be making her vulnerable to more of the prying world's avarice and cruelty. I do know I'll never sell them, or the ones of Ida.

After all that had happened on Brattle Street I couldn't bear living there a day longer than I had to, and though my lease was to go until September 1, Harvard Housing agreed to let me out of it without penalty because of what they called "extenuating circumstances."

Within two weeks of my return from Santa Monica, I had used what remained of my inheritance from Ida to purchase the top floor of a converted three-story house on a quiet, tree-lined brick street in Cambridge. The bottom two floors are owned by a retired podiatrist and his wife, a professor of Russian literature; they live on the first floor, and their son, a nebbishy, fortyish librarian with body odor that burns the eyes from two feet away, lives on the second floor. It's a huge and lovely sun-filled house—even my third of it is quite roomy.

I'm happy to have a real studio at home again—with a skylight. The apartment has a big bedroom with a fireplace and an adjoining bathroom; a small but elegant dining room with built-in bookshelves covering one wall; a generous living room with a stone fireplace; and a lovely terrace just outside the west wall. There's a small but sunny and well-appointed kitchen that overlooks my part of the backyard, in which I've planted a cutting garden filled with flowers of every color but red. I'm tired of red.

Never again could I live on the ground floor, as I did in Watertown. Now I find I need to be high up off the ground, where I feel safer and more private. I always lock my front and back doors now, too, though I recall how rarely the thought would have occurred to me in Watertown. I pull down the windowshades after dark these days, as well; but three floors up, I do feel I can leave a window or two open at night in summertime without fearing an intruder. Obviously, safety is something I think about more now, and will for the rest of my life. And always I'll be uncomfortably conscious of the vulnerability of each human body and mind to the vehemence of another person's need.

Without rent to pay, I was able to cut way back on my work hours at Aperçu Archive. Now I only go in on Tuesday and Thursday afternoons, and I limit my work to cover art—no more graphics or book design. This gives me plenty of time to paint, and I've started a series of seven huge abstract oils, quite different from anything I've done before. I find this kind of painting cooler, less emotional than what I was doing before. For me it's kind of like the feeling of moving from Puccini to Brubeck. I won't say what the new series is "about," or what it springs from, but I will point out that *seven* is the number of chakras. And deadly sins. I'm still mulling over the wonders of the world.

I have a cat named *Kundalini*, which Devi once told me was the reflection of the Holy Spirit within every living thing. Not that I've become more religious, it's just that the name reminds me to be careful of the feelings of others. Maybe I could have been kinder to Clara. Maybe things would not have reached the point where she could seem capable of what we thought she'd done, but I'll never know. And I'll always have to wonder.

My life is not empty and reclusive, despite the clichéd image of the single woman with cat and vibrator. I have a few close friends, as always, and from time to time I take a lover, but never a married one, never again. Neither have I returned to the easy intimacies of my early years, nor have I been tempted to in the least, though I make no promises. For now, though, I don't panic when I have no one to make love with. I define my new sexual philosophy as "serial celibacy."

I guess it's not a complete surprise to hear that before my post-Larkin summer had ended I became involved with Detective Burns, whose first name turned out to be Michael. I wish I'd known that beforehand—I think I might have declined—but the truth is, I let him into my bed without even knowing his first name, or being aware that I didn't know it. To me he was always simply Detective Burns. In fact, I actually called out that very name—*Detective Burns*—at the apex of our first sexual congress, which led him to apprise me of his actual first name while still inside me, a disorienting confluence of events for both of us, to be sure. All in all, ours was a sweet and comforting interlude that lasted for several weeks, but finally I realized I was letting Detective Burns fill up the silences and the emptiness I needed to be mindful of if I was to learn anything lasting from the events of my Larkin year. And from ten days in my mother's house.

For a time after our breakup, Detective Burns continued to drive up and down my street late at night in his unmarked car to provide me, he said, "an extra measure of protection from Cambridge's Finest." I had to explain to him as gently as possible that there can be a fine line between an extra measure of protection and a stalker. He admitted that maybe he was finding it hard to let go. Finally he asked the city for a transfer to the other side of Harvard Square.

I talk to my mother a lot. I call her.

Liz is moving back to Boston again next month, so we'll be able to see each other often—hallelujah—and we won't have to pay money to talk to each other anymore. I've remained friends with Georgi Brandt, though she's returned to Colorado, and now we have to pay to talk to each other. I told her recently on the phone that our friendship proves my theory about the similarities between human relationship and accreted terrain: that there need be no rational plan of connection, no common intrinsic properties, only the potential fit, and the fact of coming near one another at the right time on the earth.

I got a letter recently, announcing that Radcliffe is being subsumed into Harvard University and will continue as a center for advanced learning. The Larkin Institute will be open to men now, and I'm not sure what I think about that. The egalitarian side of me says it's only right, and that to be open to both sides of humanity can only strengthen any institution. But all the same, I can't deny that it would have been even more difficult to cope in the aftermath of Devi's murder without the sanctuary of our all-women Larkin to keep us in its safe embrace.

As for Clara, I didn't hear from her for some time after she'd left the Larkin. I did write her a letter of apology for my accusations and what they had done to her life, but words seemed hollow and absurdly insufficient to the situation, and I didn't expect to hear from her again, ever. Then she wrote to me recently to say that "an anonymous benefactor" had given her "a sum of money to pursue my writing," and she had used part of that money to move to Southern California, where she's being sponsored by her San Diego cousins who immigrated from Chile years ago and became U.S. citizens. She's working on a novel, she says, about women's friendship, and she's also working toward her doctorate in comparative literature, and getting to know many California writers.

"I recently met the poet, Carolyn Forché, who has come here from Washington, D.C. to spend a semester teaching at UCSD," she wrote, "and I was overwhelmed by her beauty and intelligence. She wrote a fine book about El Salvador some time ago," Clara went on, "so I am hoping I can convince her to write poems about Chile from a feminist perspective. I feel sure she will do it. How could she not? I know she was brought into my life for a purpose."

Last month Michael and Brenda bought a co-op apartment in New York City, where she's going to work for Morgan Stanley Dean Witter. Michael's income from *This Cold Heaven* has allowed him to stop teaching, finally, and just write. He's beginning work on his second novel, which, he tells me, will be about adultery and desire. I wonder what Brenda thinks of that. Maybe she doesn't know about it yet, though—they don't talk to each other much about their work. Bridget is going to a private school there, and Finn has moved into a tiny apartment in Chelsea with Xavier. So they'll all be together there, the Sullivan family.

I won't say I never long for Michael. And neither will I say he erred by staying in his marriage. How can I know such a thing to be true? Do I still believe that he and I could have made a wonderful life—and maybe a couple of wonderful babies—together? Sure I do. I know we could have been happy all our lives if we'd just gotten a start. But I also know that's the past now—even the fantasy of it is the past. I don't wait for him—I don't even think of him as possibility.

Anyone who knows me would say I've moved on, and I believe that's true. But it does seem to me that love, like the Catholic idea of Baptism, leaves an indelible mark on the soul. An imprint that reminds me every day of what we knew together.

Michael and I see each other rarely, and only as friends. When we meet it's always a shock to the system at that moment when we first look into each other's face—a shock to feel how the old intensity persists. We don't allow ourselves to be alone together anyplace where it would be possible to give in to those longings because we know how quickly they can turn resolve, and the world, upside down. We talk often on the phone, though, and it seems we still need each other's presence in our lives. Sometimes I wonder how it all came to be and what it was, or is, supposed to mean—this passion that springs from heart and mind and refuses to die even when the nourishment of sexual pleasure is taken away.

I miss Devi. I'm sure I will all my life. I wonder what she would have gone on to do with her great talent, what more she would have given to the world, what she might have made.

Often now I walk up Brattle Street past our old apartment building, a place I'll always see as the provenance of murder, and of other kinds of death that, unlike Devi's or Ida's, had to happen before life, stalled for so long, could reassert itself.

Even all this time after Devi's death, I can still make out the faint remains of her blood near the curb in a small depression or rough spot in the concrete where the stain has stubbornly stayed, dimmed with time and weather, gone blue like a shadow. No one would know what it was without being told, but it hurts me to see it, to see people walking over that residue of blood that should still be flowing through Devi's veins, pumping through her heart, not fading on the edge of a sidewalk underfoot.

I know one day I'll pass that spot on Brattle and find all vestiges of the stain have finally disappeared from sight. Maybe then I won't feel the whispering in my limbs that comes each time I'm near it, that whispering of the blood. I'll walk past it without stopping then, walk past it and keep walking.